SIGISMUNDO AWOKE ON THE CEILING OF HIS CELL. . . .

He looked down at the floor. His bed was there, the writing table and chair, even the chamber pot.

He did not panic. His first thought was that he had somehow triggered an explosion of *baraka*, and had levitated himself in his sleep.

He secured a grip on the nearest wall and tried to climb down to the floor.

He immediately lost his grip and slid back to the ceiling.

By then he was fully awake and beginning to try to reason about this. He tried another experimental descent, clutching the wall desperately and trying to ease himself down toward the floor. He slid slowly and inexorably back to the ceiling.

Then the terror began to grip him. . . .

"The Historical Illuminatis Chronicles is shaping up to be a wonderful multigenerational saga in the manner of Balzac's *Comedie Humaine* or Asimov's *Foundation* series. I know of no novels that offer such a unique combination of entertainment, passion, intelligence, laughter and dazzling illumination.''

—Robert Shea

The Historical Illuminatus Chronicles

VOLUME 2

The Widow's Son

BY
ROBERT ANTON WILSON

A ROC BOOK

Dedicated to Arlen

ROC
Published by the Penguin Group
Penguin Books USA Inc., 375 Hudson Street,
New York, New York 10014, U.S.A.
Penguin Books Ltd, 27 Wrights Lane,
London W8 5TZ, England
Penguin Books Australia Ltd, Ringwood,
Victoria, Australia
Penguin Books Canada Ltd, 2801 John Street
Markham, Ontario, Canada L3R 1B4
Penguin Books (N.Z.) Ltd, 182–190 Wairau Road,
Auckland 10, New Zealand

Penguin Books Ltd, Registered Offices:
Harmondsworth, Middlesex, England

Published by Roc, an imprint of New American Library, a division of
Penguin Books USA Inc. Published by arrangement with Bluejay Books
Inc.

First ROC Printing, April, 1991
10 9 8 7 6 5 4 3 2 1

CONTENTS

Peter asked: Who sent thee?
Jesus answered him and said: The cornerstone that the builders rejected is the place from which I came. The gate that is not a gate is the source of the Living One.

—*The Gospel According to Mary Magdalene*

PART ONE

Coincidence and Conspiracy

△

Our revolution has made me feel the full force of the axiom that history is fiction. I am convinced that coincidence and conspiracy have produced more heroes than genius and virtue.

—Maximilien Robespierre, 1792

Not only are teratological molecules invisible and inaccessible in the normal sense; they also appear to be deliberately clandestine.

—De Selby, *Golden Hours*, II, 114

No man can aspire higher than this: that he be remembered as one who selflessly obeyed the harsh dictates of Logic and Reason; that he was truly disinterested and objective.

—Hanfkopf, *Werke*, VI,
"Was ist Wahrheit?" p. 103

△

One

Armand Daumal didn't like the idea of wet work,* but he even more strongly didn't like what he was hearing about the king. He was reasonable about it. He leaned across the table and explained in a friendly fashion. "Georges," he said. "Georges. Georges. I know it's true. You know it's true. My ass, the pig of the aunt of my gardener probably knows it's true by now. But you don't say things like that about the king. This isn't Rouen anymore, Georges. You don't say things like that in Paris."

Georges was even dirtier and shabbier than Armand, but he still leaned back a little because Armand smelled worse. "Jesus," he said. "Jesus Mary Christ. You're getting too nervous, Armand. There's nobody here but the innkeeper and he's way the hell and gone, the other end of the room. You don't want to get so nervous, Armand."

"Listen, Georges," Armand said. "This is fucking *Paris*. Paris. The walls have ears here. Name of a name, this damned Sardines,** you heard of this Sardines I hope, he got more *mouches**** than a hound dog has fleas, is what he's got. This Sardines, Georges, he eats guys like us for breakfast. And friggin' Corsican pirates for lunch."

"Look, you guys," Lucien interrupted, smiling gently, "let's not get on each other's asses, huh? We here to drink

*Assassination.

**The underworld nickname for Lieutenant Gabriel de Sartines, whom we will get to know better as this Romance proceeds.

***Informers; stoolies; supergrasses.

or we here to get in a fight? Tell me, will you guys? I thought
we were here to drink.''

"We're here to drink," Armand said. "Until Pierre
comes."

"Then we drink, right?" Lucien said, smiling.

Lucien had the friendly, cheerful, honest face of a peasant who had successfully swindled the Lord of the Manor,
seduced the Lady, and carried off their best silverware when
making his escape. Georges had the arrogant, baffled, furtive face of a peasant who had tried all those tricks and got
caught and whipped each time. Armand simply looked like
a sheep-killing dog.

"We drink then, damn right," Georges said. "And I
won't say another word about the king's pox."*

Armand put down his wineglass with a very tired gesture,
like an old man painfully taking off his boots. "Jesus," he
said. "What I ever do, is what I want to know? What I ever
do, I get stuck with an asshole like you?"

"Relax, Armand," Lucien said, still smiling. He smiled
a great deal. "This Sardines, he ain't God. He's pretty
sharp, everybody knows that, but he don't have a *mouche*
hiding under every table in every inn in Paris. That he ain't
got. There ain't enough money in the police for that, Armand. And everybody in Paris is talking about It anyway,
everybody and his brother and both of their cousins and a
couple of sisters, too, by now. The hell, the king ain't the
only one. Half the goddam country has It by now. It's those
diegos, you know? They brought It in. Those diego sailors."

"You too?" Armand said. "At least keep your goddam
voice down, will you? It ain't healthy talking this way about
the king. Maybe this Sardines don't have a *mouche* under
every table, and then again maybe he does. You never know
around this fuckin' town, is what I'm saying."

"Your problem," Lucien said, "is that you worry too
much, Armand. Maybe what it is, is you're in the wrong
line of work. I mean, a guy worries about the police as

*This does not refer to the smallpox (of which the king, curiously,
was to die three years later). In those days, all forms of venereal infection
were called "the pox." In this case the reference appears to be to syphilis, and King Louis XV certainly had a superb collection of the obvious
symptoms.

much as you do, maybe you should stick to something safe and comfortable like shoveling the shit out of the barns back in Rouen.''

"I'm not afraid of the police," Armand said hurriedly. ''Don't you go getting any wrong ideas about that, Lucien. I just think guys like us, the last thing we want to do is attract attention, and this Sardines, what I hear, he worries a hell of a lot more about politics, the shape the country is in, than he worries about grab-and-run or any of the other things a guy might do to make ends meet. You know what I mean? Who they got in the fuckin' Bastille? A lot of guys thought they could crack wise about the king, that's who they got.''

"Can't we change the subject?" Georges asked. "I wish Pierre would come.''

"I think you worry too much," Lucien repeated dogmatically. "You're just an old worrywart, Armand. That's what I think.''

"You think whatever the hell you like," Armand said. ''I'm not as old as you, Lucien, and I'm not in Paris as long as you, but I keep my eyes and ears open, and I hear things, and I tell you the last thing we want, the kind of job we signed up for, is the police suddenly take an interest in us. Some people, respectable, they got decent jobs, think it's perfectly safe, just sitting around with friends in a tavern like this, and somebody makes a joke about the king and what happens? The next thing you know there's a great big hole in the air where they used to be, and nobody knows nothing. The fuck, nobody even saw them get arrested. They're just gone. You want that to happen to us, Lucien? Listen,'' lowering his voice even further, ''of course the king's got It. If he didn't have It, he wouldn't act so crazy, right? Of course he's got It. But you don't talk about It. You don't talk about politics at all in Paris, is what it is. I don't know how many *mouches* this Sardines has, but there is one thing I do know, Lucien, and you ought to know it by now, you as smart as I think you are, and that's that everybody who ain't on Sardines's payroll part of the time is trying to get on his payroll. That's Paris, Lucien. Everybody who's not a *mouche* yet is trying to become a *mouche*.''

"It's them houses," Lucien said softly. "Those girls, you can't stay away, right? Red hair, perfume, my God, the works. We all go to them houses sometimes. But the diego sailors bring It in and the girls get It and then they give It to everybody. And you got It long enough, ten years, twenty years, you go weird in the head. It's funny, you know? We been in whole goddam wars because the king's got It so long he's crazy. Whole goddam wars all over Europe because the king's got It so long he lost half his brain already. Because the diego sailors brought It in.

"Imagine that," Lucien went on seriously. "Some diego sailor from Palermo gives It to a girl who came up from Provence because she found out she can earn more money on her back with her legs spread than she can get paid for slopping the pigs and hacking down the wheat; and she gives It to some Marquis from Rennes-le-Château, say; and he gives It to some second assistant maid at the palace; and then the king gets the hots for that maid a few days later; and then what? Twenty years later the king is so whacked that he can't look at the English ambassador without he sees some kinda horrible giant lizard coming at him. It makes you wonder about politics, you know?"*

"Jesus and Mary and Joseph," Armand said. "Can't we lay off the king, you guys? I tell you, the walls got ears around here."

"It's because this is wet work," Georges said. "You never done any wet work before, have you, Armand? That's why you're so nervous. You're acting just like some kid, thirteen, fourteen, he just got caught by Mama with his pecker in his hand."

"Look," Armand said. "I'm up for any job of work comes along. Okay, I don't like wet work. I also don't like moving you-know. To tell you the God's honest truth, I don't much like grab-and-run. I mean, any of these jobs, you could get killed, they catch you. But I'm up for any job comes along. I need the money."

"It's because you never done wet work before," Georges repeated dogmatically. "I know. My first job, wet work, I nearly peed myself. It *is* scary the first time. But the fuck, you know, everything is scary in this world. Guys like us, we don't get hanged for one thing, sure as shit we get hanged

*Celebrated syphilitics whose policies may have been influenced by hallucination and paranoia: Henry VIII of England, Lord Randolph Churchill, Benito Mussolini, Idi Amin Dada. See de Selby, *Golden Hours*, II, 261–3.

later for something else, maybe something we didn't even do, you know? But let me tell you something, Armand, on my word of honor. It's really easier than grab-and-run.* It really is. It just seems scary before you done it." He tried to smile reassuringly, like Lucien. Since most of his teeth were missing, the effect was like a perverted jack-o'-lantern.

"Well, but," Armand said. "The thing is, the guy we're gonna hit, he ain't gonna like it, right? I mean, they don't like it when they get robbed, but getting dead is something else again. I mean, he's going to make, what do you call it, strenuous objections. Right? It stands to reason. Guy don't want to lose his money, but the same guy, he even more hates to lose his goddam life. I mean, four against one, it sounds easy, he don't stand a chance. But he'll fight like a goddam tiger, and he'll yell his head off. That's what worries me. He's sure to yell like a guy caught his whang in a coach door, and then how do we get out of the neighborhood afterward?"

"The thing is," Georges said, "a wet job, you do it right, he don't make a sound. You think of grab-and-run and the guy howling like a tenor in an opera and the whole street trying to grab you and hold you for the cops, but wet jobs ain't like that. You do it right, like we'll show you, and the guy isn't running around yelling at all, he is in fact the quietest son of a bitch you ever set eyes on. You just watch Lucien and me, and Pierre especially. This guy won't make a peep, it will be over so quick. Honest."

Lucien spoke up again, smiling and philosophical. "It's the religion shit," he said. "We all got it, way down. The fuck, they pumped it into us when we were kids. You can do a thousand grab-and-runs and not give it a second thought, but a wet job, especially the first, you start worrying about God and Hell and the Devil and all that crap. *Eternal fire,*" he intoned. "The religion shit. I don't believe that stuff no more. You believe it, Armand, you better become a monk. There ain't no way you going to survive out here in the real world, you believe that stuff. You oughta read this guy, Spartacus, puts out the pamphlets."**

*Georges is lying, of course.

**This French "Spartacus" has not been identified, but should not be confused with the contemporary German "Spartacus" who was, of course, Adam Weishaupt, well known to readers of my Immortal Novels

"I got enough troubles," Armand said, "without they catch me with one of them subversive pamphlets." He didn't want to admit that he couldn't read.

"Hey," Georges said. "It's Pierre."

Pierre was better dressed than the others and might well pass for a shopkeeper or a pimp; he even had a perfumed handkerchief in his breast pocket. He had the face of the kind of curate who gets caught robbing the poor box. "Hey, you bastards," he said cheerfully.

"Pierre, you son of a bitch," Georges said, punching him in the arm.

"Good afternoon, Pierre," Armand said respectfully.

"Health," Lucien said, raising his glass and smiling again. Pierre looked at that bright, honest smile and thought privately that Lucien was the most dangerous of the three peasants. The judge who eventually sentenced him would have his doubts and bad dreams afterward, and the public hangman would end up sincerely apologizing as he affixed the noose.

"Goddam dogs," Pierre said, still not liking the fact that even he wanted to trust Lucien's smile and be nice to the man who wore it. "You know what I just stepped in? Jesus. All over my *sabots.*"

"More wine?" the innkeeper asked, coming over to their table.

"The diego red," Pierre said. "A whole bottle. Good stuff."

"Best I have," the innkeeper said. "You'll like it, sir." He addressed Pierre as *vous.* He had been calling the others *tu.**

"Goddam dogs," Pierre repeated as the innkeeper walked away. "They should shoot all those bastards."

"Well, that's Paris, Pierre," Georges said.

"Goddam right, it's Paris," Pierre said. "I been living here nine, ten years now. My father's pigsty, now that was a nice clean place compared to this goddam town."

and soon to be introduced to new readers as this Romance proceeds. Peace.

---

*The wine he served them was mediocre and overpriced anyway. Pierre didn't know beans about wine actually. Cf. de Selby: "An expert is an idiot who has found people more ignorant than himself and knows how to bewitch them." (*Golden Hours,* III, 17.)

The innkeeper brought the wine. They waited until he had returned to the other end of the room.

"All right," Pierre said. "Lucien told you guys this is a wet job?"

"Yeah," Armand said. "We're up for it. We need the money."

"The thing is," Pierre said, "we got to find the guy first. My, um, principal, and you will convince me you are all bright guys if you don't ask his name, he knows the guy's in Paris. Also, he says the guy is a student at the university, so that tells us what kind of neighborhoods we start looking in. It might take two, maybe three days before we find him, but this is good pay for two or three days walking around taking the fresh air and a few minutes' exercise in an alley, right? Now the guy we're looking for, his name is Sigismundo Celine. Around twenty years old and pretty tall for a diego, maybe five-seven or five-eight."*

"A diego?" Armand said. "He's a diego?"

"From Napoli," Pierre said, showing his sophistication by rolling the vowels Italian-style. "What, does that make a difference?"

"To Armand it does," Lucien said, smiling again. "He was afraid he might have to kill a human being."

But Armand was smiling, too, for the first time since he agreed to doing wet work that morning. "A diego," he said happily. "Hell, they ain't nothing but a bunch of opera singers."

---

*Average height for males in Europe at that time: five feet two inches. De Selby (*Golden Hours* I, 223) attributes this to "the accumulation in the atmosphere of teratological molecules." He regarded these molecules as negatively phototropic and believed electric light banished them; hence, their scarcity in modern times.

He also believed that France was the greatest country in the world, because the priest told him that in his two years in the entire catechism class, when the father could afford to

French's

the

the

to

of the same still get help straight forward

game to bell give their own demon

also enough had children get to there

talk a bit out

Two

The innkeeper had good ears and lively curiosity; he had heard the whole conversation. Listening to conversations was his hobby, and he had almost become a philosopher by pondering on what he heard. He was no *mouche,* and didn't care about the rumor that the king had what everybody called "the Italian pox"; he had heard that rumor maybe ten thousand times before. In his experience, the existence of the rumor was no guarantee of its truth. People who drank always claimed to know something special, and the dirtier and more stupid they were, the more likely they were to claim they knew something about the king.

The innkeeper knew that he'd heard a murder being planned. That did not move him much either; murders were always being planned in Paris. Only a fool would report such a thing to the police. A man who could afford to hire four murderers was a noble, almost certainly, and you wouldn't want him as an enemy.

Listen much, talk little, and never interfere with the affairs of the rich; by those rules the innkeeper had kept out of trouble, and even become comfortable and reached the advanced age of forty-two years.

Armand, who had only seventy-six hours left to live, believed that all men from Italy were effeminate, sissified, and probably sodomites; but he also believed that they were so insatiable for women that they had spread the pox all over Europe.

It had never occurred to him that these opinions contradicted each other.

He also believed that France was the greatest country in the world, because the priest told him that in his two years in the church school, back when his father could afford to send him to school; he believed also that every single official from the king down to the local judge was either corrupt or crazy or most likely both, because experience had taught him that.

He believed that a poor man didn't have a chance in that society, because he had seen what happened to his father when the crops failed and the old man couldn't pay the taxes and rents; he believed also that it was dangerous to talk about such realities because it might get you in trouble, and what good was talking anyway?

He believed that most of the things he had learned to do for money were sins as well as crimes and that he was in danger of suffering hellfire after death, but that if he made a Perfect Act of Contrition before death he would escape that. He lit candles at church regularly, in the hope that this would build up a fund of Grace that would buy him out of Hell even if he didn't have time for that Perfect Act of Contrition, like if he died in a sudden accident or something.

Lucien had once tried to explain to him that the earth was round, like a ball, but Armand naturally objected that the people on the bottom would fall off in that case, and when Lucien tried to explain gravity, Armand decided Lucien had been turned into an atheist by reading those subversive pamphlets by "Spartacus." More than half of the things that Lucien attributed to gravity were actually done by God, according to the priest at the church school.

Armand smelled bad because, although he had seen soap once, he had never been able to afford such a luxury, and besides, everybody he knew smelled just as bad, except Pierre, who was very clever and even knew how to bribe the customs inspectors when he was moving, well, you-know—*that* stuff. Armand did not even like to think about that sort of work, because it was not just a hanging offense like most of the things he could do efficiently, but was punished by drawing, quartering, and burning. He absolutely refused to admit he knew Pierre was involved in that.* Wet work was bad enough.

Since the family had split up after the land was taken

*This will be explained in due course. Patience. Peace.

from Armand's father for inability to pay the taxes, nobody in the whole world had cared what happened to Armand.

Armand didn't care what happened to anybody else either.

He was twenty-three years old and, like Georges, had lost most of his teeth. He stood a fraction of an inch above five feet in height because peasants did not get much protein in those days.*

Georges had never even been in a school once; otherwise his life had been much like Armand's. Lucien had been in school for nearly five years before he got in trouble; that was how he learned enough to notice that most people were very, very stupid and to decide that he himself was very,

---

*According to those who do not credit the existence of De Selby's "teratological molecules." The serious student will want to consult such basic works on this controversy as Prof. Eamonn Conneghen's masterful and monumental *The de Selby Codex and Its Critics*, Royal Sir Myles na gCopaleen Anthropological Institute Press, Dalkey, 1937; Dr. Brendan Flahive's more modest, but incisive *Teratological Evolution*, Royal Sir Myles na gCopaleen Biochemical Institute Press, Shankill, 1972; Pieter Vinkenoog's *De Selby: De Onbekende Filosoof*, De Kosmos, Amsterdam, 1951—a good, workmanlike popularization; Prof La Fournier's hotly debated *De Selby: l'Enigme de l'Occident*, University of Paris, 1933; the more controversial La Tournier's *De Selby: Homme ou Dieu?*, Editions J'al Lu, Paris, 1904; Dermot Dhuigneain's poetic *De Selby and the Celtic Imagination*, Royal Sir Myles na gCopaleen Ethnic Society Press, Glenageary, 1984; *The Nature of Plenumary Time*, David Davies, University of Cardiff Press, 1968—perhaps a bit slick and unctuous, that one; Eoin MacCohlainn's charming and light-hearted *Erigena, Berkeley, de Selby: Time's Angels*, Royal Sir Myles na gCopaleen Cosmological Institute Press, Sallynoggin, 1932; Prof. Ferguson's vitriolic *Armageddon*, University of Edinburgh Press, 1928; Prof. Han Tui-Po's little-known but valuable *De Selby Te Ching*, University of Beijing, 1975; Aongus O'Ceallaigh's exhaustive *Theo-Chemisty*, Royal Sir Myles na gCopaleen Neuropharmacological Institute Press, Avoca, 1981; and the venomous and interminable diatribes of Prof. Hanfkopf—*DeSelbyismus und Dummheit*, University of Heidelberg, 1942; and *Werke*, Vols. II–III, VIII, 203–624, University of Heidelberg, 1982. These latter are well refuted by Frau Doktor Maria Turn-und-Taxis in her sparkling *Ist de Selby eine Droge oder naben wir sie nur falsch verstanden?* Sphinx Verlag, 1984, and Prof. Hidalgo La Puta's *La Estupidad de Hanfkopf*, University of Madrid, 1978. Liam O'Broichain's *A Chara, na caith tabac!* Poolbeg Press, 1981, only uses de Selby as a launching pad for a crank thesis on diet, and is accessible only to the eight people who still read Gaelic anyway, while O'Brien's popular *Dalkey Archive* (Picador, London, 1976) is romanticized and even novelized to an extraordinary degree; objective scholars do not regard it as an accurate portrait of de Selby's life at all.

very smart. He was convinced that Georges and Armand would both hang eventually but that he himself would soon earn enough through crime to buy an inn or a shop of some sort and become respectable.

Georges was twenty-one and Lucien was twenty-five. They would both be dead very soon, too.

Three

From THE REVOLUTION AS I SAW IT by Luigi Duccio, master stonecutter, Hero of the Bastille, former member of the Committee for Public Safety (1806):

In the taverns these days, people often discuss why the revolution happened; if they feel safe and are sure none of the Emperor's spies are present, they even discuss why it failed. Leaving the failure aside for the moment, there are three popular notions about the causes of the great upheaval of '89. Most commonly, people still blame it on King Louis XVI: they say it was his singular stupidity and obstinacy that drove the whole population (nobles, bourgeoisie, artisans, even peasants) to violent rebellion. Others say that the revolution resulted from the machinations of a few aristocratic cliques, especially the Orleanists, who, in trying to advance their own interests against the interests of the king, unleashed forces they proved unable to control. Finally, of course, there is the minority (mostly Catholic) who credit the claims of the Abbé Augustin Barruel, who in his *Memoirs of Jacobinism* attributes everything that happened to the plots of secret societies such as the Freemasons and the Illuminati.*

All of these theories are childish, like most human mentations in this unscientific age. One might as well attribute the revolution to the Easter Bunny, or to that remarkably endowed pigeon who allegedly made Mary heavy with Christ.

When I am drunk enough, I speak out. Having been a friend of Robespierre made me a "great man" for a while, then it made me a "great villain" for another time, but now it just makes me

---

*Barruel's thesis was later restated by John Robison in *Proofs of a Conspiracy* and has become an Article of Faith in certain quarters. See *The Illuminoids* by Neal Wilgus, Sun Books, Albuquerque, N.M., 1978.

an old curiosity, like those pendants some ladies wear that contain certain small stones that the workers sold after they demolished the Bastille, as relics of ancient infamy. I tell them, when I speak, that the Revolution was made by occult forces, invisible powers that no man sees or understands.

The fools, of course, take me literally. That does not bother me in the slightest: I have grown so cynical that I enjoy being misunderstood, since it confirms my low opinion of the general intelligence. I am not even sure I am writing this book for publication; certainly I am not writing it for publication at this time. Fouché would seize every copy, and I would become intimately acquainted with many of the bedbugs and rodents in the basement of one of those progressive, modern penitentiaries that have replaced the horrible old Bastille. I am perhaps, like all vain and angry men, writing for posterity. When one grows tired of talking to oneself, one must perforce invent an intelligent audience; since I cannot imagine that superior mind above us in the clouds, as the Church would have it, I can only imagine it somewhere in the future, and I call it posterity. Perhaps that is the last illusion to die: the hope that something not totally imbecile exists somewhere, even if only in the indefinite, ever-potential tomorrow.

Ah, Luigi, you are still only talking to yourself. You have gone half-cracked, old man. (I will cross that out when I revise this.)

The revolution, I say to the future, was made by invisible occult forces. What were these daemonic powers? They were the spirits of the earth—chthonic gods that the ancients worshipped without understanding. The chief of these dark gods was She whom the witches in Ireland and Wales still worship, and the *stregae* in my native Napoli worship also: the goddess of the swollen belly. The ancients pictured her with no face because she is no woman but rather is all women. I refer to *fertility*.

What, you object, this goddess was still powerful in your age of Christianity and Atheism? She was, my friends, more powerful than ever, thanks to the advances in medicine in the last hundred years. I studied all the relevant documents in the government offices while I served with the Committee for Public Safety. In most of the provinces of France the population increased as much as *eighty percent* in the two generations between 1730 and the storming of the Bastille on August 14, 1789. Even in the most backward provinces in the south, where medieval superstitions flourished and enlightened doctors were as rare as unicorns, I often found population increases as high as *fifty percent*. The overall increase in population throughout the nation I calculate at an astounding *seventy-five percent*.

This is where the invisible forces come into play. These occult powers are unseen because no man looks at them. People search for heroes and heroines and villains; they do not recognize the causes that actually propel events. In my opinion, after studying statistics for a long time, there is a general law that when many men are seeking few jobs, wages fall, just as when few men are seeking many jobs, wages rise.

That is, the bourgeoisie as a class will have men of varying degrees of wisdom, virtue, &c. and of varying degrees of selfishness, cruelty, &c.; but out of ten of them, say, when population is increasing rapidly, perhaps two will notice that it is now safe to offer lower wages than previously. Men accustomed to six sous will work for four, or even two, rather than starve entirely; when five or six men are seeking the same six-sou job, one of these five or six will settle for four sous, or even for two, rather than lose the job to another who is equally desperate. But, once this has been realized by even one employer, others will also see the possibility of *increasing* profits by *lowering* wages; and those who do not see it will lose the competitive edge. Is this clear? It means simply that the bourgeois who is paying two sous can sell for three sous, and the other bourgeois who is still paying four or six sous cannot sell for three sous; ergo, he either cuts wages too, or he loses his business to the first bourgeois, who has already cut wages. Thus, as population rises, wages always inevitably fall.

Some will protest that this mathematical analysis ignores the possibility of virtue among employers. Well, as to that: Imagine, if you will, a bourgeois who, despite his education and his experience of the world, still believes the mythology which the kings have paid the clergy to teach peasants. This employer sincerely credits the existence of a lovely city in the clouds called Heaven and a terrible, burning city under the earth called Hell, and he thinks "good" people will go to Heaven after death and "bad" people will go to Hell. He wants to be a "good" man and go to this wonderful cloud-cuckoo-land called Heaven. So he tries to be kind to his workers, and does not cut back on wages when others do. I cheerfully grant that such a virtuous employer may exist, although I have never seen one. I still insist that such a man will not remain in business long. Customers will go to other merchants who are offering lower prices because they are paying lower wages. Therefore this man's virtue, even if it gets him into Heaven eventually, will have no long-range statistical effect: Wages, overall, will still fall over a generation of continuous population increase.

I am afraid I have already lost my audience. People want to know who was innocent, who was guilty, and they do not want to study these invisible forces which are as immutable and pitiless as gravity. Nonetheless, attend me for a moment. *Coalitions*—or *strikes*, as the English vividly call them*—increased steadily

---

*The buried metaphor refers to lightning; cf. German *blitzkrieg*.

throughout the period I discuss (1730-1789). Everybody old enough remembers, or has heard about, the strike of the weavers in 1737, of the hatters in 1749, of the bookbinders in 1776, of the building workers in 1786, &c. These were just the largest and longest-lasting *coalitions;* there were smaller ones continually.

How to explain this? Simply understand that, as population increases, not only do *wages fall,* but later *prices rise.* It is the same calculus: when many customers bid for the same ear of corn or pint of milk, the merchants can safely raise prices; and those who do not take advantage of this will be, in one year or five years, abolished as competitors. (Will anybody understand this? Will anybody even *want* to understand it? Shut up, Luigi. Work. That is all you have left: work.)

So I say that we have two variables, falling wages and rising prices, and the relation between them, or the *ratio of wages to prices*—how much a father of a family earns, as against how much he can buy with it—is to be considered *the index of revolutionary potential,* in a given time and place. If there are high wages and low prices, this index is low, and one can expect no revolution; if there are low wages and high prices, this index is high and revolution can be predicted *as precisely as eclipses in astronomy.* This is, scientifically, the "cause" of revolutions—not "secret societies," not the idiocy or villainy of this minister or that employer, not the plots of Oreleanists and other factions.

Nor was the high index of revolutionary potential (ratio of wages to prices) a French phenomenon alone. Since the population was increasing all over Europe due to improved medicine, science, &c., I calculate an overall index of revolutionary potential (wage to price ratio) of fifty percent (see appendix one). This is why there were two insurrections in Switzerland (1765 and 1782) *before* the "radical ideas of 1789" were unleashed upon the world. This is why there were riots in Holland again and again in the years between 1783 and 1787—starting six years before and ending two years before the Declaration of the Rights of Man. This is why we had "grain riots" in France in 1774 and, I think, it is the real cause behind the allegedly religious riots in London in 1780.* Economics is destiny—and revolution is the reply to the destiny of bruised and bloody hands.

But the science of economics is not studied; it is hardly even known. People look for the "good men" and the "evil men," the "wise" and the "fools"; they do not look at the registry of births and the price of bread. And so I say that the pagans were wiser

---

*The so-called Gordon Riots against Catholic Emancipation, which destroyed more property in a week than was destroyed in the entire French Revolution. The rioters, mostly unemployed, showed no discrimination concerning who or what they attacked and, once rolling, burned everything in their path.

than we, because they at least knew that Venus, goddess of fertility, and Plutus, god of money, move events invisibly from behind the scenes.

Of course, there were secret societies and conspiracies; Maximilien Robespierre, that misunderstood man, became a god to the common people for a while, because he correctly denounced some of these conspiracies, such as that of the Orléans faction; then he became a villain, a devil incarnate, when he began seeing conspiracies everywhere. He did not, alas, understand that conspiracy is just another name for coalition; he never read the wise Scotsman, Smith, who so sagaciously remarked that men of the same profession never meet together except to conspire against the general public. He died, my good friend Maximilien, executed by those he sought to serve, and they cut him down in the midst of a speech warning that the bourgeoisie had killed the revolution; now they say he was bloodthirsty and "mad." The truth was simply that he also did not understand why the revolution could not deliver what it promised. The reason, as I shall show later, is that the real wealth of the nation was not yet adequate to provide a decent standard of living for all; the goals of the revolution can *not* be achieved until such real wealth has increased vastly over what it now is. Only Jesus, in the book of fables the church invented, ever fed five thousand with only enough fish for five. But men do not yet understand how wealth is increased, and so each faction conspires against all the others and blames the others for conspiring also. I shall return to this point.*

Maximilien, who was the kindest man possible in his private life, came to believe in the efficacy of "terror and virtue"; he found it easier to unleash terror, because virtue cannot be induced by fiat. Against his program of terror and virtue he saw the dread forces of what he called coincidence and conspiracy. Since I have spoken of conspiracy, I should now say something of the role of coincidence. A little spark can ignite a house; great events can result from trivial incidents. The philosophical doctrine of determinism (which some will think I am trying to revive in economic guise) can account for much, but not all, since *hazard* and *chance* are parts of life, too. In this connection, I think of the most singular person I have ever known, one who played a larger role than any now living realize. Have you, dear reader, ever heard of Sigismundo Celine? No? Then attend me: I have a tale to tell you.

*Signor Duccio's argument, later, is that real wealth is created by ideas that work (technological ideas), and that until such technology exists, the small comparative wealth in existence will always be seized by the most cunning predators and conspirators. To advance technology he recommends free public education for both boys and girls, and the abolition of Christianity. His formulae are: wealth for all = much technology; and much technology = much education + no Christianity.

Four

From THE SECRET TEACHINGS OF THE ARGENTUM ASTRUM, author unknown, no date:*

It is necessary to remind the candidate that each page of this manuscript should be burned as soon as it is read. In no case should a copy be kept in one's possession, even for a few hours. For any of this information to fall into the hands of our enemies, the Black Sorcerers of Rome, would be more disastrous than for all of us to be arrested *en masse* and executed.

Since our original concern was to protect the Widow and the Widow's Son, and our long-range objective is as already explained

---

*The Order of the Argentum Astrum (Silver Star) claims, like many other occult societies, that it has existed since Atlantis. Be that as it may, this order has certainly played a major role in the evolution of Freemasonry, and has inculcated a mystical obsession with the star Sirius throughout other esoteric movements. For instance, there is a silver star in every Masonic lodge, and Gen. Albert Pike, the highest ranking Freemason in nineteenth-century America, informs us in his *Morals and Dogma of Freemasonry* that this silver star is Sirius. A special meaning is also given to Sirius in Theosophy and the Gurdjieff "schools." Mr. Kenneth Grant of London, who claims to be the current Grand Master of the Argentum Astrum, also says the silver star is Sirius and calls it allegorically "the sun behind the sun" (in his *Aleister Crowley and the Hidden God*). The most famous occult order of the late nineteenth century, the Hermetic Order of the Golden Dawn, originally admitted only 32° Freemasons. Among its members were poet William Butler Yeats, actress Florence Farr (once Bernard Shaw's mistress), novelist Arthur Machen, and at one time even a coroner of London. Golden Dawn literature describes a second, more esoteric order to which only the most worthy would be admitted; this was, again, the Argentum Astrum or Silver Star. See Israel Regardie, *The Complete Golden Dawn* (Falcon Press, 1984).

(in pages which, we repeat again, should have been burned by the candidate before reaching this page), it is desirable that all the accepted ideas of humanity be undermined and subverted by any and all means possible.* Faith (viz., belief without experience of personal contact with the Living One) is the great enemy, the iron out of which are forged the chains of tyranny and superstition which retard humanity's progress toward the Great Work. Doubt, in the form of dogmatic atheism, may also become just another faith, another prison for the mind. What we wish to encourage is *uncertainty*. People must be convinced not just that the priest may be a humbug and the judge a thief, but that all systems of philosophy are equally dubious, that all papal bulls are as absurd as picaresque novels, that the latest scientific theories are no more infallible than papal bulls, &c.; in short, that all books are works of fiction, whether they are so labeled or not.

The candidate knows that as unrelenting doubt is our sword, paradox & satire are our catapults & cannons. We must learn to hide in ambush, as it were. "Who is near me is near the fire." To know the Living One, humanity must come out of the cells and closets of ideas and dogmas; life must become an experience like unto reading a novel in which it is never clear from one page to the next whether the matter is comic or tragic, who is the hero and who the villain, what is meaningful and what is happenstance or coincidence.

He is nearest to enlightenment who walks into a dark cave alone, for such a one has no fixed ideas but is alert in every cell and watchful every second. We are all in such dark caves every day, as Plato tried to teach, but we do not realize it and our fixed ideas keep us sleepwalking when it is most necessary that we awaken.**

Again we warn: before reading the next page, burn this page.

---

*Cf. "total transformation of mind, and of all that resembles it" (First Surrealist Manifesto, 1923), and also "Dada is not dead! Watch your overcoat!" (sign exhibited at the first surrealist art show, 1923, by André Breton.)

**De Selby says, similarly, "The more we know, the less we sense, and the true rationalist would be autistic, narcissistic, and strictly senseless." (*Golden Hours*, I, 17). La Fournier (*De Selby: l'Enigme de l'Occident*) describes this view as "the brute empiricism of English philosophers, swine, donkeys, and Swiss grocers." (Prof. Ferguson in his *Armageddon* argues plausibly that La Fournier never existed, and was a pen name under which de Selby wrote commentaries on himself; but La Fournier should not be confused with La Tournier (see note page 20.)

Five

They came out of the angry sea, out of the wine-and-copper waves, the star-eyed men, and they rushed howling across the sands, their long black hair waving in the wind. They were coming for her, screaming savagely, star-eyed and damp-skinned and grabbing for her skirts, snatching at her, pulling her down to the sand and seaweed and the incoming waves.

Maria Babcock rolled out of bed, out of the nightmare, and staggered to the washbasin, retching.

It was only a nightmare, she told herself. Only a nightmare combined with morning sickness. "Oh, God," she moaned, heaving again. Why of all things should she be dreaming about the Merovingians? The men with long black hair who came out of the Mediterranean, the men who were not quite human; it was a legend she had known all her life, but why should it afflict her with terrors at a time like this?

The Merovingians had been the first kings of France, and they were not really fish-people. That was just a legend. Had it come to her sleeping mind because the creature within her, the foetus, was not quite human yet?

Pregnancy was normal and natural and does not have to be an ordeal from a gothic novel, Maria told herself firmly. Mother Ursula at convent school, who had been married and widowed before becoming a nun, said half and more than half the distress was due to believing ignorant legends.

Maria banished the men with eyes like stars who had once ruled France. This was 1771 and intelligent people did not believe old legends like that any more. She was educated in the classics and in mathematics and was Lady Babcock,

here in England; at home, in Napoli, she was the Contessa
Maldonado. She was not an ignorant peasant, and morning
sickness was just morning sickness, even if it came before
morning was really here yet. Her husband, the dark and
saturnine Sir John, was a leading figure, as the press said,
of the Whig side of the House of Commons and had advanced views on all subjects. He would not believe for a
minute in men who were half-fish. The court bards of the
Merovingians, he would say, invented that legend to im-
press the gullible. And that was long, long ago: the Merovingians were dead and mourned only by the weeping
wind.

   She felt closer to God than ever, even in the misery of
this dreadful business of having morning sickness in the
middle of the night. The consciousness of new life, of the
miracle of creation, was a constant mystical presence in her
life, even at those moments when she was almost tempted
to wish she had entered a convent, never had anything to do
with Sir John, or any other *man,* and *never* experienced all
this nausea and backpain and those especially *depressing*
constipations. Even Sir John, who sometimes had rather libertine views on religious matters, said that pregnancy was
a kind of miracle, although he added that it was especially
so in that it proved that man and woman could conspire to
force God to create a new soul; a rather strange thought,
but Sir John did seem to have an attitude toward the Deity
which was, if not cynical like the terrible *philosophes* of
France, certainly a bit ironic. Sir John did not doubt God's
existence, of course; but he seemed to harbor a very personal sense of the nature of divinity, which he at times appeared to regard as being not particularly cordial toward
humanity but engaged principally in a huge *joke* at humanity's expense. But Sir John was a gentleman, and a scholar,
too, and his strange humor was probably the result of his
many years of wandering about Europe and the Near East
before he met Maria and married and settled down; he must
have seen many strange and tragic things in that aristocratic
vagabond period of which Maria knew so little. There were
deep lines of suffering on his face at times, when he sat and
pondered terrible memories, not aware that Maria was
watching him and wondering.

   But Sir John's occasional moods of melancholy were not
the only blight on Maria's happiness. Back in Napoli, her

brother Carlo was in very bad blood indeed since the duel last year. Her father, Count Maldonado, was somewhat evasive about this in his letters (the dear old man did not want to cast a pall of worry over her pregnancy, she knew), but there was enough between the lines for a young lady of Maria's intuitive nature to know that Carlo was actually in an absolutely frightful state and had figuratively "placed a knife in the heart of the Holy Virgin," as the Sicilians said; Carlo was not only beyond the laws of society but beyond the reach of religion or pity. He was fully intent on pursuing a vendetta that would make all other southern Italian vendettas look milkwatery by comparison. And you could not entirely blame him. Maria thought, when you remembered the terrible nature of his wound. What was worst of all was that Count Maldonado was thick as thieves lately with the wine merchant, Pietro Malatesta, and they had between them arranged some compromise about the duel and its aftermath. What it came down to, Maria knew, was that Carlo was officially forbidden by the Count to pursue any vendetta of any sort; and what that meant, considering Carlos's sullen anger, was that Carlo was undoubtedly conspiring to follow the letter of his father's commands while secretly evading them entirely. In plain language, he would not do anything himself, but he had probably hired *dreadful* men, from Napoli's horrible criminal class, to attend to the matter for him. Unless he had conceived of something even more *diabolical* . . .

Maria felt a rush of anger against Sigismundo Celine, the man who had given Carlo that tragic and unforgivable wound. Celine was a madcap, a *punchinello*—a would-be musician whose melodies sounded like the devil himself had collaborated on them, a known associate of Jews and magicians who had evaded the Inquisition probably only because his family was rich and powerful. Celine had once had a boyish infatuation with Maria and that had been truly insufferable. Too shy to ever speak to her, he had trailed her around Napoli like a dog who feared his owner was about to desert him, spaniel-like eyes full of suffering and unspoken pleas. It was contemptible, even if the whole town did say Sigismundo Celine was a hero on one occasion— diving longer (much longer) than the professionals did, the time his crazy cousin Antonio jumped in the Bay and killed himself.*

Maria had once felt guilty every time she thought of Sigismundo because one night in her sleep she had had a very shameful dream about him, a dream that had consequences that were almost a mortal sin, although some liberal theologians said it wasn't *really* a sin if you were totally asleep and did not willingly cooperate in it. It was crazy, of course, to have such a dream about such a wretched young fellow, and that was nine-tenths of the shame of it. But Maria did not feel any guilt any longer when she thought of Sigismundo Celine. She had a fierce hatred for him—a hatred so intense that it was a sin. Still, if Carlo was not quite in his right mind and planning horrible things in secret, it was all Celine's fault. He had shot Carlo in the place that was most important to a young man. And it was ridiculous, too, because Celine had hit *that spot* only because he—who was always showing off his skill with the sword—had never bothered to learn anything about pistols, which he considered vulgar. The imbecile even said later that he had been aiming for Carlo's *shoulder.* How you could aim for a shoulder and hit, well, *that* place, was more than Maria could understand. No wonder Carlo was beyond reason—knife in the heart of the Virgin, and all that Sicilian madness that came out in Neapolitans occasionally. It must be terrible for a man to be wounded there.

Maria wondered if Carlos's voice had started to change back into a boyish falsetto again. Count Maldonado, of course, never mentioned any details like that. It was both frightening and almost funny, in a grotesque way, to think of Carlo paying out the money to the professional murderers and squeaking like a clown at them, *"Bwing* me his head and you shall have the *west* of the gold!"* It reminded Maria of one of Sir John's sayings: "Life seems tragic to us only because we're involved in it. To the gods, it is all just a particularly violent comedy."

Well, anyway, the lifespan of Signor Sigismundo Celine would not be long.

Maria turned from the window and padded back to bed. The worst of the nausea had passed; she would try to sleep

*(Advertisement): See *The Earth Will Shake,* by Robert Anton Wilson, Roc Books, 1991.

again. She wondered about the mysterious men that Sir John
met with in private on certain nights. Political business,
probably—but very secretive, indeed. Sir John was very
open with her about everything else; he had *advanced* ideas
about marriage as about all other subjects, true Whig that
he was. Maria admitted that she was really curious about
those secretive meetings. When the men shook hands with
Sir John on leaving, they moved their thumbs in an odd
way—and Maria had seen the same strange thumb movement when Sir John shook hands with her father, Count
Maldonado, back in Napoli. Could there actually be a *secret
society* that extended all across Europe, from snowy England in the north to sunny Napoli in the south, like the
legendary Rosicrucian conspiracy a century ago? It sounded
like an idea from a gothic novel by Walpole, and, besides,
most intelligent people said the Rosicrucians never existed,
aside from the pamphlets put in circulation by some strange
prankster for unknown purposes. She was undoubtedly being silly to even think of such thing.

Of course, the Dominicans back in Napoli were always
warning about such secret societies, which they took very
seriously. They worried about the Rosicrucians, whom they
believed had existed and still existed even now, and about
the Carbonari, who might or might not exist, and about
witches and devil-worshippers and what-all. Mother Ursula
always said the Dominicans had overactive imaginations and
anyway few of them were gentlemen like the Jesuits. Mother
Ursula had even warned Maria not to show her special Talent too openly—the strange gift Maria had of going out of
her body and healing somebody who was in pain. Mother
Ursula said you might be called a saint for that five hundred
years after you were dead but in Napoli today you were
more likely to be burned for it, because the Dominicans
thought any woman with special abilities was a witch.
Mother Ursula had a very low opinion of the Dominicans
and the Holy Office of the Inquisition. She even said the
Inquisition was basically a male conspiracy to keep women
ignorant and frightened.

Well, Maria thought, Mother Ursula did her best to see
that I would not be ignorant or frightened. I can do algebra
and conic sections and read Greek, and I had the courage
to marry a Protestant and come to live in this strange Protestant land. And I have kept my ears and eyes open, and

have noticed that the Protestants are not all bad people, and I would trust many of them sooner than I would trust a Dominican.

Suddenly, without warning, the whole house shook in a crash of thunder that seemed to split the universe.

Maria jumped, just about to enter bed, and felt her heart pounding. The lightning had struck quite close, for the thunder seemed simultaneous with it, and her own shadow on the wall, in the sudden flash, seemed gigantic, almost monstrous. It's just a storm, she told herself; it is only ignorant peasants who say it is God's anger. Mother Ursula said that God was always rational and did not engage in vulgar theatrics. Still, it was shocking to think of such raw power—such mindless power—shaking the walls of your house.

Maria suddenly did not want to be alone. She padded down the hall to Sir John's room and opened the door. He was sleeping with his mouth open, as usual.

She climbed into bed beside him.

"Mmmmh?" he muttered.

She snuggled closer.

"Mmmh," he said, relaxing again.

She held him close and the thunder struck again, further away. It's moving south, she thought. Toward France.

It was just a storm, a natural phenomenon. It had nothing to do with her brother's mad rage against Sigismundo Celine; nothing to do with those strange handshakes that mysteriously linked Protestant liberals in England with Catholic liberals like her father in Italy; nothing to do with her and her child.

Not an omen. Just thunder and lightning.

"Geoffrey," Sir John said in his sleep, sounding almost tragic.

Maria had heard him say that in a dream once before, and he had sounded just as sad that time. She wondered who Geoffrey was; none of their friends had that name. Somebody John knew a long time ago? They must have been very close friends, she thought. There was terrible suffering in that one outcry in the middle of the night. She hugged John gently, feeling his pain as if it were her own, and he turned toward her. "The widow's son," he said, still dreaming. "Me. You. All a masquerade. Impostors."

Then he was deeper into sleep. The dream, whatever it had been, was all over.

The thunder crashed a third time—like fate knocking on the door, Maria thought, feeling morbid again. Hail began to patter on the window; the snow was becoming ice.

It is not fate or an omen or anything like that, Maria told herself. I must not think this way while I am pregnant; it is bad for the child.

It is not an omen. It is not. It is not.

Six

The storm paused over the English Channel, hesitated most of the night, and then rushed down on northern France like an army of icy goblins.

In Paris, the hail became rain again and the day was totally miserable for everyone.

Sigismundo Celine, not aware that he was being hunted by four men with knives, woke and trudged to the University of Paris, cursing only the weather, not knowing he would soon have other problems. Neapolitans are accustomed to rain, but not to the cold rain of Paris that comes in with winds that tear through your clothes and freeze your flesh like meat in a butcher's icebox.

Sigismundo went to an astronomy class, where he disagreed with his professor about the total mass of the solar system; he was called "insolent" for his persistence in arguing the point. He went on to a music class, where he disagreed with his professor about the theory and practice of counterpoint; he was told he was "conceited" that time.

In the afternoon, he had no university classes, so he went to see his new fencing master and practiced *ripostes* for an hour and a half. He felt so keyed up after the exercise that he spent the evening at the Maison Rouge, trying to avoid thinking about Uncle Pietro's warnings that all those girls carry the French pox. He enjoyed himself with Fatima, the black one from Algiers.

"You are *formidable*," he told her afterwards, most sincerely.

Sigismundo had passed Luigi Duccio, master stonecutter, in the middle of the afternoon, without recognizing him, thinking only: That fellow might be another Neapolitan. But Sigismundo was on his way to fencing class and had no time to strike up a conversation with an artisan.

Duccio noticed Sigismundo, however, and recognized him. The nephew of Pietro Malatesta, Duccio thought. You can tell his arrogance by the way he walks, the way he wears his sword, everything about him.

He had heard Sigismundo perform at the Teatro San Carlo in Napoli once. Amazing music, he thought. Like nobody else in Europe: no wonder the audience responded with both applause and angry boos. The same arrogance that shows in his walk. He's going to remake music in his own image, is what he thinks. We were all that way at his age. He will live and learn, as we all do.

At this time of year, Paris has a special air about it.

The rich, the medium rich, even the almost rich, all carry perfumed handkerchiefs. This is not foppery or affectation; it is an attempt to ward off that special aroma by which Paris is easily recognized even as much as eight miles away, downwind. Without the perfume, one simply reels.

Last August, the Lieutenant of Police, the urbane Gabriel de Sartines, ordered 22,000 hogsheads of water dumped into the Grand Sewer—the stream of liquid filth that flows diagonally across the city from the Bastille to Chaillot. That was Sartine's way of trying to deal with the special aroma of Paris. Ameliorating the stench is part of the duties of the lieutenant: he is in charge of the *bureau de revitaillement*, which supervises the markets and ensures that enough food arrives every day to feed the 600,000 citizens of the city; he also hires the men to clean the streets—as far as that is possible. He keeps the street lanterns lit, part of the time. He employs the Inspectors of Books, who ensure that nothing offensive or unruly gets published, unless they are paid suitable bribes first. And, of course, Lieutenant Sartines also cooperates with the *lieutenant civil* and the *lieutenant criminel* in administering what later ages would consider a rudimentary police department. That consists, in this year 1771, of 48 *commissaires,* 20 inspectors, 150 watchmen of the night patrol, 1,400 officers (who, like soldiers, may wear swords but may not carry concealed weapons), and several thousand *mouches,* or informers, who are only part-time and occasional employees but who do happen to know, collectively, most of the clandestine and criminal activities afoot in the City of Light.

All of this is a great deal of responsibility for the Lieutenant of Police, and Sartines can hardly be blamed if Paris still reeks, even in the winter. *Mon dieu,* he does not quite have the funds to keep the street lanterns lit all year long; that's why he only orders them lit on completely moonless nights. Listen, *mon ami,* it costs the State half a million fornicating *francs* just to care for the king's *dogs* every year, not to mention the astronomical sums spent in keeping Madame Du Barry in furs and jewels—do you think there is enough left over to light the ensanguined streets or get rid of this damnable stink? You must be new here . . .

I assure you that Lieutenant Sartines would like to clean up this jewelled cesspit of a city. He has certainly said, on many occasions, that if it were possible to get rid of the stink, he would by God do it in a shot. It is *not* possible. Sartines shares the national philosophy: What cannot be cured must be endured. Every May, and sometimes in July, and occasionally again in August as last year, he orders the Grand Sewer flushed; for the rest, he carries a perfumed handkerchief like everybody else who can afford one.

Observe: The Grand Sewer empties, see, into the stream of Menilmontant, which is now rising and sending little tongues of sewage into the adjacent streets. Menilmontant flows, here, into the Seine, which is also tossing desperately in the storm. The Seine eventually recirculates all the filth back through the city. No wonder the favorite oath in Paris is *merde, alors!*

It has been that way, more or less, since 1181, although a few cesspits have been added to take off the excess. You do not want to investigate these pits, I assure you. Some madman in the palace administration once ordered them emptied in 1663, and five workmen dropped dead as soon as they opened the first one. From toxic fumes or from failure of the heart—who knows? *Nobody* would open the second pit. The idea was abandoned, you can be sure. The filth permeates the soil by osmosis, as it flows in the river. All cities are dirty, of course—that is why many agree with Rousseau that we should abandon these sties and flee back

to the hills and forests like Red Indians*—but by universal
consent Paris is the foulest metropolis in Europe. The royal
family has long ago fled to Versailles, where the paresis eats
their brains and they play at being shepherds.

Eh, bien: the lovely effluvium of excrement and garbage
is only part of the discreet charm of Paris. In the west you
will notice the Charnel House of the Innocents, the huge
cemetery that has buried the paupers of 22 parishes for 800
years. When the wind blows from that direction, you will
wish to run as far as Moscow. If you are close enough, you
will observe unlovely vapors rising from the soil, especially
over the mass graves where victims of the frequent plagues
have been dumped in lots of 1,200 to 1,500 together. These
vapors turn the walls and windows of nearby houses a memorable collection of morbid colors, a Goya nightmare scene
it is; the residents of those houses die surprisingly young
even in a time and place where the average life expectancy
is 28 years. Around the corner is the opera, where you will
see, on good evenings, hundreds of fine ladies and gentlemen rushing from their coaches to get indoors quickly—
with perfumed handkerchiefs over their noses.

Since the House of the Innocents is for paupers and since
it has been filled many times over during eight centuries,
many of the dead are merely heaped on top of older corpses,
in shallow holes. The *philosophe* Voltaire (born François-
Marie Arouet) nearly "lost his dinner" passing there one
evening when he saw wild dogs digging into the mud to
gnaw human meat off the bones.

During a heavy rain like this, this pestilential soil also
washes into the Seine and recirculates through the city.

And the waters of the Seine are used in baking the bread
that *everybody* eats.

Why not? The germ theory of disease will not be devised
for nearly a century. The plagues are not attributed to the
foulness of the water but to the Wrath of God. That is the
official explanation, endorsed by the Church. Voltaire, that
old cynic, of course has different ideas. He attributes the
plagues to the *indifference* of God! That is why he has to

---

*Rousseau by 1771 was seeing enemies everywhere and showing other
signs of an Altered State of Consciousness. Probably he had syphilis by
then, too. Almost everybody did.

live over the border in Switzerland, for uttering blasphemies like that.

This is called the Age of Illumination, best joke of all. The *philosophes* tell each other how enlightened the world is becoming. They believe it, even as they munch the bread made with the water drained off cesspools and corpses.

Seven

The rain continued all day. In the evening, the Duc de Chartres—acne-scarred but handsome enough in an age when most beautiful women and dandyish men carry the pits of smallpox on their faces—Chartres, soon to be the richest man in France and already known as "the friend of the people," or "the only true friend of the people," or "the best friend the people of France ever had"—*Chartres*, soon to be *Orléans* and to lead the "Orleanist faction" in the coming struggle—Chartres, who as Orléans will be denounced by Robespierre as "the arch-conspirator of *all* known history," that *Orléans* whose motives and methods are still debated two hundred years later*—he dined, that night of January 18, 1771, on a splendid pâté of goose livers, two marvelous mixed salads of greens and cheeses, a platter of six sweetened fruits, two roast ducklings absolutely in their prime, three joints of *formidable* beef, choice green peas, a split of amusingly pretentious champagne, germy white bread, and a demitasse of devilish coffee black as sin. The great man then belched; biology and chemistry ordained it.

Most of the people of whom Chartres was the friend dined on one bottle of porter (cheap beer without a head) and germy black bread.

Chartres belched again. Ah, well—the laws of chemistry are ineluctable even for the great and mighty.

*"I dislike defiling these pages with the detested name of Orléans"—Robison, *Proofs of a Conspiracy*. But Robison appears to have been in an Altered State of Consciousness, too. De Selby, op.cit., calls Robison "A Scots logician—that is to say, a talking mule."

Chartres then retired to his study to compose a letter. He wrote rapidly, with an elegant hand, and, alas, belched again, and then farted. Inexorable chemistry.

A footman was summoned. The footman took the letter to the street, and as soon as he opened the door, held a perfumed handkerchief to his nose.

A man named Jean Jacques Jeder happened to be passing. One look was enough to identify his station in life; you can be sure the footman addressed him as *tu*, not as *vous*.

Jeder, an unemployed cabinetmaker and joiner, agreed to deliver the letter for two sous.

Jeder had been unemployed for six months, this time. He had three small children; he lived with them and his wife in a hovel that did not have any of the more attractive features of the stables where Chartres kept his horses.

Jeder was five feet tall—average height for a worker of that time. He had the black hair and swarthy skin of the south, his ancestors having come up from Rennes-le-Château a few generations ago. Do not ask how he has managed to feed his family for half a year without wages: a man must do what a man must do. It is called grab-and-run work. If you come up on them from behind, you can knock them out sometimes before they see your face, and then you do not have that ugly business of slitting their throats (which leaves a mortal sin on your soul until you go to Confession.) A landlord coming home from a tavern at night might have enough coins on him to feed Jeder's brood for a month or longer. "Life is hard," Parisians say, "but it is harder if you have too many scruples."

Jeder was irritated to find that the letter was addressed to Lieutenant Sartines. If it had been addressed to anyone else, Jeder could have collected five sous more by taking it to Sartines first. The Lieutenant has a most ingenious man in his employ who can replace a wax seal on a letter so that not even God himself would know that it had been opened.

Everybody who is unemployed in Paris and quite a few who are merely in debt know that Sartines pays reasonable prices for information received. Of course, that makes you a *mouche*, and everybody despises *mouches*, even the other *mouches;* but "life is harder if you have too many scruples," a man must do what a man must do, and, besides, do you think the rich got where they are by being perfectly honorable?

Jean Jacques Jeder delivered the letter to the *Sûreté* in ten minutes—a miserable walk in the cold rain, with sewage overflowing into the streets now. The letter remained there, a potential threat to Sigismundo Celine, until the lieutenant arrived the following morning, when it became a kinetic threat.

THEY say (but you know the sort of things THEY say) that Sartines is common. A mere fishmonger's son, in fact, who has advanced through ruthlessness and cunning. He knows they call him "Sardines" behind his back. *Eh, bien,* he is cultured, he consorts with encyclopedists and *philosophes;* when he had his coat of arms created, lovely man, he had a sardine included in the design, to show what he thinks of what THEY say. But then—he reputedly has the largest collection of wigs in all Paris, even more than Chartres or Chartres's father, Orléans; he is wearing one of them this morning: Casanova never looked grander. Maybe the fishmonger rumor does bother him a bit. He certainly wants you to know he's important. You can see it in his face.

Sartines guessed what Chartres's letter was, as soon as he saw that it was from a cousin of the king. Those fellows never communicated with the lieutenant except for one purpose.

He opened the seal; his expectations were confirmed. Another!

Sartines trudged down the hall to the *Bureau de Cabinet* and handed the document to a commissaire.

"Write out a *lettre de cachet,*" he said briefly. There was no need for explanation or elaboration.

The commissaire peered at the duc's elegant handwriting. "Wait, can you read the bastard's name?"

Sartines leaned over. "Celine," he said. "Sigismundo Celine. A Neapolitan, he must be."

"Tough shit for him," the commissaire said. "He'll wish he had never left dear old Napoli."

Theoretically, only the king could order a *lettre de cachet.* But, well, Louis XIV was obliging to friends and relatives, and Louis XV, now on the throne, is equally tolerant when it suits his whims. The *Bureau de Cabinet* writes the *lettres* and any of thousands of nobles can order them; Lieu-

tenant Sartines only refers the matter back to the court in
very special circumstances. Such ambiguous cases do arise
once in a while—recently, one duc had ordered a *lettre de
cachet* on another, and Sartines knew that each duc had the
delusion that he was the king's closest confidant and the one
and only *real* head of the one and only *real* spy network in
France. Sartines also knew how each duc had gotten that
remarkable idea: old Louis had encouraged it. It was the
king's singular habit to duplicate many functions, especially
clandestine ones, and set all of his spies spying on others
of his spies.

Typically, when Sartines referred that tricky case back to
Versailles, Louis rescinded the *lettre* and ordered the duc
who had requested it confined to his estates for six weeks.
And of course, at the end of six weeks, the outraged and
baffled duc was summoned to Versailles and again convinced that he was the *only* true head of the *only* true spy
service, and that his house arrest had been necessary to
protect his "cover."

"You can't tell a good intelligence agency by its cover,"
the king chortled.

Louis XV likes to think of himself as a fox, a veritable
Machiavelli; he firmly believes that all those rumors about
the "Italian pox" having gotten to his brain and turned him
mad are just due to the fact that most people are too simple
to realize how devious his own ingenious machinations are.
Sartines does not object to any of this; it keeps the king
happy. Meanwhile, Sartine's own spy network pretty much
does know what is going on, most of the time.

Sartines shares the general view that what is wrong with
the king is the Italian pox. He also agrees with Pierre and
Georges and Lucien and Armand that it was brought to
France by Italian sailors, or *diegos*.

He would have been astounded to know that Sigismundo
Celine, who always worried that he had caught it every time
he went to a "house," called it the French pox—as did
everybody back in Napoli. The Neapolitans were all convinced that it had been brought to Napoli by the French
army when the Bourbons annexed southern Italy.

Everybody thinks somebody else is to blame for life's
little problems.

Whether venereal disease was French or Italian in origin,

the king certainly had a beautiful case of it. Sartines could tell you a lot about that if he were the sort who talked indiscreetly. For six years now he has suffered constant humiliation about the d'Éon matter. The Chevalier Charles Geneviève Louis Auguste André Timothée d'Éon de Beaumont, that is. The "lady knight," as the English call him, or her, or it. This damned d'Éon is the king's top spy in England, and everybody in England knows it. The problem is that d'Éon went off his (or her?) head back in '66 and started dressing as a woman. Worse, he (she?) is so good in drag that there is now lively debate on both sides of the channel about whether the lady knight is a man who decided to become a woman or is really, as she (he?) claims, a woman who for a long time deceived people into thinking she was a man. Sartines is mortified by the whole unsavory mess. It is no credit to France, he thinks, to have a secret agent who is more conspicuous and controversial than a two-headed goat. It makes French Intelligence seem not only inept but grotesque. But the king will not discharge d'Éon. He says that having such an absurd spy in public view distracts the English from what his other spies are doing.

This is true enough, but it reduces the whole spying business to farce. It is not *professional,* Sartines thinks. My God, if all Europe is laughing at your spies, next they will be laughing at your diplomats and the government itself could be in jeopardy.

Authority, Sartines knows, depends on nobody laughing at the wrong time.

Eight

In half an hour the *lettre de cachet* was dispatched to the army barricades at *les Invalides* where it was officially accepted by one Captain Henri Teppis de Loup-Garou.

According to the usual procedure, Captain Loup-Garou picked six soldiers for the job—tough customers who looked like the devil's own bastard sons, veterans of a dozen or more campaigns in the endless wars Louis XV had entered because in his altered state of consciousness he saw enemies everywhere. Loup-Garou ordered these *monstres* to present themselves, armed, for a special assignment at midnight. It always helped to have the tallest, ugliest, most ferocious types on a job of this kind, and there was a definite advantage in waiting until the subject was asleep. A man hauled out of bed in his nightshirt is easy to handle, especially if he is confronted with six men who happen to look like mountain gorillas from Africa stuffed into military uniforms.

Loup-Garou made a note to remind himself to be ready at midnight when the six ogres would report to him. He was not particularly concerned. This was all routine. He had processed scores of undesirables this way.

He never wondered for a moment if this Signor Celine had done anything wrong, or deserved what was about to happen to him, or who had ordered the *lettre*. He was not given to wondering or speculating.

"I am a plain, blunt soldier," he liked to say. "I make no pretense of being an intellectual."

Gabriel Honoré de Mirabeau—who did make some pretense of being an intellectual, and who later became, if only for a short while, an official Hero of the Revolution*—did speculate a great deal about the sort of men who were unwilling guests of the state because of *lettres de cachet.*

This was because Mirabeau himself spent a great deal of time in prisons during the 1770s as a result of two *lettres de cachet.* The first *lettre,* ordered by his father, was intended to punish him for getting into debt. "The boy needs to be taught a lesson," the old man said; Mirabeau never forgave him, and never forgave the government for allowing old bastards like that to treat their sons that way. The second *lettre,* which kept Mirabeau in prison even longer, was ordered by the Marquis de Monnier, to punish him for an amusing, if trifling, indiscretion with de Monnier's wife, Sophie—they had gone off together on a holiday for a few months—well,

---

*And was therefore a member of the Illuminati, according to William Guy Carr's *Pawns in the Game.* But then, Carr believes everybody even slightly to the left of Ronald Reagan is a member of the Illuminati, and a dupe of the Elders of Zion as well. De Selby and La Fournier agree for once in calling Carr "overly imaginative." Wilgus more bluntly calls him "bizarre." Of course, de Selby's writings on the Illuminati (*Golden Hours,* vols. VII-VIII, XXXII especially) are among his most controversial; the venomous Hanfkopf is especially contemptuous *(De-Selbyismus and Dummheit,* op.cit. 44-63) of de Selby's thesis that the Illuminati were primarily a front for Benjamin Franklin and that their major concern was the utilization of electrical light to banish "teratological molecules" from our cities. Prof. Flahive's *Teratological Evolution,* op. cit. 23-4, argues that "far from the dedicated and somewhat recondite pedant described by many, the real de Selby was not above a little joke now and then," and dismisses these historical digressions as "the sage of Dalkey in a mood of playful speculation." Hanfkopf's intemperate and abusive reply to Flahive *(Werke,* V, 56-203) went far beyond the usual restraints of academic polemic, and it is to be regretted that it included undocumented and slanderous remarks about "Celtic conspiracies" and "academic apologists for the Sinn Fein bombers." Flahive replied with simple dignity *(Royal Sir Myles na gCopaleen Institute Journal,* III, 4), and it is distasteful to record that this led only to further abuse from Hanfkopf. Prof. Flahive has told me that he believes to this day that the anonymous letters sent to the Irish Police at that time, which led to his being repeatedly interrogated by Special Branch about various terrorist activities, and which emanated from Heidelberg (as shown by the postmarks), contained in places the sort of errors in English grammar typical of those who, although skilled in the language, are more familiar with German construction. "There were a few sentences," he says, "which almost sounded like the Katzenjammer Kids."

maybe several months, actually—and she was good in bed, but not so good that a man deserved prison for having enjoyed her sporting instincts. You can be sure Mirabeau had ample motive for becoming a Hero of the Revolution. He wanted to tear the whole government apart by the time he finally got out of prison.

Mirabeau made a detailed study of the men he met in prison and how they had gotten there—what else could a philosopher do with all that boredom nagging at him? Many, he determined, were like himself in the first case: being punished by their families for unruly behavior. And a surprising number were like himself in the second case, although a few were in exactly the reverse position, having been jailed for being married to women who happened to be desired by somebody higher than themselves in the aristocracy.

Real criminals—thieves and outlaws—seldom went to prison at all. They were usually drawn and quartered or sometimes still impaled, but a lucky few, who had only stolen a few sous worth of bread, got off with hanging.

The guillotine would introduce more scientific and therefore more humane executions to France, after Thermidor. Captain Loup-Garou would be among its victims. He had no foreknowledge of that on January 18, 1771, any more than poor Armand knew that he had only nine hours left to live.

That afternoon, the rain having stopped finally, the splendid Duc de Chartres added further to his reputation as the friend of the people. He drove through the Faubourg St. Denis, where the manual workers and the unemployed lived, and ordered his coachman to stop for a few minutes while he distributed coins to the needy. Several men circulated through the crowd later, shouting, "Good old Chartres—there's the man who should be our king!"

THEY said in the salons that evening that these men were secretly in the pay of Chartres himself; but THEY will say anything, God knows.*

---

*This incident can be found in a sober sociological work called *The Taking of the Bastille,* but I forgot to jot down the author's name and the man came around and told me the library was closing and—well, you know. I'm sure you can look it up for yourself if you're really curious.

Nine

"**B**ut really," Lucien said, still smiling, "you should read this guy Spartacus."

"I don't have the time for them pamphlets," Armand said. "Besides, what's the use, you know? Guys like us, there's no percentage in getting all worked up about things. Nobody gives a shit what we think, is what it is."

"I wish Pierre would get back," Georges said.

"I'm just telling you for your own good," Lucien insisted, still smiling. "You worry too much, Armand. You say you're up for any piece of work that comes along, but you're really still a farm boy. You still got the horseshit between your toes. That's no good, Armand. What this city is, is a goddam jungle. You go on believing all that crap the village abbé told you, you don't have a chance here."

"Your principal problem," Armand said, "is that you got a big mouth. You know that, Lucien? You talk too goddam much is what it is. I said I'm up for a wet job and I'm up for a wet job, period. I need the goddam money as much as you do."

"I wish Pierre would come back," Georges said.

Lucien was still smiling. "You think I talk too much?" he asked. "That means you don't want to hear what I'm saying. You're going to go to a priest and confess after this, Armand, is what you're going to do. And if he's like half the son of a bitch priests around here, he's going straight to Sardines, is what *he's* going to do. And then where does that put us? It puts us in the shit, Armand. Up to our necks."

"Look," Armand said earnestly. "What I believe is my own business, okay? I just come from the farm and you been here five, six years, makes you an expert on everything, you think. I am not a fuckin' idiot, Lucien. I don't tell no priests about wet work, believe me. I don't tell them about grab-and-run either. I want to light a candle now and then for luck, who's it hurt? Does it really bother you? You going to stay awake nights over it? Jesus, I mean, will you?''

"Okay, okay," Lucien said, smiling. "You can light a dozen candles, for all I care. The thing is, this diego, Signor Celine, he probably believes in that stuff the same as you do. So if he lights a candle and you light a candle, how does God decide which of you he likes best, is all I want to know. How's he decide?''

"I wish you guys would get off that religion stuff," Georges said. "It's morbid, a time like this."

"This is the worst part of it," Lucien said, smiling. "The standing around and waiting. When the diego actually comes, that'll be easy by comparison. I done, forget it, never mind what I done, but four against one is a piece of cake. Not a problem in the world. But the standing around and waiting, it always makes you morbid. Brings out the worst in everybody."

'Yeah,'' Georges said. "I wish Pierre would get back."

The three of them stood silent for a moment in the dark alley.

"Anyway," Armand said. "I'm glad it's a diego. Bunch of opera singers, they are."

"At least we know we're in the right neighborhood this time," Lucien said, smiling. "Christ, the last two days, I seen more fuckin' Paris than I ever wanted to see."

"Yeah," Armand said. "But that *Invalides,* you know. That's really something."

"Made out of the sweat and blood of guys like you and me," Lucien said. "This Spartacus, he explains—"

"Hey," Georges said. "Here's Pierre."

"Goddam dogs," Pierre said. "I just stepped in another pile. They should shoot those fuckin' animals."

"Yeah," Lucien said, smiling. "You find the guy, Pierre?''

"I found him," Pierre said. "Eating at a goddam *restaurant.* ''*

"A restaurant," Armand said. "He must be rich. How

---

*The first restaurant was opened in Paris in 1765.

come a goddam diego can eat in a restaurant and guys like us, we got to scratch for every goddam sou?''

"He'll be along any minute," Pierre said, "and you can complain about it to him personally. Now, what I want is, you two get your asses up the street here, see, and wait around the corner. He's wearing a sword, but don't let that bother you none, because when you guys go for him in front, Lucien and me will be coming up behind him."

"We got to be in front?" Armand protested. "But—"

"You're safer there, really," Pierre said. "He'll never get near you, believe me. Just leave it all to me and Lucien. We'll be doing the real work. You're practically getting paid for doing nothing, is what it is. It's your lucky night."

"But," Armand said, "we'll be targets for a guy with a sword, and we only got knives."

"You worry too much," Lucien said, smiling. "Leave it all to Pierre and me."

"Move your asses," Pierre said. "He's coming."

Ten

There was a gibbous moon, so the street lamps were not lit. Sigismundo Celine, digesting a good meal, was walking carefully because eight in the evening is dark in Paris in the winter.

When Georges and Armand suddenly appeared in front of him in the street, Sigismundo, catching a glint of metal, swerved without thinking and backed against the wall of the nearest house. Still not thinking, he looked quickly in the direction from which he had come and saw Pierre and Lucien creeping up, also with knives drawn. Sigismundo then thought *of course*, because he had been acting on reflexes hammered into him by his fencing teachers, and he finished the thought: *Two men with knives would not attack a man with a sword unless they had friends behind him*, and then he thought no more and acted on reflexes again, bouncing off the wall, charging forward, screaming as shrilly as a wild jungle bird, *"Die!"* (that always unnerved them, according to Tennone, his first fencing teacher), and sliced off Armand's hand with one blow and then, still not thinking, ran his sword deep into Georges's chest.

"Diegos," Armand said, eyes popping. "I thought they were op—" He sat down, not voluntarily but not quite falling either, in a state of shock from the pain and feeling dizzy from the sight of so much blood gushing from the stump at the end of his wrist where his hand had been.

Sigismundo had pulled his sword out of Georges's breast and ran forward, away from the knives at his back, not thinking again, and stopped running abruptly to whirl just as Lucien closed on him, and then Sigismundo lunged and

Lucien jumped back, not fast enough, and Sigismundo ran his sword into Lucien's guts, finally thinking: *It was four against one: I should have been afraid.*

"Shit, shit, shit," Lucien said, in the gutter. "I didn't . . ." He died before he could finish explaining what he didn't.

Sigismundo looked wildly about for the fourth assassin, the well-dressed one, Pierre, and saw him backing up slowly, very slowly, calculating, and Sigismundo, hesitated, guessing, then knew, without seeing Pierre's face in the dark, what the shoulders and arms were about to do. Sigismundo screamed *"Die!"* again, knowing he had to kill this one quickly because the right arm was up already and it was obvious that this bastard knew how to throw the blade right to the heart and Sigismundo knew that he would not be able to duck fast enough to avoid it once it was in flight, so he charged and saw, that it *was* in flight, damn it, and then he was on the ground in a tussle and another knife was coming up slowly toward his throat. A knife in somebody's left hand.

So Sigismundo sliced, stabbed, slashed, and saw the knife sinking downward as he realized he had been tackled by the wounded assassin—brave fellow, Armand, with blood flowing out of his right wrist like a geyser, he still had fight in him. Sigismundo sliced again and felt Armand going limp and sliding off him. Leaping to his feet he saw Pierre crouching near him—not preparing to leap, it wasn't that kind of crouch—he was looking for the knife he had thrown.

Sigismundo leaped forward, thrust, and missed for the first time.

He had another conscious thought—*Now I'm feeling it, my reflexes are slipping*—as Pierre ran off.

Sigismundo started to give chase and then thought better of it. He was trembling with fear now. "Watchman!" he shouted. "Watchman! Watchman!" He sobbed once, and retched. Well, that was the purpose of fencing school: to act *first* before the fear overcame you. No way had yet been invented to abolish the fear entirely.

"If they hadn't taken the cows," Armand said. He wasn't dead yet. "Jesus. The cows, the horses, everything. Mama. Why me?"

That's a good question, Sigismundo thought. *Why me?*

"Listen," he said, "who hired you?"

"The cows. They took the cows."

"Never mind the cows. Who hired you?"

"You. You killed me."

"No. You might live. Be brave."

"The Seigneur came. They took the cows. Papa cried."

"The watchmen are coming. They'll take you to a doctor." And if you live they'll hang you, Sigismundo added to himself, but he didn't say that. "Who hired you?"

"Genevieve."

"Genevieve hired you?"

"She was my first girl. God what tits she had. Papa cried."

"Never mind Genevieve and Papa. Who hired you?"

"You killed me, you diego bastard."

"*You* were trying to kill *me*. Who hired you?"

"God what tits. She's a whore now. Whole town ruined. Gone to hell. Jesus. Is it you, Papa?"

"You're off your head. You'd better try to make an Act of Contrition, if you're religious."

"God what tits. April. In the hayloft."

"I'm sorry," Sigismundo said, suddenly feeling that even this creature was human. "Do you want me to pray for you?"

"I want to go home now. I want to see Mama."

Armand died at one in the morning, without making his Act of Contrition. A priest gave him the last rites, but Armand couldn't tell him from the Queen of Sheba.*

---

*Whose mammalian globes, while perhaps not comparable to those of Armand's *formidable* Genevieve, must have been superb; see "The Song of Songs, which is Solomon's," 4:5.

Eleven

Precisely at midnight, Captain Loup-Garou summoned his trolls. Off they went in an English-style coach, big enough for the seven of them. They looked even more feral by torchlight, the Captain thought—they almost frightened him. Soon they were banging their rifle-butts on the Rive Gauche address of this Signor Celine. They banged with great enthusiasm, you must believe—the more noise, the greater the intimidation.

All they succeeded in arousing was a foulmouthed and unintimidated concierge. When she was through summarizing the ancestry, physiology, probable eating habits, and general biological defects of hooligans who come and wake a harmless old lady in the middle of the night, she finally granted, grudgingly, that Signor Celine seemed to have taken it into his head to sleep elsewhere that night, and what else could you expect, these naive young men coming here to the university from sheltered homes and meeting the shameless hussies who parade the streets these days. God must have turned His face away from France entirely—

The only way to terminate her monologue without using a rifle-butt was to salute and leave.

Loup-Garou stationed two of his men across the street, in case Signor Celine *did* return that night. Then he set off for police headquarters; it might have been bad luck, accident, *coincidence,* that Celine was not at home that night—or it might have been something else. Some *mouches* sell information *to* the police, and some sell information *about* the police. Some men vanished off the earth as soon as a *lettre de cachet* was issued; but Loup-Garou had not imagined that a foreigner, a university student, would have that kind of connections. Now, however: if the subject were in flight, it would be necessary to start a joint army-police search operation.

The captain strode into the office of the *lieutenant criminel* and found Lt. Lenoir in conversation with a young Italian—a boy about twenty, dark and stocky like most southerners, with a *banditto* mustache and a gallant goatee.

Loup-Garou and Lenoir stepped into the hall. The captain explained what had happened.

Lenoir smiled. "I wish all police work were this easy," he said. "That is the man you seek, in my office."

"Name of a name," the captain said. "What is he doing here?"

"He was set upon by assassins tonight." Lenoir raised a weary eyebrow. "This is a lad with a true gift for making enemies, it would seem."

"Will you release him into my custody?"

"Oh, certainly. But get a few soldiers in here before you attempt to place him under arrest."

"He's only a *boy*," Loup-Garou said impatiently.

Lenoir shrugged. "He is a Neapolitan."

"Oh? He didn't look *that* dark."

"He is a Neapolitan," Lenoir repeated dreamily, "and two of the professional murderers who attacked him are dead already, and a third is in the hospital bleeding to death as we speak. There was a fourth, and when he finally stops running he will tell the whole world what I tell you now, my Captain: *never* underestimate these Neapolitans."

"He killed three assassins and drove off the fourth?" Loup-Garou could not square that with the image of the boy he had just seen. "My God, what is this Celine?"

"He is a university student, it appears." Lenoir added, maliciously, "Majoring in music, he says."

They arranged a plan suitable for the arrest of one of those goddam Neapolitan wildmen. The four gorillas were summoned, but stationed temporarily in the hall, outside the lieutenant's office. Lenoir and Loup-Garou reentered the room.

Celine looked up inquiringly. He didn't seem much like a fighter, Loup-Garou thought again. Gentle, feminine eyes: artistic. Almost like some Christs in old paintings.

"This is Captain Loup-Garou from the army," Lenoir

said, essaying a swindle he didn't really expect would work. "As an expert, he will examine your sword and testify at the inquest."

And the damned unpredictable diego actually handed the sword over, as innocent as a girl at her first Holy Communion. He was disarmed.

Lieutenant Lenoir quickly stowed the sword behind his desk and Loup-Garou shouted "Hut!" and the four ogres rushed into the room and Lenoir almost had time to think it was too good to be true, and then Loup-Garou said formally, "Sigismundo Celine, I hereby place you under arrest, to be held at the pleasure of the king—"

"But I acted in self-defense," the prisoner Celine protested.

"This is a different matter," Loup-Garou said. "Please come quietly." And he motioned the four gorillas to take up position around the prisoner.

Lenoir saw Celine's eyes dilate for just a second and then the damned Neapolitan wildman was across the room having passed through a hole between the four soldiers, and then he had the window halfway open and one of the soldiers had him by the leg and then another had him around the waist and the bastard shifted his weight abruptly in some weird way and it looked like all three of them would fall through the glass, and then the other two were on him and the one turned to the captain and said "Now, sir?" and the captain said "Now. He needs it."

So while three of the solders held the prisoner Celine, the fourth expertly gave him a vigorous kick in the testicles, full-force with his boot.

Sigismundo Celine stopped struggling. They carried him out of the office without further incident, and Lenoir sat down and tried to visualize the blank time between when Celine was in his chair and when he arrived at the window. There wasn't even a blur in there, Lenoir realized: the bastard was in one place and then he was in the other place.

Maybe I should get a Neapolitan fencing teacher, he thought.

The shades of the big English-style coach were now drawn, so nobody on the street could see the prisoner Celine. That was routine in *lettre de cachet* cases. The soldiers were also under orders to forget the prisoner's face as soon as they were rid of him.

Sigismundo Celine of Napoli was in the process of becoming a non-person.

During the ride to the north end of Paris, the prisoner Celine was silent, Loup-Garou observed, and did not look at his captors. The kick in the family jewels was probably still giving him problems; his lips were white. He was no doubt thinking whatever they all think at this point.

The coach stopped finally; they all disembarked, and you can be sure Captain Loup-Garou was careful at this point. Two soldiers climbed out first, then the prisoner Celine was pushed out after them, then the other two soldiers came out with rifles at the ready. Finally Loup-Garou came out himself.

The prisoner Celine looked up at the eight gaunt towers and recognized the Bastille.

"Christ help me," he said quietly.

Loup-Garou reflected that nearly two-thirds of the men he had brought here said that at this point, when they recognized where they were. The other third mostly said only *"Merde, alors!"*

They were at the gate on the rue St. Antoine. Loup-Garou shouted; the drawbridge began creaking and wheezing and then slowly changing and clattering, as it descended toward them like the hand of some terrible and impersonal giant.

It was now nearly two in the morning, the coldest hour in the coldest month of the year for Parisians. The captain shivered and for a moment felt a flash of empathy: looking at the drawbridge coming down, down, down, he suddenly felt what the prisoner Celine must feel, what all of them must feel when they came to this moment.

Then, where there had been six men, there were only five. The prisoner Celine had disappeared.

Twelve

From THE SECRET TEACHINGS OF THE ARGENTUM ASTRUM:

It is hoped that the candidate has had the prudence to burn the previous pages.

The actual situation of humanity, to conclude this part of our argument, is that millions of fools are born each generation to murder millions of other fools for foolish reasons and are blessed by fool priests on both sides and led by fool governments. Who ignores this universal stupidity does so at great peril; as one would who, living among lions, ignored their ferocity.

The candidate has learned the identity of the center stone of the arch, which the builders rejected. First, as a Freemason, hints and allegories were given; in the second order, the truth was gradually suggested; now, in the third order, all has been made clear. Imagine, however, what would be the fate of one who, believing that this is verily an Age of Reason, an Age of Enlightenment, &c., were to publish a simple, matter-of-fact description of this center stone of the arch of the temple of immortality; if he were to state directly where it is found, how it appears to the eyes, its texture when touched with the fingers, its taste, &c.? In Papist nations, such a man and his book would burn together; in supposedly more illuminated lands, the book would burn and the man would go to prison. Nor would the world condemn him for blasphemy alone, but would pronounce (with not a dissenting voice) that he was depraved beyond the bounds of reason, decency, and common sense. And yet the stone of the arch is worshipped secretly by all those who despise and demean it, and is earnestly sought by every man who would rage in fury to read such a simple description of it. Thus the witty alchemists wrote that it is "hidden with seven seals" and yet is "known to all men."

Let the candidate meditate on this until he understands the extent of the lunacy of this species, and why only the bravest may be entrusted with guardianship of the Grail, the Tree, and the hidden manna. It must never be forgotten that once the cosmic furnace is activated, the candidate is not only in, but totally identical with, the "refiner's fire" of which the Prophet spoke. Only the fool takes our path lightly or in the mood of a game.*

Once again: burn this page before reading further.

---

*The "cosmic furnace" of alchemy is described by the seventeenth-century Rosicrucian Thomas Vaughn as follows: "The true furnace is a little simple shell . . . But I had almost forgot to tell thee that which is all in all, and it is the greatest difficulty in all the art—namely the fire . . . The proportion and regimen of it is very scrupulous, but the best rule to know it by is that of the Synod: 'Let not the bird fly before the fowler.' Make it sit while you give fire, and then you are sure of your prey. For a close I must tell thee that the philosophers call this fire their bath, but it is a bath of Nature, not an artificial one; for it is not of any kind of water . . . In a word, without this bath nothing in the world is generated." *(Works of Thomas Vaughn, Mystic and Alchemist,* ed. A.E. Waite, New York: University Books, 1968.) John Donne more wittily refers to the furnace as a "pregnant pot" in his poem "Love's Alchemy." There seems no ground for de Selby's attempt to identify this allegory with his own "teratological molecules moving backward in the time plenum," except insofar as both are what the poet Yeats called "concepts too subtle for the intellect." La Tournier *(De Selby: Homme ou Dieu?,* p. 23) argues that de Selby actually demonstrated the alchemical transformation to ten witnesses in Trinity College, Dublin: but Hanfkopf *(Werke* IV, 56) replies that all ten "were blind drunk at the time and notorious liars." It should not be forgotten by the serious student that this issue is further complicated by Ferguson's attempted proof that La Fournier and de Selby were the same man writing under two names *(Armageddon,* 78–104), though it needs to be reiterated that La Tournier and La Fournier were definitely two different men. Prof. Han Tui-Po, author of the classic but little-known *de Selby Te Ching,* op. cit., attempted to introduce some restraint and academic objectivity into this increasingly acrimonious matter in a letter to *New Scientist,* XXXI, 6, but Hanfkopf replied with invective about "Marxist conspiracies" and "Oriental treachery," which the editors' attorneys considered potentially actionable and which was, therefore, withheld from publication. It was shortly after this, while addressing the International Astrophysical Society in London, that Prof. Han was found to have 150 kilos of pure heroin in his hotel room. The fact that the British authorities quickly released him unconditionally seems to indicate that his attorneys, and the Chinese ambassador who also intervened, presented a good *prima facie* case that the narcotic was actually planted by agents of some person with an irrational grudge against Prof. Han. Chief Inspector MacAndrew, in charge of the original investigation, admitted (see London *Evening Echo,* 2 Feb. 1974) that the anonymous phone call stating that Prof. Han was "a notorious Communist dope smuggler" was placed by a man with "a thick Germanic accent, almost like Conrad Veidt in *Casablanca.*" In this context the judicious should refer back to the footnote on page 47.

Thirteen

Sigismundo Celine had dropped into a curled ball, rolled under the coach, and instantaneously arisen, running, on the other side. He thought he was into an alley before Loup-Garou noticed that he was gone.

But then he heard a warning shot.

He thought three things:—The Good Captain does not believe in miracles;—he must have run around the coach *immediately* to have seen me duck into this alley; and—I cannot run as fast as I wish because of the damned pain in my groin.

Then he thought: But I am sly and I know many, many tricks. God bless you, Giancarlo Tennone, master of fencing and of more subtle arts.

Meanwhile he had a foot on a window sill and was groping for a drainpipe above.

Before he thought consciously again he had transferred himself to a balcony.

And then the alley was resounding with the boots of his pursuers.

"It's a cul-de-sac. He must be up there," a voice shouted. It was Loup-Garou's voice.

Sigismundo hurled himself forward against a set of French windows that faced the balcony. They were not locked, and his momentum carried him halfway across the room. He saw one candle flickering on a table and a bed near the table and a man and woman in bed, ardently occupied. They did not have the *savoir-faire* of the couple in the famous joke: they stared at him, popeyed.

"Be so good as to keep quiet," he whispered conspiratorially, "and I promise never to tell her husband of this."

"I *am* her husband," said the man angrily. "And who the hell—"

"Her husband," Sigismundo repeated, as if a bit slow. "I beg your pardon. I thought I was still in Paris." But by then he had passed them and was at the hall door. "Pray continue," he added, in his most courteous and apologetic tone.

He was in a hall and again he did not think; his pursuers were below, so *up* was the obvious answer. He found a staircase to the third floor, and quickly took it at a gallop, three steps at a time.

On the stairs he thought the one word, "Two," and when he found that the stairs led to the roof, thank God, he filled in the rest of the thought: Two sets of enemies. I have two opponents, not one. Because nobody would be so redundant as to hire assassins for the same night he orders me arrested. There is one man, or one group, that wants me dead, and another man, or another group, that wants me in the Bastille. Two.

Cagliostro, he thought. That is part of the answer.

But then he was on the roof and saw the first bit of good luck that night. The next roof was quite close: an easy jump.

"He's heading for the roof," a voice shouted. The man who had been in the bed. Doing his duty as a good citizen should, damn his eyes. Well, he will have a hard time getting the lady back in the right mood. Women get skittish at times like this.*

Sigismundo jumped, and it was as easy as it had looked.

The next three jumps were easy, too. Thank God they built the houses close together in this part of Paris. This would almost be fun, he thought, if my balls stopped complaining.

Let them complain, he thought then. They have been kicked with a hard boot. They have a right to complain. It is I who must not listen to them although they complain. I am not my balls. I am not my body. I am not here at all.

---

*"The male sexual drive is insistent, ineluctable, inflexible; the female drive intermittent, interruptible, inchoate." (de Selby, *Golden Hours*, III, 874.) The one great love of de Selby's life, Sophie Deneuve, was actually a lesbian.

That is the teaching of the Rose Cross and I know it works. Without it, I would have been dead two hours ago. Without it, I would be in the Bastille now instead of enjoying healthy exercise on the rooftops. Now I must go away again and not be here.

He made four more jumps and then came back to find himself shinnying down a drainpipe. He thought: Yes, this is intelligent. They must be on the roofs by now, and I am several blocks from where I left them.

But with the return of his rational mind he was again confused. The streets ran at such crazy angles in this neighborhood that he did not know where he was or which was the safest direction to flee.

He stood very quietly and listened for the voices of the soldiers.

". . . must have gone that way . . ." The wind carried the rest of the words away from him. But the voice was closer than he liked.

He began walking very slowly away from the direction of that voice. He did not run now because candlelight was coming from quite a few windows and he did not want to attract attention. He would start running again when he was two or three blocks further south, away from the Bastille.

The sounds and the lights were soon fading behind him. He began to feel hopeful, almost. Even his groin was hurting less. He did not permit himself to think that he had no close friends in Paris, nobody he could really trust or turn to for help; that all of his possible allies were nearly a thousand miles away in Napoli.

Two. And one is Cagliostro.

No, he told himself. That is sloppy thinking. If you must analyze at a time like this, analyze carefully.

Two enemies, and one *perhaps* is Cagliostro.

Then he heard the *swish* immediately behind him and stopped thinking again. He fell prone at once and rolled quickly into the gutter. Supine, he saw his assailant above him, off balance.

Sigismundo quickly bent his knees tight as springs, to have the heels back ready to deliver a kick as the assailant tottered.

Jean Jacques Jeder stared down at him, still carried forward by momentum to the spot where Sigismundo had been, the sock full of rocks in his hand carrying him there, and Sigismundo kicked hard and hit Jeder in both shins.

Jeder made an inarticulate cry of suffering, but even as he fell he tried to turn himself so that he might get the sock into position to hit Sigismundo, and Sigismundo rolled again and came up and kicked Jeder in the side this time.

Jeder said *"Merde"* and fell fully, moaning, but Sigismundo was running again by then.

Sigismundo was thinking of a field in Napoli, a field where a strange northern bird had come to sing just one morning on its migratory flight to Africa, and the beauty of that song had gotten into the revised version of his *Two Nations Sonata;* it had been in that field that he'd faced Carlo Maldonado, the brother of the woman he loved, and thought as he pointed the pistol, "I will aim for the shoulder, because if I kill him the lovely Maria will hate me forever," and he remembered his father's voice, his true father, Cagliostro's father, Peppino Balsamo, and that voice was crying *"Libertà"* as it died in a shriek of pain, as the torturers finished: and the cry of that voice and the song of that strange northern bird in the field were part of the music only he could write, if the damned mechanical Newtonian universe were not forever pushing and shoving him from one crazy melodramatic situation to another, if he only had the time to sit down and write the music, if murder and insanity and suicide and magicians with evil drugs were not always swarming around him: and now false arrest and professional assassins again (as at the beginning), and he knew there was a mystery beyond all the mysteries he had solved in Napoli, a horror behind all the horrors he had endured and survived.

On top of everything else, he thought, I have to run into a professional brigand.

He raced around a corner.

He was face to face with Captain Loup-Garou, who raised his pistol at once.

"Do not move," the captain said. "If you have an itch, do not scratch it. Do nothing but what I say or I will blow your head off, you Neapolitan whoreson."

Sigismundo relaxed. "Captain," he said quietly, "I know when I am beaten. No hard feelings, please. The exercise was good for both of us."

Then he kicked the gun out of the captain's hand and set off again running as fast as he could.

Around the next corner, he encountered two of the soldiers coming out of an alley.

They raised their rifles and aimed carefully. They did not say anything, since they did not need to.

Sigismundo raised his arms in the ancient gesture of surrender.

"We go to the Bastille now," he said. "I wish I knew why."

They returned to the rue St. Antoine. Captain Loup-Garou no longer regarded this as a routine assignment. Celine marched in front, the others behind, with guns pointed.

When they arrived at the Bastille, the captain shouted again and the drawbridge was lowered a second time.

"Give me an excuse," Loup-Garou said between his teeth. "I'd love to shoot you dead." His hand hurt and his pride was injured also; a mere boy, even if Neapolitan and by definition a spawn of darkness, should not have given him and his veterans so much trouble.

They crossed the drawbridge in a new formation—one soldier in front, one on the left of the prisoner Celine, one on his right, the fourth and the captain behind. This Neapolitan bastard might jump in the moat and try to scale the outer wall dripping wet. Some, less tricky than this Celine, had indeed tried that, driven by sheer terror; because at the end of the drawbridge was the second wall, where the true prison began. Once inside there, you were lost forever.

They crossed the moat without incident.

The prisoner Celine was accepted by the officer on watch. The papers were countersigned; Captain Loup-Garou was finished with his job.

Dutifully, he erased the young Italian's face from his memory. But he would remember a new rule of thumb: With Neapolitans, you tie them hand and foot before you put them in the coach.

Fourteen

Sigismundo Celine was lodged in a room at the top of the *Tour de la Liberté*—the ironically-named Tower of Liberty—which faced across the moat and the rue St. Antoine to the old city gate. This room was generally used only for punishment; it was the coldest, loneliest place in the prison except for the underground dungeon where the famous "man in the iron mask" had been stowed. In Sigismundo's case, although he did not know it, he was in this freezing tower only because the prison was overcrowded.

For a Neapolitan, it was a punishment cell indeed, on a winter night with the north wind blowing.

Sigismundo shivered and hugged himself, looking around. The room was about twelve feet by eighteen feet and spotlessly clean. It had a large and comfortable-looking bed, a writing table of respectable oak, and a six-branched gold-tinted candelabrum. There was a chamber pot ornate enough for any nobleman's bedroom. When Sigismundo experimentally opened the shutters, there were no bars on the windows—since nobody had ever been mad enough to attempt the 120-foot leap to the moat below.

It hardly looked like a prison cell at all. There were no instruments of torture on the walls and nobody was screaming in terror in any of the nearby towers.

And he retched and sobbed again. You can postpone the fear, by acting and not being there, but that only postpones it. It is not abolished.

Except for the painful cold, there was nothing especially dreadful happening yet.

Still, Sigismundo had heard his heart start to pound a few

times in his first minutes of looking around and sizing up
the place. That is normal, he told himself. To be set upon
by assassins and kicked in the nuts and clapped in the most
infamous prison in Europe: a man would have to be super-
human not to have some nervous reaction.

He noticed a cold sweat on his brow, running into his
eyes.

I can ignore such phenomena of the first soul, he told
himself.

In Sigismundo's education, in which Aristotelian psychology had been mixed with more modern notions, the
"first soul" was the part of the mind that was most intimately tied to the body and expressed itself through body
signals. He also called it the vegetative soul, following Aristotle, and he had been taught by his fencing master, Giancarlo Tennone, how to ignore it and concentrate on what
must be done in a given situation.

The first step, he reminded himself, is to breathe properly. Do not let yourself gasp for air; that only increases
panic.

Abraham Orfali, who had been Sigismundo's teacher in
Speculative Masonry, said that moving to a foreign country,
fighting a duel, or being arrested all produced the same
effects in the first soul: sweats, palpitations, and a strong
desire to tell your problems to somebody older and prefer-
ably female. You are reliving the anxieties you felt as a baby
when Mama did not come at your call, old Orfali said. Just
understand that this first soul is the baby level of the mind,
and do not let it deceive you.

Yes, Sigismundo thought. When I first came to Paris, I
had some of these feelings. I wanted, more than anything
else, to go back to Napoli and talk to Mama.

He felt his heart pounding again. He breathed carefully,
slowly, and told himself: That is the *baby* mind. I must draw
energy from it up into the *adult* mind and think clearly.

The pounding subsided again.

And then he thought: Why am I here? What horrible mistake, what monstrous injustice has happened? Cagliostro
perhaps hired the assassins, but he would not have the influence to arrange the arrest.

He crawled into the bed, clothes and all, and hugged
himself again for warmth. Might as well try to hold out

against the cold, while wondering about what had happened
. . . what might happen next . . .

In a few moments he was shivering less. Only his nose
and eyes were above the covers. He thought: Well, anyway,
maybe I won't freeze to death before morning.

And the answer came:

Count Maldonado.

After the duel with Carlo Maldonado—that damned idiot
escapade which still made Sigismundo ashamed—a truce had
been negotiated between his uncle, Pietro Malatesta, and
Count Maldonado. If Sigismundo left Napoli and never returned, the feud between the Malatestas and Maldonados,
which had ended only a few years ago, would not be resumed. The Count had said that he wished peace between
the families as much as Pietro Malatesta did.

Sigismundo thought: The Count was *lying*. He is rich
enough and powerful enough to accomplish this. Somehow,
through his friends, he has bribed the right people in the
French government, and that is why I am here.

Then he thought: Now wait a minute. That is also an
inference, a deduction. Old Abraham Orfali had taught him
that the worst fool is he who makes an inference, assumes
it is a fact, and does not go on to consider alternative ex-
planations.*

---

*Cf. de Selby: "All perception is inferential; all inference uncertain;
all theory, a combination of perception and inference, is therefore educated guessing." *(Golden Hours*, I, 93). Ferguson *(Armageddon*, 32)
claims de Selby's mind was ruined by reading David Hume while smoking hasheesh. Frau Doktor Turn-und-Taxis in her *Ist de Selby eine Droge*,
op. cit., points out that the evidence of de Selby's alleged cannabis habit
is entirely based on "the discredited and often fraudulent pages of the
embittered Hanfkopf"; but La Fournier *(de Selby: L'Enigme de l'Occident)* argues at some length (p. 88–142) that nobody can understand Hume
who has not experimented with hasheesh, nobody can understand hasheesh without mastering the epistemology of Hume, and nobody can begin
to appreciate de Selby without extensive *"immergence"* (immergence) in
both Hume and hasheesh. (It must not be forgotten that Ferguson has at
least some very suggestive evidence to back his claim that La Fournier
is a non-person, a masque, a pen name for de Selby himself.) The disinterested scholar must agree that Frau Doktor Turn-und-Taxis seems to
have demonstrated beyond further *caveat* that the legend of the "dope-
crazed" de Selby is at least ninety-five percent the product of Hanfkopf's
fevered imagination, and the other five percent we have only on the testimony of very questionable witnesses, who were themselves so often
"stoned" or "wasted" (as the argot has it) that they seldom remembered

Carlo?

The Count might be acting in perfectly good faith. Carlo himself might be seeking revenge.

Would Carlo be able to manage an affair like this?

Sigismundo pondered a while longer and then realized he was thinking in circles. Three suspects—Cagliostro, the Count, and Carlo—and no hard facts to determine which of them was guilty of which part of the night's conspiracies.

And there might be a fourth player in the game, and a fifth, persons he did not even know were concerned with him. All three of his suspects might be innocent of this business, and the unknown fourth and fifth might have engineered it all.

This is the type of thinking that drives men mad, he told himself. Leave it alone for a while. Think constructively, about for instance the very interesting topic of how you are going to get out of this place.

Into his mind came a picture of something he had hardly noticed earlier: the old city gate across the rue St. Antoine from the Bastille.

Once you were past that gate you would be in open country. There were hundreds, *thousands* of places to hide out there.

Most excellent, he told himself. you are in fine form tonight. You have solved all your problems at once. To get past the gate all you have to do is climb down the sheer face of this tower, all 120 feet of it, and then scale the first wall, a mere eighty feet it looked like, and then swim the moat and climb up the second wall, another eighty-footer, and then simply stroll across the rue St. Antoine and overpower however many sentries there are at the gate.

I begin to perceive, he told himself, why nobody in all history has ever escaped from the Bastille.

He who understands Speculative Masonry, old Abraham Orfali said, does not know despair, for every hour brings him new information to be absorbed and utilized.

If nobody had ever escaped from the Bastille, then it was Sigismundo's job to prove that it *could* be done.

who they had been talking to. (The infamous letters to the Berlin police, which led to Frau Doktor Turn-und-Taxis being investigated as an alleged gunrunner for the Gehlen *apparat*, seem to have all had Heidelberg postmarks.)

Fifteen

been a guest of the place on two occasions when he published "seditious" and "offensive" books, pronounced the building excellent. In fact, few of the recent installations

Actually, aside from the cold quarters he had been given, Sigismundo Celine was in one of the most progressive prisons in Europe—for the time. You do not believe it. Nobody believes it; the legend, the horror, live on despite a thousand corrections by objective historians. They have proven that the man in the iron mask was in a *silk* mask, and that he was not the king's brother but just a Spanish spy: everybody still prefers the romantic legend. Other prisons of the time were true hellholes, and the Bastille a gentlemen's club by comparison, but nobody wants to hear that. They prefer the horror stories.

In fact, old Jumilhac, the governor, tried to make his prisoners as comfortable as possible, and not just because he had read the humanitarian arguments of the *philosophes*. (Read them? He has met them personally, in many cases.) Jumilhac has pragmatic reasons for his gentle penology. Very few of the guests of this establishment are ordinary criminals. Most are here for being on the wrong side of some upperclass power struggle and—politics being what it is—most of them not only get released eventually but find their way back into government. Jumilhac does not want any of them holding a grudge against him: Today's prisoner may be tomorrow's Minister of Justice.

Originally built in 1370 as a fortress guarding the northern approach to Paris, the Bastille had been converted into a state prison by Cardinal Richelieu, who also established the peculiar secrecy that ever after surrounded it. It was this secrecy which made the Bastille a symbol of terror, not any of the practices of the recent governors. Voltaire, who had been a guest of the place on two occasions when he published "indelicate" and "offensive" books, pronounced the food excellent; indeed, few of the general population ate as well as the men in special state custody at the Bastille. Diderot corrected the proofs of his first *Encyclopédie* there; Morellet, the satirist, had been there for six weeks once; Jumilhac liked to boast of the distinguished men who, due to lapses in *good taste* or *common sense,* had been remanded to his custody for a while.

There was an arcade of shops in the south wing, across the courtyard from the prison proper and next to the governor's office, where the prisoners could buy almost anything available in the best shops outside the double walls. Each prisoner received a weekly allowance that was comfortable, and those whose presence in the Bastille was not a state secret were allowed to receive additional money from their families. Some especially sensitive cases were even allowed to leave on personal business occasionally, on their word of honor to return by nightfall.

The infamy of the Bastille was entirely due to the fact that its activities were secret and terrifyingly random. There were nearly 400,000 nobles in France, most of them peevish if insulted or inconvenienced; once a *lettre* had been ordered by one of them, the prisoner was held, under law, "at the pleasure of the king." Since old Louis's actual pleasures were mostly limited to his human and mechanical toys, especially Mme. Du Barry, he neither knew nor cared about such cases. The persons so held were detained indefinitely—or until powerful friends (if they had any) intervened in their behalf.

There were a dozen or so prisons for such persons, but the Bastille, because it was so old and ugly, and because it stood at the north gate where every visitor to Paris would see it eventually, had become the symbol of the whole frighteningly arbitrary system.

When a man disappeared, he might have been murdered by brigands and dumped into the Seine to feed the fishes; people said, knowingly, "He's probably in the Bastille." He might have been sent into exile, with instructions to leave by night and speak to nobody*; but people still said, "He's probably in the Bastille."

Sigismundo Celine did not know much of this, but he did

*As happened, e.g., to Necker in 1789.

know that the fortress-prison was regarded with universal horror and loathing by the general population. He thought torture might be as common there as in the dungeons of the Inquisition. He had images of the thumbscrew, the Iron Maiden, manacles and whips. He wondered how many of the other prisoners might be the most violent kind of bandits and highwaymen.

Courage, he told himself; remember Nasrudin and the horse.

That was the favorite story of old Abraham Orfali back in Napoli. Nasrudin was one of the founders of Speculative Masonry in the east, Abraham said, and there were thousands of legends about him still told everywhere from North Africa to India. In this particular story, Nasrudin was condemned to death by a fundamentalist Shah who did not like his "liberal" interpretations of some of the best-known verses in *al-Koran*. Mullah Nasrudin then made a strange proposal, one that illustrated the Masonic teaching that every hour presents new opportunities. "Postpone my execution for a year," the divine Mullah said, "and I will teach your horse to fly." The Shah, intrigued, agreed to this bizarre proposition; but he took care to keep Mullah Nasrudin imprisoned within the palace walls until the horse did begin to fly.

"What do you expect to gain by this?" Nasrudin was asked after a few weeks, by a disciple who had been allowed to visit him in the stables where he was muttering Greek incantations over the horse.

"A year is a long time," the wonderful Mullah said. "In a year, the Shah may die, and new Shahs always pardon all condemned men on their coronation day. Then again, in a year's time, there may be a revolution, or a foreign invasion. In a year, the palace guards will have many opportunities to become careless, and I will always be watching for a chance to escape.

"And if worse comes to worst," Nasrudin concluded, "maybe the damned horse can fly!"

The north wind blew down on Paris like a wave of ice. Sigismundo tried to ignore it and get some sleep. Courage, he told himself again. Maybe the damned horse *can* fly.

The prisoner Celine finally slept.

It is the Age of Illumination, nonetheless; we insist upon that. Voltaire, at seventy-seven, has poured forth irony and sarcasm against every form of tyranny and superstition for nearly fifty years now; he sleeps across the border in Swit-

zerland, so they cannot throw him back in the Bastille with
Signor Celine, but his words are known to all who can
read—a number which is increasingly rapidly. Travelers tell
of seeing coachmen read while they wait for their lords and
ladies to finish shopping, soldiers reading, even *laborers*
reading. Diderot, at fifty-eight, has almost completed his
revised *Encyclopédie,* enlarged and more lavishly illustrated
than ever but still full of bad taste and offensive ideas—he
even questions the Virgin Birth! He is in Russia now, engaged in offering further enlightenment to the enlightened
despot Catherine II, who after murdering an undesirable
and reactionary husband has decreed many liberal reforms
and is eager for philosophical wisdom.

Danton? He is a mere schoolboy of twelve. But Marat is
already twenty-eight and in London; he is writing *The
Chains of Slavery,* a book which claims that all religions
are tools invented by the wicked to render the masses stupid
and exploit them. Like Luigi Duccio, he has also started
thinking about economics.

De Sade, that blond, blue-eyed, angel-faced young man,
was placed under house arrest back in '68 for his usual
entertainments—flagellation and aggravated sodomy upon
four prostitutes was alleged, with the further horror that he
ordered one of them (she testified) to assist him to ejaculate
upon a crucifix, crying out "terrible blasphemies against
Our Lord" until he climaxed. His wife and mother-in-law
still thought at that time that he could be reformed, so they
procured a *lettre de relief* from Louis XV, who after all is
a close relative of this egregious family. De Sade was merely
confined to his estates in Provence, without guards, so he
did wander a bit—THEY say (but you know the sorts of
things THEY say) that he now has four "love nests" in the
south, where whores less squeamish than those who denounced him in '68 nightly participate in *divertissements*
that would curl the hairs of the Borgias.

Beaumarchais, at thirty-six, has not yet written any of the
plays that will make him famous; he has spent his youth
acquiring a fortune, by marrying two noble ladies in rapid
succession—he claims it is just coincidence that both ladies
died very soon after making out their wills in his favor. THEY
say that he poisoned both of them, but you know the sort of
things THEY say. And now he, this laughing and ambiguous
Beaumarchais, is spending a large part of his new wealth to

make himself well-known in the important circles of Paris and Versailles; his reward will be that soon he shall become one of the few full-time *mouches* in the employ of the ingenious Lieutenant Gabriel de Sartines, and the highest paid of them all. That will prove most beneficial when Sartines moves to the forefront of the government under Louis XVI.

Buonaparte? In the godforsaken goodfornothing island of Corsica, he has a load of crap in his pants and is howling for Mama to come change him. He is two years old.

Count Cagliostro of the violet eyes and strange talents has been traveling south for three days in the fastest coach possible, away from Paris and from any provable connection with the Duc de Chartres, for the same reason that Sigismundo Celine is freezing in the cold at the top of the Tower of Liberty.

The Grand Orient lodge of Egyptian Freemasonry, that strange contraption which will swallow and ingest all French Freemasonry in the next seventeen years, is now a year old and will not make its first public moves for another year. But Lieutenant Sartines, you can be sure, already knows a great deal about it—as he does about other Masonic orders, and the *Carbonari,* and every other society that imagines it is secret.

Sartines knows that this Grand Orient lodge will admit any initiated Freemason and nobody else. He knows that it alleges that it has found the lost Mason Word which other lodges are seeking—whatever that means. He knows that it claims the same powers of magick and theurgy as the legendary *Fraternitas Rosae Crucis*—good bait to hook fools, in his opinion. He knows that some very shady and spooky individuals are involved, such as the notorious international spy and adventurer "Count" Casanova, and a more recent Italian fraud, "Count" Cagliostro. And he even knows that the secret Grand Master of this carnival is the beloved philanthropist, humanitarian, and "friend of the people," the Duc de Chartres. He doesn't miss much, this Sartines.

He has even looked into the royal genealogies and has made himself a little chart (which he promptly destroyed, after memorizing it) tracing the lines from Chartres to Louis XV, with the age and life expectancy of each person. It is possible, he thinks, that if the right people die at the right times, and if a few others are assisted in dying early, in ten or fifteen years Chartres could be king.

Chartres will certainly be Orléans as soon as his father dies. Aside from the king's fool grandson, whom he is known to despise and who might easily have an accident, at that point Orléans would be only two steps from the king.

Sartines is not the sort of dunce who believes that any man with a reputation as a philanthropist and liberal must be a philanthropist and liberal. He was not born yesterday and he did not come down with the morning rain, either; he has read Machiavelli and Hobbes; he knows what games they play, these nobles.

"Life is hard," he often says, giving his own twist to the Parisian proverb, "but it's much harder if you are simple-minded."

Armand, Georges, and Lucien were buried in the Charnel House of the Innocents. Like all the paupers since the twelfth century, they were just thrown in the dirt, not very deeply, and no stone was erected above them.

After a while, the wild dogs came and gnawed their bones.

Before the year was over, Charles Emmanuel III abolished serfdom in Savoy, Bougainville suggested the first theory of evolution in his *Voyage Autor du Monde*, Sir John Babcock and Edmund Burke with other Whigs attempted to abolish the Penal Laws in Ireland, and James Watt's marvelous steam engines were coming into wide use throughout Scotland and England.

The first edition of the *Encyclopedia Britannica* was also published, including the notorious article which identified California as an island in the West Indies.*

*Le Monade has pointed out that the seemingly chaotic vol. IV of de Selby's *Golden Hours* is, in fact, a point-by-point refutation of all the errors de Selby found in this 1771 *Britannica*, a labor that occupied him for no less than four and a half years. La Fournier claims that de Selby was sublimating his unrequited love for the lesbic Sophie Deneuve, who at that period was in the habit of pulling the curtains and pretending not to be home when de Selby called. Le Monade replied in *Paris Soir*, 23, 5, that such reduction of "intrepid scholarship" to repressed Eros was "sewer psychology." The matter is discussed further in Hanfkopf's *DeSelbyismus und Dummheit*, where it is further alleged that "teratological molecules" existed only in de Selby's brain; Prof. La Puta attempted to refute this view, which he interpreted literally, by securing de Selby's brain for pathological analysis. De Selby naturally resisted this with some asperity, and heated words were exchanged.

PART TWO

The Tower

△

There are no rocks in the sky; therefore, rocks do not fall out of the sky.

—Antoine Laurent Lavoisier

The nefarious thesis that the transubstantiation of the Holy Eucharist is effectuated by these so-called teratological molecules . . . is false, absurd, heretical and blasphemous . . . It shall not be taught in Catholic universities while I am alive. Not in Ireland anyway!

—Padraic Cardinal O'Rahilly, 1952,
"Pastoral Letter on the de Selby Heresy"

△

One

When morning comes and the sky turns rose and tangerine, it is bright and clear, hardly winter at all, in the seaport village south of Dublin that the galls call Dunleary. Seamus Muadhen, who is seventeen and has the brightest brick-red hair in the province of Leinster, will not accept the galls' orthography; he spells the name of the town Dun Laoghaire and pronounces it *doon lara*, as it was in the Heroic Age, before the galls came to Ireland. Dun Laoghaire means the fort of King Laoghaire, and Seamus can tell you the whole story of King Laoghaire and of the debate at his court between St. Patrick and the archdruid, which led to the conversion of Ireland to Christianity in 432 A.D. Aye, and Seamus can tell you the story of all the Ui Niall kings* too, all the way back to Niall of the Nine Hostages, and of Partholón, who was in Ireland even before the Ui Nialls; and of the three sons of Milesius who came out of the Mediterranean area even before the pyramids of Egypt were built, and whose crowns are still to be seen on the flag of Kerry. He is a fisherman's son, Seamus Muadhen, but the wandering bard, O'Lachlann of Meath, once had a hedge-school in Dun Laoghaire, and Seamus asked a lot of questions and was rewarded by being taught a good deal of the ancient historical stanzas.

The hedge-schools are the only schools available to Irish Catholics. Under the Penal Laws of 1702 it is illegal to educate the children of Catholic families in Ireland; it is

*Whose name was eventually anglicized into O'Neill, of course.

also illegal to send these children out of the country to be educated on the Continent.

Seamus is out with his nets at the break of dawn. He does not wait for his father or his uncles. He owns his boat outright and he knows the currents, at seventeen, as well as any of them. He is not only educated but a hard worker. Despite the galls and their Penal Laws he has become an expert fisherman because he does not intend to remain a fisherman very long; he has savings hidden.

Gall means stranger or foreigner. A great many Irish families were galls themselves once—the first Fingals were *finn-galls*, blond strangers or Norsemen, and the Dugalls or Doyles were *dhub-galls*, dark strangers or Danes originally; and God knows the FitzGeralds, who are now—as everybody says—"more Irish than the Irish," were galls when they arrived in the Norman invasion of 1170 led by Strongbow, Earl of Pembroke. But all that is history; today the galls are the English landlords and the nefarious English army and the curse of a cross-eyed devil land sidewise on all of them. Bleeding Christ, wasn't a Muadhen from Dun Laoghaire and himself Seamus's own grandfather hanged as a White Boy? Did not the Muadhens ride out together as a clan in the uprising of Silken Thomas FitzGerald in 1532?* And, arah, did not the Muadhens fight beside Brian of Borumu against the Vikings on this very bay in 1014 A.D.? Anyone who comes here and thinks he will reduce the Muadhens to illiterate serfs forever is a gall and a fool into the bargain.

Seamus has nearly three hundred pounds in his hidden savings box and speaks and writes not only Gaelic and English but French and Spanish and classical Latin. He also has a Plan.

The Penal Laws, written in 1602 after the Ui Niall uprisings and then made more stringent in 1702, were intended to keep the Catholic Irish subservient to the English and Anglo-Irish Protestants. These laws not only attempted to reduce the Irish majority to illiteracy by preventing them from educating their children, but also reduced them to poverty by forbidding them to own a farm or a horse worth

---

*Silken Thomas is best remembered for his repentance after burning down Cashel Cathedral: "I sincerely regret my impetuous act on that occasion, but I swear to God I thought the archbishop was inside."

more than five pounds, or to run a business or engage in a profession. To make them politically impotent they were also barred from holding office in what was theoretically "their" Parliament, and they were also forbidden to vote for "their" representatives, who were elected by the Protestant minority. Priests were outlawed and Catholics were forbidden to attend Mass or receive the Sacraments.

There were a few old Catholic families who, by skillful footwork, had managed to hold on to their lands even during the Penal age; but they were being slowly crushed. One article of the Penal Laws decreed that, when a Catholic landowner died, his lands would not be inherited by the oldest son, as in the rest of Europe, but by the first son to abjure Catholicism and convert to the Church of England.

All of this was justified, in the minds of men who were not totally vicious or fanatical, by the atrocities which the Irish Catholics had committed in their several rebellions, and by the hundreds of years of religious wars throughout Europe in which ferocity was the rule and massacres on both sides left each sect convinced the other was barbaric and inhuman.

Jonathan Swift, who had been part of the Protestant ruling class in Ireland in the worst of the Penal era, wrote once that the English Protestants might as well eat the babies of the Irish Catholics, since they had already devoured the rest of the country. This led people to say, later, that Swift was mad, or embittered, or something like that.

Swift also said, "We have enough religion to hate each other, but not enough to love each other." That led people to say he was a cynic.

Most of the Irish in 1771 could read neither their own language nor the English of the conquerors. They were not only illiterate and impoverished but dirty, smelly, ignorant, and superstitious. The Penal Laws had accomplished that much.

When humanitarians like Swift or Burke or such types would argue in favor of relieving the Irish from the Penal Laws, common-sense people therefore had an answer to this sentimental liberalism. The answer was that the Irish could not be helped because they were obviously an illiterate, ignorant, dirty, and smelly people.

Almost everybody had forgotten by then that Ireland once

had more universities and more learned men than all the rest of Europe together.

Those who hadn't forgotten were mostly the wandering *shanachies*, or bards, who would recite the old poems for anybody who would buy them a drink, and would set up a clandestine hedge-school for any group of Catholics brave enough to try to educate their children. There were also some underground priests, Jesuits, who taught at these hidden hedge-schools.

If the priests were caught, they were executed by breaking on the wheel, a method of slow death in which the man's insides came out in a bloody mess for the edification of the spectators long before he died screaming.

That was the Age of Faith. Secular humanism had been invented in France by Voltaire and Diderot and that lot, but it had not yet been incorporated into law anywhere.

It is still a fierce and nefarious age for Ireland, as the shanachie O'Lachlann often says.

And it's the truth I'm telling you, although a truth that Seamus Muadhen does not think of often: as bad and worse than all this was done to the Protestants by "Bloody Mary," the last Catholic Queen of England.

It was an Irishman, it had to be an Irishman, who wrote, "History is a nightmare from which I am trying to awake."

Seamus set sail southward toward Bray Head where the best shrimp are to be found and a man might even fetch some fine big lobsters on a good day. Across Dublin Bay from his boat loomed the long, whale-like peninsula of Howth, where Graunia the Fair and her leman Dermot the Brave hid when they were fleeing from the fury of Fin Mac Cool, Graunia's husband. Seamus knew the whole legend by heart, every verse; he had been taught by the shanachie, Sean O'Lachlann of Meath. Sean had taught Seamus a great deal of history and legend and a fair amount of lore that had not gotten into books yet because it had been passed on orally from one shanachie to another—that King James II, the glorious hero of the Jacobites, had fled the Battle of the Boyne (up north of Dublin) so cravenly that the common soldiers called him Shem the Shit; that Puck in Shakespeare was actually the old Celtic *pookah* or woodland spirit (one of many proofs, Sean

O'Lachlann said, that Shakespeare, being a wise man, had come to Dublin to learn how to use English properly); that the real Hamlet had not died when he killed his uncle but came to Dublin and was governor during the Danish occupation.*

Seamus Muadhen trimmed his sail to steer around Dalkey Island, taking the seaward side to avoid the rocks near Vico Road. Who was Vico again? Some Italian philosopher, Seamus had heard from O'Lachlann. Someday Seamus would learn Italian, too, and read this Vico to find out why the gall governor had named a road after him.

Then, on the seaward side of Dalkey Island, Seamus saw a strange sight.

It was just a group of farmers—but what were farmers doing out here, so early in the morning? And a *galore* of them there were, not just from Dun Laoghaire but from Cill

---

*And he wasn't even named Hamlet, for that matter, but Ollave. The Irish corrupted that into Amlaoibh (pronounced AW-law), Saxo Grammaticus corrupted that still further into Amlethus (in his *Historica Danica*), and the English finally corrupted the corruption of a corruption into Hamlet. See Brendan O'Hehir's *Gaelic Lexicon for Finnegans Wake*, University of California Press, Berkeley, 1967, pp. 387–390; and Dounia Bunis Christiani's *Scandinavian Elements of Finnegans Wake*, Northwestern University Press, Evanston, 1965, passim. De Selby, as is well known, believed himself descended from this Ollave/Hamlet, Danish governor of Dublin (see *Golden Hours*, I, 1, II, 3); MacCohlainn's *Erigena, Berkeley, de Selby*, op. cit. examines the genealogical evidence and finds the matter "beyond proof or disproof." The irascible O'Broichains's *A Chara, na caith tabac!*, op. cit., naturally accepts the dubious genealogy as authentic and adds to it by tracing both Hamlet and the Merovingian kings back to Noah, by way of Partholón. The thesis of La Tournier's *de Selby: Homme ou Dieu?* does not deserve serious discussion; it is symptomatic of the decline of critical intelligence in our time that there is said to be a cult in California based on vulgarized de Selbyoid "theo-chemistry" and the "ancient astronaut" version of the unfounded fantasies of O'Broichain and La Tournier. (It is sad to learn, as this goes to press, that O'Broichain, a delightful man in person despite his unscientific mysticism, appears to have suffered a fatal auto accident while on a visit to Heidelberg, where he intended "a serious, adult discussion" with Professor Hanfkopf about their differing interpretations of de Selby's works. Since this is the second fatal accident to occur to a de Selby scholar this year—one recalls with pathos the sudden death of Professor Le Monade while hunting in the Ardennes last May—it is to be expected that fanciful Jungians will begin talking of "synchronicity," and some may even claim an occult link to the series of five fires in his home, of which Professor La Puta so miraculously escaped the first four.)

Inion Leinin and even from Bray. And all of their rowboats hidden here to seaward, so that nobody could see them.

Seamus knew at once what sort of game was afoot. But that cause was hopeless now, and it was farmer's business anyway. He wished he had not seen them, or they had not seen him. Those boyos dealt very harshly with informers, and suspected informers, and even possible informers.

He recognized a few faces: Marcus Rowan, Matt Lenehan, Padraic Joyce, Luke Connyngham. Praise the saints, he thought, those fellows know I'm no informer.

But just as Seamus sailed near, Matt Lenehan had raised his arms in a peculiar square shape and cried dramatically, "Oh Lord my God, is there no hope for the widow's son?" That was how Seamus knew it was some secret society business, and secret societies do not like their grips and passwords known to outsiders.

They were all silent, staring at Seamus in his sailboat.

There was nothing for it. God and Mary and Patrick and Brigit with me, he thought, trimming his sail to move closer.

"Grand morning, is it not?" he shouted, putting a big stupid grin on his face.

"That it is," said red-faced Matt Lenehan, notorious drunkard that he was. "God be praised for fair weather. Well, you are just out to be catching the shellfish, is it?"

"Sure, and what else would a poor fooken fisherman be doing at this unchristly hour?" Seamus watched their faces carefully. Some of them knew him and there was no earthly reason why they should suspect him of being a possible informer or of loving the galls. No reason except that this was a poor and wretched island and the galls paid in hard coin, and there has been no revolutionary movement in Ireland's bitter history that was not betrayed by *someone* for those English coins. Some of the men Seamus didn't know, from Cill Inion Leinin, were looking extremely wary and unhappy.

Seamus knew exactly what they were thinking. It was not to their liking to kill a lad his age, but if they let him go they might all hang for their fine sentiments. A revolutionary movement, anywhere, makes for hard decisions.

"Who is this fooken sod?" one of them asked suddenly, with open hostility.

"*Orra*, he's only a poor fisherman," Matt Lenehan said.

"A goodly spalpeen.* His grandfather was hanged as a croppy."

"He *saw*. He *heard*," another voice said angrily. Seamus caught that chap's eye and he was not what you would call loving and endearing at all. He looked like one of those wild faction fighters from the west country who met in fields on a Saturday to have at each other with clubs and heavy rocks, just for the sport of it.

"*Bhoil*, all I saw," Seamus said carefully "is a group of farmers who are after having a day of fishing, not knowing what a miserable fooken life fishing is."

"His grandfather was hanged by the galls," somebody else repeated, as if repetition would quiet doubt.

"And Timothy fooken Flanagan of infamous memory," said the faction fighter, "did he not have a father and *two* bloody uncles hanged by the galls before he turned the colors of his fooken coat and informed on the True Men of Cork?"

I can sail away, Seamus thought, and they will never catch me in their rowboats. Farmers—what do they know of the currents and the shoals? But later they will come looking for me, even if I run as far as Liverpool. By God, I would have to run all the way to America and live with the Red Indians in wigwams.

Then he heard the click. The faction fighter had taken a pistol from inside his coat and cocked the hammer.

You could not sail faster than a bullet.

And everything entered a new dimension of fatality for all of them. Most of them did not want to kill a lad who was probably harmless; but the gun changed the options. It was a hanging offense for an Irishman to own a pistol, and it was a crime (called misprision, Seamus knew) not to report knowledge of such an illegal weapon.

Bold advance was the only move at a time like this. Seamus, staring straight at the westerner, dropped his anchor over the side and skipped lightly over the bow, wading ashore through the freezing winter water.

He walked right toward the pistol. "You are a Connacht man?" he asked politely. "An O'Flaherty perhaps?"

The giant had been startled by Seamus's cold courage in

---

*Working man, laborer; from the Gaelic *spailpin*, one who toils.

walking toward the gun so easy-like, and the question un-
settled him further. "How did you know?"

"My grandmother had *the sight,*" Seamus said glibly. "It
comes to me at times." In fact, this dark and undoubtedly
partly Danish hooligan had a family resemblance to all the
fierce O'Flahertys. Seamus remembered the words cut into
the city gate of Galway: FROM THE FURY OF THE
O'FLAHERTYS, GOOD LORD DELIVER US. "You will
have a long life and no gall jail will hold you long," he
went on. "There is a maid named Mary who longs for you
to return to the west."

That was quite safe; at least three out of four Connacht
girls were named Mary.

"And what are you doing with a shoehorn, for Jesus'
sake?" Seamus asked, pretending to see the pistol for the
first time.

"That is no shoehorn," O'Flaherty said, awed and confused.

"The eyes are great deceivers," Seamus said. "I thought
you were a shoemaker. I see many worlds but I am sore
afflicted in seeing this ordinary world at times. I have seen
a slattern turn into a princess, when the love madness was
on me. I have seen faeries where other men said there was
naught but swamp gas. It is like that, faith, with the natural
and the supernatural vision, do you know that way? I can
scarce recognize a single face I see here today. *Orra*, it's
worse even; I cannot be sure it is men before me and not
apes or bears."

Seamus had their undivided attention. They recognized
what he was doing. He put on an expression of bland idiocy.

"*Bhoil,*" he said, "if my poor eyes get any worse, I may
have to take up begging instead of fishing. All I know for
sure is that it is Irish voices I hear and it makes my heart
sing and dance like a goat in spring because I love the tongue
of the Irish and hate the harsh sounds of the gall's language.
Bhoil, you must forgive me for not saying more, but, don't
you know now, my memory is failing me, too, and I do not
remember the topic of this conversation at all, at all. Two
pence for Tom," he cried suddenly. "Two pence for Mad
Tom?"

"Faith, and are you a shanachie?" a voice asked amid
appreciative laughter.

"I am just a poor blind fisherman with a failing memory,

good sir,'' Seamus said, still playing the fool. "I may have studied with a shanachie," he added quietly.

He was counting on the old Celtic belief that it is the worst possible luck to kill a poet or a minstrel. In the old times, even kings had tolerated the satires of hostile bards out of fear of the doom that comes on swift feet to anyone who harms a hair on the head of an inspired singer.

Seamus had demonstrated that he could *become* another character, as a true shanachie becomes each character in an epic as he tells it. He had shown his ability to create images—the goat dancing and singing in the spring. The repeated *bhoil* (well) indicated his familiarity with the refrains of the old songs. "Farmers" like these men—*peasants,* actually, since their lands were now owned by the rich Babcocks of England—clung tenaciously to the old ways and old beliefs; tradition was all they had left to distinguish themselves from other beasts of burden the English owned. They would turn a mirror to the wall when a man died, and rush outside to tell the bees of his death, so the faeries could not capture his soul, just as their ancestors did 5,000 years ago. They plowed sometimes in zigzags, to avoid disturbing a faery mound. They would not dare harm a shanachie.

"Get along with you," said the giant O'Flaherty, obviously the leader from his tone of voice. "Study more with the shanachies, lad, and God go with you. But see that your memory does not improve suddenly."

"God and Mary go with all of you," Seamus said politely, and waded back to his boat, not too hurriedly, careful not to seem to be rushing in fear. He did not look back, not once.

It was strange and passing strange, he thought as he sailed toward the looming hump of Bray Head. It was desperate and nefarious entirely. Like the story O'Lachlann told of the man who lost a twopence piece by the road, and because of that another man got drunk at an inn with the twopence, and because he was drunk he insulted another man, and because of that a whole chain of events happened, ending with the seventh man in the chain being hanged for murder, showing how life and death often turn on meaningless hazard or coincidence. Seamus had not even heard enough to know *what* secret society they were—White Boys or True Men of Cork or Coal Burners or something new he had not even heard tale of . . . they might even be Jacobites, he reflected, still nursing the dream that the Stuarts would return someday and restore religious liberty to the British Isles.

All Seamus really knew was some meaningless phrase about a widow's son. Surely no great consequences could come of a thing so small? Surely it had all ended when they allowed him to sail away?

The widow's son . . . a memory almost took form in Seamus's mind, but then it floated away like an unmanned dinghy. He had heard those words "the widow's son" once before in a special context, but he could not recall the time or the place. Sure, in these desperate and nefarious times, there were always widows and widow's sons.

Seamus reminded himself of his Plan. He had three hundred pounds buried in a safe place already, all of it gathered by the most judicious and cool-headed gambling. Soon, in only a year or two, he would have enough to buy a shop in Liverpool. There was no law against that there; everybody loved the Irish, as long as they weren't in Ireland.

Getting involved in secret societies had no part in that Plan. Irish rebellions were all fomented by secret societies, and faith, they were all like so many farts in a windstorm: gone before anybody even noticed them. If informers did not betray them, the English army was always better armed, and quickly defeated them. It was ten years usually before the legend grew and the ballad singers were howling another melancholy dirge about the latest martyrs for old Erin.*

Old Erin, Seamus coldly thought, has had enough martyrs, and more than enough, to free any country, if martyrdom were all that was required.

Seamus Muadhen arrived at Bray Head, the huge cliff that drops down to the sea by the town Seamus called Cill Inion Leinin and the galls called Killiney. As he began lowering his nets, he was humming softly, not remembering the words of the tune. It had just come up out of the submerged depths of mind, like a drowned man surfacing after three days, and Seamus did not connect it with his efforts to remember

---

*Rule of thumb for visitors to Irish pubs: When they start singing "Kevin Barry," stay not on the order of your going but go at once. If they sing "The Croppy Boy," don't even try to leave; just hide under the table.

where he had heard of "the widow's son." The tune was
Scots and full of minor notes like all their whining, eerie
old folk songs. He hummed on, still not recalling the words:

> Many's the lad that fought on that day
> Well the claymore could wield,
> When the night came silently lay
> Dead on Culloden's field.

Suddenly, lowering the last net, some of the words came
to him—just part of the last phrase actually: ". . . lay . . .
on Culloden's field." Lay cold on Culloden's field? Lay dead
on Culloden's field? Something like that. Culloden: where
the Jacobites had made their last stand, in Scotland, in '46.
Twenty-five years ago, a quarter of a century that was, and
many a fool even here in Ireland still believed Bonnie Prince
Charlie would come back yet, and win this time.*

Lord, the number of Irish lads who had died there on
Culloden for the Stuart cause, and the songs people still
sang about that . . .

Seamus had his Plan, and that kind of folly was no part
of it.

He sat on the stern, waiting for the time to sample his
nets and see if he was catching only shrimp or had been
lucky enough to take your man the lobster. He concentrated
on his Plan, and banished politics and those songs that drive
men mad and make all the fools and martyrs. But the song
came back, nagging at him, and he caught the words of a
whole stanza:

> Speed bonnie boat like a bird on the wing,
> Onward the sailors cry:
> Carry the boy that's born to be king
> Over the sea to Skye!

Suddenly, in a flash, he thought that he might have stumbled on something bigger than the White Boys or the Peep

*The historical Charles Edward Stuart was a man with such unen-
dearing traits as vanity, foppery, gambling mania, alcoholism, wife-
beating, and cowardice. "Bonnie Prince Charlie" was a myth imposed
on the man by Catholics, Presbyterians, Dissenters, and others who were
repressed by the official state religion of Anglicanism. Humans live
through their myths and only endure their realities, *nicht wahr?*

o' Day Boys or any ordinary local uprising against the landlords. Something that might have deep roots and extend all over Ireland, or beyond Ireland.

He hadn't lied to O'Flaherty; he had *the sight* at times. All Muadhens did.

"No," he said aloud, involuntarily. "Sweet Jesus, no." I won't get involved. Erin has had enough martyrs, and my mother raised no idiot sons.

"No," he said again, aloud. "Not Seamus Muadhen."

But Matt Lenehan's words came back to him—*Oh Lord my God, is there no hope for the widow's son?* and the *sight* was on him and he knew he had touched something that incorporated him, made him part of it, and would use him now despite his Plan, as it was using others in places he had never been; something that was older than Culloden, older than the Jacobites; something that did not give a twopenny damn about men and their private Plans.

He remembered the time he had gone with his Da to visit their cousins in Enniscorthy and had seen the mountain called Fidhnagcaer, which the galls called Vinegar Hill because they couldn't pronounce Fidhnagcaer. It had been a warm day, but Seamus had shuddered as the *sight* came on him and he knew he should never go back there, that something terrible was waiting for him in Vinegar Hill.

Now he knew that somehow, someday, against his judgment, he would be drawn back to Vinegar Hill and something that waited there for him.

In Virginia, across the great ocean in America, is a gigantic man of six feet four inches who has the same startling red hair as Seamus. He is an owner of slaves, a fact that is beginning to bother him. He has spent years in the wilderness doing surveying work for the colonial government— years alone in a feral, inhuman world with no bed but the earth, no civilized comforts, and nobody to call for help if he made a mistake. He has learned to trust his reflexes and intuitions, to rely on himself alone, as only a woodsman learns. He is painfully shy and awkward in social affairs, because he knows himself well but hardly knows ordinary people at all; he does not yet realize that the secret that will make him great, the secret that when a man of his size and temperament decides to move, the rest of the world will quickly decide to move out of his way.

He is actually related to Seamus Muadhen through the Leinster O'Neills (whom Seamus calls Ui Nialls in Gaelic); that is why they have the same cinnamon-red hair. His name is George Washington, and he knows all about the widow's son.

He is writing a note to the gardener back at Mount Vernon, telling him once again to be sure to separate the female hemp from the male. The effect of the medicine, he has discovered, is much weaker after the females are fertilized.

The hemp, he has found, is not only good for his toothaches, but has other amazing properties as well. His thoughts, always slow and methodical, are even slower when he uses the hemp, and he often sees what others do not see.*

Now George has smoked a little more of the hemp and is more philosophical. He takes out his diary and scrawls carefully, in his usual eccentric spelling:

ROULES

1. No wyfe.
2. No horse.

He stops and reflects for a while. Nothing is ever hurried in his mind. Finally he adds:

3. No mustashe.

*For documentation of General Washington's hemp habit, see *The Illuminatus! Trilogy*, Wilson and Shea, Dell, 1984, Appendix Aleph, pp. 735–737.

Two

In Paris, Sigismundo Celine has had his first interview with the governor of the Bastille, M. Jumilhac. He was issued enough coins to buy his needs for the week from the shops in the courtyard, and the rules were explained to him. For the first time he understood that he was not going to be tortured or mistreated, but also that he was here indefinitely, unless the king should actually take some interest in his case. He was also informed of severe penalties for writing his name on the walls of his cell or in any of the books from the library, or for talking to the guards without a legitimate reason.

Sigismundo complained bitterly about the cold at the top of the Tower of Liberty. He was eloquent and even stentorian, remembering the proverb about which wheel gets the grease.* Old Jumilhac expressed sympathy and assured him that extra blankets would be sent up.

In mid-morning** Sigismundo was allowed to walk in the courtyard.

All the way down the stairs from the top of the Tower of Liberty he was thinking: My God, am I really going to climb down the outside of this? Yes I am. It is the only way, and therefore I am going to do it.

And then my fairy godmother will drop a sword out of the clouds and I will hack my way to the Italian border through ten thousand dragoons and musketeers. Sure I will.

*The squeaky one.

**By then Seamus Muadhen had caught a bushel of shrimp and two fine lobsters.

The shops in the courtyard were well painted and expensive-looking. Of course: some of the finest families in France have had members lodged here for a while.

Sigismundo was still wary as a wolf. God knows what other types you might meet here.

He soon spotted a few professional criminals who had escaped hanging for one reason or another: you could tell them by their cheap clothes and, even more, by that unmistakable predatory expression in the eyes and around the mouth. He steered around them.

There were also a few obvious lunatics: Sigismundo deduced that one way a noble family could get rid of the embarrassment and anxiety of having such an individual around was to arrange to send him in here.

Most of the prisoners were seedy but genteel, middle-class men fallen on hard times. Writers and journalists who had been indiscreet, probably, with maybe a few forgers or embezzlers.

One of the lunatics approached Sigismundo. His family obviously sent in enough money to keep him in fine clothing, but he was disheveled and unkempt. Sigismundo thought of his cousin, Antonio, who had jumped in the Bay of Naples, and felt an instant pang of pity, and an increased wariness. You never knew what they were thinking or were going to do next.

"No wife, no horse, no moustache," this one said. Sigismundo remembered Antonio raving about Jesus being a woman.

"Yes," Sigismundo replied carefully. "You express the problem very well." But he was balancing on the balls of his feet, ready to fight if this case decided he was one of the demons. Antonio had seen demons everywhere at first; later he saw sodomists everywhere. Then he jumped . . .

"Oh, what do *you* know?" the lunatic said bitterly, disappointed. "Down, down, croppies lie down!" He stalked off, angry, muttering to himself.

"Hi, handsome," said another voice: one of the brutes, the predators. But thank God he was sitting in the sun, not approaching.

Sigismundo walked past, as Tennone had taught him to walk past any challenge that might be avoided, every swaggering step saying, "My sword is dangerous but I do not waste it on creatures like you." It would have been more effective, he thought, if he actually had his sword with him.

The other did not rise and follow. Maybe I've bluffed him, Sigismundo thought. But there will be others; you've got to expect that in here.

Carlo Maldonado, he thought. If he is responsible for this, it is an apt revenge. I destroyed his manhood, and now I will have to fight day after day to retain my own. All because of that damned fool duel.

Sigismundo had been fighting drunk for the first and only time in his life when he provoked that duel. He had told himself that he had a right to be a drunk and a fool for one day, because Maria had just married the Englishman, Babcock.

And now, he thought, the consequences of being drunk one time are still with me.

Yes. Even if Carlo were not responsible for this imprisonment—even if it was, perhaps, the work of Sigismundo's half-brother, "Count" Cagliostro—Sigismundo would pay for that duel every day. He had lost as much as Carlo, in a way. He had lost his belief that he was one of the "good" people who never did anything truly evil. He had tasted evil; he had been drunk and brutal, forcing the duel, and he had shot poor Carlo right through the groin.

He suddenly felt weak and very, very tired. Not only was he trapped in a cage from which none had ever escaped, but he was guilty enough to think that in some sense he deserved it. The boy who was going to be the greatest musician since Scarlatti—now he is both an exile and a convict.

He was staring up at the prison wall. Over a hundred feet probably. Last night he'd estimated that it was maybe only eighty but it was more than that. And the moat and outer wall were beyond it.

A man had moved beside him. Sigismundo turned, on guard.

It was a very old man, hair like thin seafoam. My God, Sigismundo thought, he looks like he's been here since Louis XIV was king. And he had a priest's black robe on.

A Jesuit, then. They were the only priests who ever got into enough trouble to land in a place like this.

"You just arrived last night," the priest said without pre-amble. "I imagine you are still confused and frightened."

"I—" Sigismundo turned back toward the wall, fighting against a delirium of emotions, afraid that he might weep openly and look like a weakling to the predators who might be watching.

"I know," the priest said softly. "It is a shock to hear a kind voice suddenly when you are on the edge of despair. The first day here is the same for each man. Have you thought of trying to climb the walls with your bare hands yet?"

Sigismundo smiled, evading the question. "I was just wondering if my heart would start pounding again as soon as they put me back in my cell."

"The heart," the priest said. "Yes. That is intermittent during the first week, in most cases. It is a profound shock to experience directly how much power government has over us and how hopeless resistance is when they come with their guns and tell us we must go where they want to put us.* Have you felt dizzy?"

"Just very tired."

"That is normal, too," the priest said. "We have all been through it. Every man here." He meant: And we have sur-vived it.

Sigismundo was no longer shaken by the emotions that had been unleashed by hearing a kind voice in this place.

---

*"Government is organized violence, a fact that all know when they wish to turn its guns on their enemies and that all regret when its guns are turned against themselves. The only sane attitudes toward this con-traption (sane in the sense of consistent) are those of the sadomasochist, who enjoys the violence whether the target be others or himself, and the anarchist, who rejects it entirely on moral grounds." (de Selby, *Golden Hours*, II, 18) Le Monade regards this passage as "an outburst of ado-lescent leftism" unworthy of de Selby's otherwise transcendental imagi-nation, and attributes it to de Selby's altercations with Irish customs authorities when trying to bring condoms into that country. La Fournier dissents, claiming that the legend of de Selby's "Dublin donnybrook" (he allegedly engaged in fisticuffs with three customs inspectors and two *gardai*) is unsupported by contemporary documents, uncharacteristic of de Selby, and was published originally by the "rabid anti-de Selbyite," Herr Professor Hanfkopf of Frankfurt, whose connections with the Knights of Malta and the CIA are only recently becoming recognized. It is hard to see why a man as monumentally unsuccessful with women as de Selby would try to import condoms, to Ireland or anywhere else.

He turned, not realizing that his eyes were wet, and formally extended his hand. "Sigismundo Celine," he said.

"Père Henri Benoit," the priest said. When their hands joined, Sigismundo felt an enquiring motion of the thumb. He easily joined their thumbnails, not really surprised. A Jesuit who landed in the Bastille would likely be involved with the Craft.

"Greetings on all three points of the triangle," Sigismundo said softly.

Father Benoit pretended to stretch, as if getting a crick out of his back, but his arms briefly made the squared-U sign of the third degree.

"Oh Lord my God," Sigismundo whispered, "is there no hope for the widow's son?"

Benoit walked with him to a lonelier part of the courtyard. "Will you spell it or triangle it?" he asked softly.

"I will triangle it," Sigismundo whispered. "Ba."

"Ra," the priest replied quietly.

"Ka," Sigismundo completed the formula.

Ba was the Egyptian name for the first or vegetative soul, *Ra* the solar or animal soul, *Ka* the human reason or third soul. Together these Egyptian words made *baraka*, Arabic for the fourth soul or the alchemical "cosmic furnace." Sigismundo and old Benoit now knew that each had attained the fourth degree in Speculative Masonry.*

"As Free Man to Free Man, and as Brother to Brother in the Craft, how can I help you?" the priest asked.

---

*Freemasons distinguish between *Operative Masonry* (the ancient art of working in stone, including the allied art of architecture) and *Speculative Masonry* (a mnemonic system of psychology to train the will and imagination, using the tools of Operative Masonry as implements of ritual and meditation). Thus the compass is used in Operative Masonry to make a geometrical arc in building, but the compass in Speculative Masonry is employed in ritual and also to form a focus for meditation and study along Pythagorean and Platonic lines. As Carl Jung points out in *Psychology and Alchemy,* the circle is similarly used for meditation in many mystical traditions; but Speculative Masonry combines this "spiritual" or psychological function with examination of the philosophy of geometry. The letter "G" inside the compass on all Freemasonic temples means both God and Geometry because of the secret Freemasonic training in which understanding of geometry is equated with understanding of God. Cf. Pythagoras' "All is number," Sir James Jeans's "God always mathematizes," and the identification of mathematics and mysticism in G. Spencer Brown's *Laws of Form.*

"Is it possible to smuggle a message out of here?" Sigismundo whispered at once.

"It is possible to smuggle anything in or out," the priest said in a low voice. "The guards all take bribes. Unfortunately, if you are on the Special List, they will take your money and betray you. Your letter will go to the governor and no further. I will find out if you are on the Special List. That will take one or two days."

"How long have you been in here?" Sigismundo asked suddenly, remembering the awful possibilities that had occurred to him when he first noted Benoit's aged face and snowy hair.

"Twenty years in March, it will be." The priest saw the effect of this and added quickly, "Every case is different. Some are out in only weeks. It depends on who your enemies are. And who your friends are."

"Has anybody ever escaped?"

"There is a legend among the prisoners about one man who did. It is certainly a fantasy, to cheer up those who choose to believe it. There are two walls to be climbed, after all. I cannot offer you much hope on that score unless you know how to grow wings."

They walked in silence a moment.

"You are Italian?" Benoit prompted.

"Neapolitan."

"I hope I haven't offended you."

"No, certainly not—" Then Sigismundo saw the joke and laughed.

"I'm sorry. I couldn't resist the obvious."

"We have the same joke about Sicilians. They no doubt have it about the Corsicans."

"How long have you been in this country?"

"Only a few months. I came to study at the university. The only friends I have here are a few other students. Nobody important."

"That is most, ah, unfortunate, because your enemies must be important or you would not be here. Is your family, um, well, connected?"

"We were once rulers of the Western Roman Empire and princes of Rimini," Sigismundo said at once, by reflex. "Now, well, we own a very large and successful wine business. But my uncle Pietro, he is very high in the Craft. I

think he is in the F.R.C.," he added,* lowering his voice
still further. "He has many contacts in all nations."

"That is hopeful," Benoit said. "But when they send a
man to investigate your disappearance, let us pray he is very
suspicious and not satisfied with what appears on the surface. Do you have any idea why you are here?"

Sigismundo hesitated. "I have had a strange life," he
said lamely. "You will find the details remarkable." He
paused and then brazened it out. "There were strange con-
junctions of the planets when I was born. It appears that
more than one occult orders seems convinced that I must
be made to fit into their plans or else be eliminated entirely.
The worst of it is that I am not even sure how many of these
groups there are who have taken an interest in me."

---

*The F.R.C. or Fraternitas Rosae Crucis first came to public notice
c. 1610-1620 due to a series of sensational pamphlets in which they announced their existence and promised that a great new age of enlightenment
was about to dawn. The most remarkable of these pamphlets, which continues to exercise a great influence in certain quarters, was *The Alchemical
Marriage of Christian Rosycross*, which was deliberately written in code,
allegory, and metathesis so that it could be deciphered only with great
diligence and perseverance (and some intuition), or by those who were
given the "key" in face-to-face communication. As historian Frances A.
Yates documents in *The Rosicrucian Enlightenment*, Grenada, London,
1975, a great deal of the optimism of the F.R.C. centered on the marriage
of Princess Elizabeth of England, daughter of the Stuart king James I, to
Frederick V, Elector Palatine of the Rhine, scion of the Hapsburgs. Elizabeth was a learned woman and a keen student of Francis Bacon, whose
New Atlantis is regarded by Yates as a Rosicrucian allegory. Frederick was
a mystic much concerned with both music and architecture (like the Freemasons later). Yates believes that the F.R.C. expected this Stuart-Hapsburg
union to begin a reconciliation between the warring factions of Northern
and Southern Europe, but she does not explain why it was considered so
much more propitious than similar dynastic alliances with identical pacifis-
tic hopes attached to them. Baigent, Leigh, and Lincoln, in *Holy Blood,
Holy Grail* (Delacorte, New York, 1982), explain, in part, the mystique
associated with the Stuart and Hapsburg bloodlines, which were both par-
tially Merovingian. The Argentum Astrum (see page 27, footnote) regards
the "Living One" (a term explained elsewhere in this Romance) as occurring only when certain "alchemical marriages" are consummated.
    Waite in *Encyclopedia of Freemasonry*, King in *Ritual Magic in En-
gland*, Bernard in *Light on Freemasonry*, and others, have all indicated
the continuity, via Jacobite secret societies devoted to "Bonnie Prince
Charlie," between these seventeenth-century Rosicrucian activities and
the rise of eighteenth-century Freemasonry. The ninth degree of Freemasonry is still called the Rose Cross degree.

Well, he thought, now the good priest will decide I suffer from that mental disorder that sees enemies everywhere.

The priest was silent a moment. "Tell me more," he said noncommittally.

"There was an attempt to assassinate me a few hours before I was arrested, and I am not at all sure the two events were connected."

"Um?"

"As Brother to Brother in the Craft, I must confess: I fought a duel a year ago. It was my own doing. I was drunk and provoked it. I was a beast at the time, entirely governed by the violence of the second soul."

"Um."

"My bullet went through just above the generative organ. The other fellow—they say he may never be a father. I imagine he has reason to hate me for that, and he is very wealthy."

"Ah?"

Father Benoit, Sigismundo realized, had gone into the passive-detached state. He would not make any inferences or pass any judgments at this point. His mind was as empty of ideas as Sigismundo's had been when under attack the night before.

"And," Sigismundo went on, more detached himself, "I am also a bastard. My real father was a Sicilian bandit. I helped murder him, or, well, I was in the room when he was murdered."

"Uh . . ."

"He raped my mother. He murdered my uncle. He had invented a world of his own where good was evil and evil was good. He had another son, my half-brother, who may be here in Paris, passing himself off as a Count . . ."

"What sort of man is this half-brother of yours?"

Sigismundo paused. Benoit was in the Craft; he knew about the *baraka*. He would not think this was mad. "He is a Satanist."

The priest stared. "You do have a colorful career behind you . . . and ahead of you, I imagine. A Satanist?"

"A witch, too. *A Rosso*. He has been involved with every secret society of revolutionary temper in Italy, I think."*

*(Advertisement): You would know a great deal more about this, of

Benoit was still staring, saying nothing. Of course, Sigismundo thought, psychology is the principal study of those high in the Craft. "He is not my *shadow* or my *dark woodland*," Sigismundo said. "He is very tangible and solid." He meant: He is not part of me, a part that I am hallucinating is outside. "He is wanted in Italy," he added, "for murder and theft and treason, and other crimes, too, I think."

"You have spoken as Brother to Brother in the Craft," Benoit said. "I believe you."

"It was natural for the thought to cross your mind," Sigismundo said. "I have seen how, when a man is near to developing the fourth soul, his mind may split and he will see parts of himself as other beings." He was thinking of his cousin Antonio, who had jumped in the bay to escape the hordes of sodomists he believed were pursuing him.

The priest pondered. "Could such a man, a bandit really, have allies in high places?"

"Anything is possible for him. If he is the one I suspect, he is currently passing himself off as a count, as I said."

The priest was startled. "Not Casanova?"

"No, he is using the name Cagliostro."

"I haven't heard of him."

"I suspect that you will, eventually. He is formidable . . . like our father."

"To go back a bit," the priest said, "these occult orders who are so concerned with your horoscope: ah, do they include"—and he lowered his voice further—"the Black Sorcerers of Rome?"

Sigismundo said, "It rains."*

The priest mouthed the initials, not pronouncing them: "K. of M.?"

"Good God, I hope not," Sigismundo exclaimed.**

course, if you rushed right out and bought a copy of *The Earth Will Shake*, Roc Books, New York, 1991.

*Craft code for: This refers to matters known only to those of higher rank than me.

**Evidently Father Benoit referred to the Knights of Malta. As revealed in, e.g., Bernard's *Light on Freemasonry*, Masonic lore regards the Knights of Malta as being engaged in a perpetual struggle to enslave mankind and destroy all efforts at human liberation. Officially known as the Sovereign Military Order of Malta, this group was formed in the Middle Ages, opposed the rival Knights Templar of Jerusalem, and played

"They are pledged on oath to destroy the Craft and every member of it," Father Benoit said somberly.

"I know that much," Sigismundo said.

"It is they," the priest said bitterly, "who have corrupted the Church from the beginning. They who—well, you will learn the whole hidden history when you reach the appropriate rank."

This was the part of Masonic teaching about which Sigismundo was, privately, still skeptical. He was convinced the Knights of Malta regarded themselves as sincere agents of God and believed the Freemasons were the villains of European history. *Everybody,* he thought, believes his own crowd is on the side of the angels.

But the priest could not control his tongue at this point. "They are the true Satanists," he blurted, "not those poor, ignorant peasant women they incite the deluded Dominicans to burn. The Inquisition, that social suppuration, is their work. *They*—oh, well. I speak too much." He spoke quietly again. "The duel," he said. "I can see that that weighs heavily on you. Are you still a Catholic? You may not have intended it, but you have made a confession. I can give you absolution."

"No," Sigismundo said at once. "I don't know if I am still a Catholic. That is for the Church to say, is it not? But I do not believe in absolution. I will carry that duel with

a significant role in the persecution and public burning of Jacques de Molay, Grand Master of the Knights Templar, in 1308. Dashiell Hammett's *The Maltese Falcon* is based on a weird legend about the same order, which is incidentally still active today, as witness the following news story from the *Irish Times* (Dublin), 23 August 1984: "The Vatican is promoting a secret initiative to replace British troops in Northern Ireland with a United Nations peacekeeping force, according to a book by Gordon Thomas and Max Morgan-Witts published today. . . . 'For the past four years the papal envoy has played a crucial role in a secret Holy See move to try to bring peace to Northern Ireland,' the authors claim in their book, *The Year of Armageddon.* . . . The book also states that the Pope receives a weekly CIA briefing on world affairs through the U.S. Embassy in Rome. The authors, both British former journalists, point out that the present director of the CIA, William J. Casey, is a member of the Sovereign Military Order of Malta, 'a vaunted Vatican order' which dates from the Crusades when warrior monks served as a fighting arm of the Catholic Church." A review in the *Irish Press*, 20 August 1984, quotes the same book as alleging that "the U.S. branch of the Knights of Malta is routinely used to convey sensitive information from the CIA to the Pope."

me all the days of my life; I cannot shift the burden to God. But what are you in here for, Father?''

Benoit smiled gently; after twenty years he had learned resignation. ''I have never been sure. They don't give reasons, you know. I suppose it was one of my pamphlets on economic justice. But then, who knows? Maybe it was the one on the Trinity.''

Another Unitarian, Sigismundo thought. The Craft was full of them. ''Tell me the story—the legend—of the man who escaped.''

''It is only a myth. There is little hope that way, Signor Celine. Two walls, remember. And the guards watch always and know all the tricks.''

''Tell me the legend, anyway. I am Neapolitan, remember? If my family cannot discover that this is where I am, I will have to help myself. Tell me.''

He was thinking: Maybe the damned horse can fly.

Three

That afternoon, Maria Babcock wrote a letter to Mother Ursula back at the convent school in Roma.

My Dear Mama Bear,

I am most sincerely sorry that it has been so long since my last communication, but as you know the duties of being the lady of a large English country estate are complex and various, as well as often being perplexing to one of Neapolitan birth.

My dearest teacher, I miss you and your wise words more often than I would have thought possible! However, I think I can say that I am comporting myself well, on the whole; and I have never allowed compassion to seduce me into one of those overt displays of my healing art that would cause astonishment or social consternation.

John is, I am enchanted to say, an ideal husband and gives me not one excuse for complaint—aside from certain moods of melancholy, which are not his fault, and undoubtedly the result of having such high ideals in this imperfect and fallen world. He works himself into exhaustion at times, mostly over the injustices to the poor Catholics in Ireland, whose plight has much exercised him since he last visited his lands there in the regions of Dunleary and Sandy Cove.

My pregnancy is proceeding comfortably most of the time and I am grateful for all the good advice you gave me when I was a green girl, which has saved me from believing the more terrible of the horrid old wives' tales I once heard from my aunts. I still think, however, that if the Lord God had been a woman, he would have arranged these matters a bit differently. (I wouldn't dare make that kind of joke to anyone in religious orders except you!)

There is a little political news to repeat. The King of England is, as you know, as much of a fool as the King of Napoli. Captain Cook is still sailing somewhere in the Pacific and nobody knows what marvels he is discovering, which will be reveal'd to us on his return. The ingenious American, Mr. Ben Franklin, was here one evening recently, to explain his remarkable discoveries concerning the electric fluid to John. When I asked some questions of detail, Mr. Franklin was amaz'd and said I must be English after all; he does not believe an Italian woman can have a trained mind. But he was delighted to answer me in all germane matters, altho' later, when John was not looking, he tried to feel my leg. He desisted when I discouraged him and became a perfect gentleman again. He was most charming in general, despite his low opinion of education in Catholic nations; but I did see him trying to grapple the breasts of one of my maids on his way out.*

*Similar stories about de Selby forcing unwanted attentions upon servant girls, widely spread by Prof. Hanfkopf, have been ably refuted by La Fournier, op. cit., 101–133. The objective scholar must, of course, recall Ferguson's claim that La Fournier was only de Selby himself under a pen name, and we cannot of course afford to ignore what the sensational press has dubbed the "Hanfkopf Bombshell," namely Prof. Hanfkopf's *documentia*, which even the most skeptical must admit provide some suggestive (albeit hardly conclusive) evidence that, under both the names "de Selby" and "La Fournier," somebody in Dalkey was, for a time in the 1970s, acting as Irish representative of the terroristic Freemasonic organization, mostly headquartered in Italy, known as *Propaganda Due* or P-2. Certainly, all have been shaken by the financial records Hanfkopf has unearthed, which seem to show shady financial transactions between "de Selby," "La Fournier," and the notorious Roberto Calvi, a known member of P-2 and former president of the bankrupt Banco Ambrosiano. (See *Unsolved: The Mysterious Death of God's Banker*, by Paul Foot and Paolo Filo della Torre, Orbis Publishing, London, 1984). As La Tournier—again, not to be confused with the elusive La Fournier—comments in *Paris Soir*, XXIII, 4, the elements of Freemasonic ritual in the manner of Calvi's death (he was found hanged, half-submerged in water, with his pockets full of bricks) seems to indicate clearly "that he was killed either by Freemasons or by persons who ardently wished us to suspect that he was killed by Freemasons." Scotland Yard, as everybody knows, originally pronounced Calvi's death a suicide (a matter discussed sarcastically and with hostility in *The Brotherhood: The Secret World of the Freemasons*, by Stephen Knight, Grenada, London, 1984, in which startling allegations are made about the extent of Freemasonic infiltration of Scotland

You will be happy to know that I learned enough about the electric fluid to realize that it is connected somehow (I know not how) with the healing power in my hands; and I discover'd this without alerting Mr. Franklin to the direction of my thoughts or alarming him with the suspicion that I might be a witch or a lunatic.

Burn this letter, lest it should fall into the wrong hands if the Dominicans ever begin an inquiry into the strange doctrines taught at your convent.

And yes, dear Mama Bear, you guess correctly: I have written this entirely in English just to show off my growing command of that language. Am I not still a vain young thing in some respects?

Maria

Contessa di Maldonado

P.S. What do you know about the Merovingian kings? I had a strange dream about them recently and have exhausted all the Arts you taught me to decipher such messages from the Great Mind to my little mind. What does it mean, Dear Teacher, to dream of men from the ocean in the mid-point of one's pregnancy?

That afternoon, Jean Jacques Jeder, the unemployed joiner, heard that a factory in the Faubourg St. Antoine was hiring joiners and cabinetmakers.

You can be sure he was there as fast as his legs could carry him, even though it was probably just another wild rumor of the sort that always circulated among the unemployed.

Bless the Holy Virgin and Saint Jude, they *were* hiring. He gave a demonstration of his skills and was immediately accepted, to start at eight in the morning.

The working hours were marvelous, too; the factory closed down tight as a drum at only ten in the evening: an

Yard itself). It still remains unclear why La Fournier (whether or not he was de Selby in disguise) received so much money from Banco Ambrosiano and deposited it in the account of Leo Schidlof, the man who allegedly wrote the Merovingian genealogies that play so large a role in the "ancient astronaut" theories of de Sède. And nobody seems to know why La Puta went to Budapest in 1980 to meet Mehmet Ali Agca, the young Turkish national who later attempted to assassinate Pope John Paul II in May 1981. Le Monade, among others, has suggested that "more than an academic feud" is involved in the de Selby *scandale*.

easy fourteen-hour day. The owner, who must have been reading the *philosophes* and become liberal, even allowed a whole half-hour break for lunch in the mid-afternoon. It was really only thirteen and a half hours, then.

Jeder felt as if he had died and gone to heaven.

Best of all, the salary was twelve sous a day. With bread only four sous a loaf, that was practically luxury.

Jeder was singing all the way home, happy to have some good news to tell his wife. People turned and stared, wondering if he was drunk.

Let them stare, he thought. No longer will I creep about in the freezing dark of night like a predatory animal, hitting men from behind to steal their purses.

The Lord God was a just God after all. He had given Jeder a chance to be an honest man again.

He stopped at a small chapel and lit a candle to the Virgin Mother, to express his gratitude to heaven.*

Never again, Jeder promised himself, will I tangle with another Italian mountain gorilla like that sneaky bastard last night. My shins still hurt.

As darkness came down on Paris, the Italian mountain gorilla climbed out the window of the Tower of Liberty and hung by his hands for nearly thirty seconds.

When he hastily climbed back into the room, he staggered and the floor seemed to tilt sickeningly; but he had expected that.

The people who walk the tightropes at carnivals do it all the time, he told himself. *Avanti!*

But he was still staggering with vertigo.

Sigismundo sat down for a moment on the bed, and concentrated on the fourth soul. *Toward the One, the perfection of love, harmony, and beauty, the only being, united with all those illuminated souls who form the embodiment of the Teacher, the Spirit of Guidance.*

Sigismundo climbed out the window again.

*De Selby has an odd comment on the alleged parthenogenesis of Jesus: "All myths may be foretastes of future evolution. Zeus the Thunderer *(Zeus Bronnton)* = wars in outer space, after rocketry advances further? Wings of Daedalus already realized in Wright Brothers? Virgin birth = future asexual reproduction (clones, etc.)?" (de Selby, *Uncollected Fragments*, ed. Sir Myles na gCopaleen, Dublin, Poirin Press, 1935.) Prof. Hanfkopf calls this another of de Selby's *"Dummheiten."*

A gust of sudden wind, cold as a dead man's clutch, seized him at once and he swung crazily outward and then rammed against the wall as he was hurled back again. In imagination, more vivid than reality, he was falling through endless space; he felt his fingers cramp as he grasped in panic at the reality of the window.

He was back in the room with one leap, trembling.

Courage, he told himself. You are going to do this, fellow, whether you like it or not.

His bowels moved greasily within him. Go ahead, he told himself bitterly. Shit your pants. I do not care about that. You are going back out that window in a moment, a very *short* moment, before you lose your courage entirely, *just as soon* as the damned room stops spinning, you hear?

His sphincter tightened again; he would not shit himself after all. Now: *Avanti! Corragio! Presto!* He forced his right leg out, then his left; he sat on the sill, turning carefully. He was hanging again, holding on with tight but not cramped fingers.

Hey, he told himself, you are a brave fellow after all.

Nausea swept through him. He saw again the vision of his body falling and falling forever. The wind battered him like a herd of runaway horses. He hung on and counted. "In case of necessity any layman or woman can do it," he quoted.

Forty-two, forty-three, forty-four.

His heart began to pound. He held on. When the audience booed my *Two Nations Sonata*, that was harder to bear bravely than this. Really? Well, maybe not. Hang on anyway. Half the human race is born male, but after that accident it requires work to become a man.

Fifty-nine. Sixty.

Sigismundo pulled himself back into the room, which now looked like one of those Byzantine paintings where all the angles are wrong. He was panting and felt hot sweat in his armpits and crotch, despite the cold. He rushed at once to the chamber pot and urinated, splashing a bit because his hands shook.

After that, he rested on the bed again for a moment.

Seven more times that night he climbed out and hung from the window sill while the winds pounded him.

Then he sank on the bed, satisfied. He had some muscle spasms but they did not bother him. That's it, he thought calmly. Ten times a night, getting accustomed to doing it without getting dizzy, and then I will be ready for descent.

When I figure out how to make 120 feet of rope out of six blankets.

Four

That same evening, across the channel in London, the fog was so thick "you could spread it on bread," as the celebrated Dr. Johnson was heard to remark. In Freemason's Hall, Sir John Babcock—"that damned harebrained radical," as Dr. Johnson was also heard to remark more than once—awaited initiation as a Mark Master Mason.

Having passed through the first three degrees of Speculative Masonry, Sir John was already convinced that the Craft was the best hope for bringing enlightenment to a stygian world. The *shocks,* as they were called, of the first three initiations had each raised him to a higher level of perception; each had been like an experiment in consciousness. Freemasonry, to him, was scientific mysticism, since it revealed by demonstration and did not demand blind faith.

He wondered what *shock* would come with the fourth, Mark Master degree.

He waited, as always, in the antechamber, until they summoned him into the lodge and whatever new ceremony was prepared to frighten, awe, and illuminate him.

Frankly, Sir John was not at all sure of the literal truth of the claims of the Craft. He doubted that it had really come down in unbroken order from King Solomon, or that the pyramids had been built by Fellows of the Craft, or that he believed any of that romantic history. The Craft, for all he knew, might have been invented less than a century ago. It didn't matter. Wherever it came from or however it was devised, the Craft had given him something he had never had since losing his faith in the Church.

This is not my body, it is the temple of Christ, he thought solemnly. That kind of idea had been just wishful poetry to him for many years: the kind of jargon that a parson would mouth and everybody would accept politely, but in most cases nobody would feel or sense anything differently after hearing it. Sir John felt and sensed the whole world differently after hearing it at the climax of his third-degree initiation. After the *shock.*

Whoever invented Speculative Masonry, whenever that was, the creator or creators were masters of psychology.

The Senior Deacon came out of the lodge-room and, without a word, handed Sir John a large, white marble stone. It was heavy—maybe twenty pounds or more.

It begins, Sir John thought, half wary and half eager.

He was motioned silently to the door of the lodge.

The Junior Overseer challenged them as they entered. "Who comes here?"

"Two Brother Fellow Crafts," said the Senior Deacon, "with materials for the temple."

"Have you a specimen of your labor?" the Overseer demanded.

"I have," said the Senior Deacon.

"Present it."

The Deacon presented a piece of timber, which was then measured with the square and pronounced suitable for the temple. Then Sir John was challenged, and presented his heavy, white marble stone, which was also measured.

The edges, Sir John could see, were not perfectly square, although they had looked square to the naked eye. The stone represents my mind, he thought. I am approximating the ideal of the Craft, but have not reached it yet.

The Junior Overseer pronounced the work unsuitable geometrically (as Sir John had expected after seeing that it was not squared properly), but then added, "But from its singular form and beauty I am unwilling to reject it. Pass on to the Senior Overseer."

This was all very mild so far, compared to the first three degrees. But Sir John was intensely alert, waiting for the shock; and that was part of the purpose of the ritual—to rouse him to that special, intense awareness midway between fear and hope, in which every detail made an impression of powerful meaning upon him.

The same routine followed with the Senior Overseer at the west of the temple: the Deacon's timber was accepted as square, Sir John's marble was criticized again, and again tentatively passed because of its "singular form and beauty." The repetition began to have its impact. "This is not my body," Sir John remembered again, "it is the temple of Christ. This is not my heart, it is the altar."

They were sent on to the Master Overseer at the east. The pattern was beginning to remind Sir John of the third degree and the death of Hiram, the widow's son.

Then came the switch. The Master Overseer asked suddenly, "Is this your work?"

Sir John waited, knowing he would be prompted.

"It is not," the Senior Deacon whispered to him. "I picked it up in the quarry."

"It is not," Sir John repeated. "I picked it up in the quarry."

"Picked it up in the quarry?" the Master Overseer cried, in a good pretense of outrage. "This explains the matter. You have been loitering away your time this whole week and now bring another man's work to impose upon the Overseers! This deserves the severest punishment."

Here we go, Sir John thought. He was waiting for the shock.

Instead there was merely a conference of Overseers. The Junior and Senior Overseers repeated their previous lines in turn, as reports given to the Master. Sir John again heard that his stone was not square but that it possessed "singular form and beauty."

At the conclusion, it was decided that despite its beauty Sir John's stone was not suitable for the temple, and it was thrown to the rubbish—actually, a junior lodge member caught it, and carried it back out to the anteroom.

They will use it in other initiations, Sir John thought. It is very cleverly done; it looks square until it is tested. Like most of us?

Suddenly a line was being formed. The "masons" were to be paid their wages for the "week's work" in the quarry; Sir John's punishment seemed to have been forgotten. But he was still very alert, and watching.

He was pushed to the front of the line, and somebody said near his ear, *"The first shall be last, and the last, first."**

---

*A text often cited by de Selby in defense of his strange doctrine of plenumary time. Cf. *Golden Hours*, I, 1; II, 2; III, 3; IV, 5; V, 8; VI,

The line marched about the lodge, stopping at each of the four "quarters" to give the signs of the first, second, third, and—finally—the fourth, Mark Master, degree. It was the first time Sir John had been allowed to see that sign, of course, and it was deliberately brief.

The procession had reversed in its march and Sir John, the first, was indeed now last. This is based on one of the parables of Jesus, he thought; but he could not quite remember the parable at the moment. The line marched toward a window in the false wall that cut off the lodge from the temple. Each "mason" inserted his hand, made a sign, and received one penny.

Sir John arrived at the window, waiting for the surprise that would be intended to throw him into temporary panic. Of course, he knew it was all playacting; he really trusted these men, or he wouldn't be there. Still, he had been gen-

13, etc. The great difficulty (indeed, the *pons asinorum* of de Selby's cosmology) is that the teratological molecules produced by the counterclockwise twist in plenumary time cannot themselves be observed by any known or hypothetical instrumentation, since any attempt to observe them will, by de Selby's calculus, cause them to mutate into ordinary molecules. In this connection see the stimulating and witty discussion of de Selby and the von Neumann Catastrophe in the chapter "Uncertainty Principles Multiply: Copenhagen Test Irrelevant" in Prof. Davis's *The Nature of Plenumary Time*, op. cit. It was after this valuable exegesis was published that Prof. Davis was questioned by Scotland Yard in connection with the "Yorkshire Ripper" murders. The "evidence" against him, he claimed later, consisted of anonymous letters from Heidelberg, which did, however, show considerable knowledge of his habits and movements over the period of seven months between the publication of his book and the first letter to Scotland Yard—"as if the writer had employed a detective agency to keep me under surveillance," Davis asserted. He was ultimately released, without charges; Prof. Lakanooki in his *The Scandal of Modern Science*, University of Hawaii Press, 1980, argues that the letters in question contained in places the sort of errors "characteristic of those who, although fluent in English, were originally educated in a Teutonic tongue," and that some of them "sound like the old Doctor Krankheit act in vaudeville." It was after this was published that Prof. Lakanooki began to receive the obscene and threatening letters, addressing him as "slant eyes" and "gook," mailed from Langley, Virginia; see Ferguson's exasperated "The CIA, the Knights of Malta, and the Crusade Against de Selby," *Fortean News*, XXIII, 5-9. (Lakanooki's main contribution to de Selby scholarship has been his attempt to explain the mysterious and persistent loud hammering associated with all of de Selby's experiments; he dissents from Hanfkopf's view that "spirit rapping" was involved.)

uinely panicked in the third degree, and he suspected that the effects would be more startling in higher degrees. He was ready for anything.

He inserted his hand into the window, wondering what would happen.

The hand was seized fiercely from the other side and shouts of "Impostor! Impostor!" were soon ringing through the lodge.

"Chop off his hand!" was the next cry.

Of course, Sir John told himself, they won't *really* do that. Still, he felt his heart pounding a bit.

He was held by the unseen fellow on the other side of the window while a fierce debate about him was simulated. The Junior Deacon, of course, was the only one who spoke in his defense. Finally, he was released—his arm hurt by now, from carrying the heavy marble so long and then being held uncomfortably stretched forward by the chap beyond the window—and he was taken before the Right Worshipful Master for judgment.

This must be what it feels like to be arrested, Sir John thought. I wonder if the criminals try to tell themselves it's not quite real, but just playacting? I wonder if they expect to be released, with a moral lesson, as I expect to be.

The testimony was a repetition again. Sir John, more and more convinced that they were talking about him, not his stone, heard three more times that the shape was not *square* but that it possessed "singular form and beauty." He also heard again that it was not his own but something he "picked up in the quarry." Of course, that meant that the normal consciousness was not self-created but acquired from society, from parents and teachers and friends, more or less by accident. The aim of the Craft was to create a real consciousness, a True Self. A square fit for the temple.

At least they admit I have a singular beauty, he thought, trying to hang on to his sense of humor.

The Most Worshipful Master repeated it all again, one more time—his stone was not square, he found it in the quarry, he was loitering all week long, and now trying to receive wages for work not done.

"Are you a Fellow Craft?" the Master asked suddenly.

"I am," Sir John said.

"Can you give us any proof of it?"

Sir John made the right-angle Sign with his arms and quoted Solomon's words on the death of Hiram.*

"Have you ever been instructed on how to receive wages?"

"I have not."

"That serves in a measure to mitigate your crime." There was more ritual and repetition, but eventually Sir John was taken to the anteroom and "prepared" to learn how to receive wages. This consisted of stripping him to the waist and removing one by one all his coins and valuables, together with placing upon him the symbolic device of this degree.

He was led back to the door of the lodge, and the Senior Deacon knocked four times. This whole degree, Sir John thought, is all about fours and squares, in some sense. "A true initiation never ends," old Pietro Malatesta back in Napoli had once said; that meant (among other things) that you could think about it all your life and always find new meanings in each part of it.

Four knocks replied. "Who comes there?" the Junior Warden asked from within. It was as if the initiation were beginning all over again; but Sir John was even more sensitized and keyed up than at the first beginning.

The Deacon declared that Sir John had been entered as an apprentice and passed to Fellow Craft and elevated to Master Mason, and had worked in the quarry and now sought the honorable rank of Mark Master.

"Is it of his own free will and accord that he makes this request?"

"It is."

"And is he duly and truly prepared?"

"He is."

Sir John was escorted back into the lodge. He looked about warily. A new member was present, holding an engraving chisel and a mallet.

The chisel, Sir John noticed, had bloodstains on it. The shock was coming soon.

"Brother," this person said most gravely and solemnly, "it becomes my duty to put a mark on you, and such a one as you will carry to your grave."

*"Oh Lord my God, is there no hope for the widow's son?" Taught to all Freemasons in the third-degree initiation.

Sir John thought of the weird rites of the M.A.F.I.A. in Sicily, the bloody tests of the dervishes in North Africa, the terrors imposed on candidates in the ancient mysteries of Egypt. But surely Freemasonry was sophisticated and subtle—these were all English gentlemen—this must be only more drama. It *must* be.

Or were the shocks symbolic only in the early degrees? Were there real tests of valor as you proceeded?

It is working, he thought with attempted dispassionate analysis; they really have me in the state where what happens next will make a permanent imprint on my mind.

The chisel was placed on Sir John's left nipple.

There was no sound, no sound at all.

All these English gentlemen were watching and waiting with no expressions on their faces whatsoever. Sir John thought he might as well be in a cave in Sicily. *Anything* might happen next.

The hammer was raised.

Sir John involuntarily cried out: "Maria!" Then he clenched his jaws and tried to remain as emotionless as everybody else in the lodge.

The Brother with the mallet and chisel hesitated, then turned to the Right Worshipful Master. "This is a painful undertaking. I do not feel able to perform it. Right Worshipful, I wish you would select some older brothers to perform it in my stead."

The Right Worshipful Master looked sincerely pained. "I know the task is unpleasant, and a painful one, but as you have undertaken to perform it, unless some other brother will volunteer his service and take your place, you must proceed."

Sir John began to feel a perspiration on his palms. It is only a ritual, a drama, he told himself. They will not really do it.

I hope.

The marker, or whatever this functionary was called, was now speaking to each of the other brothers in turn, asking them to take his place. They all protested that the duty was too painful.

The longer they drag it out, Sir John thought, the more time I have to worry and wonder. He was not terribly afraid of the pain *per se*, but a chisel driven into the skin right over the heart was well-calculated to cause worry. If the blow was just a little bit too hard . . .

The delay went on and on. Nobody else would volunteer to put the mark of Mark Master on Sir John. Finally, a physician was called upon to assist. He came forth, bearing a bowl ''so that no drop of blood would soil the floor of the temple,'' he said.

The bowl, like the chisel, had bloodstains on it.

If I were not perfectly sane, Sir John thought, I might almost believe they were actually going to do it. A sickening image drifted through his mind: the chisel piercing his heart, a geyser of blood, every face full of horror at the accident . . .

The marker placed the chisel again on Sir John's left nipple.

He looked Sir John straight in the eye and slowly raised the mallet and Sir John thought, *It will only hurt for a moment, they know how to do it without impaling the candidate,* and the marker said in what seemed a few seconds that expanded beyond time into eternity, ''Operative masons make use of the chisel to cut, hew, carve, and indent their work''—he hefted the mallet, drawing it back—''but we as Free and Accepted Masons make use of it for a more noble and glorious purpose,''—the mallet was descending—''to cut, hew, carve, and indent the *mind!*''

At the last word—*''mind''*—the mallet struck the chisel.

Sir John thought he almost fainted then.

But he was not unconscious; he was more conscious than ever. They were parading him around the four quarters again and he understood that his skin was uncut, only his mind had been *marked* as the words of the ritual said—it was a conjurer's trick, but it was not a trick because it did indent the mind, he was seeing colors clearer and hearing words with infinite overtones of meaning—

The Warden of the East showed him a Bible opened to Psalms and read aloud the words, ''The stone which the builders refused is become the head stone of the corner.''

The Warden of the South showed him a Bible opened to Luke and read, ''What is this then that is written: The stone which the builders rejected, the same is become the head of the corner?''

The Warden of the West showed him a Bible opened to Matthew and read, ''Did ye never read the Scriptures, the stone which the builders rejected is become the head of the corner?''

The Warden of the North showed him a Bible opened to the Acts of the Apostles and read, ''This is the stone which was set at naught by the builders, which is become the head of the corner.''

It is the secret of alchemy, Sir John thought: The part of ourselves that we reject, that is what transfigures and redeems us, when we accept it without fear: the First Matter, the Rosicrucians called it.

He was back at the altar, facing the Most Worshipful Master, who also showed him a Bible, opened to Revelations, and read, ''To him that overcometh will I give to eat of the hidden manna, and will give him a white stone, and in the stone a name written, which no man knoweth save him that receiveth it.''

Another brother appeared from the circle, carrying the white marble stone that had been rejected because it did not fit normal standards. It was given to Sir John and now bore the letters ET IN ARCADIA EGO.

''You are now a Mark Master,'' the Most Worshipful intoned solemnly.

All gathered around to present congratulations.

The stone that was rejected . . . they are dramatizing that imperfection is illusory, not real . . . I am in Arcadia, the Golden Age, all the time . . . it is not faith, hope, or love that sees through delusion to the essence of things; it is courage . . .

Sir John suddenly thought that this ritual, in some form, dated back to the first men who dared band together to hunt a dangerous carnivore, with sticks and bones for their weapons.

Somebody was asking something.

''What?'' Sir John demanded, still thinking about the part of himself that he rejected, the part that was not straight by normal standards. Everybody has something like that, he thought; the average is that which no person quite ever is. ''What?'' he repeated.

''I was asking,'' the Most Worshipful said, ''if you could loan me a trifle of five quid for a few days.''

It was a dreadful, absurd anticlimax.

Gentlemen did not borrow from each other in public; they came and asked in private.

Or was that another aspect of the rejected stone? There
are no secrets between True Brothers in the Craft—the private is public, at least within the lodge—

"Five quid?" he repeated, feeling totally off guard and
foolish. The image was coming up to the surface, being
under the water for so many years, bloated, ghastly white,
the corpse of Geoffrey Wildeblood, who had died because
he had been placed in a situation where he could neither
hide nor confess his love. In a pool at Eton, thirteen years
ago, a boy's dead body: suicide; because he lacked the courage to either lie to the authorities or admit the truth. And
Sir John Babcock survived, became *a leading figure,* as the
press said, because he did have the courage to lie and deceive and hide and sneak . . . while Geoffrey's death was
ineluctable as the stone and sand; Geoffrey was gone,
mourned only by the wine-wet wind.

"I'm sorry," Sir John said, smiling nervously. "They
took all my money when I was being prepared for the ritual."

The Most Worshipful Master seemed suddenly angry.
"Have you not sworn, in each initiation, never to leave a
Brother in distress? Are you just playing at the Craft? Do
you understand none of the meaning?"

There was an embarrassed silence.

Sir John tried again, awkwardly. "They took all my
money, outside . . . they do that in every initiation . . ."

"Are you sure you have nothing to give a Brother in
need?"

Oh, Christ, Sir John thought, it isn't really over . . .

"I have nothing," he said, wary and waiting.

"Search yourself," the Master said. "Perhaps when you
thought yourself penniless some kind stranger might have
helped you without your knowledge."

Sir John wonderingly reached into his trouser pockets—
and found the heavy weight of a five-pound piece in the left
pocket, the one he never used for coins. Another conjurer's
trick: while his mind had been whirling from the shock of
the mallet that did not impale his heart, and the symbolic
Bible verses, some brother had quickly slipped the coin into
his pocket.

Sir John removed the fiver and passed it to the Most Worshipful Master.

"Remember this lesson all the days of your life," the

Master said solemnly. "Your situation is never as hopeless as it may seem at first glance. Help may arrive invisibly and unexpectedly from unknown sources. Never say 'I have nothing to give,' but always search to learn what your true situation is, and be aware that all things can change in an instant while you are not even observing what is happening."

Then the Master opened the Bible and read: "For the last shall be first, and the first last: for many are called, but few chosen."

Sir John Babcock knew that he had been marked indeed, even though no blood had been shed.

Five

From *AN HONEST DEFENSE OF FREEMASONRY, WITH CRITICISMS ANSWERED, by Citizen Priest Henri Benoit (1797):*

In final reply to such jealous and suspicious minds I wish to say frankly that it was the Craft, more than my training as a priest, that allowed me to endure my thirty-eight years' confinement in the Bastille without losing faith in God and man. For, as I have many times already insisted, while the Church is the incarnate Body of Christ, as Holy Writ assures us, a body can sometimes lose its spirit; and the spirit, as it were, must then take lodgement elsewhere. The corruptions of the Church are so well known these days, since the revolution has taken care to document all forms of greed and simony among the clergy, that I need scarcely belabor this point; rather, in this day and age, many will think me naive for continuing to revere the Church at all.

The case is this: The sacraments have lost their vitality. Not because of the corruptions I have mentioned, not for want of piety and sincere holiness among many of the hierarchy; no, but because the meaning of the sacramental has been attenuated by centuries of what Our Lord called "vain repetitions." Those of the Craft will understand at once, although others may be unclear on the subject, that a true sacrament makes, as Aquinas said, an *indelible* mark on the soul. Now this can only be accomplished when the soul is prepared; and the soul can only be so prepared by devices that are similar to those the great Aristotle analyzed in his book on tragedy. There is no sacrament without the dramatic *catharsis* Aristotle describes, *viz.,* a group making a play together in which terror and pity are most forcibly impressed on the whole mind, including the vegetative and animal levels as well as the human reason. This is and always has been the true function of ritual and drama in all ages and times.

Thus it is that Freemasonry grew up (I know not from where) in this age when men were no longer satisfied with "vain repetitions" and the empty reiteration of antiquated dogma. The men of this age do not want to be told; they want to see and experience for themselves. Freemasonry gives them experiences, and these experiences do illuminate every level of the mind. This is the reason for the "secrecy" about which there is so much misunderstanding among critics of the Craft. Anybody can read in Holy Writ how Saint Paul was lifted up to the seventh heaven and came back with his eyes so inflamed by the light that he was blinded for three days after; but in reading this, one does not share Saint Paul's illumination. One who has gone to a secret place at night, in a spirit of earnest questing for spiritual knowledge, and has passed through risk, danger, and uncertainty, will remember such light as is passed on at that time. This is the nature of an *indelible* experience in the sense of Aquinas. Some secrecy is necessary, then, since to reveal too much in advance would eliminate the excitement, the testing of the candidate's courage, and the shock of the revelation made; it would deaden the experience and make it as boring as (alas!) the average church service now is.

As for the allegations that the Craft has been used, at times, as a mask for political intrigues, I must in all candor admit that this is possible. I can only say that I know of no case in which it was perverted for *evil* political purposes. The fact that the Masonic motto—liberty, equality, fraternity—has become the motto of the revolution shows that the Craft has been the proponent of progress, not of tyranny and superstition. However, the true meaning of the Craft goes beyond the revolution to higher ideals and more glorious aspirations; to goals that few of present-day humanity can begin to grasp. This can be heard in those composers who were initiates of the Craft, such as Haydn and Mozart. Indeed, in *The Magic Flute* Mozart defends the Craft far more ably and eloquently than I do in this poor little book; for from the first sounding of three knock-like notes (whose meaning is clear to all who have experienced the tragedy of the widow's son) to the triumphant reversal of accepted ideas in the finale, the whole opera is a magnified Masonic initiation adapted for the theatre.*

*Cf. *Mozart and Masonry*, by Paul Nettl: Philosophical Library, New York, 1957. Mr. Nettl is one of the best musicologists among living American Freemasons and, although (due to his oaths) he cannot quite explain *everything*, he reveals enough that the reader possessing any practical occult experience can guess the rest. Nettl is worth reading also for his transcription of the mottoes (indicating degrees of illumination attained) recorded in the logbook of the Vienna lodge of New Hope to which Mozart (and Haydn) belonged. One of the members wrote in Hebrew "Genesis 14:18" (which is worth consulting), and another, also in Hebrew, "Here the dog lies buried." (Gurdjieff in our own century often

Freemasonry, then, is like Greek tragedy in calling us to attend with sobriety to eternal mysteries and to experience within our hearts the meaning of death and the triumph beyond death: but it is more like the music that is the special glory of our age, the music that it in many cases directly inspired, the music that goes beyond mere beauty to challenge us and inflame us and inspire us to be more glorious beings then we ever thought we could be. (See in this connections 1 John 3:2.)

For—make no mistake about it—our critics are right in one sense: The revolution itself was only the *beginning* of the work of the Craft in this world. Greater upheavals lie ahead; tyrannies so old and entrenched that men regard them almost as laws of nature remain to be overthrown; superstitions that have become enshrined as "common sense" remain to be challenged and exposed; liberties which none can yet conceive must be demanded and seized by all human beings everywhere. Every Christian, of every sect, prays in church on Sunday, "Thy kingdom come, thy will be done, *on earth* as it is in heaven." Not one man or woman in a thousand stops to think what those words mean; not one in ten thousand dares to imagine that they could mean exactly what they say. I have claimed that Speculative Masonry is like ritual, like tragedy, like heroic music; but it could all be said more simply by merely writing that it is the coherent will of all those committed to the Great Work of achieving the meaning of the Lord's Prayer, so that the mind of the Great Architect of the Universe will be manifest, not only in the marvelous harmony of the stars at night but in the daily lives of all men and women everywhere— "*on earth* as it is in heaven." I endured the Bastille, dear reader, because to know the ineffable central secret of the Craft—the stone that the builders rejected—is to die to this world and to live in another and more glorious world, which shall be the shared commonwealth of generations not yet born.

spoke of "burying the dog" by writing his books in code, and J.J. Bennett in *Witness* says Gurdjieff told him "the dog" was the Dog Star, Sirius—the Argentum Astrum.) Mozart wrote in the logbook the typical F.R.C. sentiment, "Patience and tranquility of mind contribute more to cure our distempers than the whole art of medicine."

Six

In the town that the galls call Dunleary, Seamus Muadhen is going through an initiation that will leave an indelible mark on him. It started at around midnight—the English army knows as much about disorientation and intimidation as Captain Loup-Garou in Paris—with gunbutts rapping on the door and soldiers bursting in with bayonets. Ma cried piteously, the younger childher whined, Da cursed and got slapped for it, and then Seamus was taken for a long coach ride, surrounded by hostile military faces, through the freezing cold of an Irish winter night.

Seamus was lodged in the army barracks adjoining the pier. They left him alone in a small cell for a while—giving me time to worry and wonder, he thought—and then hustled him down the hall into a darkened room, lit only by one small candle, where a black-bearded, red-faced gall sergeant interrogated him.

"You are See-mus Mud-hen?" The sergeant was looking down at a piece of paper, probably a list of those who had been arrested.

Lord, they never learn to pronounce our names. "Shaymus Moo-on," Seamus enunciated slowly.

"Moon then. You are he?"

"If my mother was an honest woman, Your Honor." Seamus used the grin that had gotten around many a sweet colleen and extricated him from many a nasty confrontation. He was playing the comic stage Irishman to the hilt and would have turned his hair brighter red and grown more freckles if that were possible.

"None of *you lot* ever had honest mothers," the sergeant

said viciously, refusing to be amused. "What were you doing at Dalkey Island at six in the morning?"

It was that then. Like the man who dropped two pence by the road and after it passed through seven transactions a man was hanged for it, in O'Lachlann's story: on such small things a life can bloody turn. Seamus thought: If I had decided to cast my nets off Howth Head instead of off Bray . . . and if my grandmother had balls she'd be my grandfather. If, if, *if!* "Well, Your Honor, being a fisherman, I was after doing what fishermen do. Fishing, don't you know? And without much luck."

"That is your story, then? You were innocently fishing and you did not attend a seditious meeting. Give it up, young croppy. We know more than you think."

We know more than you think, Seamus repeated to himself. They always use that line, Da said, and the great fool you were if you believed it.

"You must be misinformed," he said with a dumb, innocent look. "Fishing is a busy life, Your Honor. I have no time for seditious meetings. I must be out early, don't you know, and work late, too, to make a good catch for the day."

"We have witnesses."

That was the next line. "We know more than you think." "We have witnesses." Next would come "Name the others and we will let you go." It was like the refrain in the old ballad that everybody had heard; the only trick was to make it sound new.

"Orra," Seamus said, still trying, "on this impoverished island you will find men to swear they saw Lord North at a rebel meeting, if you pay them enough. I am an honest fisherman."

When pigs grow wings and the faeries come out from under the earth they will believe me, he thought. But he kept the grin and the dumb, honest expression. You can't win if you don't bloody try.

"You are a boldfaced croppy liar with a practiced smile that you think will deceive anyone," the sergeant shouted, exaggerating his anger. Sure and he's after playing a stage role, just like me, Seamus thought. If we could only stop playacting and be honest? No: it is his job not to trust me. "How long have you known Marcus Rowan?" the sergeant barked: more theatrics.

"That would be Rowan the farmer, Your Honor? I hardly know him at all. I may have raised a pint with him at the Dun Laoghaire fair once."

"Doon Leary?" the sergeant repeated, getting it all wrong as usual; Seamus had pronounced it correctly: *doon lara.* "You refuse to call this town by its legal name, I see. Typical croppy pigheadedness."

"It was Dun Laoghaire for a thousand years, Your Honor," Seamus said with one more engaging smile. "We are a slow people. It takes us a time to adjust to change. Sure and if we went and changed the name of London to Baile Átha Cliath, it would take you a while to get accustomed to it."*

"Doonleary, Doonlara, the name does not concern me," the sergeant said. "What does concern me, and keeps me from my bed at this unchristly hour, is that you have banded together with other croppies in lawless rebellion against your constitutional monarch. Now, do you know what the word *treason* means in common law?"

Seamus could not control his wit then. "I believe that to an Englishman it means the terrible and inexplicable blasphemy of somebody else loving his own country."

"Ah. Your true face is beginning to show." (And the more fool I, Seamus thought, for letting him bait me.) "Now: How long have you known Marcus Rowan?"

"I have told you, Your Honor. I hardly know him at all. By now I am getting to know yourself better nor I ever knew him."

The sergeant made a motion with his hand. The two soldiers who had brought Seamus here moved closer, behind him, and the room suddenly exploded into a million million stars and one cosmic, all-encompassing riot of pain. Space and time reeled drunkenly for a long, long time—long for Seamus Muadhen—before the room came back into focus and he knew the pain was located principally in his lower back.

*Baile Átha Cliath, "the town of the wicker bridges," was the original name of Dublin; pronounced BLAH-clee-ah, "although," as de Selby notes (*Golden Hours*, II, 27) "most citizens of that metropolis seem to believe it should be pronounced *fookendooblin*, as in 'Ah, sure, when I have enough money I'll get out of fookendooblin and move back to Kerry where a man can breathe.' "

A riflebutt in the kidneys, that must have been. Bugger all, Seamus though, I'm in for a fooken night of it.

"How long have you known Marcus Rowan?"

Seamus gritted his teeth and managed to contain his urine. "You should pay higher wages and buy yourself a better class of informers, Your Honor. You should not be taking the word of any fargobawler who would sell out innocent men for two pence ha'penny each."

"Fargobawler? What is that?"

"Any jack on the highway, Your Honor."*

The sergeant looked over Seamus's shoulder again. The room exploded into chaotic agony one more time.

The sergeant waited until Seamus's eyes seemed to focus again. "Now listen to me carefully," he said calmly: another set speech. "You think you are a brave young fellow. We all have that illusion at your age. I have seen more battles than you have seen fishnets, croppy, and I assure you that after the first battle, men will advance again only because of the sure and certain knowledge that they will be *shot* if they desert the field or retreat without an order. I will tell you another secret of my profession. I have dealt with many rebellions and treasons and have conducted interrogations of this type for more than twenty years. Every man alive will talk eventually. Every man has his breaking point. Sometimes it takes longer, I admit. Sometimes it take many days. But every man who has ever sat in that

---

*The old Gaelic *fag a'bealach* ("clear the way") had been anglicized to fargobawler by this time and meant a miscreant, a wretch, a bodacious individual. De Selby's notoriously intemperate remark, "The Irish are a decent and harmless people as a nation, but the Dubliner, being a mix of Irish, English, and Dane, has the worst traits of each nation and is generally an amoeba-brained fargobawler," *(Golden Hours,* II, 1056 *bis.)* is adduced by Hanfkopf as supporting evidence for his thesis that the Dalkey sage grew bitter in old age as a result of the alleged incident of the condoms at Dublin Custom House. (See La Puta, "The Contraband Condom Canard," *Journal of Plenumary Time,* III, 2.) Le Monade documents *(Oeuvre,* XXII, 56, passim) that, whatever the facts of the condom incident, it was at this time that de Selby's letters to Sophie Deneuve in Paris began to be returned with the scrawl "Moved, left no forwarding address" inscribed on the envelopes in what he recognized readily as Sophie's own handwriting. Sophie Deneuve was involved then in a sapphic *amour* with Alice B. Toklas, undetected by the usually jealous Gertrude Stein. *Vide* also "Les Belles' Alliance: de Selby's Waterloo," Kathe, *The Journal of Plenumary Time,* IV, 3.

chair where you sit now has eventually told me all I wanted to know. Lord, some of them have told me things I could not possibly care to hear, they were so eager to spill everything and have the ordeal over. Now, why not be reasonable for once in your life, young Moon? You can spare yourself a great deal of pain, *un*necessary pain, if you tell the truth now, because you shall surely tell the truth sooner or later, and we have all the patience we need. Now, when did you join the White Boys?''

Jesus, Mary, and Joseph, that was what it was. Seamus forgot to say "Your Honor" this time. "Do you know nothing at all, man? The White Boys are farmers. They have a quarrel with your English landlords for taking their lands away for cattle and sheep grazing. What has that to do with a fisherman? My business is in boat and nets, not in land.''

"The White Boys are Papists. Do you claim to be a Protestant?''

"I swear to God, Your Honor, if it got me out of this chair I'd claim to be a fooken Moslem.'' Seamus tried the grin again. "The White Boys are not all Catholics, Your Honor. There are Protestants among them. It is a farmer's fight, not a religious war.''

"Everything that happens on this island is part of a religious war. This is the Pope's last stronghold in the North.''

"When they take a man's land and give it to cows and sheep, he wants it back, whether he is a Catholic or a Protestant. Do you know nothing of the affairs of the place you administer, man?''

The sergeant raised a finger. The pain shot through Seamus again and this time he did lose a little urine. The soldier, whoever he was, knew how to hit the exact spot each time, so the kidney was more tender, more susceptible to agony, at each blow. Like any other professional, he was probably proud of his accuracy of his work. "I never miss,'' he might brag to his wife, in bed at night. "I make the bloody blighters scream their heads off.'' "Ooh,'' she would say, "you are a wild bull of a man, you are. Turn over and stick it in me again.'' Jesus, Seamus thought, I must be getting lightheaded to think like that.

"When did you join the White Boys?''

Seamus gasped and panted a bit before he could speak. "Well, now, Your Honor, the Lord's truth is that I just now this minute joined them. And you and your trained gorillas recruited me, do you know that way of it? Now, do your worse, you fookers, for that is the last word you will have out of me."

The sergeant gazed at him a moment, judging. "You are that type," he said finally. "A true classical Platonic pigheaded *mick*. I hate these scenes," he added, almost to himself. "By God, I do hate them. But you will have it that way, croppy. Corporal Murphy, do your best." He arose and left the room, showing no further emotion.

Corporal Murphy, Seamus thought. It would be a Corporal Murphy. They always find an Irishman to do their dirty work for them.

And then there was nothing but pain, and more pain. They did not ask any more questions; that would start again when the sergeant returned. This was just a lesson, to demonstrate what happens to those who will not talk.

O'Lachlann of Meath had taught Seamus an old Druid secret to deal with pain. You go away, far away, in your mind, and look down from a great height, as if you were at the peak of Howth, say. And looking down, way down, you see the body in pain and say: That is not my body, it is just *a* body.

The pain went on and on. Seamus could not stay atop Howth Head; he kept coming back to this room and the agony.

If it does not work at first, O'Lachlann said, you think of your shirt. This is not my shirt, it is just *a* shirt. If I lost it, somebody else would find it and wear it. When I lose the body, the worms will find it. I am neither the shirt nor the body. I am far away, looking down, and this is only *a* shirt and *a* body.

After two or three hours, when Seamus thought the Druid magic was beginning to work, they stopped.

He would learn this in the next few days: Whenever a man seems to be going unconscious or into a trance, they stop. They wait. They start again when he seems susceptible to pain again.

This time Seamus went far away, over the North Pole, upward to the stars. But he could not keep that vision in focus. He came back, thinking: A body hurts like bloody hell.

Around dawn, they moved him to a cell where a doctor visited him. There was no attempt at treating his wounds;

the doctor merely checked him over to see how much re-
cuperation he needed before the next session. They did not
want a man to die before he talked.

The doctor made the same speech as the sergeant, in his
own words: "This is senseless and appalling. Everybody
talks eventually. Tell them what they want to know and get
it over with. Nearly thirty men are being held and none of
them will ever know who talked first. Spare yourself, young
man."

"Sasanach ithean cac," Seamus panted.*

The doctor turned red and stalked out. Was it possible
that the man actually knew Gaelic, or did he just recognize
the kind of thing it was from the tone of Seamus's voice?

After an hour they took Seamus back to the interrogation
room.

"I hope you have had time to realize your true situation,"
the sergeant said, looking refreshed and rosy; he had probably catnapped for a while, Seamus thought. "Let us assume for a while that you are not a traitor. Let us say you
just stumbled on that meeting on Dalkey Island by accident,
and our, um, source of information was mistaken in thinking you were there all along. If that is to be your story, we
will perhaps believe you—if you prove your honesty and
loyalty by cooperating with us. Now, who did you see
there?"

Be damned to that. Seamus saw it all clearly now: the
informer, whoever he was, had told the truth. The soldiers
had known all along that Seamus, a fisherman, was not involved in a farmer's conspiracy. All the torture of the night
had just been to prepare him for this moment now, so that
he would see the practical wisdom of telling the truth rather
than suffering more pain to protect men he hardly knew well
enough to say "hello," "goodbye," or "fook off" to. All
night long, through the pain, he had believed he was
doomed: that this would end with him hanging from a rope,
a conclusion predestined since they arrested him. That cer-
titude had given him the defiance of despair. Now, suddenly,
he was back in the role of innocent bystander. All he had
to do, to deserve that role, was the simplest and most nat-

---

*An Irish patriotic slogan, often to be heard even today in the colorful
old streets of Derry or Belfast.

ural thing in the world—just to tell the truth—and then the nightmare would be over.

He could see himself walking out the door. They would even apologize, of course, and probably offer him a small sum of money to compensate for what he had suffered.

Yes: it was the simple, natural, and honest thing to do, to tell the truth; and Seamus had planned to be a shopkeeper some day, and had no desire to add himself to the long list of martyrs for Erin.

"Well?" the sergeant prompted.

No use: they had recruited him, as he said earlier. The moment the pain loosened his bladder, they had recruited him into the White Boys.

"Sasanach ithean cac," he said thickly.

The sergeant sighed, suddenly looking older. "It is to be that way, is it? You Irish do love a lost cause. What is your name?"

"Sasanach ithean cac."

"Where do you live?"

"Sasanach ithean cac."

"That will be your answer to all questions now?"

"Sasanach ithean cac."

The sergeant turned slightly. "Corporal Murphy, could you tell me what that means?"

"I'm sorry, sergeant. I don't know the language, myself. It is spoken mostly in the west, in Connacht."*

"You are lying, corporal. I shan't go all weak-kneed at a croppy insult. Tell me what it means."

Seamus grinned, involuntarily. This might offer a moment of amusement on a dreadful night.

"Well, sergeant," Corporal Murphy said, shifting from foot to foot, "I believe I have heard it from other prisoners, sergeant, and, um, sergeant," he paused to scrutinize the floor as if searching for a lost shilling, "I may have sort of gathered the general meaning, perhaps." He took a breath. "I am afraid that it means, sergeant, well, that Englishmen have, er, um, peculiar eating habits. I beg your pardon, sergeant."

The sergeant's face remained impassive but his ears pink-

---

*Where the oldest Gaelic clans survived, Cromwell having decided after the uprisings of the 1640s that they could "go to Hell or go to Connacht."

ened. "I would imagine it was more vivid than that," he said mildly. He addressed Seamus again. "You have chosen the hard path, young croppy. Corporal Murphy, fetch the bucket." The sergeant leaned back in his chair and sipped some tea. "Moon is a good name for you, because I swear to God you are entirely lunatic. I am offering you an accommodation. We will assume that you came on that island yesterday morning entirely by accident. We will press no charges against you. You can return home and resume your career as a fisherman. We will even pay you, and a handsome sum by your standards, if you are honest with us. Now, before we inflict serious damage on you, damage that will mark you for life, what were the names of the men on Dalkey Island?" Before Seamus could say anything, he added, "It is a farmer's quarrel, as you said. Why should you ruin your life for them? Well, croppy?"

The wit had almost run away with Seamus then; he nearly said, "The three things I have learned to distrust are the hoof of a horse, the horn of a bull, and the promise of a Saxon." But no: he realized that that was the way you lost. Get into an argument with them, and soon the words create their own momentum, and then you have let something slip; after that, it is much easier to say more than to face the pain again. The only safe path is monolithic resistance. The same three words, and those only, or else no words at all.

"Sasanach ithean cac."

Corporal Murphy had returned with a tin coal bucket.

"What happened before was nothing," the sergeant said, almost sadly. "Now we shall really give you hell. Do you want to spare yourself? This is your last chance before your mind starts to crack. What is your answer, croppy?"

"Sasanach ithean cac."

The sergeant rose and left the room again; he had tender sensibilities for a gall. Corporal Murphy and the other soldier tied Seamus's hands behind his back. They placed the bucket over his head, cutting out all light. Corporal Murphy leaned very close and Seamus smelled the rotten teeth in his mouth. "This is your moment to decide, Seamus my boyo. A few of the others have started talking already; we know more than you think. Do not play the bloody fool all your life, croppy."

Seamus almost cracked then. He had heard about the bucket and he knew that some men were never right in their heads again after that ordeal. He remembered the conversations he and other boys had had, years ago, testing their anxieties in imagination, frightening themselves and one another: "Suppose you had to choose between being blinded or losing both legs . . . Suppose you had to choose having your fingernails pulled out or having your prick cut off . . . Suppose you had to eat a toord or lose your right eye . . ." In all those imaginary ordeals, wondering which they could bear and which they could not, all had agreed, always, that they would choose *anything*—blindness, paralysis, immediate death—rather than having their minds destroyed, becoming idiots or madmen. And yet that happened to some who underwent the bucket torture.

They can take everything else away, Seamus thought with a sudden clarity as cold and shocking as the waters of Glendalough, *including my life itself if they want it, but they can never take my courage, which only I own and only I can surrender.*

He bit his lips and closed his eyes, waiting for it to start, and then all at once his head seemed to explode and he was deaf and blind in the pain of it as they banged on the bucket again and again and again with their riflebutts.

Seamus vomited down his shirt-front—just like the seasickness, the first time he was out in a strong gale—and the nausea did not cease with the vomiting but became worse, became vertigo, and he retched and vomited again, beginning to feel the disorientation, the loss of solidity and reality. Time and space began to change in odd ways; Seamus had no need to try the Druid exercise of going out of the body—he had lost the body when time and space went skewery on him. It was like the gale tossing the boat about, up and down, port and starboard, "six ways to a Sunday" as the old fisherman said, and you were headed straight for Howth Head one minute and racing crazily across the Irish Sea backward toward Wales next minute, and you would go up up up not believing a wave could be that high and then you were coming down so fast it was like falling down a mineshaft forever and ever into pulsating blackness. It was like the very first time he had sex with a girl, the moment of climax eclipsing his consciousness entirely in a way he had not expected even in the rising momentum of the pleasure of the copulation; but it was not pleasure that shattered him now; it was like the worse toothache he ever had, when his jaw swelled big and round like a melon and he had to go to the barber-surgeon to have the tooth torn out with pliers. And a spiritual terror, worse than the nausea or the pain or the dizziness, the terror of being not a man any more but a dumb animal, not thinking, just suffering, no mind or self left but only a million separate sensations of terror and loss going off in all directions to infinity. He was afraid he was going insane, and afraid he was already insane. He was exhausted beyond all measure, and yet he knew it had hardly begun.

Reason and will stopped functioning entirely. Except for pain there was no center or form to existence. They had put a bucket over his head and started banging on it but that was long ago, in another place; he did not know now where he was or what was happening, except that his immortal soul was lost when his mind went, and he was unable to hold on, unable to remember whatever it was that you had to remember to be sane and to know who you were and where you were.

If only the bloody explosions and spasms and noise would stop, he might remember how to get home. It was very important to get home, but he was too tired, too confused—he could not remember which direction to take to find Planet Earth even.

The faeries were coming over the hill, closer and closer and closer.

"Is this real?" Seamus asked.

"Is what real?"

"This. This—this—what happened to space? Where's time?"

"What's wrong?"

"Please help me."

"Are you real? Where are we? Who is doing this?"

"Help me."

"Is God insane? How did this happen to the world?"

"If you tell me what the problem is, maybe I can do something."

"Who is talking now?"

He felt as if he were dying. But then a worse horror came to him: he knew he could never die, that this would go on, over and over, forever and forever. It was all mechanical. Nobody had ever been alive. It was all machinery repeating the same mechanical cycles over and over, again and again.

He had thought he was a human being, he had thought the world was solid, space and time had meant something back then—he was losing control utterly. All the time he had thought he was in control and the machinery had been controlling him. He had never been born and he would never die. It was all gears turning. He vomited again.

"Please help me."

"What do you need?"

"Please."

"You don't make sense."

"It's starting all over again."

"It's starting all over again."

"Who are you?"

"We are one."

He had lost everything he had been trying to defend. It was all happening too quickly for him to take control again. If he could make it slow down a little he might remember who he was and why this was happening. He was either a human being or a machine that had been wound up and set to act as if it were a human being. It would be like this forever. There was no beginning or end, no time, out here. He had spent his life, many lives, millions and millions of lives, trying to find something to make it better, but it never would get better. It was always the same, the identical gears turning, the puppets moving in jerky gestures to kill and maim each other, the eternal insanity of a blind universe where God had died of a broken heart.

And then it was like looking down a very deep cave into total unpulsating blackness until he felt himself pulled down into it, falling and falling and falling: but as he is slowly falling and falling slowly he is telling himself stories now, don't you know that way? He heard a terrible, inhuman scream and absently decided it was himself, back in the interrogation room there, but he was falling now into the inward-turning spiral the most ancient Celtic symbol of rebirth, the shape of the old pagan burial mounds that the farmers said were faery hills, and Seamus grabbed onto it and passed through it, an old Druid trick according to O'Lachlann, and then he was wearing the spiral on his tunic. This was the symbol of the armies of Brian Kennedy of Borumu, who had driven the Vikings out of Ireland, and it would surely take another man like Brian Boru to drive out the accursed Saxons. Brian had started his war when he was eighteen, one year older than Seamus, in 944, and he had fought for seventy fooken years, not stopping until he was eighty-eight and the last Viking stronghold in Dublin was defeated on April 23, 1014. And Seamus had fought with him at Clontarf, his name was Padraic Muadhen then, he was his own ancestor, time had nothing to do with what happened to a man out here beyond the spiral of birth and death. In the eternal, the ineluctable, adamantine as stone and sand and starlight.

He knew that his hair had turned gray, and he was old, incredibly old.

"Can't we speed it up? It is all so slow and unreal."

"No wife, no horse, no mustache."

"Why can't I die, or go insane, or something?"

"You are God's own, and none of mine, and you are the angel's darling."

Spaniel-like eyes full of a Hebrew or Arabic word—the widow's son, that singing sungold man who died the first death and lived the starry second life, gone as grass and mourned only by the wine-wet wind—

"We are One. Only One. Forever."

Nowt can halt the moon and sun, more *mouches* than a dog has fleas—a hidden grave, an underground stream, a code, a secret ciphered knowledge—love, lust, loneliness, and the endless, longing lament of the lion-loud sea, gone as laurel leaves and mourned only by the hawk-haunted wind—It always has to be professionals and they always *coincidentally* connected with the rock—

"I am coming apart, piece by piece—"

Death, dishonor, and the dung of despair—green hope like the bullock prancing in rough rubicund rutting time—thunder, lightning, and mobs with human heads on pikes spiked—When you find the world, you will find a smallpox of walls—

"Ghosts of dead ladies and lilac perfume on an old gown . . ."

A child's cry in goblin nightmare time and a brave man's tears—the ineluctable: stone and sand and seashells crunched—gone, gone, gone and by only the weeping wind mourned—

I have been chosen for the torture and the cross once again, because *there is no other victim*. I am alone. I have created all this.

"Yes. I can sacrifice nobody but myself because there is nobody else to sacrifice."

When they finally threw him back in his cell, he was still having both physical and mental spasms. He kept going out of the cell, to the peak of Howth, to the North Pole, to Connacht in the west, to the stars, and back and forth in time, to the battle of Clontarf where he had fought the Vikings, to a cave where they had sacrificed a bear and smeared themselves with its blood, to a room where he worked on a machine that thought like a man and was called GWB-666, to a coffeehouse called The Friendly Stranger where he conspired with a sodomite priest and a Italian named Hagbard Celine.

It took over an hour before he knew he was Seamus Muadhen, this was Dun Laoghaire—be damned to Dunleary—and it was the year 1771.

He stank of vomit and urine. His nose was a festering wound. "*Sasanach ithean cac,*" he shouted one more time, to the bare walls, ashamed that he was weeping, ashamed that he had screamed, ashamed that he had peed himself.

One thought was clear to him: Babcock. That was the name of the English bastards who owned most of the land around here. They were the principals; the soldiers were only their agents. He would strike back at the principals and let the devil take the agents. Babcock. He would remember.

Then they took him out of the cell, back to the interrogation room, and went to work on his fingernails with pliers.

Twelve years earlier a young Protestant in Dublin, studying law at Trinity College, had begun a book on the persecution of the Irish Catholics by the English government. He argued his case with the slow, point-by-point precision characteristic of eighteenth-century lawyers. His case was that nowhere in the whole history of the world was there any record of a persecution so cruel, so prolonged, and so savage. As a Protestant himself, he could hardly be accused of being prejudiced on the Catholic side.

His name was Edmund Burke, and he never finished the book. He decided it was too blunt, too offensive to English sensibilities. He went to England, and later got elected to Parliament from Bristol, and patiently, gradually, tried to introduce legislation to relieve the suffering Catholic majority of his nation.

Burke had to work patiently and slowly, because he knew he was opposing fears and prejudices based on hundreds of years of violence on both sides. To speak of the civil liberties of Catholics was like speaking of the civil liberties of rattlesnakes; it was eccentric even for a Whig.

Edmund Burke's slow methods were not enough to give hope to a man like Seamus Muadhen, who had lost three fingernails to the pliers before they threw him back in his cell again, where he sprawled on his bunk moaning and hallucinating for three hours.

Then they took him back to the interrogation room and started over.

Seven

From THE DAYBOOK OF MARIA, LADY BABCOCK (1771):

Being with child and being in England will always be inseparable in my mind, for it was only weeks after we arrived from Napoli that I discovered my pregnancy. The excitement, the joy, and the fears of knowing I would be a mother all combined with the discovery of a new nation, a new people, a new way of life. It is as if Maria Maldonado, the girl, ceased to exist and a new person, Lady Babcock, were born; if I had converted to Protestantism—which dear John (bless him!) has never requested—I could not be more completely transformed.

Nobody in Napoli would believe that human beings can survive in this climate, especially in winter; and yet I have grown accustomed to that fairly easily. What is harder, much harder, is to become easy about English speech and opinions. It is silly, I know, but when we have guests and the conversation flows to the usual topics that concern John and his friends, I have sudden moments of acute discomfort; and then I realize that, in the back of my mind, there is the lurking fear that somebody might denounce us all to the Inquisition. When I remember that there is no Inquisition here I feel like a heroine in a novel who is in a shipwreck and finds herself among pirates or Arabs.

And yet there is nothing savage about these people; they are all so polite and tactful that already Neapolitans begin to seem like noisy children by comparison. One cannot imagine an Englishman biting his thumbnail in threat or stabbing another in a fit of anger; John tells me they do have passions, including revenge, but that it is expressed by speaking certain words to certain important persons and stopping a man's career, rather than by physical combat. Strangest of all, these very courteous and gentle people are all given to profane cursing and swearing, such as only the lower orders in Napoli practice, and they even take a peculiar pride in it, each one trying to outdo the others in the ingenuity and originality of his blasphemies. I have started reading John's favorite author, a Mr. Swift, and while there is much humor and much moral instruction in his writings, the sheer indecency of his language is hair-raising. Yet he was a clergyman!

John and his friends also speak of the king in a manner that makes me uncomfortable at times, and I must often remind myself that this is not Napoli; for anybody there who spoke of Ferdinand so coarsely would soon be in a dungeon. Nor do they hesitate to speak of the king's ancestry in ways that, although coarsely amusing in the style of Mr. Swift, are biologically impossible and quite tasteless. I do, in fact, think I have fallen among blackamoors at times; but it is clear that these people are, mostly, quite devout Christians in their own peculiar Protestant way. A monstrous exception—whom I have fortunately not met—is Mr. John Wilkes, who is a great hero to all John's friends and a greater hero to the general population, even though he has been expelled from Parliament several times and has served a prison term for libel and obscenity. Mr. Wilkes was associated with the infamous "Abbey of St. Francis"—which the press more accurately has named the Hell Fire Club—a kind of society of freethinkers and atheists who took perverse pleasure in burlesquing the sacraments of Christianity.*

This Wilkes has also published things about the king which even John and his friends regard as extreme; he has also written and published a most indelicate poem, "Essay on Woman," of which John has a copy hidden in a drawer where he thought I would not find it. I must say that this versification makes even the language of Mr. Swift seen decorous by comparison. Mr. Wilkes does not disparage my gender (as so many male philosophers have unfairly done) but rather praises us in rhapsodies that would sound religious if it were not for the vulgarity and impropriety of the words used and the sentiments expressed:** one could

*The Abbey of St. Francis came to public attention when it was denounced in the House of Lords by the Earl of Sandwich. It has since been discovered that the Earl himself had been a member and that his exposé was partly the result of a bout of political infighting, and partly motivated by his fury at having been bitten by an orangutan during a Black Mass at the Abbey.

**The "Essay on Woman," written in the style of Pope's "Essay on Man," actually had the salacious nom-de-plume "Pego Borewell" on the title page; but later historians do not challenge the Earl of Sandwich's claim that Wilkes wrote it. Considering the revival of pagan mysticism

get burned for publishing such matter in Napoli. Yet he is the best-loved man in England, among the generality, because he has fought harder for the interests of the poor workers and farmers than any man living. As for his blasphemies and indecencies—John says he is a saucy rascal but has too much honor to become a true scoundrel.

How can I, raised in Catholic Napoli, adjust my expectations to a land in which a gaolbird like John Wilkes is an alderman, and is expected to win reelection to Parliament?

While I am endeavoring to understand this libertine nation where the well-born blaspheme God in every sentence, ridicule the king continually, and admire atheists like Mr. Wilkes, I am growing larger every day and am continually aware of the miracle occurring inside my womb. I remember the time when I first experienced the healing power in my hands, and the time I went out of my body to the stars while listening to Mr. Handel's *Messiah* oratorio, but this is more wonderful and more awe-full than either of those ecstasies. Even with the morning sickness I am so happy and so full of the light of God that at moments I think I could float off the earth. I become so *enthusiastic** (as the English say) that I wish to run mindlessly about the countryside, making all the light go into my hands, and heal every sick person I meet—precisely the temptation that Mother Ursula so severely warn'd me against when we first discovered I had the Gift. (Most strange and perplexing: the English would not burn me as a witch, I think, but would declare me a fraud and set out to expose my "tricks.")

I am a stranger in a strange land. I do not understand the people around me, and I do not understand the miracle inside me; but I know that God is using me to create a new human soul, who will be half English and half Italian, half Catholic and half Protestant, and will therefore have a remarkable destiny. I will write a silly thing: If God appeared before me in corporeal form, I would not wash his feet, like the Magdalene. I would run forward and hug

in various quarters at that time, it is possible, despite the boisterous bawdiness of the poem, that Wilkes intended it quite piously, according to his own lights. A sample of his theology:

> Since life can little more supply
> Than just a few good Fucks and then we die,
> So fuck the Cunt at hand, and God adore;
> Nor seek to penetrate Life's Riddle more.

*The word had a stronger meaning in the eighteenth century than it has today. It would not be inaccurate to translate it roughly as "insane"; and Thomas Jefferson was not being kind when he described Adam Weishaupt as "an enthusiastic philanthropist."

him. Those who do not love God as I do now have never tasted the full sweetness of life.

I will write no more. It is time to pray. Oh God, my living God, I do adore thee.

Eight

Under the looming hulk of Vesuvius, in the sunny Mediterranean bustle of Napoli, an old man named Pietro Malatesta was reading a letter for the second time, trying to convince himself it was a mistake or a cruel joke of some sort.

It is with a heavy heart . . . my most sincere condolences . . .
I met your brilliant nephew only a few months ago . . . he talked often of you . . . it is too cruel to put this into a letter to the boy's parents . . . please break the tragic news to them in the gentlest possible . . .
I saw it happen . . . just an inexplicable accident . . . the water carried him away in seconds . . . several brave men dived many times . . . not even a body to return to Napoli for Christian burial . . . again, my deepest and most heartfelt . . .
. . . seemed like a cheerful lad . . . his music . . .

Yes, Pietro thought, Sigismundo told me once that he had a vision that he would die by water.

Sigismundo is dead. It is impossible, he told himself, but it is true. A cousin of the king of France has written to tell me of it. The Duc de Chartres, no less. And I hear he's a Brother in the Craft.

Two deaths by drowning in only a few years: Sigismundo's cousin Antonio in '67, and now this. I will soon start to believe in the Malatesta curse myself, if I don't watch out.

Sigismundo survived a duel last year only to fall in a river this year: such is the mad logic of destiny.

Then the old man, Pietro Malatesta, realized that he was weeping.

Sigismundo had been his favorite, his prize; all of the men of the Craft in Napoli, even old Abraham Orfali who had more *baraka* than any, agreed that Sigismundo was the *one*, the special one foretold in the prophecies. And now a meaningless death in a chance accident, drowned in a foreign river.

The still air touched his face. Breathe it deeply, he told himself. You have a hard duty. Bear it like a man.

Destiny is fan-shaped, he reminded himself: that was an early lesson of the F.R.C. The future foreseen by those with the *baraka* is only one future out of many possibilities. The world is a contingency. The future we foresaw for Sigismundo exists somewhere—in the mind of God perhaps—but it will not be manifest here, in this world.

With a pain in his chest, reminding him of the time last year when he had thought he was having a heart attack, Pietro went down the hill to the Celine household, to break the news to his sister Liliana, Sigismundo's mother. I will hate those words in my mouth, he thought.

Sigismundo Celine, vanished into the Bastille, had become officially nonexistent even to his family.

In Paris, Sigismundo had complained of the cold often enough to have a large supply of blankets in his room by now.

Each night, after dark, Sigismundo hung by his hands from the outside of the window ten times. Like a tightrope walker, he was training himself to trust his muscles and reflexes and not to worry about falling.

Then he would sit on the bed, wrapped in a blanket and shivering, while he worked on another blanket. He had taught himself to unravel the fabric thread by thread. It was maddeningly painstaking work, monotonous and exhausting; only a prisoner would have the patience to do it.

When the heap of threads on the floor was a good size, Sigismundo would begin reweaving them by hand, thread by thread.

He was getting more skilled as he went along. The first

night he had woven one foot of rope, the second night almost two feet, the third night about five feet.

Every night, when eyestrain and weariness forced him to stop, he hid the rope under the mattress and sank quickly into sleep. And every night, the same nightmare came, sooner or later: he was climbing down the wall with his rope; he became terrified; he lost his grip; he was falling, falling, falling—

It does not matter, he would tell himself when he woke. I can banish the fear while I am awake. It is not important that it comes when I am asleep.

The way out, he reminded himself, is to climb down the sheer wall of the tower; therefore I will climb down. The word "impossible" was invented by fools and cowards to explain their failures.

And meanwhile there were other alternatives.

Sigismundo had learned from Father Benoit's "sources" that he was not on the Special List, so he had smuggled out a letter to the liberal Duc de Chartres, telling him his suspicions about Count Cagliostro and how he himself had been thrown into this place so unfairly. The Duc might start his own enquiry; one could hope so, anyway.

Sigismundo had also tried to smuggle a letter to his family in Napoli—even though Benoit warned that letters to foreign parts never passed the walls, even if you were not on the Special List.

It was also instructive to observe the guards and their habits. A stolen uniform and a good bluff might just possibly get you over the drawbridge, at night in the dark, if you were fast and had luck on your side. But, alas, that would require finding a guard alone and coming up behind him very silently; and the guards always walked in couples.

Meanwhile, Sigismundo improved his French by reading every interesting book in the prison library. When works of merit and depth were exhausted, he turned to the novels and amused himself by classifying them into types. One, the hero is the victim of monstrous injustice; he suffers excruciatingly, and is further victimized along the way; finally, he triumphs and gets revenge on his enemies. Two, the heroine is the victim of monstrous injustice; she suffers excruciatingly, and is further victimized along the way; finally, she marries a very rich man, and forgives half of her enemies (the other half conveniently die in accidents, usually caused by their own machinations). Three, the hero, of low birth, wanders from country to country, seducing women everywhere (miraculously, he never catches the pox); at the end, his father is revealed to be a Marquis, and he inherits the entire estate. Four, the heroine goes to an Old Gothic Castle and Unspeakable Horrors happen to her, but like the heroine in Case Two, she finally marries a rich man. Five, the author actually has something interesting to communicate, and quickly forgets about the plot, whatever it was supposed to be; most of the novels of that sort usually said ''translated from the English,'' and seemed to be by a man named Sterne.*

Sigismundo then turned to poetry. The long ones, he found, all showed that their authors shared his own veneration for Homer; the hero wandered all over the world encountering adventures both natural and supernatural, but finally returned home. The short ones mostly argued that a certain woman was remarkably like a certain natural phenomenon (sunlight, flowers, birds, stars, etc.) and that the poet's heart, in response to this fact, was like another natural phenomenon (parched desert, wounded animal, dark cave) and, finally, that there was only one natural resolution to this natural conjunction of natural phenomena. He gathered that she would have to take her clothes off.

The rope grew longer every night.

And Sigismundo kept thinking: Perhaps Chartres will act. Perhaps the letter to Napoli got out, after all. Perhaps Uncle Pietro, wondering why he got no letters at all, would send a bright, inquisitive man to investigate.

One night Sigismundo managed to hang by his hands in the cold wind for ten minutes before pulling himself back inside the tower; and that was his first attempt for that evening. He rested only briefly and climbed out again, to hang just as long the second time.

There was no dizziness. He was becoming accustomed to the experience of dangling 120 feet above the earth and trusting his nerves and muscles. All things are like fencing,

---

*Sigismundo did not live long enough to encounter Six, the hero goes hunting a large, ferocious mammal, but stops often to philosophize about God, Nature, and Fate; at the end, he meets the mammal and he kills it, or it kills him, or they kill one another.

he told himself; what is difficult at first becomes easy later and eventually is pleasure. After working on his rope for three hours, he fell into a deep and feline sleep, with no nightmares of falling.

Nine

In Dun Laoghaire, Ireland, English justice had been done. Six tarry corpses (tarred to preserve them: as a warning) swung at the end of hemp ropes on a freshly built gallows in front of the army barracks.

The other twenty-four prisoners were released, according to the policy that had worked so well throughout the Empire On Which The Sun Never Sets: Hang the leaders and extend clemency to the others. This policy has two functions: it creates a surface impression of mercy, and it spreads suspicion among the survivors.

Seamus Muadhen, with the twenty-three other walking invalids who had been through interrogation, came out onto the sea-walk and looked at the six blackened cadavers: six hunks of meat that had once been men.

Overhead, a sun-glitter on bright feathers: a noisy flock of arctic terns squawked angrily, then banked and glided toward Clontarf.*

*It was de Selby (Golden Hours, XLIV, 763) who first identified this species, which only appears in Dublin during the winter months, as arctic terns. Hanfkopf (Werke, VI, 3–205) challenges this view at exhausting length and insists that it was the first sign of what he considers de Selby's "complete mental breakdown" after the Sophie Deneuve affaire. La Fournier, true to his position that the sage of Dalkey "was, in medical terms, neither sane nor insane, and, in philosophical terms, egregious," regards the tern debate as "an irrelevance," and speaks of "Teutonic obtuseness" (De Selby: l'Enigme de l'Occident, 104). The birds were positively identified as arctic terns by zoologists of University College, Dublin, in 1983. Hanfkopf's claim that these savants were "rabid de Selbyites and known cocaine abusers" seems intemperate and unsubstantiated, as is his canard that all of them "had previous records of I.R.A. affiliation."

Seamus's right hand is a mutilated claw; it will be three years before he totally regains the use of it. He still hears ringing in his ears and sees serpentine, cat-like things at the edge of his vision; but they go away when he tells himself firmly that they are hallucinations. The hard wind blew off Dublin Bay and the corpses danced a dead man's jig. Christ, man, you could almost smell the death off them even under all that tar.

All twenty-four survivors were casting uneasy glances at the others. Every man of them seemed equally in pain, and they all limped, but still the clemency left the doubt that was intended: each wondered if the informer were among them; each was appraising the others, looking for one who perhaps pretended to be hurt more than he really was.

Nobody was sure. They all looked equally hideous. Perhaps the informer was not among them at all, had never been arrested even for a cover. In that case it might be somebody they had not seen at all that morning on Dalkey Island—the morning that now seemed so long ago, because they had all been normal men then and could walk without groaning, and could look under a table without having to convince themselves that the vile thing they saw there was only a hallucination.

Twenty-four walking wrecks, Seamus thought, who will never, in a million years, dare to trust each other. Because the informer might be among them.

And the final bitter irony of it all, he realized, was that despite his obvious marks of torture, he was probably the leading suspect in the other twenty-three minds. After all, he had never taken their oath and pledged himself to their cause. He was the outsider, not even a farmer like the others.

"Six more martyrs for old Erin," he heard Matt Lenehan say behind him. Six more bloody fools, Seamus thought, who did not know the size and weight and mass of the British Empire and did not even get a chance to strike one petty, impotent blow against it before it arrested them and hung them up to stink and dry like dead fish in the sun.

And after interrogation he was well on the way to becoming a bloody fool himself. He was learning to hate the English more than he feared death.

Then they saw the local merchants lined up in front of their shops. They will memorize our faces, Seamus thought.

The army will hardly have to pay for informers any more, in our cases. Every property-owning Protestant in the district will be watching us, by God.

Seamus and Matt and the others limped down the street, passing all those hostile faces.

And then the merchants, the Church of England men who owned the island, began to sing *their* song, the song that went back nearly a hundred years to the Battle of the Boyne. They sang it loudly and proudly, their voices full of triumph and threat:

> Poor croppies, ye knew that your sentence was come
> When you heard the dread sound of the Protestant drum,
> In memory of William we hoisted his flag
> And soon the bright Orange put down the Green rag.
> DOWN, DOWN, CROPPIES LIE DOWN!

They had been singing that hymn of hate for eighty years and, in Ulster, they would be singing it for another two hundred.*

And just then Seamus remembered at last where he had heard of the widow's son before. In Dublin it was, on Eden Quay next to the dark, dancing Anna Liffey, the river the shanachies said was a witch-woman and a goddess in pagan days. A man had almost been trampled by a runaway horse, and another man had leaped in the way to rescue him and Seamus was so close that he smelled the horse's sweat and heard the rescuer explain tersely, "For the widow's son, man," when the other tried to thank him; and later in the crowd somebody said they were both suspected of being Jacobites.

Then Seamus raised his voice, and the other twenty-three picked up the song, and they sent it back in defiance against the galls who owned Ireland and did not know it or love it:

> Burned are our homes, exile and death
> Scatter the loyal men;
> Yet ere the sword cool in its sheath
> Charlie will come again!

*E.g., when Prime Minister Margaret Thatcher announced recently that she saw no need for new policies in Northern Ireland, the *Irish Press* (Dublin) for 15 October 1984 published her views under the headline CROPPIES LIE DOWN!

Speed bonny boat like a bird on the wing,
Onward the sailors cry:
Carry the boy that was born to be king
Over the sea to Skye!

But the merchants outnumbered the rebels, and no other
Irish face showed itself on the street, and the loyalist song
rang louder than the hymn to Bonnie Prince Charlie. The
chorus followed Seamus and his cohorts as they limped out
of town in defeat:

DOWN, DOWN, CROPPIES LIE DOWN!

In 1687, James II, recently succeeded to the throne of
England after the death of his brother Charles II, issued a
Declaration of Independence of Conscience. In it, James
restored civil liberties to Episcopalians, Jews, Roman Catholics, and other heretics, including the dissenting sects with
such odd names as Ranters and Howlers and Quakers. It
was the most libertarian decree since the Unitarian heretic, John Stanislaus, King of Transylvania, had established
absolute religious freedom in that nation in 1568.

Parliament, made up almost entirely of Church of England men, did not like James's Declaration of Independence of Conscience; most of them appear to have thought
it was a swindle by means of which James, a Catholic, hoped
to establish a Roman dictatorship. In 1688, they removed
James from the throne and replaced him with his half-
brother, William of Orange, who immediately rescinded the
Declaration and reestablished the Church of England as the
only legitimate church in the realm. For this act, orange
remained forever the symbolic color of anti-Catholicism in
the British Isles and Ireland.

The Jacobite wars followed, and James was defeated at
the Battle of the Boyne River, north of Dublin, in 1690.
Nonetheless, the Jacobite cause had survived—among Irish
Catholics and Scots Episcopalians and Unitarian Dissenters
in England. The Stuart family was alive and actively involved in international machinations from their refuge in
Paris. By 1746, after the defeat of James's heir, "Bonnie
Prince Charlie," at Culloden, the Jacobite cause became
more subterranean, esoteric, protean; it formed strange alliances and accepted peculiar doctrines. When Seamus Mu-

adhen and the White Boys of Dun Laoghaire sang the old Scots song about Bonnie Prince Charlie they did not literally mean the man, Charles Edward Stuart, any more. They sang of someone long prophesied, "the boy who was born to be king," because he would represent all the peoples of the British Isles, and not just the Church of England.

Seamus did not know that the White Boys were believers in a more mystical and specific goal. He did not know their version of the legend of the widow's son, or their secret teachings about the King of the World.*

Seamus had only one thought in his mind: the Babcocks. They were the principals who owned the land around here; the English army was only their tools. Seamus had an appointment with the Babcocks.

---

*LaTournier's claims about de Selby in this connection (de Selby: Homme ou Dieu?) are undermined by Ferguson's insistence that La Tournier was de Selby; but that, in turn, is cast into doubt by Hanfkopf's assertion that Ferguson was also de Selby. The objective historian can only suspend judgment, although Ferguson's views on the role of the Knights of Malta in all this (see footnote, page 112) are certainly excessive. Whatever the true nature of de Selby's financial dealings with the late Roberto Calvi of Banco Ambrosiano, it appears that there were those within the Vatican even more immediately involved than were the Knights of Malta; see, for instance, the Irish Times, 21 June 1983, OPUS DEI LINKED TO CALVI AFFAIR, in which is quoted the testimony of Mrs. Clara Calvi, the widow, to the second coroner's inquest in London. A few paragraphs are worth quoting:

"She (Mrs. Calvi) said Opus Dei was 'the right wing in the Vatican' and the Institute of Religious Works (the Vatican bank) was on the left wing. . . .

"She told the inquest jury that her husband's appeal was due to be heard in Milan on June 21, three days after his body was discovered. Mr. Carman (the coroner) asked, 'Did your husband ever tell you what he was proposing to do about his appeal?'

"She replied, 'He wanted to make the deal, but if he couldn't succeed he wanted to go back to Italy to appeal. He wanted to name names.'

"Mr. Carman said: 'Without naming those names, would they have been important people in the Vatican?'

" 'Yes, sir,' she replied, adding that they would be 'at the top.' " Calvi was probably planning to reveal details of the stock fraud in which he helped secure one billion dollars worth of counterfeit stocks for the Vatican Bank, at the request of Cardinal Tisserant; the stocks were printed by the American branch of the Mafia. See Richard Hammer's The Vatican Connection (Penguin Books, New York, 1982) for full details on this most astounding of all modern banking frauds.

Ten

In Ingolstadt, Bavaria, Count Cagliostro, he of the violet
eyes and silky voice, was meeting with a Jesuit named Father Adam Weishaupt. The priest was young and handsome,
bland as a touring mountebank; generally, he listened more
than he spoke. You had to look closely to see in his eyes
the same inner crucifixion as Cagliostro's.

"*Who?*" Weishaupt asked, almost shocked for once.

"My damned brother. Sigismundo. Him again."

"But he is the one . . ."

"He is the one *when the stars are right.* As of today, he
is still our most dangerous enemy. Not that he guesses, yet,
what his real potential is. He is a bomb unaware of its own
lit fuse."

Weishaupt reflected for a few moments. "What has he
been doing since you, ah, had him sequestered from worldly
temptation?"

"Planning escapes, I imagine. He has also smuggled out
one letter. To Chartres."

"To Chartres?"

"Warning him against me." Cagliostro smiled briefly. It
was like moonlight on a tombstone.

"He *is* naive," Weishaupt said. "But that is part of
the prophecy, isn't it? If he is the one . . . *Et in Arcadia
Ego* . . . I almost believe it myself at times. What about his
family?"

"Chartres has written them a letter of condolence. It
seems he saw Sigismundo fall into the Seine and drown.
The body was never recovered."

"Very good. Still, you were wise to leave France for a

while. Is Chartres not insisting on what would seem the obvious solution?''

"There is the prophecy. He fears it.''

"And the code in the Parcifal legend. Where exactly is Sigismundo on the ladder?''

"We believe he has reached the third or fourth degree in the Italian lodge. They are outsiders, mere *cowans** as far as the real secret is concerned. Sigismundo still thinks he is a *good* man.''

"Well, as for that—'The enemy has the cross; we have Christ.' Have you ever heard that?''

"Yes. And I laughed.''

"Tell me, does it ever get lonely out there—beyond good and evil?''

"It was your order, Father, that first proclaimed that the end justifies the means.''

"Not *any* end. Not *any* means. But I am not teaching a class on moral theology today. We are discussing one particular and urgent problem. Let me suggest something practical." Weishaupt leaned forward and whispered.

"It is impossible,'' Cagliostro said after a moment.

"You may have the thirty-second degree, but you do not understand the Work really.''

"There is none like me in the Craft today. When I say *heal*, the most hopeless cases are healed—''

"Many old peasant women do as well in that department. They are careful enough to avoid notoriety, so nobody denounces them as witches. That is elementary-level work. What we of the Priory aim at is much more ambitious, you must realize.''

"I . . .''

"Think about it a moment.''

"It is impossible.''

"That is the language of the Great Lie. Nothing is impossible to the custodians of the Grail and the Tree.''

"To turn the whole world upside down . . .''

"What did King Solomon say at high twelve? And what happened to you at low twelve?''

"You are not mad. It *can* be done.''

---

*Masonic jargon for the unenlightened; probably from the Greek *coun*, dog.

"And it will be done," Weishaupt said. "Miracles are easy. It's this damned immanentization that takes a while."

"*Ewige Blumenkraft,*" Cagliostro said.

"*Und ewige Schlangekraft,*" Weishaupt concluded.

Young Father Weishaupt, although the most amiable and vacuous of men (on the surface), already had more of a reputation around Ingolstadt than he realized. People discussed him when he was out of earshot. "He's a deep one," they would say, tapping their foreheads significantly; "you never know what he's really thinking."*

Only his fellow members of the lodge of Theodore of Good Council knew that Father Weishaupt was a Freemason. Only the Grand Master of the Craft in Bavaria knew that Weishaupt had gained admittance to what Grand Masters referred to unspecifically as "the Priory." Only Cagliostro and Casanova and two or three others knew that Weishaupt either was or brazenly pretended to be the Outer Head of the Argentum Astrum.**

*Adam Weishaupt has probably inspired more controversy than any other figure in the Freemasonic-Illuminati movements of the late eighteenth century. Regarded as a demonic villain by such conservative authors as Guy Carr *(Pawns in the Game)* and Nesta Webster *(World Revolution: The Plot Against Civilization),* Weishaupt is promoted to full rank as a "monster," no less, by a spokesman for the John Birch Society, Gary Allen *(CFR: Conspiracy to Rule the World),* but is dismissed as a naive humanitarian by Will Durant *(Rousseau and Revolution).* Aleister Crowley in his *Confessions* lists Weishaupt as one of his predecessors as Grand Master of the Argentum Astrum (Silver Star). One of Weishaupt's "fronts," the Ancient Illuminated Seers of Bavaria, was outlawed by the Bavarian government in 1785, but merely changed its name to the Reading Society (as Neal Wilgus documents in *The Illuminoids)* and went right on operating. Indeed, as the Reading Society, it commissioned Beethoven's first major work, the *Emperor Joseph Cantata* (see Maynard Solomon's *Beethoven,* Schirmer Books, New York, 1977, p. 36), which is as supreme a work of Masonic ideology set to music as Mozart's *Magic Flute.* John Robinson's *Proofs of a Conspiracy* (1792), op. cit., started the line of speculation which holds that Weishaupt personally hatched the French Revolution.

**See previous footnote, and footnote on page 59. The Inner Head of the Argentum Astrum is allegedly a being not quite perceptible to ordinary humanity; in Hanfkopf's sardonic phrase, "He dwells in that realm of pure metaphysics shared by Hegel's Absolute Idea, the faery-folk of Celtic peoples, and de Selby's teratological molecules." (It was this remark that led O'Brien to challenge Prof. Hanfkopf to a duel, the seventh

THE WIDOW'S SON 155

And only the other members of "the Priory" knew that Adam Weishaupt was the owner of one of the seven copies of what they called "the Tree." This was actually a genealogical chart, in which the name at the bottom had been replaced by the gnomic formula *Et in Arcadia Ego.* Near the top of the chart, representing the present generation, were the names of the Duc de Chartres*, Charles Edward Stuart, Bishop Maximilian von Hapsburg-Lorraine of Munster, and several others—including Sigismundo Celine.

The day after the meeting with Count Cagliostro, Father Weishaupt had another of his increasingly frequent flashes of what he called "time vision." He was thinking not in years or decades, but in aeons. He quickly jotted his insight down in his secret diary:

> I think we should become infamous. In fact, as soon as I have the time and can think of a clever *nom de plume,* I shall write a book denouncing us as scoundrels and miscreants.
>
> Since men are mostly fools (and women, for tolerating them, must be damned fools), many will believe this masque and more books will quickly follow warning the world against us.
>
> It is necessary that the majority of these books should appear fanatical, irrational, and deranged; it is hardly necessary, and not desirable, that all should appear so. The important factor is that most of these books be so absurd that scholarly opinion will regard the whole subject as delusory. The world will then believe either that we do not exist, or that we are the embodiment of Machiavellian villainy. Only in that way can we guarantee that those who come to us shall be drawn exclusively from that egregious breed that does not believe all that it reads, that thinks for itself, and that is never influenced either by popular prejudice or by the opinions of alleged "experts."
>
> We might even write certain books which, while pretending to warn against us, are secretly working to recruit those of proper mentality, *those who can read between the lines.***

time that that degree of vitriol had intruded into the de Selby controversy.)

*Soon to be Orléans, remember?

**The italicized words are underlined in Weishaupt's original. This is

Father Weishaupt was so delighted with this thought that
people all over Ingolstadt noticed how much he smiled that
day—at every man and woman, at the children playing in
the parks, at every bird that sang in a tree branch.

That night Father Weishaupt met with his superiors in the
Knights of Malta and gave them a detailed report—most of
the details totally imaginary—about what the Bavarian Freemasons were currently scheming.

He was delighted to see that they believed every word of
his fantasy.*

But then, Weishaupt never had a very high opinion of the
general intelligence level among the Knights of Malta.

"Machiavelli was not a political philosopher," Sir John
Babcock drawled, somewhat bemused by the profundity of
his own mind and the fact that the room seemed to be spinning very slowly around him. "Old Nick was writing theology in disguise, to avoid trouble with the Inquisition. God
is, in fact, the Prince he was describing: the arch-conspirator
and masque-player of the cosmos. He hides everywhere."

He was enjoying a few mugs of the new Irish drink—
Guinness extra stout**—at the Turk's Head tavern on Gerard

one of the most puzzling passages in Weishaupt's writings, and the present author scarcely pretends to understand it. Those seeking further light
might enquire at: Order of the Illuminati, 126 Park Street South, Gold-
thorn Hill, Wolverhampton, West Midlands, England WV2 3JG.

*Such double-agency exists far more often in fact than in thriller nov-
els, because the authors of thrillers are careful not to strain credulity too
much and the facts are usually incredible. See, for instance, Sir John
Masterman's *The Double Cross System in the War of 1939-1945*, Yale
University Press, 1972, which reveals that during World War II, the Brit-
ish had "turned" (recruited) not many, nor most, but literally *all* the
German spies in England, a success so great that even M15 could not
believe it until the war was over and they captured the records of the
German intelligence agencies. More apropos, see David Yallop's *In God's
Name* (Jonathan Cape, London, 1984), which avers that the Freemasonic
conspiracy, *Propaganda Due*, infiltrated the Vatican, took control of the
Vatican Bank, and poisoned Pope John Paul I. Yallop, a responsible journalist whose previous books have been marked by scrupulous accuracy,
alleges that some of his information comes from sources in the Vatican
still battling the Freemasonic infiltration. See footnote, page 100, for
more on the Knights of Malta, the probable source of Yallop's exposé.

**The first pint of Sir Arthur Guinness's magnificent product was
brewed on December 31, 1759—"a day that will live in glory," as de
Selby says.

Street. It had been a long, hard day at the House of Commons, which was determined to "punish" the American colonies for the insurgent activities of recent years. Sir John, along with Edmund Burke and Pitt and a few others, had been arguing in vain for a spirit of conciliation rather than further aggravation of the colonists. They had lost. Sir John was more and more worried that war with the colonies was inevitable, and he hated the prospect.

Perhaps, he thought after uttering that mildly blasphemous joke, he had had more than a few mugs. His bitterness might be taking over again; he would have to watch his tongue. Even if the room did waltz a bit.

"Ah, well," Burke said vaguely—that man who was never vague—"God is so large and unique an object that we each make a partial image of him, I imagine. Usually the image is ourselves magnified, as the cynics say."

Sir John felt a sudden spasm of anxiety, as if his own mask had fallen off, as if the always watchful and analytical Burke had somehow discerned Sir John's own role-playing. "I did not imply that God has sinister motives," he said hurriedly, "but merely that he acts in ways that are deliberately obscure to us."

"Philosophy is a great relief," Burke said blandly, "after a day of trying to teach logic to those blockheads on the other side of the House."

Burke was a shade too bland, perhaps—or maybe, Sir John reminded himself, I have merely indulged in too much stout. But the image was imprinted upon him: God as a Machiavellian was just an image of his own true nature. He very soon made his excuses and left.

Moon, the new coachman, was waiting outside the Turk's Head.

"Back to the hotel, sir?"

"No," Babcock said. "I want to go home tonight. Take me to Babcock Manor." It was a long ride and he would certainly be late for the House of Commons tomorrow, but he desperately wanted to see Maria tonight.

As they left London's lights behind and the darkness of the countryside settled about him, Sir John thought: Burke does not know, A man as pious as he would draw away, regard me with loathing. He would not be so cordial and friendly. It is just my guilty conscience acting up.

Besides, he had been faithful to Maria for over a year
now. There had been no more boys.

Many men, he thought, more than the world knows, go
through such a stage in their youth and grow out of it.

Moon was whistling as he sat up above in the driver's
chair, guiding the horse. Sir John thought of the coachman
with compassion. He had undoubtedly come to England because of legal troubles in Ireland. The ruin of his right
hand—the three missing fingernails—told a story Sir John
could read without doubt, having been raised in Dublin
himself, when his father was a judge there.

There was something wrong with Moon's right eye, too.
It would not quite focus.

Sir John had voted for every bill Burke had proposed to
relieve the Irish, to remove the hateful Penal Laws. They
had been defeated by overwhelming majorities every time.
I am appeasing my conscience, Sir John thought, by hiring
an Irishman with a very probable rebel background.

Well, Moon was a good worker. It was not charity to keep
him: he earned his wages.

Sir John remembered the first interview. "James Moon,"
he had said. "That was probably Seamus Muadhen back in
Meath, wasn't it?" Moon, or Muadhen, claimed to come
from Meath—which probably meant he came from Cork or
Wexford or any place but Meath.

The look of astonishment on the lad's face was pathetic,
Sir John thought. He had obviously never met and never
conceived of an Englishman who cared enough about Ireland to learn Gaelic.

He was still whistling as he galloped the horses. Sir John
recognized the tune:

> 'Twas early, early all in the spring;
> The birds did whistle and sweetly sing,
> Changing their notes from tree to tree,
> And the song they sang was of Ireland free.

A rebel song. Sir John smiled. The boy was concentrating
on the horses and did not realize what he was whistling,
how incriminating it was.

We all give our away our secrets sooner or later, Sir John
thought, and the fear came back as he applied that idea to
himself.

The concept of God as a Machiavellian could only occur to a man who was himself Machiavellian.

Do I not always work for the humanitarian cause? Am I not trying to be a good husband? What is past is past. I have "put away all childish things."

You are living a lie, another voice within him said. You know what you feel at the sight of certain special boys, boys with that brutal beauty that still attracts you.

It was at that point in his thoughts that Sir John Babcock saw what seemed to him at first, one of God's more Machiavellian tricks.

The object came down with a thunderous roar, it glowed like a ghost in a legend—or one of the faeries of Ireland—and it landed with an earsplitting crash only a short distance from the road.

A "thunderstone."*

An object that did not exist, according to the Royal Scientific Society. A myth that only peasants believed.

And it was still glowing.

"Moon!" Sir John shouted, banging on the roof of the coach with his walking stick in excitement. "Stop! Stop at once!"

The two men stood beside the coach, looking at the glowing rock. "You saw it come down?" Sir John asked, feeling like a character in a Walpole novel of demons.

"Aye. I saw it, sir." Moon did not seem frightened at all. Of course, Sir John thought: he had detected evidence of some education in the lad previously.

"You are not afraid?"

"Afraid of a rock? Sure, it's those *human* sons of bitches that scare me, when I am scared. Sir."

Sir John had already gotten past thinking it was something God had thrown in his direction to teach him something about how inscrutable a Machiavellian divinity could be. This was a natural phenomenon of some sort, and its connection with his own thoughts were only coincidental.

"I wish to dig it out of the earth," Sir John said carefully,

*Cf. "The universal rejection by eighteenth-century scientists of meteorites (or 'thunderstones,' as they were then called), is again repeated in the hysterical condemnation of de Selby's six-dimensional plenumary time." La Puta, *La Estupida de Hanfkopf*, 13, passim.

controlling his excitement. "It may have great scientific value. Let us see if it is still too hot to be touched."

The two men walked across the field, and Sir John became increasingly aware that James Moon was not an ignorant peasant. He seemed to understand Sir John's intellectual curiosity, and he showed no anxiety that faeries might leap out of the rock and transport them a hundred years backward or forward in time.

When they stood looking at the "thunderstone," which had faded from bright yellow to mild gray already, Sir John felt exactly as he had during his four degrees of initiation into Freemasonry. The Royal Scientific Society was wrong about these objects; the peasants were right; *everything* was thereby thrown into doubt. This kind of awe and wonder had never come to him in any church, and yet he felt a sense of infinite mystery that was supposed to be what the churches were all about.

Who was it who had said, "There are no rocks in the sky; therefore rocks do not fall out of the sky"?*

Well, there were rocks in the sky, and Sir John had seen one of them fall. What else is up there that we do not know? he wondered uneasily. The City of Heaven? That was superstition, but then, where did this Damned Thing fall from?

"Find a large fallen branch," he said intently. "Something to pry it loose from the earth."

Sir John had devoted his life to an ideal of justice, which had been increasingly exacerbated by knowledge of how infuriatingly difficult it was to achieve, or even approximate, justice in this world. Now he felt a new passion: a commitment to pure truth such as the dedicated natural philosopher must feel. The Royal Scientific Society—indeed, all educated opinion—was wrong about thunderstones. Sir John had seen this one fall with his own eyes; it was not some peasant's tale. It was his duty to inform the scientific community. He had, at that moment, only a dim premonition that this might be an unpopular undertaking. That did not matter, of course; he had been vilified considerably for some of his positions in Parliament—his defense of the American colonists, his opposition to slavery, his efforts to remove the Penal Laws and restore religious liberty. He was not afraid of public opinion. Besides, he had the rock, and he was

---

*Lavoisier, of course. See page 77.

sure nobody could argue away the existence of so tangible
an object.

Sir John heard Moon move behind him.

Seamus Muadhen was hesitating, as he had been hesitating for months. It was only partly that Babcock was not the
villain Seamus had imagined in the interrogation room in
Dun Laoghaire; mostly, he had delayed because he lacked
the stomach for this job. He had told himself, many times,
that he was being clever and crafty: waiting for the right
time, the time when he could do it and escape without suspicion. That had all been lies; he had had many opportunities. Opportunities lost, gone, keened only by the wild,
wicked wind.

It was easy to commit murder in imagination, Seamus had
learned. There was the man you hated, the man who deserved to die: and there you were, alone with him. You shot,
or you stabbed, or you clubbed him, and the work was done,
But now, in the real world, it was more complicated: the
man had a wife, for instance, and you could not stop yourself from thinking of the look in her eyes when she heard
the news; and she was pregnant, and you thought of the
unborn child; and you learned, the way servants learn things,
that she, Lady Babcock, had a brother who was half-mad
because of a wound from a duel, and you wondered what
more violence coming into her life might do to her mind . . .

The plain fact is, Seamus thought in the dark, coming up
behind Sir John, the great conquerors and empire builders
like the English are people who have learned not to think
that way. Here is a man who must die, they think: and they
kill him: and there is an end. And the revolutionaries who
succeed can also think one step at a time: here is a man
who must die: so we kill him. Those of us who think of the
next step, and the step beyond, Seamus realized, are not the
ones who make history. We are its passive victims. If a
prime minister anywhere in Europe had the kind of mind I
have, Seamus thought miserably, he would never sign a mo-
bilization order for an army: and there would be no history.
History is made by men who do not think of the ultimate
effects of what they are doing.

Babcock was English (never mind his wife and the new
life in her womb; never mind the next step and the step

beyond), and Ireland would never be free until enough Englishmen were killed; and that was the logic of history.

And Seamus still hesitated. I am not to be an actor in history, he thought, but only a victim of it.

Hamlet, O'Lachlann said, was unable to act because he had read too many books at the University of Heidelberg; and I have read too many books, Seamus thought, for a fisherman's son in a conquered, crucified nation.

Seamus had a good large branch of beech in his hand. One blow and Babcock would be down, unconscious. Four or five more blows and his head would be open like a rotten melon. It was no more effort, really, than killing a rat. Easier: rats are more sly than this rich, idealistic young man who had never inquired into the sources of his wealth.

And a child would be born of a widow in grief and that child would be marked in ways that you could not predict.

If a child was born at all; if Lady Babcock did not miscarry in the midst of shock and grief.

But many Englishmen had to die—it was the merciless logic of the real world: no conquered nation had ever been freed voluntarily—and each Englishman had a wife, or an old mother, or sisters, or childher, or somebody who loved him.

I can force myself, Seamus thought. I will think of the pliers pulling at my fingernails and the rifle butt smashing my kidneys and making the urine run down my thighs and the hours in the bucket when space and time warped into chaos, when my mind became chaos and I knew what it was like to be a madman, when my mind collapsed like a house falling into a debris of bricks and black dustmotes; and he thought then: This thunderstone fell to teach me, once and for all, what sort of a man I truly am.

So he thought of the agony in the interrogation room and he moved quickly and raised the beech branch high over his head and was behind Babcock at the right distance and thought, *I am not doing it for hatred or revenge but for Ireland's liberty: history will absolve me** and then he heard

*The Hegelian and Marxist view of history as the judge of human action has never received such incisive criticism as that offered by de Selby in *Golden Hours,* vols. X-XII, wherein he argues with his usual intrepid logic that acceptance of his own doctrine of six-dimensional plenumary time reveals all history to be *one* multidimensional act, "co-

it, almost like thunder in the distance in the first shock,
freezing him (as O'Lachlann said the concept of God was
invented when some early man, about to commit a deed he
knew to be evil, suddenly heard some terrible Thing roaring

hering both forward and backward." (He is here using *cohere* in its original Latin meaning of "sticking-together.") It was during their vehement
dispute over this issue that Hanfkopf confronted La Puta with the much-
debated "lavender diaries," allegedly in de Selby's own hand, which
seemingly proved the Sage of Dalkey to be not only a maniac, but a
devotee of drugs, drink, and more sexual perversions than Gilles de Rais.
(See "De Selby Diaries Proven Forgery," *Journal of Plenumary Time*,
IX, 3; "Lavender Diaries Vindicated: No Fraud Found," *The Skeptical
Inquirer*, XIV, 4; and "UFOs in De Selby Diaries," *Fate*, XXIII, 16.)
It is to be regretted that La Puta weakened his own case, in this instance,
by collecting "testimony" against Prof. Hanfkopf from various public
prostitutes whose evidence, as the judge said at the third hearing on Hanfkopf's countersuit for libel, was "hearsay at best and bears clear evidence
of deliberate perjury in places." It was after this that Prof. Hanfkopf
began to lose even such minimal restraint as he had previously exhibited
and wrote his notorious open letter to the press of six nations, charging
not only La Puta but Le Monade, La Fournier, O'Brien, and indeed the
entire academic world with being engaged in "a conspiracy of deception
without parallel in the annals of infamy." Actually, de Selby's thesis of
plenumary time (without its odd historical applications) reappears in the
writings of quantum physicist Dr. John Archibald Wheeler as the notion
that perhaps all electrons are *one* electron moving backward and forward
in time and thereby creating the mesh of apparent reality; see John Gribbin's *In Search of Schrödinger's Cat*, Bantam, New York, 1984, p. 192,
passim; and Hoffman's *The Strange Story of the Quantum*, Pelican, 1963,
p. 217. In such a multidimensional weave of forward-and-backward cau-
sality, de Selby would have found justification for his notorious paradoxes
(such as "Shakespeare as much as Brutus plotted Caesar's death," "The
Church is right, after all, in asserting that Jesus suffered 2,000 years ago
for my sins today," and "Since electrons are created by acts of obser-
vation, the Big Bang is being caused by quantum experiments now occurring"). It was while de Selby was developing the geometry and
calculus of this uniquely Hibernian cosmology that Sophie Deneuve,
wishing to terminate once and for all the interminable series of love
poems (written, typically, in Homeric Greek) that he was sending her
from Dalkey, persuaded all her friends in Paris to write him letters of
condolence, expressing regret at her alleged death. It was in the first
terrible weeks of de Selby's grief over this putative loss that he made the
one glaring error over which Hanfkopf has exercised so much heavy-
handed Teutonic sarcasm (see *Werke*, IV, 44–46, 49, 73, 101–16, 223,
236–78), absently dividing his Phenomenological Constant by $x - y$
where in fact x was equal to y, thereby dividing in effect by zero; this
lapse created such astounding results that only the hypothesis of teratological molecules could then rescue the edifice of plenumary time from
intellectual ruin.

at him from the sky), and then recognized it as the sound of a coach coming at a gallop, the driver forcing the horses to desperation.

And it was coming from the direction of Lousewartshire: of Babcock Manor.

Sir John whirled, not noticing the branch in Seamus's hand.

"I want more witnesses to this," he said, and then he dashed back toward the road. Whoever was coming, they would have to slow down to pass his coach and he could wave them to a halt.

They will stop for him, Moon thought. Sir John would not be mistaken for a highwayman in his fine cloak and wig and knee breeches.

James Moon, the servant, followed his master toward the road, the beech branch dangling from his hand.

The other coach was slowing. As it stopped and they ran toward it, Moon recognized the face of Dorn, the gardener.

"It's Lady Babcock," Dorn shouted. "Her time has come. I was sent to London to fetch you."

"How long . . . ?" Sir John asked, anxiety in his voice.

"She's been hard took for over an hour now I'd say, sir."

Sir John nodded. "I must go the Manor," he said to Moon crisply. "Dig the thunderstone up and bring it there."

Then he leaped into the second coach, beside Dorn, and sped homeward.

Moon turned and trudged back to the rock that had fallen out of the heavens.

I don't know what you are, he thought, looking at it, but you're no greater mystery than my own mind. In the name of God I swear I know not at all whether it was cowardice or mercy that kept me from killing him.

Eleven

Sigismundo Celine waited until seven on a moonless night.

By then, in Paris in the autumn, it is quite dark. He had made a metal hook out of part of the bedsprings. The rope was double-looped, so the hook could be detached from the sill by tugging properly, after he reached the bottom.

The winds were not bad this night, He would not have the extra worry that a strong gust might blow him off the tower entirely.

Sigismundo attached the hook to the sill, tested it for purchase, and then checked the loop that would pull it loose when he reached the moat.

All set. Ready to go.

Nobody had ever escaped from the Bastille.

Well, then, Sigismundo thought, now I make another crack in that terrible concept, "the impossible," which is the world's folly and despair.

He swung out the window and, bit by bit, began uncurling the rope from around his waist.

It was necessary, he knew, to keep a firm grip at all times. If one hand slipped, even with the rope around his waist, the force of gravity would hurl him down so rapidly that rope burn would rip the palm into a bloody mush. No amount of courage would help then; it would be physically impossible to regain a tight grip with a hand so seared. This was meticulous work, just like the nights he had spent unweaving the blankets and reweaving the threads into rope.

Hand over hand, slowly and patiently, he climbed downward.

There was no dizziness, no images of falling; he had trained himself, in the months of hanging from the sill ten times a night. It was like fencing or playing the harpsichord: do a job every day and eventually it becomes easy and natural.

Although it was moonless, there were no street lamps visible from here: the Tower of Liberty faced the open country to the north. That was good, because he was virtually invisible in the darkness; but it made it almost impossible for him to be sure how far he had descended yet. He thought he was more than a third of the way down, but that might be a bad guess. He might have descended only half that far.

He could have ninety feet yet to go, or 105 feet.

When he was further down, he would be able to judge better, by listening to the sound of the water in the moat.

His biceps began to ache. Well, he had expected that. Even with six months' practice hanging from the sill, this kind of slow, hand-over-hand descent was hard work.

After what seemed a long, long time, he still did not think he was more than halfway down: the sound of the water was still far below. His back was hurting worse than his arms now. Well, I want to get *out,* he told himself; this is the price.

There was no way to stop and rest. If he loosened his grip the rope curled round his waist would tighten painfully—that would be worse than the ache in his spine and shoulders.

The wind started to blow again.

He could see his breath becoming steam in the air.

Just what I need, he thought, a drop in temperature, so my little swim in the moat will freeze the bejesus out of me, before I climb the outer wall.

Nobody had ever escaped from the Bastille.

Sigismundo's fingers were icy now and beginning to cramp.

I know why people like to read picaresque novels, he thought. This kind of thing is exciting if you can sit in an easy chair and read about somebody else doing it.*

---

*Cf. de Selby: "Footnotes are loved by academics, not because they are necessary, but because they are intimations of infinity: prose commenting on prose adumbrates mind contemplating mind and opens an exuberance of mirrors." *Golden Hours,* I, 33.

He felt the panic beginning. He had beaten away the fear of falling, hanging out the window all these months, but now a new fear had to be faced. He could see himself, hands cramped, back cramped, unable to continue; caught like a fly in a web.

The only thing to do then would be to drop. He was far enough down, probably, to survive the fall to the water. And they would find him there in the morning, shivering wet. Defeat.

Hand over hand, he continued his descent.

I am my father's son. He learned how to remove ordinary human mercy from his heart, crush it out entirely. I can remove fear. All it takes is will, and a kind of madness, and I think I have inherited both.

He was beginning to hear the water more distinctly. He must be more than halfway down then.

Most marvelous. Only sixty feet more to go.

Another gust of wind, much stronger than the last, came along and he was blown far out into space, away from the tower. He held on to the rope with both hands and remembered to breathe rhythmically.

Then the tension in the rope pulled him back, very fast, and he knew he was going to smash against the wall and he raised his feet to take the impact there and the wall raced toward him and he banged his boots hard, hitting. His right hand slipped and he let go, to avoid the rope burn, and clung desperately with his left hand.

The weaker hand, he thought. Damn it, I have to hang by the weaker hand while my whole body is trembling from the collision with the wall.

His right hand found purchase again. He hung limply a moment, not trying to move, breathing.

Then he began his descent again.

His eyes were more and more adjusting to the dark. He began to realize where he was. The eighty-foot outer wall was visible now, the top just slightly above him.

So: he had only climbed forty feet down so far. It had merely *seemed* longer.

But that gave him a new idea, so plausible he wondered why he hadn't thought of it sooner.

It was dangerous and perhaps impossible. But if he could do it, he would not have to climb down eighty feet further and then swim the moat and then climb up eighty feet again.

Sigismundo began to swing back and forth, building up momentum. The trick was to push himself away from the tower wall with more force each time, and yet not hit the wall so hard on the return swing that he would be knocked off into space.

If he could swing far enough, and catch hold at the exact instant, he would be atop the outer wall. The hardest part would be over.

He swung further out.

And, on the way back, he managed to miss the tower and swing higher into empty space.

Just as Newton said (or was it Galileo?), that increased his acceleration on the way back out.

You must be crazy, he thought bemusedly. Only a carnival acrobat could do what you are attempting.

He swung back and out again.

And as the outer wall came closer and closer and he reached with his right hand he knew that it would either work this time, *right now,* or he would lose his grip entirely in the weaker left hand and fall into the moat. His fingers stretched, clutched, and one more moment of panic came over him, and he was hanging on the wall. He spun quickly, let loose his left hand, stretched again, and was hanging from the wall by both hands.

He pulled himself up quickly; the rest of the rope was still curled around his waist, tied securely.

Sigismundo sat on the wall, resting. Then he twisted the rope and tugged quickly. It uncurled from the sill far above and fell toward him. He pulled it upward before the hook hit the moat.

He sat and rested. He had made it to the outer wall, he was exhausted and aching. There was a long night ahead before dawn would come.

He looked at the city gate across the rue St. Antoine. Two sentries were on guard.

This was the wrong place for the descent. He would have to walk around the wall to the city side before starting to climb down.

An hour later, from the west wall, Sigismundo began his second descent. He felt rested and increasingly confident; luck had been with him so far.

There were street lamps nearby, but that was not a serious

worry. Almost everybody would be indoors at this hour, with their shutters closed against the wind.

Halfway down he had one more wave of panic, when it seemed again that he was getting a cramp so severe it would paralyze him.

He prayed and visualized the white light:

"Toward the One, the perfection of love, harmony, and beauty, the only being, united with all those illuminated souls who form the embodiment of the Teacher, the Spirit of Guidance."

The cramp passed as he visualized the light flowing through his whole body. He continued his descent, hope rising as the street came closer and closer. The true Freemason does not know despair. "Maybe the damned horse can fly." "Learn to Dare, Learn to Will . . ."

Sigismundo's feet touched the ground.

He had not felt so good since he wrote his *Two Nations* Sonata, the one that drew so much wild applause and so many angry boos at the Teatro San Carlo.

He leaned against the wall a moment, panting, ecstatic.

Then he saw a figure approaching with a lamp.

A watchman. His eyes were widening. He was noticing the rope, and realizing what Sigismundo had done. "Guards!" he shouted. "Escape! Over here!"

Sigismundo was on him by then, using the side blow to the neck that Tennone had taught him for an occasion when you were attacked and did not have your sword.

My luck is still with me, he thought as the watchman sank into oblivion. This is a misfortune, not a calamity. If Paris watchmen were armed, it might have been a calamity.

He was into an alley when he heard another watchman shouting "You, there—halt!"

This time it was not a cul-de-sac. Sigismundo was soon into another street, sprinting rapidly, but still hearing the watchman behind him, that chap was quite a sprinter, too, it seemed, and he was perhaps gaining a bit.

Sigismundo saw a bridge ahead. Excellent. Once across, he could get lost in the labyrinth of alleys and the watchman would not know where to start looking.

He dashed onto the bridge, hearing the watchman close behind.

And saw another watchman directly ahead of him, where the bridge joined the grounds of the church of St. Marion Calpensis.*

"Jesus Christ and his black bastard brother Harry," Sigismundo thought, having heard that oath from Sir Edward Babcock in England.

The two watchmen closed on him rapidly.

Sigismundo dived over the rail.

When the water hit him he thought all at once of diving for his cousin Antonio's body back in Napoli, and of his dream that he would die by drowning, and of his first-degree initiation into Freemasonry. Then, staying deep and holding his breath, he swam as quickly as he could downstream, letting the current help him, thanking God that it was still

---

*It was at this very church, oddly, that de Selby first met Sophie Deneuve; his first words to her (they were both seeking shelter from a rainstorm) were "You are wet: may I offer you my jacket?" and hers were "Fuck off, Buster." No cold academic account of de Selby's astounding speculations can, or should, express the depth and severity of his grief and metaphysical *angst* when the fraudulent letters concerning her alleged death reached him in Dalkey; it was in those black days of cosmic despair that de Selby conceived his plan to "neutralize plenumary time" and thereby abolish all life in the universe, which he regarded as an "obscene jest." (See O'Brien, *Dalkey Archives,* Picador Books, London, 1976, p. 23, ff.) It is a tribute to both de Selby's mental resilience and his unique capacity for transmundane states of consciousness that he soon recovered and became convinced that he was deeply in love with Nora Barnacle, whom in fact he had never met. His letters to her, attempting to woo her by demonstrating his intellectual agility—he was under the misapprehension that Nora lived with James Joyce because she admired Joyce's macaronic metaphysics—contain many ingenious and piquant passages, such as his famous argument that the mysterious number 1132 which recurs monotonously and tantalizingly throughout *Finnegans Wake* (then called *Work in Progress*) refers to both Ireland and the Periodic Table of Elements, thusly: Thirty-two is the number of counties in Ireland; these counties comprise four provinces; therefore divide thirty-two counties by the four provinces and obtain eight; when the eight is multiplied by the eleven remaining in 1132, the result is eighty-eight, the number of elements in the Mendeleyev table. Mr. Robert Nicholson, curator of the James Joyce Museum, informs me of an odd coincidence that might interest Jungians: When he, Nicholson, spoke about de Selby's theories at University College, Dublin, there were exactly eighty-eight tickets sold for the lecture. In another letter *(De Selby/Barnacle,* closed shelves, Cornell University Joyce Collection) de Selby adds: 8 + 8 = 16, a direct link to the date of *Ulysses* (June 16, 1904). Nora's only recorded comment on de Selby's epistles was "That fellow in Dalkey seems a bit daft."

early autumn and the waters were not cold enough to numb him.

He came up, once, and saw a watchman—which one?—running along the bank, but far back. He dove again and swam as if sharks were at his heels.

When he came up again, he saw no watchmen.

He crawled ashore, dripping, and began to feel the chill.

Oh, well, he told himself, that is only wet and damp; it may give me the pneumonia and kill me after all this exertion, but I will not worry about that now. Now I must be in focus on the moment. From here on, even more than during the escape from the Bastille, everything depends on luck and blind chance, so I must seize every opportunity.

Posters of his face would be all over Paris by midday.

There was no way of getting past the sentries at the city gates without papers, and he had no papers.

He also could not survive long without money.

I will have to find a way around or over or under the gates, he thought. A man who got by the two walls of the Bastille is not to be trifled with: he would get past the unpassable gates.

How? Well, he would have to think about that.

And after flying over the gates? He could not return to Napoli; he had given his oath, after the duel, never to return, so that the peace between the Malatestas and Maldonados could be preserved. Besides, that path would take him across hundreds of miles of French police. He would go north then, following the Seine—but staying off the main highways, of course. It was only a short way to the Channel, and a man who is named in a *lettre de cachet* and has already assaulted an officer of the law will not stick at stealing a small boat.

And then he would be in England. In the same country with Maria.

Well, he would not be damned fool enough to go within a hundred miles of her. He was cured of that folly, and she hated him for what he had done to Carlo.

Good enough, he told himself. I will go to England, land of constitutional liberties, where they have no *lettres de cachet,* and I will stay far, far away from Maria Babcock.

That is what I will do. As soon as I figure out how to get through gates where the sentries will be looking for an Ital-

ian male of my height and description and will probably
even have pen-and-ink sketches of my face.

He sneezed.

Pay no attention to that, he told himself. You have no
time for the pneumonia or the influenza or anything of that
sort.

He staggered into an alley doorway and hunkered down,
wet and dripping. He sneezed again.

Now is the time, he told himself, now above all, to praise
God with every cell of my being, to be at one with Him in
the fourth, universal soul, to rejoice at the miracle of existence.

Because if I cannot do that, I will despair quickly and
lose the game.

"Toward the One, the perfection . . ."

A rat scampered across his foot. He shivered and prayed
on, ". . . the perfection of love, harmony and beauty . . ."

PART THREE

The Living One

△

nor shall diamond die in the avalanche
be it torn from its setting

—Ezra Pound, *The Pisan Cantos*

△

One

Maria looked perfectly normal when Sir John, after galloping up the stairs, burst into her bedroom. In his fevered imagination he had been expecting a scene from the *Inferno,* or enough weeping and howling for the fifth act of *King Lear.*

"The spasms are twenty minutes apart," she said, smiling in reassurance. "I've been timing them with the old grandfather clock in the corner."

"Don't need no clock," chuckled an old woman's voice from the shadows, as a brown, weathered hand reached out and came to rest gently on Maria's bulging torso. "Don't need no clock. Old Kyte knows when they comin'. And this little lady here she don't make no noise hardly in the pains. Jus' a little bit of 'Mmmmmmmmmm.' And that's good. Don't waste no breath yellin', I tell 'em. You goin' to need all that breath later on. And she just rest in between and that's good too. She's a rare good 'un for a first-time lady, I can be tellin' you that, sir."

Sir John recognized Old Kyte, the town's alleged "witch."* He regarded her as a harmless soul, actually, and some of her brews often seemed to help her customers. Old Kyte had been a midwife and herbalist so long that nobody knew how old she was; John's father, Sir Edward,

---

*From the Old English *wicce,* to know, or one who knows, a word related to modern "wit," "wisdom," and the German *Wissenschaft* (science). Long before the Inquisition and its witch-hunts, the word was applied in England to persons (usually but not always women) who practiced what nowadays would be called herbal healing or folk medicine.

remembered her from *his* youth. Once a preacher of the Ranter sect, one of the dissenters, had tried to have her run out of Lousewartshire, but the people had run the preacher out instead. The local doctor, Mr. Coali, was always fuming and fulminating against her, but most (and not just the peasants, Sir John knew) still resorted to her occasionally, when the doctor was away, or when he pronounced a case hopeless.

Many had been healed by her, or claimed they had. Still, Sir John wanted the best, most modern, most *scientific* care for Maria.

"Where's the doctor?" he asked, trying not to sound as panicky as he felt.

"I'll just see if this here tea's ready, sir," murmured the shabby old woman, as she moved with surprising speed and grace across the room to where a steaming kettle stood among packets of her herbs.

"Mistress Kyte is brewing me some special tea, John," Maria said, smiling again but somewhat glazed. "I've already had one cup and it did wonders for me, whatever it is. She says I can only have two cups and must 'piss it right out quicklike,' and then no more liquid."

"Where the *hell* is Doctor Coali?" Sir John whispered, frightened but not wanting to offend the old lady.

"The doctor was sent for hours ago," Maria said, "but word came back from his house that nobody knows where he is. Maybe he was stopped by an emergency somewhere on the road. Or maybe he just went off to play cards with his cronies. I am nearly a month early, you know."

If I find out he *was* playing cards, Sir John thought, I'll wring his neck. I'll get him disbarred or defrocked or whatever they do to doctors. I'll kick his arse on the public street and dare him to challenge me to a duel. I'll do *something*, by Christ.

He paced nervously around the bed, running a hand through his hair. Old Kyte was humming tunelessly, almost inaudibly, as she stirred the tea. I hope it isn't eye of newt and toe of frog, he thought desperately. Maria was propped up in almost a sitting position.

"Shouldn't you be lying down?" he asked, hearing his voice crack.

"I'm quite comfortable, *caro mio*." It always brought

back the wedding night when she called him that; he red-
dened, almost fearing the old "witch" could read the chaos
of love and lust and irrational guilt that swept through him.
"In fact," Maria went on, "I've been up walking about
several times, in between. But now another one is just about
due, so I got myself settled."

"Oh my God." He started to pace again. The doctor had
warned him that some women scream most terribly during
the contractions. If a husband cannot stand that, Dr. Coali
said, it is best for him to go to another part of the house,
where he cannot hear it. But Sir John could not leave Maria
alone with the ordeal.

He sat down and held her hand again, steeling himself.
"How did that woman come to be here?" he asked quietly.
If the husband *is* in the room and shows panic, the doctor
said, that just frightens the wife and makes her ordeal worse.
I will not be that kind of idiot, he told himself.

"It is an indelicate story," Maria said, smiling again.
(What *was* in that tea?) "I had a few . . . cramps . . . earlier in the day, but nothing really. I was determined not to
send out a false alarm, as it were. Then—don't laugh—I was
on the pot when suddenly *whoosh*, there was a deluge. I
told Alice, my maid, 'The waters have burst, call the doctor.' and then I got out of my clothes—the skirt was all wet
anyway—and into my nightgown and waited. The next thing
I knew Mistress Kyte was here. She had been selling herbs
to Cook, she said. I doubt that's all of it. Such women *know*
things that are going to happen."

Well, Old Kyte had never been accused of killing any of
her customers, Sir John thought. Many swore by her reme-
dies.

"She has been very kind," Maria went on. "And she's
told me so many interesting things. Just what I can expect,
how I can help the birthing, things I never knew. Women's
mysteries."

Sir John nodded. Still, there was something bizarre,
Gothic, *medieval* about Old Kyte's rough, patched home-
spun dress swishing about among the exquisite satins, mus-
lins, brocades, and silks of Maria's bedroom. And about
her continual humming and muttering in a language that
sounded as alien as Basque. But every town had a witch-
woman like her, kindly old souls mostly, who did know a
great deal about what Maria called "women's mysteries."

And she was clean, compared to the average peasant woman. The hair he could see beneath her kerchief did not hang in greasy strands like most farmwomen's. White as wool, it puffed out and went fluffing down her shoulders like Maria's jet-black hair right after she had had it washed.

The worst that had ever been said about Old Kyte was that, many years ago, she had led peasant dances in the woods on May Eve, which some of the Methodists and Ranters had called licentious.

"Old Kyte knows when they comin'," she said, moving toward them with the tea. Maria reached for it. "No, not now, my sweetling." She set the tea down and laid her hand on Maria's stomach. "About now," she said. "Ah! Here it is. Now remember what Old Kyte told you, that's a girl. Breathing out, breathing in, what will finish must begin. Breathing in, breathing out, all is well without a doubt. You're doing lovely. That's it, lips closed. Nothing to fight, everything right. Now ride like I told you, ride the pain, then the rest time comes again."

Maria leaned hard on the outbreath. "Mmmmmmm."

Sir John's knuckles were white around the bedpost. His face was drained of color. Old Kyte looked at him quickly, then back at Maria, who was in the middle of another long groan. "That's my lady. That's right, no pushing, no strain. I'll tell you when to do that. For now, just let it be, it's comin' 'long fine. No grabbing now. Uncurl your toes, don't frown. Ah, now, that's good."

"Mmmmmm," said Maria. It was almost a casual sound this time. "I think it's over."

"For a little time, my sweet," Old Kyte said softly. She muttered to herself, "Robin, Marion, Orfee, Bride, all ye gentry come from Side."

Maria's breathing was normal again, her eyes open. "Those are spirits who protect women in birthing," she said to John, with no mockery of the old woman's beliefs. "*Side* is where they live, isn't it, Mistress?"

"Side ain't no place," Old Kyte said simply. "It's a different kind of time. The gentry, they don't *come* here from there. They're *always* here. I call their names so's I can see them better."

I do believe she's talking about Platonic forms in her own way, Sir John thought, bemused at this bit of folk metaphysics. Entities that are not in time but create effects that are in time; that is pure Platonism.

"Drink this," Old Kyte's voice commanded. She handed him a cup of tea. He shook his head.

"I thought that was for me," Maria said plaintively.

"He needs it more nor you do," said the old woman. "Drink now," she said, not adding "sir" and speaking with authority.

Sir John drank, more amused than offended. It was bitter, but no more so than Guinness stout.

"What about me?" asked Maria.

"Time you pissed out the last tea, my lady. We wants you empty now. The last one was a good stong 'un. And the next will be not far behind an' I know my work. You don't want nothin' on your stomach from now on."

"Who are those, ah, spirits from Side?" Sir John asked as Maria relieved herself.

"The guardians of the four quarters," Old Kyte said directly. "North, east, south, west, they are fairest, they know best. That's what the wise women say."

"The wise women?"

"Them who know the Craft."

Sir John was startled—but of course she did not mean Freemasonry. It was just a coincidence, of course.

But Charles Putney Drake, the Most Worshipful Master of the Liberty lodge in London, had said once that he believed there was a time, long ago, when all who had the *baraka* were in one lodge, and then the Inquisition came, and they were all driven underground, and many different lodges grew up with different traditions . . .

"I'm thirsty again," Maria said. "May I drink nothing?"

"We'll fix that." Old Kyte went to the chest of drawers. "Clean handkerchiefs?"

"Top drawer," Maria said.

"Oh, ain't they pretty! It's years since I seen the likes of these." Old Kyte took out a large, lace-edged handkerchief and dipped it into the kettle. "Now we'll just let it cool," she said, wringing it loosely. "You can suck on it."

"Ugh," said Maria.

"It'll do the trick, keep your mouth moist. You don't want to be chuckin' up nothin'. Beggin' your pardon, but did you shit today, my lady?"

"This morning," Maria said, unflinching.

"Twasn't since then? Oh, well, it will all come out in the end."

Sir John groaned. Both women looked at him. Old Kyte came and stood over his chair, staring down at him.

"Now she told me she wanted you here, my lord. Though why, I don't know. Never saw a man was any good at the birthing time."

"There are doctors," Sir John said. "They're men."

"The less said about them the better," Old Kyte said bitterly. "Not one of 'em ever bore a child nor knew what it was."

"I appreciate all you have done," Sir John said evenly, "but when the doctor comes, you shall have to leave. I want scientific care for my wife."

"He won't be here," she said bluntly. "Not in time."

Panic rose in him again. "How do you know?" He looked at Maria. She looked so young, so helpless, so frail. She was breathing quietly, her eyes closed, a faint, brave smile playing around the corners of her lips.

"It will be all right, *caro mio,*" she said. She reached for his hand and pressed it. His heart almost burst with emotion.

"Old Kyte know when they comin'. No doctor be here till it's too late."

"What do you mean, too late?" he asked nervously.

"Too late for him to have anything to do, 'cept give you his bill." She laughed. "They never too late to give you the bill. Baby beats doctor here, though, you wait and see."

Sir John nodded, saying nothing. Something in him began to relax. Probably the tea she had given him was starting to work. He wondered what herbs she used: were there relatives of the opium poppy in England? None that he knew. This was more like the hasheesh he had sampled in Cairo, but not as strong. "What *was* in that tea?" he asked.

"Devil's claw and heartsbalm and wild hemp and a few other things. You have to mix 'em just right, else they gets you excited 'stead of calming you."

There was another, louder groan from Maria.

Old Kyte put one hand on Maria's belly and one on her forehead, crooning and cheering her on. "Oh, that was a lovely 'un," she said, when it was over. "They're comin' closer now. That's grand."

Maria looked into the old woman's eyes. "Am I doing it right?" she asked.

"You're doing it right as rain, you are. You're lettin' it do itself right. Nothin' you have to do till the very end. Then you'll work, my pretty. Then you'll have some work to do. The hardest work you've ever done in your young life. But only for a few minutes and then it'll be all over and you'll have a beautiful bairn, a beautiful bairn."

"Bairn is baby?" Maria's voice sounded faint, child-like.

The old woman's hands gently massaged Maria's bulge. "Aye. A beautiful baby, my lady. Hester, wester, tanner, quill, banish every kind of ill. Be it her or be it him, sound of body, strong of limb. It's dropped already."

"Dropped?" Sir John said quickly.

"Just means it's come down. Gettin' in the right position. Like it should, sir. Head first, face down."

"I know," Sir John said. Actually, he had been a little unclear about it.

"Now, my lady," Old Kyte said. "I have to tell you, them two silly maids of yours has been out in the hall peekin' in here every two minutes. Mind if I puts 'em to some use?"

"Go ahead," said Maria. She turned to John, and he rested his lips on her slightly damp brow.

Old Kyte's voice could be heard giving orders in the hall. It rose in irritation. "Well, why don't you know, you silly creature? Go find somebody who does. And the hot water. I want it in here and coolin' and right away. And those clean sheets, folded so, three times, you mind? No, you for the kitchen, you for the rest. And don't forget the . . ."

"I'm awfully glad she's here," said Maria.

"They say she knows her business," he replied. "Been a midwife since the year one, the country people say."

"I like her funny rhymes. They keep going through my head when . . ."

"My poor, brave darling. Does it hurt very much?"

"It does, but it's not *bad.*" She looked at him seriously, seeking words to tell him what he could not experience. Like a sighted person explaining "red" to the blind, he thought wanly. "I feel good about the pain, because I want the child. It's not an *insult* like ordinary pain. I know it's necessary. There's a feeling of getting closer and closer all the time. I don't resent it. And with the rhymes going around and around in my head, I know what she means about riding the pain. It's not riding me.'' She subsided, suddenly weary.

"Rest,'' he said, kissing her damp temple.

She opened her eyes again, the tiredness past as quickly as it had come. "Do you know what she did when she first came in? She made me take off all my rings and sort of flop my hands. Then she loosened my hair and not only that, she untied all the ribbons on my nightgown and then she went around untying everything in the room that had a knot or a loop, even the curtain sashes. And she kept saying, 'Nothing hinder, nothing bind, *something something* now unwind,' with that odd humming, and believe it or not I felt straightaway more easy. And then she spoke to the four guardians, as if they were in the corners of the room. Robin, Marion, Orfee, Bride. Where does she get those names?''

"From generations and generations of peasant midwives, I daresay.'' *Bride,* he knew from his years in Dublin, was the old Celtic goddess of fertility. The Catholic Church had accepted her, or incorporated her, by making her St. Brigit. He seemed to feel the centuries behind him; before the Normans, before the Saxons, before even the Romans, when this land was Celtic, that rhyme had its roots. It might be as old as Stonehenge, he thought, awed by the persistence of tradition among the country people.

Old Kyte came back into the room followed by Floss, the upstairs maid, carrying a stack of linen.

"Put it down there,'' Old Kyte ordered. "And then go and do what I told you. And then help the other 'un with the pans. And don't you forget the soft cloths and the bit of soap. Well, don't stand there a-gawpin' at the lady. Go!'' The maid scuttled off.

Old Kyte's tone changed completely as she approached Maria. "How's my pretty now?'' Maria grasped her hand hard. Another contraction was starting. "There's my lambkin. Good girl. Hah, that was the best 'un yet, I can tell.''

Maria looked tired again. "Will it be much longer, Mistress?''

"The Lady only knows. But remember, you are in her arms. If it's my opinion you be wantin', and I seen more souls into this world nor I can count, it shan't be much longer. A few more, and then there'll be no letup, my lady, and you'll know you're ready. It started this morning with that first cramp you thought was a false alarm, I suspeck. Now you remember what to do at the end?''

"I remember. Like a hound," Maria said.

"Like a hound after a hard hunt," Old Kyte said emphatically. "And then?''

"Bear down. Will I have the strength? I get more tired after each contraction.''

"Will you have the strength? Look at her, sir." Old Kyte cried to John. "A healthy, strapping girl. Look at her color.'' She turned back to Maria, speaking very seriously now. "You have no idea, at your age, how much strength you got. You too young to have been tested. Lady, you *can* do what you *must* do. The strength is all there, when you need it. I seen some silly ladies a-scared out of their skulls and a-screamin' and weepin' and a-cursin' like an earl, and when the time came, they had all the strength they needed. And you're a good brave 'un, not like them fools.''

"I want my crucifix," said Maria, reaching toward the beside table. It was out of reach. Old Kyte sprang for it and kissed it briefly, with her eyes closed, whispering, "Gentle Mary, strong and mild, bless this mother, bless this child.'' As she handed the gold chain with its small pendant to Maria she smiled down on her, a radiant smile, a smile that contained as much love as if Maria were her own daughter. It was gone in a minute.

Old Kyte turned away quickly and was throwing dresser drawers open. "Now where you got them baby things hid?'' she asked with annoyance.

"They're in the—'' Maria's voice was tense. "In the press, in the basket.'' Another one had started. Maria closed her eyes, holding the crucifix between her breasts, "riding'' the pain. John felt that wave of love and lust and guilt again. The guilt, he thought, is because we shared the pleasure of the conception, but she has to bear the pain of the delivery alone. He watched her lips move, but could not tell if she was praying or repeating one of Old Kyte's rhymes.

"Mmmmmmm," Maria moaned as it ended.

"Good," Old Kyte said briefly, and went for the layette. "Ooh, they're lovely. I never seen the like. Will you look at that little gown? And that lacy shawl? Oh my, my, my, my . . .''

Toward dawn, Sir John heard Maria groaning more terribly than before. With another guilty start, he realized he had begun to doze in his chair. Hastily, he took her hand and pressed hard. She pressed back, her palm moist. Several times she looked into his eyes gratefully and even tried to smile. He tried also but failed utterly and finally stopped trying. He simply held her hand and tried to believe that touch could express all his love.

The spasms were coming harder now, without any interval.

There is not one man on earth, John thought wretchedly, good enough to deserve a woman's love. He suddenly remembered, in total agony, his grief at his mother's death and, reliving that grief, knew it had never left him; he had just pushed it to a corner of his mind where he didn't see it any more. He wanted to take all the pain that all the women in history had borne and bear it all himself. It was like the time he had smoked hasheesh in Cairo and knew that the palm tree before him was *alive;* it was like his Mark Master initiation (''a mark that will stay on you to the grave''); and Maria was panting like a hound now—part of what Old Kyte had taught her—and he felt that the pain was flowing into him and he was sharing it. Old Kyte ducked her head and lifted the sheet that covered the lower half of Maria's body, and seemed to be lifting her slightly to place the thick folded sheets under her, and then she bent Maria's knees, spreading them wide; and Maria stopped panting a moment and cried out, and Old Kyte came up grinning, saying ''Like a hound, lady, like a hound. Soon now, very soon.''

Maria was in continuous contraction now, her mouth open, panting rapidly. She seemed to be in a kind of trance, a kind of ecstasy.

''There's a bit of the head,'' said Old Kyte.

What did she mean, a bit of the head? What horrible thing was going wrong? John jumped up and looked. The organ, which he had called ''the rose of the world'' when making love, was purple and engorged. Even though he understood that the baby had to pass through he was astonished that the vulva had spread to that incredible width—and there was something else. An oval—no, a circle—about the size of a hen's egg. ''The top of the head?'' he whispered. Old Kyte nodded.

''Now,'' she spoke loudly and decisively. ''Now, my girl,

you've got some work to do. You want to bear down, don't
you? It's like wanting to go to the closet only more so, ain't
it? And you,'' she turned to John. ''She needs somethin' to
press against. I want you to put your arm under her shoulders and give her both your hands. Both! And hold her an'
let her press against you. Give her your strength. I shall be
busy down here now.'' He did as she ordered. ''Now, my
lady, you bloody well *push!*'' Maria did so until her face
turned red. John held her hands tightly through the strain,
feeling it.

''That was grand,'' Old Kyte said encouragingly. ''You're
a fine, strong girl and you're doing your job well. Now
again! Ah, there's a fine head coming through. No, no res-
tin' now. A few more and—'' She muttered under her
breath, ''Nowt can halt the moon and sun, nowt can stop
what's once begun.'' She raised her head. ''No slackin' now,
my girl. You're all lovely and open and the baby wants to
come. One more great big shove . . . and shove . . . and
shove . . . That's it, that's it! We'll just turn his little shoulder so, or is it hers? We'll know in a trice. Just hold your
breath a minute, no more strain. Ah, here it is! All well
and sound and whole. Now breathe, my loves, the both of
you. Come, baby, try the air now, that's a love.''

There was a patting, then a muffled sound, then a high,
piercing cry. Old Kyte held the strange little creature up by
its heels.

Maria's eyes shot open. ''It's here?''

John's eyes were misted over and all he could see was a
streak of blood on the head.

''Is it a—'' ''Give me—'' John and Maria spoke simultaneously. Maria was trying to raise herself up.

''In a minute,'' Old Kyte said crisply. ''She'll be prettier
for a quick bath.'' She made a gesture over the baby's head,
then busied herself with the warm water and soft wrappings.

''She?'' Maria cried.

''Aye, you have a beautiful daughter.'' Old Kyte grinned
a partly toothless grin. ''God bless this house and all here.''
She presented the infant, washed and wrapped, to Maria.

John had been so dazed that he had not noticed Old Kyte
cutting and tying the umbilical cord.

''A soft birth,'' said Old Kyte contentedly.

I should hate to see a hard one, John thought.

He was downstairs looking for a servant, to order some breakfast. He had held his daughter in his arms for a few moments—terribly nervous, fearful of dropping her or doing something awkward, fearful of the fragility of existence—and then Maria had taken the child back to her breast.

"Beyond a certain point, the whole universe becomes a continuous process of initiation." Who had said that to him, what Fellow Craft in what lodge, in England or on the Continent, how long ago?

He was in the main hall, but he could not remember what he was looking for. Oh, yes. Breakfast.

It was incredible that any entity so tiny could have so much power. The king himself, he thought, could not summon me to come so quickly, or to risk my life so willingly, as one cry from that child.

This is fatherhood, he told himself. No wonder it is so popular.

He tried again to remember where he was going. Oh, yes, he was trying to find a servant. For breakfast.

The maids were all upstairs, admiring the child and congratulating Maria. Where was Fenwick, the butler?

"I fetched the bloody rock, sir."

Sir John Babcock turned, gradually remembering the first miracle he had witnessed that night.

Moon had been sitting by the front door, waiting.

I shall give him the hidden manna, and a white stone . . .

"I am a father," he said, dazed, unable to contain the news.

A strange expression crossed Moon's face, something Irish and furtive, not to be known by the conquering race. Then a simple smile broke through.

"God and Mary and Patrick and Brigit be with you, sir," he said, coming forward, reaching into his jacket. "And may I be the first to offer you a drop of the creature, sir?"

He took out a bottle of whiskey.

Sir John drank, all of Dublin and his childhood there rising into memory. *A drop of the creature . . .* He had first heard that expression, not understanding it, at the age of four perhaps. I was a child then, he thought, and now I am the father of a child: what strange tricks time plays on us. His mother's face and the river Anna Liffey were as vivid in his mind as the child he had just held.

Upstairs, Old Kyte had disposed of the afterbirth and placed the baby in its crib. There had been little tearing, but she said "Best I stays awhile, just in case." She sat by the window and hummed softly over the crib.

Maria, neither awake nor fully asleep, had forgotten the pains and would not remember them until much later. She was dreaming about walking through her father's villa in Napoli, with her daughter, aged about five. Since she was not asleep yet, she was making the dream up as she told herself each detail. It was the perfect kind of spring day that happens only in Napoli, and Papa was so proud of her he could almost burst. Carlo had recovered from his wound and was being very nice. The sun was warm, all over her body. The little girl, her daughter, had John's eyes and mouth but jet-black Italian hair like her own.

This was better than the time she came out of her body listening to Handel's *Messiah,* she thought. This was better than making love with John. It was better than feeling the power in her hands when she did a healing. She remembered what she had written in her diary, months ago, about wanting to hug God. That was not silly at all. During the last moments of pushing down and straining, He had entered her body utterly, He had been more real and present than John or Mistress Kyte, He had taken all of the pain and given her all of His love and His love was, just as Handel's great music said, like a refiner's fire. He was not outside the universe, aloof and above, as people think. He was inside the most inside part of it, in her womb, in her muscles, in her blood, in her arse. He shared all our joys and suffered all our pains and he fought on both sides in every war. He is not grand and great at all, she thought; He is humble enough to be in a louse.

So she dreamed of explaining this to Mother Ursula, back at school, and Mother Ursula said, "I am so glad you have experienced Him, Maria, because the people who never experience Him are alone all their lives and very easily frightened and almost mad with a melancholy they do not understand." And then Mother Ursula took her into chapel and they knelt before a statue of Mary and prayed together, and Mary smiled at them with the same infinite love as God entering Maria to take her pain and then she was not making the dream anymore and she was really asleep.

"You be a lucky 'un," Old Kyte whispered to the child.
"Your parents are both of the Craft, I do suspeck. Wonder
if they know it yet? Eh, my pretty? Think they know Side
yet? They will, they will."

Two

From THE REVOLUTION AS I SAW IT, by Luigi Duccio:

Therefore, even if it be granted that the Freemasonic lodges (and other similar or related secret societies) were the principal channels through which the *ideas* of the "Enlightenment" were spread, one still needs to ask, in a scientific spirit, why did these groups have so much power? You cannot grow wheat on stony soil, and innovations will not take root until the social environment is ready to receive them. The fact is that ninety-two percent of the twenty-three million souls in France were peasants, and few of these were recruited to Masonry before the 1770s. Granted that Orléans (then Chartres) and his clique of satraps made a determined effort through the Grand Orient lodge, using the charlatan Cagliostro as a front man, to enlist men of all classes, this would not have been a successful undertaking if men of *all* classes were not, even under Louis XIV, suffering increasing distress, due to the pressure (aforementioned) of rising population with its inevitable wage/price differential. The fact that both Louis XIV and Louis XV raised taxes and land duties only aggravated this problem, but did not itself count for much; men will always complain of taxes, which are a tangible nuisance, rather than of other economic burdens that they feel but cannot identify or name. Similarly, the enclosure movement—in which a few large agriculturists drove the majority of small farmers to ruin and changed France from a land of many small farms to a land of a few large farms—only *aggravated* the stresses inherent in runaway population growth.

The same pattern was going on throughout Europe without being noticed, because the human mind, untrained in analysis, is quick to see a visible good (more babies surviving the first months of life, due to better medicine) and not quick at all to note an invisible threat (rising population destabilizing all previous economic structures). Thus, the rebellions in Switzerland and Holland, already mentioned, were attributed to "radicalism" or "subversion," not to economic desperation; thus, in a small country like Ireland, one reads of insurgent groups with such remarkable names as the Peep o' Day Boys or the White Boys, and this is attributed again to "radicalism" (or to Papist plots) with no analysis of economic factors; thus, again, the "Gordon Riots" in London (1780), which burned nearly as much property as the Great Fire a century earlier, are attributed to anti-Catholic hysteria, which was only its façade, since examination of the arrest records afterward showed that virtually *all* the incendiaries and arsonists were unemployed or marginally employed—*viz.*, men seeking an outlet for rage and despair, created by the simple fact that there were more men in London than there were jobs for men to do.

I am writing this book, in fact, to show how people in general, whatever they may think are the motives of their private actions, are part of a historical process beyond their comprehension, a process that can only be seen when one looks at the movements of millions of persons over generations of time, a process as *predictable* and hence ultimately comprehensible as the Newtonian laws of planetary motion. I am asserting quite definitely, without equivocation, that if the mad Louis XV had lived longer and not been replaced by the saner (if stupider) Louis XVI, the revolution might have come sooner, *but not much sooner;* or, in the New World, if Wilkes and Burke had won more concessions for the American colonists, the revolution there might have been postponed a while, *but not prevented ultimately;* and if dozens of such accidents had been otherwise, the broad general outline of events would have been much the same in the long run.

And I therefore assert, as a consequence of this fatality, that the revolution "failed" (insofar as it did), and all similar revolutions must inevitably fail, until the day when industry is so altered by new sciences that it is possible to do what revolutionaries can at present only impotently dream of doing; namely, to give all citizens an adequacy of food, clothing, shelter, &c.; which can only be done when knowledge of natural law has increased to the point where the governor can give these things to Citizen A without taking them from Citizen B and thereby provoking B's rebellion. That is, when there is *more than enough of everything for everybody.*

And this, I repeat, can only be accomplished when Christianity and other superstitions are long forgotten—when Diderot's last doddering priest has been killed by a brick falling from the last crumbling church—and all boys and girls everywhere are educated in science and logic.

From THE SECRET TEACHINGS OF THE ARGENTUM ASTRUM:

The gate that is not a gate—the source of the Living One—was worshipped by all the ancients, as can be seen in the art of the Greeks, Egyptians, &c., is still worshipped in large areas of India, Tibet, and China, and appears disguised even in the art and architecture of our enemies, the Black Brethren, *who know this* and would hastily destroy any person who dares to declare it openly. The Sacred Heart is such a disguised symbol, as is the gothic arch, the parable of the loaves and fishes, the emblem of the fish itself, the Grail, &c. For the Long Memory, which is asleep in most persons, still controls them through dreams and visions, and they create, when the spirit of art moves them, only the multitudinous images of this secret and sacred eidolon that the wise rabbis of Judaea called *daleth* and that appears in the Tarot as the Empress card (which the aspirant should therefore study devoutly, until all its secrets are reveal'd).

Know then, O Brothers and Sisters of the Craft, that the desirable is life, the delightful is love, and this *daleth* is the gate of both life and love.

Burn this page.

Three

Marcel said Pierre was the man you wanted for wet work.

"Pierre don't take that kind of job no more," Louis said. "He's into, you know, moving things now. You see, he ain't as young as he used to be. Hell, which of us is? And he had a hard case last winter. Son of a bitch diego, scared hell out of Pierre. No, he don't do wet jobs. He just moves, you know, merchandise."

"Well, okay, then," Henri said. "Pierre's lost his balls, you mean. But this is good money I'm talking, and we need at least four. Now are you guys in or are you out, is what I want to know."

"Oh, I'm in," Marcel said. "I need the money. And I don't care, even if it is another son of a bitch diego like the one who scared the bejesus out of Pierre. I'm not afraid of them diegos."

"I'm in, too," Louis said. "Those diegos, what are they? Just a bunch of opera singers. Is it a diego?"

"Well," Henri said, "as a matter of fact, to be honest with you guys, it is. I don't know about the one gave Pierre the trouble last year, but this one should be easy. Guy just came over the wall of the Bastille."

"What is he, for Christ's sake," Louis said, "a goddam carnival acrobat or something? Came over the wall. Christ, that's two walls there. He must be one of them, you know, Neapolitans."

"I didn't ask where he came from," Henri said. "The thing is, he sure as shit ain't got no sword and he sure as shit didn't sleep well last night, and he sure as shit isn't eating regularly today, you know? I mean, this guy is probably staggering around Paris getting hungrier and weaker all the time.''

"Poor bastard,'' Marcel said. "I almost feel sorry for him. But I'll feel sorrier for myself, I don't make some money soon. Let's go find him, is what I say.''

Lt. Sartines was pondering a strange document. It had come to him from one of the *mouches* assigned to penetrate the Grand Orient Lodge of Egyptian Freemasonry and find out what the devil Chartres and his colleagues were really plotting behind all that mystic mumbo-jumbo. According to the *mouche*, this was a most important document, normally shown only to those of the highest degree of initiation. "I made this copy,'' the *mouche* said with quiet dignity, "at the risk of my life.''

Which meant that he expected to be paid extra.

Sartines compromised and paid a *little* extra. This document was meaningless to him, but he believed that the *mouche* was sincere in claiming that it was very important to these Grand Orient cultists.

It was not a genealogy, although a few of the people on it were related in some degree or another.

It might contain some important facts, Sartines thought, or it might be the key to the system of lies by which the Grand Orient convinced its members that it knew a great secret. Sartines had investigated enough to know all Masonic orders claimed one deep, dark secret or another. The secret usually turned out to be a Hebrew or Arabic word that meant nothing to anyone but a mystic.

Sartines examined this document again:

Louis Phillipe, Duc de Chartres

Well, naturally, Sartines thought, he'd have himself put at the top. But the next name stopped him a moment:

Charles Radclyffe, C.R.C.

Radclyffe, an Englishman, had been quite active in France about two generations ago. He was involved in—what? Something to do with the Jacobites, who were trying to return the Stuarts to the throne of England. And yes, there had been rumors, Sartines recalled, that Radclyffe was an alchemist and an organizer of the Strict Observance sect of Masonry. C.R.C.: that would be Chevalier de la Rose-Croix. The usual Rosicrucian nonsense.

Sartines suddenly remembered more: Radclyffe was the illegitimate son of Charles II. If James II had been restored to the throne, if the Jacobites had succeeded, this Radclyffe would be as close in succession, almost, as Chartres was to the French throne now.

Which might mean something or might be a coincidence.

Isaac Newton

Sartines smiled. He knew enough about secret societies to have a good guess as to how that name got on this list. They all claimed a few of the illustrious dead, since the dead could not rise up and contradict them. It took great cheek, though, to claim a Newton.

Robert Boyle
Johann Valentin Andrea
Robert Fludd

All scientists with an interest in alchemy. Just like Newton . . .

Louis de Gonzaga
Ferrante de Gonzaga
Connétable de Bourbon

All members of the interrelated royal families that had governed Europe for the last several hundred years. Chartres could, with some plausibility, claim to be related to each of them, and even to Radclyffe, if Radclyffe was an illegitimate Stuart. But there was no known bloodlink to Newton, Fludd, or Andrea . . . ?

The rest of the list was like that: royal families represented every two or three steps along the way, interspersed with distinctly non-royal and rather colorful individuals: Giordano Bruno, Leonardo da Vinci, Nicolas Flamel. Then at the bottom:

Jacques de Molay, K.K.J.
Dagobert II

Le Fils de la Veuve
Et in Arcadia Ego

Beautiful; it runs back in time to the Merovingians and then . . . "The widow's son"—"And in Arcadia, I . . ."

The last part, then, was in code. That would not be put into writing at any time, but only communicated *viva voce.* Probably in a graveyard at midnight, Sartines thought sardonically.

Let us make an assumption, Sartines told himself. This Grand Orient contraption has one purpose: to promote Chartres to the throne.

This list is, then, some mystical and metaphysical justification for that project? Not necessarily. If the proper people die at the right intervals, Chartres can succeed automatically; he needs no more legitimacy than his known genealogy.

Well, then, Sartines thought, I must imagine some further, higher goal, *beyond* the kingship of France.

Emperor of a United Europe? That would explain the Stuart and Gonzaga connections . . .

Sartines felt he was missing something. This was more arcane, more esoteric, than that.

Et in Arcadia Ego . . .

I have seen that before, Sartines thought suddenly. It is as clear as my father's face and the smell of the docks where I grew up.

But where, when?

A picture of shepherds.

Sartines waited, not forcing it. Memory works best when you do not push at it.

A picture hanging in the king's rooms at Versailles.

It all came back in a flash. It was a painting that Louis XV especially prized and kept in his own suite, away from the portrait gallery. Sartines had passed his eyes over it dozens of times when called there for conference, and had never really thought about it. And yet it was there in his brain quite clearly now. The artist, Poussin, was hardly one of the masters, nor was this one of his better or more famous works. Why did the king prize it? It was called *The Shepherds of Arcadia,* and it showed some shepherds, of course, but they did not seem to be in ancient Greece, as the title suggested, but somewhere in southern France. Sartines knew the general area—in Provence, around Montségur perhaps—where the Albigenses had been massacred by the Dominicans—where Jacques de Molay and the Templars had once flourished—*

The shepherds were standing at a tomb. Their expressions did not show grief, not at all: they seemed to be looking out of the canvas right at you with expressions that seemed to say nothing else but "we know something you don't know." And on the tomb were the four words that had brought this memory back:

ET IN ARCADIA EGO**

Sartines felt a wild hypothesis forming. The Grand Orient has a *real* secret, he thought, and the king knows it, too. He keeps that painting out of the main gallery because he is so suspicious these days that he fears every contingency; he worries that somebody else might guess the code, the allegory, or whatever it is that Poussin was hinting.

I *know,* Sartines told himself. I can trust my intuition this time.

It is the grave of somebody very important who once lived in Provence. Somebody we are not supposed to know too much about.

*Without wishing to find Freemasons dogging his steps forever, the author hopes it is permissible to mention at this point, as something widely published many times, that the 32° initiation of Freemasonry is largely concerned with the death of de Molay; and that the Knights of Malta are therein named as the conspirators who allegedly framed de Molay and the Templars. See for instance *Light on Freemasonry,* by David Bernard: Vonnieda & Sowers, Washington, D.C., 1858, pp. 287–304. See also footnote, page 100.

**This painting was indeed specially treasured by Louis XV and is analyzed at length in *La Race fabuleuse,* by Gérard de Sède, Editions J'ai Lu, Paris, 1973. By extremely tortuous argument, de Sède arrives at the conclusion that the secret hidden in the painting is that the French royal family was of extraterrestrial descent. The more usual interpretation is more vague and suggests that Arcadia (linked to the Golden Age) contained secret knowledge that abolishes the fear of death (symbolized by the tomb). A third line of interpretation is suggested by Baigent, Leigh, and Lincoln in *Holy Blood, Holy Grail,* op. cit., which seems to support the notion that the grave depicted is, as Sartines thinks, in southern France, and may be that of the widow's son.

Le Fils de la Veuve . . .

At that moment, Lenoir, the *lieutenant criminel*, stuck his head in the door. "Bad news," he said. "Some bastard just escaped from the Bastille last night."

Four

$\mathbf{S}$igismundo Celine, his clothes dried by now in the September sunlight, was wandering through the faubourg St. Germain, which was a middle-class and mercantile section where a man dressed as well as himself did not seem out of place. He had been lurking in les Halles for a while, hoping to be lost in the crowd when the workers rose to go to their jobs, but he soon realized that among all those sabots his own boots and finery made him as conspicuous as a green horse.

Sigismundo staggered a bit, to create the impression that he had been drinking all night. That would keep people from wondering why his fine silks were a bit smudged and torn in places.

Nobody had ever escaped from the Bastille before, and he had done it. That was a triumph he could remember and savor in old age.

Right now it did not seem like a triumph. He was beginning to realize that getting out was almost easy, compared with *staying* out. He had no way of obtaining food, except to steal—which meant one more risk. All the roads out of Paris had gates, where the sentries no doubt had his description already.

In Italy, in such a situation, he would find a Masonic lodge. He was afraid to try that here, since Chartres and Cagliostro seemed to have turned French Masonry in a direction that abolished the oath of brotherhood. Sigismundo was convinced by now that the two of them, Chartres and Cagliostro, were behind his imprisonment. For Italian Masons to plot against a Brother Craft that way was unthink-

able—it was unthinkable in England, too, or anywhere—
except in France today.

It was getting on toward noon, and Sigismundo had wandered some of the same streets more than once. It was time
to get out of the faubourg St. Germain.

Signor Pietro Malatesta
Malatesta and Celine Fine Wines
Via Roma
Napoli

My Honored Lord,
You do not know me but I am of old Neapolitan stock,
and have often enjoyed your wines. To get to the point,
honored lord, I am a cutter of stone and came to Paris two
years ago, hearing that wages were higher here. Since I
write to my family in Napoli often, I heard nearly a year
ago that your nephew had drowned here, and I was most
sorry for your sister, his mother, the Lady Liliana. Well,
honored lord, I must tell you that you have been grieving
without cause. Your nephew is alive, and has been in the
Bastille all this time. What's more, he has made monkeys
of the French authorities by escaping, and there are posters
of him all over Paris this day offering a handsome reward of
ten thousand francs.

This is what I propose to do. If I can find him, Sigismundo, I shall send him south in the false bottom of a coach
used by a friend of mine who, I am sorry to say, engages
in certain movements of merchandise without proper li-
censes and tariffs. If I cannot find the lad, at least you will
know by this letter that he is alive, and you can take steps
of your own to do whatever seems advisable to you.

I pray you, do not think I am the sort who helps a coun-
tryman in need only for hope of reward. I am proud of my
skill with the stone, and I earn good wages, and I do not
take charity. However, my sister, Signora Bianca Mazzini,
in Napoli, has recently lost her husband to the smallpox,
and if you feel a need to express your gratitude in the form
of coin, please address it to her.
    Yours most humbly,
    Luigi Duccio
    Stonecutter

My Honored Lord,

As you have no doubt heard through the grapevine, S. has gotten over the walls of the Bastille; I don't know how, except that the bastard must be part Barbary ape or something like that. I assume that, under the circumstances, our former arrangement is still in force, and I shall therefore attempt to have him found before the authorities get their net around him again, and I will make absolutely damned sure my men slice his throat from ear to ear this time, I promise you; and I assume that the sum agreed to beforehand, namely ten thousand florins in gold, will be paid into my account in the Banque de Paris upon word of his death reaching your lordship. I am sorry we could not get to him in the Bastille, but I promise you, on my mother's grave, we will do the job properly this time around, as I depend on the satisfaction of my customers to remain in this business. I have already hired three good men for the work, which should not be necessary as this time he has no sword, but I am taking no chances, and I hope you will be delighted with the news that reaches you in a day or two.

I kiss the hands of your mighty lordship,

P.

My Dear Chartres,

Yes, I know he's out. Have no fear; preparations for *transition* were already complete and I am sure our agents can find him before the bumbling police do. We shall use Italians who will pretend to be acting for his uncle in Napoli. It will be smooth as butter, believe me.

Cagliostro

Sigismundo was in the faubourg St. Paul by midafternoon. The air was thick with dust from the foundries and stoneworkers' shops, but that was better than the stench of midtown.

Besides, there were Italians living here, artisans who had come north because the French were currently infatuated with Italian-style architecture and carving. It was risky, but the only alternative was to wander the streets until the police found him. Sigismundo was hoping that luck was still with him. There might be somebody here from Napoli, somebody who knew Tennone or Father Ratti or Uncle Pietro; somebody who would help a compatriot in great distress.

Sigismundo has already seen two reward posters. That was one more danger. The moment he had landed on the ground outside the Bastille he had entered this new Paris, which was the old Paris for everyone else, but was a place of constant emergency for him. It is in many ways less of a stress to remain a convict, he thought, than to become an escaped convict.

If he could once get beyond the city gates, the flight to England would be easy. As long as he was within Paris, every face was a book which had to be read quickly—is this one a *mouche?* Is he wondering why I am in this neighborhood with rich clothing on me? Does that one recognize me from one of the posters?

One face did jump to the center of his awareness just then. It was definitely staring at him, and it was Italian. South Italian. Maybe even Neapolitan—

"Are you lost, Signor?" this face said, coming closer. It was a man in laborer's clothing, with an artisan's apron. Speaking Italian.

"I was looking to have some stone cut," Sigismundo said carefully, "but I couldn't remember the name of the shop I had used before . . . Are you Neapolitan, too?"

"But of course. As you are. I recognize the accent now."

Sigismundo remembered that the reward on the posters was ten thousand francs. But at a time like this you had to gamble.

"And do you also recognize my face?" he asked.

"I see a family resemblance to the Malatestas perhaps. Am I correct?"

Sigismundo plunged. "You will see my face on walls in many parts of Paris today," he said. "I am surprised that you have not seen it yet."

"But I have," the artisan said. "I understand your position. You need help but you dare not trust the wrong person."

"The posters say I am dangerous," Sigismundo said. "A man eager for the reward might want to win my confidence and then maneuver me to a place where colleagues can help overcome me."

"Of course. But you will have to gamble on somebody, or you will never get out of this city."

"Ten thousand francs is a great deal of money."

The man smiled. "The mighty Malatestas, they will pay more than that for your safe return."

"I'm sorry," Sigismundo said. "You are altogether too plausible and glib. Forgive me if I am wrong."

He landed a swift punch in the man's gut and took off, running into the nearest alley. Sure enough, there were two right behind him, who had been closing in during the conversation. He saw the glint as one raised his arm.

Sigismundo ducked through a gate into a stonecutter's backyard as the knife plunked into the wood beside him.

He was in a forest of angels; the owner of this shop obviously specialized in graveyard monuments. White, serene stone eyes gazed down at him as he ducked, dodged, and heard the gate open again as the assassins entered the yard in pursuit.

He saw no workers; he saw nobody. The owner must have closed down for the day to go fishing or something of the sort.

He groped his way amid cold stone candles toward the house. That was the direction of escape now.

Then he saw the back door of the house and one window. One of the assassins had fathomed the geography of the yard faster than Sigismundo had and was waiting there for him, knife drawn.

Five

Sigismundo was backing up, automatically, into the forest of white serenity, looking for something, *anything*, that might serve as a weapon, and at the same time he was thinking that it was not fatigue that wore you down eventually, and not even fear, but just outrage: the sense that the universe had no *right* to be so pitiless and intractable. You surpass yourself in courage and will power, you do what you think you cannot do, and then you do more, and in the back of your mind is the thought always, *Now* I have done enough, *now* no more will be asked of me. And then the universe quietly demonstrates that it does not give a rat's arse.

And now, as if to show that it was sneaky enough to give you renewed hope just when you had decided it was really a pisspoor contraption all around, the universe revealed to Sigismundo's desperately searching gaze a mallet.

One mallet against two knives. It wasn't much, but it was something. Sigismundo remembered his Mark Master initiation ("Help may arrive invisibly and unexpectedly from unknown sources") and seized the mallet and crept forward again.

The white, empty eyes of the angels gazed down.

The assassin was still waiting, knowing Sigismundo would come that way. He was maybe four inches taller than Sigismundo and maybe sixty pounds heavier.

As Sigismundo raised his arm to hurl the mallet, the assassin saw him and ducked, down and sideways.

Sigismundo checked his arm in mid-throw, held onto the mallet, ducked low, and moved in fast.

The assassin was coming at him, crouched low, holding

the knife low the way the professionals do, weaving, making a small, wobbling target out of his huge body.

They met. The knife missed on its first slash as Sigismundo dodged. The mallet missed as the assassin dodged.

They looked into each other's eyes for a moment, judging. No two lovers in passion ever tried harder to merge, to intermingle, to know each other's minds and feelings fully.

Then the assassin decided and Sigismundo saw him decide and the knife lunged forward again, fast as a cobra striking, and Sigismundo swung as hard as he could and brought the mallet down on the hand that was thrusting the knife toward his belly, and hit it a second before it would have cut into him.

"Awa," the assassin said involuntarily, dropping the knife in pain, and Sigismundo raised the mallet quickly and brought it down again, this time on the man's head, and then again a second time quickly, blood gushing up from the wound onto his hand, making him feel sick and dizzy for a moment, but still swinging a third time, hard, more blood spurting onto his arm and chest as the man fell to the ground, a pool of wet crimson spreading around him.

He's dead, Sigismundo thought. Jesus, I killed three last year, with a sword, but that wasn't as God-awful as this. (I mustn't vomit.) Maybe I'll get so hardened eventually I can kill them with my bare hands and enjoy it. (I must *not* vomit. Not yet.) Because I *did* enjoy this: I am my father's son. (I don't think I can control it: I will vomit.) No: be clear: you didn't enjoy it, you just had a sense of victory: enjoyment does not contain this feeling of loathing and self-disgust. But I am glad, sincerely, that he is dead and I am alive. (Maybe I will not have to vomit.)

Then he heard the in-breath behind him—the involuntary gulp for air of a man trying to be silent—and immediately, not thinking, fell forward and started rolling as soon as he hit (his first fencing teacher, Tennone, would touch his heart with the point of the sword, meaning *You're dead now,* if he tried to get up at the place he fell) and kept rolling as fast as he could until he was next to the house, before leaping to his feet again.

The second assassin was another big man, and all Sigismundo noticed besides that was that he had blue eyes and was already raising his arm with the knife in it. Sigismundo started to swerve and the arm stopped moving as the man calculated, obviously realizing that if he missed he would then be without a weapon: so he ducked suddenly and was running forward but also weaving right and left so Sigismundo could not throw the mallet accurately.

Another professional, Sigismundo thought. That's the sort of day it is, for me: they're all professionals, and they're all bigger than I am. Then they closed on each other and Sigismundo feinted with the mallet, and the assassin swerved but Sigismundo swerved faster and at least hit him on the shoulder, and he grunted with pain but the knife came up fast anyway and Sigismundo swerved as the knife cut into his abdomen (he felt no pain in the first seconds but only sensation, knowing it was in him and he was bleeding) and he swung the mallet in both fear and rage now, a wounded animal, clubbing again and again, blood spurting from both of them now.

The two men stared at each other with shared pain and defeat for a moment, each thinking, *You beat me, you bastard.* Each man thought he was about to die.*

*According to de Selby (*Golden Hours*, XXXIII, 1049-73), this precise nanosecond, and every other nanosecond in the space-time continuum, is the resultant of every *other* nanosecond, whether these others come "before" or "after" it in conventional linear time (which he calls *ich-zeit*, following Einstein temporarily). Indeed, conventional or subjective time, as de Selby sees it, is nothing more nor less than, in his memorable words, "a story we tell ourselves, similar to the pictures on a film screen which appear to move although each is in fact a distinct *quantum* or *ding an sich*, the illusion of motion or narrative sequence being created in and belonging only to the gregarious nature of mind and the *instinct to gossip.*" It was during their debate over this controversial passage—an acrimonious and increasingly heated discussion that was pursued relentlessly through the columns of such journals as *Edinburgh Philosophical Review, Der Naturwissenchaft, New Scientist, The Zetetic Scholar, Annuaire de la Société Métérologique, Bulletin de la Société Astonomique, Ciel et Terre, Omni, Comptes Rendus, Entomological Journal of London, National Enquirer, Journal des Debats, Monthly Notices of the Royal Phrenological Society, Nature, Scientific American, Popular Mechanics, The Journal of Plenumary Time,* and eventually even the *Simcoe Reformer,* over a period of thirty-two years—that Prof. Ferguson and Prof. Hanfkopf made themselves the subject of prolonged investigation by the CIA, the KGB, and M15, all three of which were convinced that much of the discussion, being unintelligible to those not fully acquainted with the triple intricacies of de Selby's cosmological theorems, quantum mechanics, and Cabala, must be some sort of code in which classified information or subversive opinions were being broadcast. (There are grounds also for crediting La Puta's assertion in *La Estupidad de Hanfkopf* that similar misconstruction of the metaphysical issues involved led Hanfkopf to be approached, albeit guardedly, by recruiters for the Pro-

Then the assassin fell. Sigismundo jumped on his body, landing with both knees on the ribcage, clubbing again and again, too frightened to be nauseated now, too enraged to

visional Irish Republican Army and the Palestine Liberation Organization.) It is certain that academic respectability and decorum was breached by both men at various points in this recondite and perhaps stentorian *contretemps*, although one hesitates to accept Hamburger's reckless charge *(Werke,* II, 66) that Ferguson was indeed responsible for the crude and defective letterbomb sent to Hanfkopf following publication of his *Fergusonismus und Schweinerei;* the official police verdict is that the explosive (which misfired anyway) was sent by the Royal Orange Lodge of Ulster, who were under the misapprehension that Hanfkopf had indeed become a manufacturer and supplier of gelignite for the IRA.

Amid this unprofessional and sometimes unethical and tasteless polemic, few at the time noted the short article, "Plenumary Time and the von Neumann Catastrope," *Journal of the Canadian Physics Society* LXII, 5, in which Wolfe demonstrated that, given the basic and well-verified theorem of Dr. John S. Bell,

$$\frac{dci}{dx} = 0 \qquad \frac{dci}{dt} = 0$$

in which c_1 is any hidden variable, or any set of hidden variables, consistent with quantum mechanics, and dt is the rate of change in time of this hidden variable or hidden variables, and dx is the rate of change of said variables or variables in space, then by Walker's formula for consciousness selection,

$$\frac{N^{2/3}}{t}$$

where N is the number of neurons in the brain and t is the delay time between synaptic transmissions, de Selby or any other person who has changed the rate of transmission *(t)* has entered, not merely an altered state of consciousness, but an altered state entirely, in which mind itself will function exactly like a Bell nonlocal hidden variable. In other words, perhaps de Selby really did see the future as well as the past in each moment, just as Blake alleged he saw "infinity in a grain of sand." This elucidation was ignored at the time because of the *scandale*, which excited not only the academic world but the popular press also, when Hanfkopf produced a photograph of a man in an explicit pornographic scene with Georgina Spelvin, the man having the body of Harry Reems but the face of Prof. Ferguson; although quickly identified as a composite and fake, this photo seems to have caused Ferguson unusual emotional stress, and played a large part in his subsequent mental breakdown and his conversion to Shinran Buddhism, the radical sect that holds that all sentient beings will become Buddhas eventually whether they do anything to deserve it or not.

be disgusted by the bloody pulp of the skull as he smashed it. He was panting, and, without knowing it, whimpering and snivelling. He realized gradually that the man was long dead and he was attacking a corpse.

He stood up and staggered, sick again.

The first one, he thought, the one I punched in the street—

He looked around wildly. The forest of serene white marble was as silent as outer space.

Sigismundo leaned against the house wall and pulled up the fabric of his jacket and shirt. The wound was gushing like a faucet but he did not feel pain even yet, so he thought maybe, just maybe, no important internal organ had been reached. Or maybe he was just in shock.

A dog barked somewhere, a come-feed-me-I'm-hungry bark.

Sigismundo looked up again, wary as a hunted otter, a feral glint in his eyes. The white marble statues were all he saw.

A second dog barked, an I-hear-you-come-play-with-me bark.

The first dog answered with an I-don't-want-to-play-I'm-hungry-where's-my-master bark.

Amid the white marble all else was silence.

Maybe, Sigismundo thought, the first one, the one in the street, fell so hard he didn't see what alley I ran into. Maybe he saw the alley but not the yard. Maybe, God help me, he went for reinforcements.

Or maybe he's waiting behind one of those pedestals, perfectly still, until I half-turn to try to force the door, and then he'll be on me—

Sigismundo listened.

A third dog barked, a shut-up-you-mutts-this-is-my-territory bark.

The first two dogs replied with a go-to-hell-first-you-have-to-find-us-wise-guy duet.

The third dog came right back with an authoritative be-careful-I'm-tough-and-I'm-in-charge-around-this-habitat bark.

I wonder, Sigismundo thought, can I really hear that much in the language of dogs, or am I just light-headed?*

---

*De Selby's alleged "conversations with dogs and goats," as reported in the disturbing and much-debated *Quadruped Quatrains*, are now known

Sigismundo decided that the third assassin (if there was a third assassin) had not found the yard, or that he did go for reinforcements. The yard *felt* empty.

The first dog uttered a weak and unconvincing well-maybe-you're-tough-but-let-me-see-you-prove-it bark. The second dog was discreetly silent.

Sigismundo turned and forced the door with his shoulder.

As soon as he was inside, he lurched again and had to clutch the wall. Even the effort of forcing the cheap lock had caused him to lose more blood.

But there was nobody at home, as he had expected.

An empty yard, an empty house: maybe the universe had not been constructed, in every minute detail, just to destroy Sigismundo's faith in its Maker.

He was still bleeding profusely.

to be an elaborate hoax, since all scholars (except the rabid Hanfkopf) agree that the MS is not even in de Selby's handwriting, although none share the view of Ferguson that the handwriting is certainly that of the shadowy Hamburger. The matter is discussed in La Puta's *La Estupidad,* passim, and Herbert's *The Two-De Selby Theory,* Panic Button Books, Chicago, 1983. Few give credence to the Kerflooey elaboration, which holds that de Selby was only and always a pen name for the Prince of Wales, which Brennbaum aptly calls "the worst academic schlemozzle since the Bacon-Shakespeare lunacy." (See *Royal Masquerade,* by Artemis Kerflooey, Christian Book Club, Oklahoma City, 1984; and *Kerflooey Is Kaput,* but Francis X. Brennbaum, Thelema Books, Los Angeles, 1985). The "collective de Selby" theories are hardly worth refuting; there is no real evidence in the wild imaginings of Swenson (whose *The Truth At Last,* Cosmic Awareness Press, Seattle, 1982, alleges that de Selby was another pen name for the consortium of mathematicians who previously published their collective works under the *nom de plume* of "Nicholas Bourbaki") or of Jacoby *(Science, Pseudo-Science and Satire,* Ed Smith University Press, Biloxi, 1983), who claims de Selby was the joint creation of Schrödinger, Borges, Velikovsky, Winston Churchill, and the American film comedian Julius ("Groucho") Marx. The fact that Jacoby was in Dealy Plaza, Dallas, on November 22, 1963, and died recently (of a heart attack, according to his own physician), will only add to the paranoia which increasingly infects the investigation of plenmmary time and its remarkable, if enigmatic, discoverer. Ferguson's attempts to link Jacoby to both the Vatican Bank and the Church of Scientology are implausible, and his "solution" of the puzzling *loud hammering* involved in all of de Selby's experiments, are more suitable for a surrealist manifesto than for sober scientific consideration. Perhaps the ultimate answer to these enigmas is in Walker's concept of mind as a nonlocal variable; see "The Compleat Quantum Anthropologist," Edwin Harris Walker, *Proceedings of the American Anthropological Association,* 1974.

Sigismundo found a shirt hanging over the back of a chair. He sat on a divan, looking at the growing pool of blood at his feet, and tore the shirt to strips. Then he began winding the strips around his waist, making a bandage to stop the crimson flow.

The bandage soaked through quickly.

Everything has a purpose, Sigismundo told himself. Perhaps this stonecutter has led a dull life. Now, when he comes home from his holiday, he will find me dead on his divan and two more cadavers in his backyard. It will give him a good story to tell in the taverns for years to come.

He got up and, listening to the blood squish in his boots, searched for a bedroom. When he found it, he tore up a sheet and made more bandages to wrap around his middle. He made it even tighter than the first layer.

No blood showed through, at first anyway.

I am entitled to hope, he told himself. Perhaps the cut was not very deep. Perhaps this will staunch the flow for good. Perhaps I will make it all the way to the kitchen and eat something before I faint.

He found the kitchen. There was good brown bread and real beer, not porter. He ate and drank, examining his bandages occasionally. No more blood was showing.

Now I am refreshed, he thought. When I open the front door and find five more assassins I will be ready for them.

Sure I will. And then I will sprout wings and fly to England.

He ate some more of the rich wheat bread and drank more beer.

The obvious next move was to find where the stonecutter hid his money.

The thought was repugnant.

What, Sigismundo asked himself, you have killed two men today and you worry about a little thievery? Well, yes, but that was different; I acted in self-defense. But how about the three you killed last winter? That was self-defense, too. Yes, but five in nine months? You are a *desperado*, Signor.

Besides, necessity knows no law. Some Roman senator said that, I think. Or some Greek, gazing around him in his toga and pondering the ultimate nature of things. They had lots of time to ponder, those fellows. They weren't always being kidnapped and drugged by Satanists and attacked by assassins and clapped in the Bastille.

Sigismundo examined his bandage again. Still no blood showed.

A key turned in the front door.

Oh, shit, piss, and corruption, Sigismundo thought. Now I must attack a perfectly innocent man. Necessity knows no law.

Was I really an idealistic young boy once, planning to write greater music than Scarlatti?

He hefted the bloody mallet and moved quietly toward the kitchen door, hearing the blood squish in his boots.

The footsteps that entered the front room stopped suddenly. The stonecutter, coming home, had heard the squish also.

Sigismundo leaped through the door, waving the bloody mallet, the perfect picture of a dangerous criminal. A small, brown Neapolitan stared at him, frozen.

"One sound," Sigismundo said, "one little peep, Signor, and I will beat your brains out, I swear to God."

Then he fainted dead away. His reserves of energy were at last used up.

His last thought was: *Back to the Bastille.*

Six

When he awoke, Sigismundo was not in the Bastille but in the stonecutter's bed. Two men were sitting nearby watching him—the small Neapolitan stonecutter and a stranger, a French laborer, pockmarked more than usual even in this age when six out of seven Europeans had had the smallpox.

"Good evening, Signor Celine," said the stonecutter, in Neapolitan dialect.

"Good evening," Sigismundo repeated mechanically, staring around wildly.

"There are no police," the stonecutter said, guessing the meaning of Sigismundo's fear. "I do not like the police, not one little bit. I do not like the Bastille much either. I will tell you what I *do* like," he said somberly. "I like Neapolitans. I like wild, crazy Neapolitans. I especially like a crazy Neapolitan son of a bitch who climbs over the walls of the goddam Bastille and makes monkeys of the police. I like such a man a great deal." He smiled radiantly.

Sigismundo burst into tears. "I'm sorry," he gasped. "I attacked—I threatened you—with a mallet—" He could not continue. The sobs shook him as all the terrors of the past day burst through his armor.

"It is worse than that," the stonecutter said grimly. "I am afraid you have left my house and my backyard in a terrible mess. That is no way for a guest to behave."

The Frenchman laughed.

"Luigi Duccio," the stonecutter said, extending his hand. "A carver of unreal ideals."

Sigismundo fought back the tears. "I must seem like a

terrible weakling,'' he said, ashamed and feeling himself blush.

Duccio turned to the Frenchman. "A terrible weakling," he repeated. "He climbs the walls of the Bastille, beats up a watchman, and kills barehanded two professional assassins, armed with knives no less. And now he's embarrassed because loss of blood and exhaustion make him weep."

"You Neapolitans," the Frenchman said, "you're all crazy, you know that?" He extended his hand and Sigismundo shook it.

"My friend here," Duccio said, "prefers not to give his name. Let us merely say that while I have confessed to a mild dislike for the police, he is a man who has stronger feelings about them."

"What it is," the Frenchman said quickly "is that we're getting too *centralized*, you know? Goddam Sardines, he's so damn smart he's stupid, is what he is. Worst thing that can happen to a country is an efficient police force, you know? We all end up getting regimented like a goddamn army."

"And it's hard to make a dishonest living these days," Duccio said, smiling.

"It's even harder to make an honest living," the Frenchman said, ignoring the irony. "You think I never tried, Luigi? Christ, the times I've tried. I've tried everything, honest and dishonest, and I'm still broke most of the time. Well, everything but wet work; I never tried that. Don't have the stomach. But there's no use, they got it all tied up, like this Spartacus says. A poor man hasn't got a chance these days."

"Spartacus," Luigi said, staring into space. "I wonder who he really is."

"Everybody wonders who he is," the Frenchman said. "Sardines especially wonders who he is. He'd pay a few livres, Sardines, any *mouche* comes in and tells him who that Spartacus is."

"He's too smart for them," Duccio said.

"Yeah," the Frenchman said. "He's pretty smart. I bet even his best friends don't know. I'm a coachman," he said to Sigismundo. "I got a coach that's something special. You're going to love this coach. What it has, see, is a secret compartment underneath the seats. I hope you're smart enough not to ask me what I usually have in that compartment. Just be glad that you're going to be in it, when you're ready to travel.''

One of them is Spartacus, Sigismundo thought. I almost caught it, but not quite.

"I may need a doctor," he said. "Do you know one who is . . . who shares your feelings about the police?''

"We know a few doctors like that, yeah," the Frenchman said. "One's been here already.''

"While you were off on the other side of the moon," Duccio said. "My God, were you out of touch, there. It must have been shock, from all the blood you lost.''

"What did the doctor say?" Sigismundo asked quickly.

"You must have been born with a good horoscope," Duccio said. (Not that again, Sigismundo thought.) "You lost a lot of blood, a hell of a lot of blood, but the doctor said no internal organ was cut.''

"Yes," Sigismundo said. "It was all very fast, but I was busy hitting the other fellow with your mallet while he was trying to stab me. There was one moment there, my God, when we looked right into each other's eyes, and we both knew we were hurt, and we were both wondering who was hurt worse. And I swear, in that moment, staring at each other, we were closer than brothers. I mean, we both shared the same pain and the same fear . . . Then he started to fall and I started clubbing him again, so he couldn't get up and stab me another time . . . Christ . . .''

"That's why I never take wet work," the coachman said. "You need nerves of steel for that kind of job. Like Pierre, friend of mine, he used to do wet work but no more. He ran into a guy just like you, about a year ago it must have been.''

"Pierre," Duccio said. "Pierre and the dogs." He laughed.

"It's his eyes," the coachman said. "He won't admit it, you know. Hell, it scared him to think about it. It would scare you or me, too, right? But he won't admit it, that his eyes are going.''

"I will see that you are both well rewarded," Sigismundo said. "My family in Napoli—''

"I want no reward," Duccio said immediately. "It is enough that once you are out of Paris safely the glorious Lieutenant Sardines and his whole crew will look like perfect dunces. That is my reward and I will treasure it for many, many years.''

During the night the two bodies were removed from the yard. Sigismundo gathered that chunks of uncut marble were used as weights and that the cadavers joined the rest of the morbidities at the bottom of the Seine.

Duccio and Sigismundo had breakfast together in the kitchen the next morning. ''The only subjects worth discussing are politics, sex, and religion,'' Duccio said. ''Which would you prefer?''

''Religion,'' Sigismundo said. ''After being in the Bastille for six months without knowing why, both politics and sex are painful subjects to me.''

''Good,'' Duccio said, opening his third bottle of beer. ''I suppose, like most university people, you are a Deist?''

''The God of the churches does seem rather small and petty, compared to what we now know of the universe,'' Sigismundo said.

''You believe in Newton's cosmic clock-maker, then?''

''No. I believe God is bigger than that, too, just as He is bigger than the oriental despot the churches offer us.''

''How big is your God, then?''

''He fills all space,'' Sigismundo said, quoting Bruno.

''Then there is nothing that is not God?''

''Exactly.''

''This is most serious. You have entered the heresy of pantheism.''

''I fear that I have.''

Duccio finished his third beer and opened a fourth. He had unique ideas of what constituted breakfast; he had barely touched his bread. ''You are really saying that the universe is intelligent.''

''How else does the cherry stone know how to grow into a tree?''

''The dogs and cats are God, too, then?'' Duccio asked, his eyes sparkling with mockery. ''And the lice, the bedbugs, the fleas . . .''

''Yes.''*

*Only a person as consumed by rage and prejudice as the irascible Hanfkopf would continue the debate about *Quadruped Quatrains* long after scholars elsewhere are unanimous in pronouncing the work spuri-

"This sounds grand but it is meaningless," Duccio pronounced. "If it is asserted that everything is blue, then nothing is blue. If red is really blue, and yellow is really blue, and white and black and all the other colors are really blue, then we do not need the word 'blue' any more, except perhaps to distinguish hallucinations. If everything is God, then we do not need the word 'God' any more. You are an atheist without knowing it."

"No. The atheist says that all is accident. I say that all things cohere. To explain the coherence I must either use the word 'God' or employ some abstraction, which a clever man like you will quickly tell me is just an alias for God."

"That which makes the universe cohere and is inside all things and you call God: is it in the men who so unjustly clapped you into the Bastille and hired assassins to kill you?"

"Yes."

Duccio opened a fifth bottle. "Do you really believe that, or is it just what you tell yourself to build up some courage to confront this terrible world?"

"I believe it. What do you believe?"

"I believe that if I sell enough monuments in a month, I can pay the rent, and if I do not sell enough I will be thrown out on the street like a dog. That is what I believe."

ous. While many people talk to dogs, and some even feel sure that they understand the dogs' "answering" barks to some degree, a work is dubious on the face of it when it claims that goats communicate only in iambic pentameter, and this is true whether one accepts the orthodox one, real, Irish de Selby presented in O'Brien's admittedly novelized biographies, the two de Selby of Herbert, the de-Selby-as-Prince-of-Wales of Kerflooey, or Swenson's and Jacoby's collective de Selbys. Hanfkopf's alleged photo of de Selby talking to a goat in Kerry is clearly, like the pornographic Ferguson photo, also produced by Hanfkopf, a composite, a fake, a dastardly fraud, although many share La Tournier's view that something clandestine may be revealed in the fact that all other photos show de Selby bearded while this photo, of a cleanshaven de Selby, looks remarkably like O'Brien. This may be a red herring, however; remember Ferguson's suggestive arguments that it was La Tournier, not O'Brien, who wrote the major part of the works alleged to be by de Selby. In any event, stories of de Selby talking to dogs are no more remarkable, when one consults original sources rather than Hanfkopf's exaggerations, than the habits of many animal lovers; and de Selby's pantheism is no more eccentric than that of Spinoza, Hegel, Emerson, Blake, or the *Upanishads*, except in the small matter of his insistence that God is, clinically speaking, schizophrenic.

"You read books. I can tell."

"I read books, but I pay the rent in sous. I believe more in sous than in books."

"Why do you hate the police?"

"That is my religion."

"You are taking great risks to help a man who is a stranger to you."

"No Neapolitan is a stranger to me. That is also my religion."

"You hate the police, you love your countrymen, and you believe money is the most important thing in the world: that is your religion?"

"Money is the most important thing in the world when you have no money. When you do have money, you can read books and think pretty thoughts."

"Why do you carve so many angels?"

"Because that is what most fools want on their graves." Duccio opened a sixth bottle of beer.

Sigismundo opened a second. "You know I am of aristocratic stock. I have little experience with artisans and laborers. Do they all think like you?"

Duccio laughed. "No, they believe what the priests tell them in church. And the priests tell them what will keep them docile and submissive. When the Bastille is torn down, brick by brick, and there is a hollow hole in the earth where it stood, then you will be able to say, 'My word, the masses have started to think like Luigi Duccio.' "

My Honored Lord,

This is just a short note to assure your Mighty Lordship that we now know the general whereabouts of S., two of our men having disappeared while seeking him in the St. Paul neighborhood where many Neapolitans live, from which we assume he must be in the area and hiding with compatriots, so that we are proceeding now with a house-to-house search, which I firmly believe will find and destroy him at last. I kiss the hands of your Lordship.

                                                        P.

The anonymous stagecoach driver appeared outside Duccio's as soon as darkness fell. Sigismundo, waiting with Duccio at the gate, observed that the coach was most humble and in bad repair. He was quickly inside and the panel beneath the rear seat slid back, as had been explained to him.

Sigismundo was in a dark space no bigger than a peasant's coalbin. There was a faint odor of gunpowder and he wondered what sort of brigand this coachman was. Running guns to the highwaymen who stopped the more prosperous coaches, perhaps?

That's what comes of being a convict, Sigismundo thought; you have to associate with the criminal classes.

The coach rode a short distance, then stopped. Four men got aboard and filled the seats. Members of the "gang" probably, he thought, traveling as camouflage. An empty coach would certainly arouse suspicion.

"They should shoot them all," one of the men said, continuing a conversation. "Take every one of the bastards to a lot somewhere and just blast away."

"You are no animal lover, Pierre," another voice said.

"It's disgusting," Pierre said. "As if this city doesn't stink enough already, for Christ's sake. I just stepped in a pile of it this evening. In les Halles, no less. Now what I want to know is, what the Jesus is Paris coming to when you can't even walk in les Halles without getting dogshit on your sabots?"

"They got to shit somewhere, Pierre."

"They don't have to shit on the fornicating streets, is what I'm saying. Dirty filthy animals, it's disgusting."

"My kid loves her dog," a third voice said. "My God, the pleasure she gets out of that animal."

"That's the way it is with kids," the second voice said. "We wouldn't have dogs, or cats either, if it wasn't for the kids. 'Daddy, can I have that doggie?' 'Daddy, can I have that kitty?' What are you going to do? A kid, you just can't say no to her."

"*I'd* say no to her," Pierre said. "If I had a kid and she wanted a goddam dog, I'd say no. I'd say, 'Honey, do you know how much dogshit there is in Paris already? Do you know where it will be in a hundred years?' I'd say. 'Up to the goddam second-floor windows,' I'd say. All over my sabot," he added furiously. "In les Halles. Where the *bread* comes in."

"You don't have kids," the second voice said. "You can't say that to them. When they want a dog, they want a dog. You'll go and bust your hump to get them a dog. Jesus, if we knew what we were getting into the first time we shoved it into a woman, we'd all be monks. I swear to God. But what are you going to do, I want to know. Kids, you can't help loving them.''

"What happened to Jules?"

"You didn't hear about Jules?" Pierre asked. "They slit his throat, is what happened to him. A wet job.''

"Yeah, I knew that. But I mean *what happened?* Why did they slit his throat?"

"He was a *mouche.*"

"Yeah, but everybody knew that . . .''

"This time he *mouched* on the wrong crowd, those bastards from Rouen.''

"Christ Almighty in the morning. He wasn't a bad guy, Jules. Slit his throat. Jesus. It's a tough world.''

"Everybody *mouches* occasionally, you know? I mean there are two kinds of men in our business. Those who *mouche* once in a while and those who wouldn't *mouche* and got hung by the neck in a tar overcoat.''

"Sure. But you don't *mouche* on the wrong people.''

"What happened to Jules's girl? What's her name? Blanche?"

"She's selling her ass now.''

"Yeah. It's a bitch, this city.''

"What city is any better? Tell me and I'll move there.''

"All cities are the same. Unless you're rich.''

"Those bastards. You know the difference between them and us? I was reading a pamphlet yesterday by that fellow calls himself Spartacus and he explained it. You know what the difference is?"

"They got more money.''

"No. Well, yeah, that's true, but I mean the difference before that. What it is, is they write the laws, you see, so that when they steal it's legal. This Spartacus, he's a bright guy.''

This is part of my education, Sigismundo thought. I am learning things they never taught me at the university. Already in only a few minutes I have heard of important matters of civic hygiene and of the manner in which even professional criminals can be browbeaten by their children. I have even heard a most original and provocative theory of the origin and purpose of law. Above all, I have learned that one should never, under any circumstances, *mouche* on those mean bastards from Rouen.

"Poor Jules," said the man who could not resist his daughter's pleas for a dog. "He was a damned decent sort, really. He'd reach down into his pocket and loan you a sou if you needed it."

"Yeah. He got cursing and swearing at times, like all of us, but I never once heard him damn his mother's eyes. Not once."

"He was nuts about that Blanche. I never saw a guy so crazy over a dame."

"Yeah. Well. He never should have *mouched* on that Rouen crowd."

I never met this Jules, Sigismundo thought, but I already know that he was generous to the needy, respectful to his mother, and capable of deep romantic love for somebody named Blanche, or at least that he appears that way in retrospect. I wonder what form of criminal endeavor he pursued, and if his victims ever realized what a nice guy he was when not engaged in felonies?

"But about those dogs," Pierre said again. "They're worse than the horses. Horseshit now, you smell it and see it a block away and you got plenty of warning, is what it is. But with dogshit, Jesus, you practically gotta go around bent over like a hunchback or you're in it before you know what happened, and the next thing is you're skidding in it and like to break your goddam back. It's a public hazard, is what it is."

"You're too sensitive, Pierre. You shoulda been born a gentleman. Then you could ride around in a coach all the time."

"It's not just me personally. It's what you call a social problem. You let enough of them filthy bastards in the city and pretty soon we're all up to our goddam eyeballs in dogshit."

"Look, what you should do, you're so worried, is get a shovel tomorrow and start on the rue St. Denis where you live—"

"We're coming to the gate."

The coach slowed and then stopped.

"Weeping Christ," Pierre cried. "It's Sardines himself."

All four coach doors slammed open at once and there was

a sound of many feet running rapidly followed by a shout of "Halt in the name of the law!" followed by more running and then rifle fire.

I begin to surmise, Sigismundo thought, that I perhaps got into the wrong coach.

The panel slipped back and an inspector, resplendent in full dress uniform and holding a torch, looked in at Sigismundo.

"Would you believe," Sigismundo asked gravely, "that I was just hiding from a jealous husband?"

The inspector did not smile. "No guns," he shouted. "We picked the wrong night. But I did find something interesting."

Lieutenant Gabriel de Sartines, in all his glory and with a magnificent wig, appeared also looking down into the secret compartment. "Well, well," he said mildly, "a man who likes to travel *under* the coach. This might be more intriguing than a weapons shipment."

Back to the Bastille, Sigismundo thought. I wish I knew why.

Seven

From SPAWN OF THE SERPENT: A WARNING TO ALL FELLOW CRAFTS OF THE BRITISH ISLES, by John J. A. MacKenzie, M.A., F.R.C.S. (1795):*

The facts, as documented by the pious Abbé Barruel in his persuasive and well-researched *Memoirs of Jacobinism,* and as shown further in the secret records of the Illuminati recently released by the Bavarian authorities, are that a highly organized and

---

*MacKenzie (1735-1826) was one of the pioneers of modern hypnotism and one of the first to differentiate it clearly from mesmerism. A competent surgeon, by the standards of the time, he also made significant contributions to comparative botany (his commentary on Bank's *Floralegium* is still classic) and was a skilled performer upon viola, French horn, harpsichord, and piano, often appearing with the Royal University of Edinburgh Chamber Music Ensemble. His later years were embittered by two prolonged controversies, the first concerning MacPherson's *Ossian* (which he accepted as genuine after the forgery was evident to savants elsewhere) and the second an interminable polemic with John Robison, author of *Proofs of a Conspiracy,* op. cit.; MacKenzie thought Robison was not nearly hard enough on the Illuminati in general and Adam Weishaupt in particular. As the debate continued and grew both heated and foetid, MacKenzie was not above implying that Robison was perhaps himself an agent of the Illuminati. In one of his rare lapses, de Selby asserts that both MacKenzie and Robison were in fact agents of the Knights of Malta (*Golden Hours,* XLI, 1459). (Ferguson, *Armageddon,* 31-38, describes both men as "idiots.") Hanfkopf appears cogent for once in finding (*Werke,* VI, 333-36) "chilling" and "suggestive" parallels between the Illuminati as described by MacKenzie and current activities of the Italian Freemasonic group called *Propaganda Due,* on which see Yallop's *In God's Name,* op. cit., and Richard Hammer's *The Vatican Connection,* Penguin Books, New York, 1982.

unscrupulous conspiracy existed within continental Freemasonry for many decades at least; that this conspiracy was directed by atheists, scoundrels, and revolutionary enthusiasts, sworn enemies of God and Christianity all; and that, behind a great deal of "occult" and "magickal" hocus-pocus, such as would make an honest English Mason laugh with scorn, this cabal plotted nothing less than worldwide anarchy—*viz.*, the destruction of civilization as we have known it and the creation of a world governed, or rather not governed at all, by the Satanic motto of the Hell Fire Club of sinister memory, "Do what thou wilt."

When I speak of this to my Brothers in the Craft in England and Scotland, all too many are prone to smile and raise a skeptical eyebrow. The Abbé Barruel, they remind me, was a Papist priest, and the Papists have long spread slander against the Craft; as for the Bavarian documents, they have been published only in German and are little known here. Nonetheless, I hope to present enough evidence in the following pages to convince all sober and judicious minds that I am not spreading false alarms and crying wolf when there is but a stray dog passing; that this conspiracy of diabolists exists within our ranks, and not just in France, but in the German states, in Austria, and in only God knows how many lands. That the rebellion of the American colonists, in which principles of extreme libertinism were enunciated in their so-called Declaration of Independence, is part of the same Satanic plot is, I think, if not proven, certainly highly probable. Benjamin Franklin, the American traitor, for instance, was a member not just of the R.A. and the S.R. which are true Freemasonry but also of these infamous French lodges which only pretend to be Masonic and serve far more sinister ends; and Franklin presided over the rites in which the monster Voltaire was initiated into the Paris lodge of the Nine Sisters—the very lodge that, together with the horrible Grand Orient as I shall describe, provided most of the cast of characters in the revolutionary government and shocked sane men everywhere by the crime of regicide and open avowal of atheism.

Some, not aware of the facts, say that Louis XVI was a bad manager of governmental affairs, and that his incompetence was the "cause" of the revolution. But the conspiracy I describe dates back to many years before Louis XVI came to the throne; to the days of Louis XV, and perhaps even earlier. For, as we shall see, there is evidence, and not a little evidence but a great deal, that there are direct links backward from the Jacobins to the Jacobites; from the Grand Orient to secret societies calling themselves Carbonari, Hermeticists, Rosicrucians, and so forth; to the witch cult, and to such outbursts of mad anarchy as were associated with the infamous names of the Alumbrados in Spain, the Albigenses in France, the Rossi in Italy. Nor should this astonish us, for the Bible, which is revered in all true Masonic lodges (although banned, as I shall show, by these French pseudo-Masons), assures us that there is one source of all evil, one father of all lies, one demonic intelligence behind all rebellion against God's natural order . . .*

*A saner, more sober, but equally hostile view of the underground anarchist tradition in European occultism can be found in Prof. Cohn's *The Pursuit of the Millennium*, Grenada, London, 1970.

Eight

Sigismundo Celine was taken to Sartines's office, and left with four guards. Two officers with swords stood at the door and two more, also with swords, at the window. Sigismundo assumed that Lieutenant Lenoir had told Lieutenant Sartines about the sneaky Neapolitan who had gotten halfway out the window before you saw him start to move.

He had rehearsed the interrogation in his mind. "I met him at a bar." "No, he didn't tell me his name." "No, I don't know what he carried in that compartment on other nights." He was determined to keep Luigi Duccio out of it.

Sartines reentered and sat behind his desk. "You are Sigismundo Celine," he said flatly. "You escaped from the Bastille two nights ago. I congratulate you on your ingenuity and perseverence. I hope you will not insult my intelligence and waste my time by pretending to be somebody else."

"I am Sigismundo Celine, yes."

"You are a Freemason." It was hardly a question.

"I escaped from the Bastille, yes."

"And you are a Freemason. That is no crime. Why do you not admit it?"

"I am Sigismundo Celine and I escaped from the Bastille."

"Very well. You took an oath, when you joined the Freemasons. You swore never to reveal any of the secrets of the Craft to any outsider. You also swore never to do any harm, either by force or by fraud, to a Fellow Craft. Do you want to hear more of the oath?"

"So, you have *mouches* in the Masonic lodges here. Why do you ask me what you already know?"

"Who is the Grand Master of the largest Masonic lodge in France?"

"I would not know."

"Yes, you would. It is, in fact, the Duc de Chartres."

"I would not know."

"Do you know why you were in the Bastille?"

"Does anybody ever know?"

"You were named in a *lettre de cachet*. Would you like to know who ordered that *lettre?*"

"I believe you are not allowed to reveal that information."

"These four officers become deaf when I tell them to. If you ever say you heard this here, I will call you a liar, and I will be believed. Do you want to know who ordered the *lettre?*"

"Yes."

"The Duc de Chartres."

Sigismundo smiled.

"That amuses you?"

"I wrote to him from the Bastille. Asking for help. It must have given him a good laugh."

"It must have indeed. It would seem he has violated his oath as a Freemason and treated you most abominably."

"I see," Sigismundo said. "And now you expect me to violate my oath and reveal all his guilty secrets. It is not that simple, Lieutenant. I do not know his guilty secrets. I do not know why he has persecuted me."

"Perhaps you know more than you think. Who was the widow's son?"

"I am Sigismundo Celine and I escaped from the Bastille."

"We know more than you think," Sartines said, pretending impatience. "The widow's son, in ordinary Freemasonry, is Hiram, the builder of Solomon's temple."*

"I congratulate *you* this time. Your *mouches* have reached as high as the third degree."

"They have reached higher. Who was the really important widow's son, the one hidden behind the allegory of Hiram?"

"I have no idea what you mean."

*See 1 Kings 7:13–21. But see also the elucidation of Idries Shah, *The Sufis*, Jonathan Cape, London, 1964, pp. 187–188.

"What did the Knights Templar find in Solomon's Temple?"

"I have no idea what you mean."

Sartines leaned back in his chair and made a pyramid of his hands. "You arrived in Paris," he said impatiently, "only a few months before your, ah, troubles began. I deduce that you became involved in Freemasonry much earlier, back in Napoli. I deduce further that you know little of what is happening in French Freemasonry these days. Suppose I tell you that the Italian lodges have broken off all relations with the French lodges because of the things that are happening here. Will you believe me, or will you think that is some policeman's trick?"

"I believe that you wish to get information out of me. I suspect that you are, for your own reasons, more interested in harming Chartres than in helping me. When will you send me back to the Bastille?"

"Perhaps I will not send you back to the Bastille."

"Now that *is* a policeman's trick. I did not come down with the morning rain, Lieutenant."

"You have an uncle, Pietro Malatesta, who manages a large wine business back in Napoli. He has been in communication with Ferdinand, your king, and the Neapolitan ambassador is now at our court asking embarrassing questions about our mistreatment of one of his subjects."

Sigismundo studied Sartines's face. "I think perhaps you are not deceiving me. Perhaps."

"It might be the easiest and wisest thing to send you home and apologize to Ferdinand for the, um, tragic mistake of your arrest. On the other hand, Chartres is in conference with Louis right now, and I have no idea of what he is saying." Sartines leaned forward intensely. "My interest is not in helping you—you are nothing to me, a stranger, and I will not pretend otherwise—nor is my interest in harming Chartres, which could be most dangerous. I am a policeman and, I hope, a good one. I like to think I have the best spy network in Europe. I dislike conspiracies that are going on under my nose and still remain puzzling to me. I dislike them intensely. I want to know what the hell is going on: is that clear enough?"

"Yes. You begin to remind me of my uncle Pietro. He would rather know the truth, even if it kills him, then lazily accept the plausible as most men do."

"*Bien*. We begin to know each other a bit, perhaps. I can send you back to the Bastille this second. I can also send you back to Napoli before word comes from the palace with other orders, if that is to happen. It will look as if I were merely overeager to save us from an international conflict. So: satisfy my curiosity and that will help me to decide. We may not have long."

Sigismundo reflected. "I think I will arrive back in the Bastille eventually. You seem to know more about this conspiracy than I do."

"We shall see. Do you know that you are related to Chartres?"

"No," Sigismundo said, surprised. "It must be a distant connection, surely?"

"It is quite distant but quite unambiguous. I have been studying genealogy lately. Was Freemasonry invented by the Jacobites?"

"Some say so, but I do not believe it."

"Do you believe it really goes back to Solomon's Temple?"

"No, I do not believe that either. It goes back to the Rosicrucians, and beyond that all is hazy."

"The Jacobites certainly played a role in spreading Freemasonry all over Europe. Do you know that Chartres is related to Charles Edward Stuart?"

"Of course. Through the house of Lorraine."*

*The principal French authority on this subject, Gérard de Sède, has explored these genealogical links in *Le Vrai Dossier de l'enigme de Rennes*, Vestric, Paris, 1975. In *La Race fabuleuse*, op. cit., de Sède gives his principal authority as a mysterious Marquis de B., allegedly murdered in the Ardennes forest on December 23, 1971. Baigent, Leigh, and Lincoln in *Holy Blood, Holy Grail*, op. cit., aver that the Marquis de B. never existed and was, in fact, a mask to cover de Sède's real informant, Pierre Plantard de Saint-Clair, a hero of the Resistance during World War II (he resisted torture by the Gestapo without informing on his colleagues) and a direct descendant of the Merovingian kings. Oddly, the Plantard Coat of Arms had a Jewish Star of David and the motto *Et in Arcadia Ego* (see *Holy Blood, Holy Grail*, p. 155). Even odder, the date given by de Sède for the death of the seemingly unreal Marquis de B., December 23, is actually that of the death of the last Merovingian king, Dagobert II, in 679; and the real Dagobert, like the false Marquis, was stabbed to death in the Ardennes forest. De Sède makes a great mystery about both the Ardennes and Arcadia being named after bear-gods, as was King Arthur of the Grail legend, but this is almost certainly

"Who was Charles Radclyffe?"

Sigismundo hesitated. "The first Grand Master of the Strict Observance rite of Scotch Masonry. A member of the *Carbonari*, some say."

"And?"

"And the natural son of Charles II of England and therefore another relative of Bonnie Prince Charlie. And therefore of Chartres. And me, if your genealogical research is accurate."

" 'They have the cross; we have Christ.' What does that mean?"

"It is symbolic. It refers to a certain state of consciousness, a special focus."

"Is that all? Does it not have a more specific reference?"

"No. Not that I know."

"Once again, what did the Knights Templar find when they excavated the Temple of Solomon?"

Sigismundo hesitated again. "It is a secret known only to the Illuminati. I have not attained to that grade. But they found something, yes."*

misdirection; as Baigent, Leigh, and Lincoln complain, de Sède is given to hinting rather than revealing.

It is remarkable that the Swiss journalist Mathieu Paoli (see his *Les Dessous d'une ambition politique,* Lyon, 1973) believes Pierre Plantard de Saint-Clair is the Grand Master of the Priory of Sion, and claims to have found that the Priory's magazine, *Circuit,* was published out of the office of the Committee for Public Safety of the de Gaulle government, when Plantard de Saint-Clair and the distinguished André Malraux were co-chairmen of that committee. It is even stranger that *Circuit* claimed to be published, not by the Priory of Sion, nor the Committee for Public Safety, but by the Committee to Protect the Rights and Liberties of Low Cost Housing. The cover of one edition of *Circuit,* reproduced by Paoli, shows a Star of David, superimposed on a map of France, and what looks like a spaceship hovering above, recalling de Sède's controversial theory that the royalty and nobility of France are descended from extraterrestrials. It is no doubt only a coincidence that Paoli was shot by the Israeli government, as a spy, shortly after publishing *Les Dessous.* Hanfkopf's shrill invectives against de Sède, Paoli, Baigent, Leigh, and Lincoln are best passed in silence; there is no evidence to support his charge that they were all "closet de Selbyites."

*The extensive excavations of the Knights Templar in and *beneath* the Temple of Solomon have been the subject of occult and conspiratorial speculation for nearly eight centuries. Many believed, in the early Renaissance, that the Templars brought back a "talking head," which modern theorists have identified as everything from an extraterrestrial radio

Sartines wrote on a piece of paper. "What does this mean?" The paper said ET IN ARCADIA EGO.

"It means that time is unreal. The illuminated mind sees across and beyond time."

"Suppose I permutate the letters," Sartines said. "Like this." He wrote again: I TEGO ARCANA DEI.

"Go," Sigismundo translated. "I conceal the secrets of God." He was surprised.

"Your ancestor, Sigismundo Malatesta, built a temple which is said to be an allegory in stone, a compendium of Masonic secrets. Why are there sea-gods all over that temple?"

"He was a materialist, it is said. He admired Thales, the Greek philosopher who said all life has evolved slowly and came out of the sea originally."

Sartines sighed. "I begin to agree that you know less than I do," he said wearily. "But one more time: Who was the *real* widow's son?"

There was a knock on the door.

Sartines stepped into the hall.

Sigismundo thought of his ancestor's glorious Tempio in Rimini. He had noticed the goddesses, mostly, when he was there in '65, but sea-gods certainly were prominent on the exterior walls. The Malatesta family motto was *Tempus loquendi, tempus tacendi:* A Time to Talk, A Time to Keep Silence. The temple spoke and yet it kept silence. The Church had condemned it as pagan, without perfectly understanding it; but they knew it concealed some heretical doctrine. Learn to Know, Learn to Dare, Learn to Will,

set to a minicomputer; it has been identified with their "god," Baphomet. (See, for instance, Gershon Legman, *The Guilt of the Templars.*) The mysterious Shroud of Turin has also been claimed, in some sources, as the treasure of the Templars; this is a cloth on which is impressed, by means not currently understood, the image of a crucified man alleged to be Christ. Thirty-second-degree Freemasons are told that all charges against the Templars were perjuries instigated by their archenemies, the Knights of Malta. Aleister Crowley (who alleged he was the Grand Master of the Argentum Astrum as well as a 33° Freemason) identified the head of Baphomet (in his *Book of Thoth*) as an image of Papa Meithra (Father Meithra), the Manichaean sun-god, claiming that *Papa Meithra* had been corrupted by near eastern Manichaeans into Bapho Met. Baigent, Leigh, and Lincoln *(Holy Blood, Holy Grail,* op. cit.) support the theory that what the Templars found in Jerusalem were documents positively identifying the widow's son.

Learn to Keep Silence: the four Masonic ''pillars'' that made the Temple of Solomon. The widow's son was certainly Parcifal, Sigismundo had surmised long ago, and the legend of Hiram was invented later. Parcifal, the pure fool, who found the Grail that the wise ones of the earth could not see . . .

Sartines returned, looking uncommonly grim. He did not look at Sigismundo.

''You will take the prisoner back to the Bastille at once,'' he said crisply. ''And needless to say you will forget everything you heard here.''

Sigismundo was led out by the officers. The word must have come from Versailles, he thought. Chartres convinced the king that I am such a threat that I must be buried alive again.

He wondered vaguely what lies they were telling the Neapolitan ambassador.

They arrived in the street. The coach was waiting.

Well, Sigismundo thought again, back to the Bastille.

That was his last conscious thought as the bullet hit him. He never even heard the pistol shot.

Nine

Sartines, ten minutes later, was dancing in fury. "What do you mean, the assassin escaped?" he howled.

Officer Mortimére squirmed. "He must have fired from some house across the street." He squirmed again. "Men are still searching, but it stands to reason that he is out of the neighborhood by now."

"So," Sartines said, "you are telling me we cannot even take a prisoner out the front door without somebody shooting him and just walking away. Am I running a police department or a home for the feeble-minded?"

"The prisoner is expected to live," Officer Mortimére said hopefully. "He was just turning to enter the coach when the shot was fired . . . it went through the upper arm, actually . . ."

"This man was stabbed in the gut two days ago," Sartines said, pounding his desk. "How many shocks can one human body survive? I *am* running a home for the feeble-minded, and I am the biggest idiot of all for trying to make sense out of what goes on here. Chartres wants this obscure Italian student in the Bastille. Now the king wants him in the Bastille, too. Somebody else wants him dead. I am forbidden to investigate any of this. We may be at war with Napoli tomorrow, and I will never even know why. Jesus, I once thought I had the best spies in Europe. I will give up this farce. I will enter a monastery tomorrow. You will see."

"Yes, my lieutenant. I am sorry."

"Oh, shut up. I am forbidden to investigate this Celine fellow. I am *not* forbidden to investigate assassins who shoot prisoners at my own front door. I want every known gun dealer in this building in two hours, and I want them *sweated.''*

Officer Mortimére saluted and left hurriedly.

I will write a pamphlet myself, Sartines thought. I will sign it Spartacus, so everybody will think it is the same crank who writes the others. I will tell the whole truth: the king is a fool, the nobles are scoundrels, the people are dolts who deserve no better than they get, the Church has invented a great lie to conceal what is really going on. I will then publish it and demand that these excellent inspectors of mine find the author and arrest him at once. Let me see if one of them has the wit to suspect *me.* *

Sigismundo returned to consciousness in the Bastille hospital. They gave him a few days to recuperate and then moved him back to the Tower of Liberty.

There was one change. They had installed bars in the window.

Dear Chartres,

It all works out for the best in the end. Plans for transition are now complete.

Cagliostro

---

*The egregious de Selby is, as usual, alone in his attempt to prove *(Golden Hours,* LXI, 78–203) that Sartines was the author of the Spartacus pamphlets. (Hanfkopf's typical comment *(Werke,* III, 14) was, "What can one expect of a man who talks to goats and claims they answer him in verse?") La Fournier's attempt to identify Spartacus as the Marquis de Sade *(Oeuvre,* II, 7–21) is more plausible, but not without flaws; and one must not forget Ferguson's reiterated claim that La Fournier *was* de Selby.

Ten

From THE DAYBOOK OF MARIA, LADY BABCOCK (1772):

It was wonderful to hear that Carlo has become a husband. Although Papa is far too discreet to spell out the details in so many words (he still treats me as if I were an ignorant virgin), it appears that the bullet with which the scoundrel Celine wounded him did not actually destroy the reproductive capacity. I gather that, during all the months that Papa was worrying about Carlo plotting a *vendetta,* poor Carlo was actually only trying to work up his courage to attempt sexual union, and that when he found he was still normal, he had the decency to marry the lady in question, a d'Este, no less.

Oddly enough, I had another dream about the villain Celine a few nights ago. In the dream, I saw him hunted by dangerous men with knives, and he looked to me as if imploring help. Of course, as Mother Ursula taught me, it is easy to interpret dreams, which come from the Great Self rather than the little self we know in waking life. This message was saying in picture language that, as a Christian, I must forgive all sinners, even one as wretched as Sigismundo Celine. I shall therefore pray for him tonight; he, too, has a soul to be saved.

I wonder if Celine actually does have enemies of that sort? It would scarcely surprise me: he is the type who makes enemies. Even I, only a year ago, wondered if Carlo had hired such unscrupulous men to hunt Celine down, in France or wherever he is. Was that fear, like the dream, actually a premonition that Celine is in serious trouble and needs somebody to pray for him? I must admit that he would be an attractive boy, if he stopped strutting and acting so important all the time. Mother Ursula always said that boys who act that way are just trying to conceal their nervousness.

Enough: I will pray for the wretched fool, but I will think no more about him.

Mistress Kyte drops by once every fortnight, to see Ursula and to offer me advice on every aspect of childrearing. I know the servants resent it and think I should not associate with such a humble creature except in emergencies, but dear John (bless him!) is becoming as fascinated by the old woman's lore as I am. (Not that he has much time to spare from his energetic involvement in protecting the American colonists and getting Mr. John Wilkes back into Parliament and persuading the Royal Scientific Society to examine his thunderstone. He spends many nights in London and sometimes only returns here on weekends—but I must not be jealous. These causes are of tremendous importance to him, and I do admire his courage in holding to so many unpopular stances, even if I do get lonely at times.)

Mistress Kyte, strangely, knew all about my healing power even before I told her, she says. It is her claim that she sees a light around my hands, and that all who have that light are healers. It is not a normal light, of course, and can only be seen by those with *the sight*. She says these gifts come from Our Lady, not from God directly; she is the only one I have met in England who discusses Our Lady at all, since Protestants do not admit Her importance in the divine scheme. Yet I think Mistress Kyte is a Protestant herself, as she certainly is not a Catholic in any way.

The only servant who does not resent Mistress Kyte's familiarity with me is Moon, the Irishman. He seems to regard her with a special reverence and once asked her to read the cards for him. That made me almighty curious and I insisted that the operation be performed in my room, so that I could see how it was done. Well, it appeared that *his* card was the Hanged Man, and Mistress Kyte was much distressed and tried to offer him reassurances; but he only grinned crookedly and said, "Sure, that is every Irishman's card."

Naturally, I commanded a reading also. It appears that my card is the Star, which means that my ultimate destiny is not of this world in some sense. John's card is the Prince of Wands, a figure which looks half-male and half-female, but Mistress Kyte says that means Wisdom.

I would not be typical of my sex if I did not think little Ursula—whom I have named after my dear Mama Bear back at convent school*—is the most adorable child in the world. But if this be

---

*Maria called her prioress, Mother Ursula, "Mama Bear" because in Italian *ursa* means bear. At this point one cannot resist recalling the strange coincidence or synchronicity mentioned in the footnote on pages 227–228, namely that Dagobert II, the last Merovingian king, and the

illusion, fathers are subject to it as much as mothers, because John finds her enchanting and, when he is at home, spends hours "conversing" with her, feeding her, playing with her and generally reassuring himself that this miracle is true: that (as he used to say when I was first pregnant) we have forced God to create a new soul. He says that our little darling is living refutation of the doctrine of Original Sin, because she is composed of nothing but pure love, plus the few natural appetites necessary to her survival. At times I agree with him about Original Sin being fallacy; the more I talk with Mistress Kyte, the more I realize my true religion is closer to hers than to anything I learned from the Church, even from so liberal a teacher as dear Mama Bear.

The American Mr. Franklin was here again, and this time made no attempt to fondle me (altho' I did see him grapple again with one of the maids). He would not discourse on the electrical fluid further, being full of excitement and amazement at the return of Captain Cook from the Pacific and the strange botanical specimens secured there by the naturalist Mr. Banks of Cook's company. To a Deist such as Mr. Franklin, every one of these hitherto-unseen flowers is as much a revelation as any story of miracles could be to a conventional Christian; John to some extent shares that view. They exchanged that mysterious handshake when they parted.

Marquis de B., de Sède's informant on the Priory of Sion, were both killed in the Ardennes forest, which is named after a bear-god, and both died on December 23. But of course de Sède manufactured that coincidence out of whole cloth; there was no Marquis de B., that being only a mask for Pierre Plantard de Saint-Clair. Still, it is odd that the Arcadia in *Et in Arcadia Ego* is also named after a bear-god. See Weston le Barre's *Ghost Dance: Origins of Religion*, for a detailed discussion of the influence of the Stone Age bear-deity on later cultures; see also de Selby's remarkable letter *(De Selby/Barnacle*, closed shelves, Cornell University James Joyce Collection) pointing out that three of the major characters in *Finnegans Wake—Arthur*, Duke of Wellington; King *Arthur*, of the Grail legend; and Sir *Arthur* Guinness, the brewer—all contain the bear-god, etymologically, and are combined by Joyce into the composite "Cid Arthur" of FW-66, a dream-myth archetype including all these Arthurs, the primal bear-god himself, the Spanish hero El Cid, and the Buddha (Siddhartha). It was this letter that prompted Nora Barnacle's famous comment that "the fellow in Dalkey" was "daft"; but the bear-god is also found in the *Wake* by Adeline Glasheen, *Second Census to Finnegans Wake*, Northwestern University Press, 1973, pp. 166–168; and see the discussions of Prince Ursus and King Arthur in *Holy Blood, Holy Grail*, op. cit., pp. 235–237, 254–280.

Eleven

In Boston—part of the Massachusetts Bay Colony—a group was formed with the innocuous name, Committee of Correspondence. The authorities were not deceived: they knew the organizers were those two notorious radicals, Samuel Adams and Joseph Warren. Reports soon reached London, and the Tories became more convinced than ever that the damned rebellious colonists needed to be taught a lesson.

Whigs like Burke and Babcock and Wilkes had a different view—they thought the complaints of the colonists should be considered thoughtfully and ameliorated—but the Whigs were the minority party and the Tories ruled.

In Bavaria, before 1772 was over, all Ingolstadt was shocked by the scandal when Father Adam Weishaupt abruptly resigned from the Jesuit order. Soon, however, everybody knew that Weishaupt was no renegade; he did not attack the Church but spoke respectfully of it on all occasions. He confessed to all and sundry that it was his weaknesses that persuaded him he was not of the character to be a true priest. When he was appointed Professor of Canon Law at the University, Weishaupt was still working for the Church, since they owned the University. He was no apostate, all agreed. His respectability remained intact.

In Salzburg, Wolfgang Amadeus Mozart's Symphony No. 21 was premiered. At seventeen, young Mozart reflects glory upon all Austria; everybody agrees that the *wunderkind* has written more great music than any contemporary two or three times his age. THEY say (but you know the sort of things THEY say) that he is a bit of a libertine, almost a second Casanova, and is seen sometimes in association with known liberals and Freemasons. He worries the devil out of his old father, Leopold—poor Leopold, blooming happily at his son's success, but striving desperately to keep the boy genius respectable; innocent Leopold, not yet knowing that no way has ever been found to keep genius within the bounds of decorum.

Back in London, Captain James Cook set sail on his second voyage to the Pacific, and George III and his illegitimate brother, Lord North, prime minister of the Empire On Which The Sun Never Sets, were well satisfied: the Empire continued to rule the waves.

In La Coste in sunny Provence, the merriest part of France, the Marquis de Sade, blond and angel-faced and damned as ever,* has been raising hell again. The authorities had confined him to his estate after the king's *lettre de relief* had quashed previous charges against him; wouldn't you think even de Sade would lie low for a while after that? Not in the least. This ogre has seduced his wife's sister, affronting and infuriating his mother-in-law—she who had obtained the *lettre de relief* for him. He has gone on to debauch and pervert the daughter of a local judge—and the judge is fuming also, you can be sure. There is no stopping this de Sade. Now, one Saturday afternoon he had staged a saturnalia with four whores—you can imagine the details: whips, crucifixes, his usual notions of sport—and then in the evening took a fifth whore for further dalliance. He was enjoying her, in fact, when the police arrived.

The four ladies of the afternoon were near death; they claimed de Sade had poisoned them. He denies it indignantly—"My God," he asks, blond and blue-eyed and flouncing in vexation, "do you gentleman take me for a *monster?*" The police eye each other; they do in fact take him for a monster, as most people did. De Sade became reasonable and conciliatory. He had given the ladies a drug, he confessed—not a *poison,* for heaven's sake. Cantharides, he explained. It heats the blood, you know. The ladies must have nervous stomachs. What is this country coming to, if a gentleman, of royal connections by the way, cannot en-

---

*The eighteenth-century de Sade, the philosopher of pain; not the twentieth-century de Sède, the philosopher of ancient astronauts, mentioned frequently in these footnotes. Patience! Diligence! Hang in there!

tertain himself according to his taste, without being pestered by the police about it?

The ladies, in fact, recovered; but the story was all over France by then. Name of a name, crucifixes and whips and drugs such as only witches know; he calls that *entertainment?* With his mother-in-law now against him, with the local judge still furious over the games de Sade had taught his daughter, with every tongue wagging, there is no *lettre de relief* this time. Sade is condemned to death—"and good riddance," most people say.

But, no, this creature is *formidable;* you will see. He escaped, and he would lead the police forces of all France a merry chase indeed before we shall encounter him again.

In the faubourg St. Marcel, Paris, Jean Jacques Jeder has been employed long enough to celebrate occasionally by allowing his wife to buy meat for dinner. His oldest son, at eleven, is employed now too, at the wallpaper factory of the great M. Reveillon, who pays the highest wages in the city, being a former worker himself and a liberal. With two salaries coming in, the Jeder family is well off, compared to what they have endured in the past.

Jeder has read a few of the subversive pamphlets by Spartacus and Lycurgus and other occult beings with classical sobriquets: Luigi Duccio, the stonecutter, is always urging them on other artisans. Jeder is not aroused by that sort of thing. So the king was a fool, yes, and Mme. Du Barry costs the people a lot more than she is worth, and maybe the Red Indians live without governments or nobles, good for them in their *tipis*—but Jeder is saving a little each week, under the mattress. The price of bread has not gone up one sou under Lieutenant Sartines's draconian administration of the markets. Under the circumstances, Jeder sees no reasons to take an interest in politics.

In the Bastille, the prisoner Celine found that his celebrity faded after a few months. Nobody came up to him in the yard to congratulate him any more; small groups did not stop their conversations and stare as he went by. Only the guards remembered vividly: their eyes were always watching.

Sigismundo fell back into the endless boredom of prison life. In the mornings, he walked the yard with Father Benoit and discussed philosophy. In the afternoons, he read books from the library or wrote in his journal. In the evenings, he worked—listlessly, now—on a new rope, not sure how he would cut the bars when he *had* a rope.

He did not even notice that he was sinking into despair.

Twelve

Sigismundo's journal was an attempt to pass the time—prisoners, he realized, have nothing but time. As the days passed, it became also an attempt to learn if there were, as he had been taught, consolations in philosophy. He wrote no music. His first note explained that:

Some birds will not sing in cages.

In the beginning, he did not record his own reflections—which mostly concerned conspiracies and deceptions and human malignancy; subjects on which he knew his views were highly colored and subjective. He dredged out of memory the ideas, from the great minds of the past, which he hoped might illuminate his morose solitude.

To love is to see. (Richard St. Victor)
Love does not know of the impossible. (St. Victor)
The intelligence should direct the will. (Aquinas)
Ripeness is all. (Shakespeare)
If the mind does not will well, it dies. (St. Victor)
Treason is so vile a word that in common courtesy it is applied only to losers. (Uncle Pietro)

He filled reams with such borrowed wisdom, but the bars were still impassable and the days were still long and the weeks even longer. He began writing about the things that preoccupied his mind.

The largest bully in the prison will not attack if you convince him you are crazy enough to be unpredictable. He must believe totally that you do not care a fig about whether you live or die. This is the great Secret of Survival.

N.B., this only works inside. If you try to apply it consistently on the outside, you will frighten people so much that they will put you back inside.

Whatever happens, if it does not kill me it will probably teach me something when I stop trembling and get a good night's sleep.

Father Benoit is tranquil because he has resigned himself to fate. I am too young to resign. Misery is the tax we pay nature for having the audacity to continue hoping.

But then he began writing more concretely and unflinchingly about what was really happening to him, what the prison experience meant:

The consolations of philosophy are real at times, but in here one must resort to them more and more often, as the drunk goes hourly for his bottle.

To believe that there is a gigantic conspiracy against you is the illness that drove Antonio to suicide. But I now find it very hard not to believe in such a conspiracy. For instance, I believe Lt. Sartines is as puzzled as I am, because the conspiracy is too huge for even his spy network to comprehend. Is that madness or am I deducing logically *what must be the case* to explain my experience?*

Sometimes I imagine that the conspiracy is everywhere, in every part of Europe. Surely that is a symptom of madness; or am I just awakening, finally, from the naiveté that

---

*Cf. Carl Oglesby, *The Yankee and Cowboy War,* Berkley Books, New York, 1977, p. 26: ''The point arose in a seminar I was once in with a handful of businessmen and a former ambassador or two in 1970 at the Aspen Institute for Humanistic Studies. . . . I advanced the theory that government is intrinsically conspiratorial. Blank incredulous stares around the table. 'Surely you don't propose there is a conspiracy at the top levels?' But only turn the tables and ask how much conspiring these men of the world do in the conduct of their own affairs, and the atmosphere changes altogether. . . . Routinely, these businessmen all operated in some respects convertly. . . . Only with respect to the higher levels of power, around the national presidency, even though they saw their own corporate brothers skulking there, were they unwilling to concede the prevalence of clandestine practice.'' Prof. Oglesby believes all cliques conspire, and know they do, but artificially conditioned veneration prevents them from recognizing similar trickery in those above themselves in the power hierarchy.

has made people call me "artistic" and "sensitive" since I was a little boy?*

My mind goes back, again and again, to the superstitious astrological prophecy**—that I will shake the world. I swell with grandeur and think that all my enemies, who have brought me here and even tried to kill me, will be crushed in my hour of triumph. Now I know for certain that *that* is a symptom of madness. And yet the thought comes back again and again.

To reach the bottom, to touch utter despair, does not make you morally better, or "purge" you as Aristotle thought. But it does make you considerably less superficial.

I am beginning to hate and that is the supreme danger for those of the *baraka*. It is how Black Magicians begin. It is the path my father and brother took, and from which Uncle Pietro and the F.R.C. have striven to protect me.

I resort to the vice of Onan more and more often, not out of lust, but just to escape my own brooding about universal conspiracies and diabolical vengeance.

After that he became afraid of writing such moods down— it made them more real and powerful; it did not exorcise them at all. He returned to jotting down ideas from the philosophers:

"The intellectual love of things consists in understanding their perfections." (Baruch Spinoza)

Bruno says there is one mind in the gopher digging a hole in somebody's yard in Napoli; and in the woman in labor inside the house to which that yard belongs; and in all the people and animals and insects in Napoli; and in all Italy; and in all the world; and in millions and millions of similar

---

*Cf. Oglesby, op. cit., pp. 25–26: "The implicit claim, on the contrary, is that a multitude of conspiracies contend in the night. . . . Conspiracy is the normal continuation of normal politics by normal means . . . and where there is no limit to power, there is no limit to conspiracy."

**De Selby was forced to accept a kind of astrological determinism in order to keep plenumary time consistent and to synthesize it with his evolutionary pantheism or theo-chemistry; but, of course, this astrology works backward in time: as explained in *Golden Hours*, I, 17–23, the *hour of a person's death* creates all the cosmic and terrestrial "resonances" that cause the life that *precedes* it (in conventional time) and the sexual mating of the couple that produces that life, etc. Hanfkopf is particularly sarcastic and verbose in his rebuttal to this; see *Werke*, II, 5–1065.

worlds. And I did contact that universal mind once. I did. I
know I did.*

"The true nature of existence is always hiding itself from
us." (Heracleitus). Come out, old Machiavellian, I saw you
face to face that one time!

Bishop Berkeley says that the hind leg of a cheese mite,
which we cannot see, must be as big, relative to the mite, as
our legs are, relative to us. Therefore size is not a reality,
but a *construct* of the mind; and space a *construct to contain
constructs.*

David Hume says I do not see this pen and paper but my

---

*This seems an appropriate place to clarify, once and for all, that
de Selby does *not* argue that electric lights alone are removing teratological molecules from our ken, as Hanfkopf so often implies in his
interminable polemics. *Golden Hours,* III, 44–72, makes it abundantly
clear that de Selby believed all teratological molecules result from the
Big Bang, which he places of course at the *end* of the universe, not the
beginning. His equations III.3–III.7 indicate precisely how the acceleration of his Variable Constant causes these molecules, rushing backward from the Bang, to accumulate exponentially in the "earlier"
periods of existence ("earlier" as regarded from the viewpoint of *ich-
zeit* or conventional time-sense, which de Selby calls "a projection
outward of the instinct to gossip"). [And even if de Selby *was* involved
somehow in the shady financial dealings Hanfkopf alleges (the monies
mysteriously moved from Banco Ambrosiano to "La Fournier" in
Paris—who may not be de Selby at all, despite all the unsubstantiated
claims to that effect—and thence to the mysterious "art dealer" Leo
Schidlof, who allegedly deposited in the Bibliothèque Nationale the
dubious genealogies connecting the Priory of Sion with the Meroov-
ingian monarchs).] In any case, Paoli, *Les Dessous,* op. cit., and Baigent, Leigh, Lincoln, *Holy Blood, Holy Grail,* op. cit., agree that
Schidlof did not deposit the said genealogies in the Bibliothèque and
was only an innocent victim, the genealogies probably being the product of the largest Freemasonic order in Switzerland, the Grand Loge
Alpina; see especially in this connection Baigent, Leigh, and Lincoln,
op. cit., pp. 203 ff. The mysterious death of the young Pakistani Fakhar
ul Islam on 20 February 1967—he was found beheaded on the tracks of
the Paris-Geneva express near Melun while allegedly carrying more
Merovingian genealogies—is discussed by Baigent, Leigh, Lincoln, op.
cit., pp. 73–76, and certainly is in need of explanation, but Hanfkopf's
melodramatic theories on the subject are untenable. Baigent, Leigh,
Lincoln (p. 76) are dubious that Fakhar ul Islam had any real connection with Schidlof at all. Ferguson's "propinquities" linking ul Islam,
Schidlof, and Leopold Ledl (the man who secured the billion dollars'
worth of counterfeit stocks for Cardinal Tisserant and Archbishop
Marcinkus in 1971) are tenuous at best. But see Richard Hammer's *The
Vatican Connection,* op. cit., pp. 215–225.

ideas of pen and paper. Then I do not see the Bastille, but
only an *idea* of the Bastille?

"Time, which is serial, is the moving image of eternity,
which is one." (Plato). I think he means what Berkeley means
about size. It is the mind which makes "things" appear to
"move" in "space" and "time," all of which are *con-*
structs.

One day Sigismundo wrote only:
$$F = m\,a$$

That was enough, at the moment. It meant more to him,
in that day's struggle against despair, than anything St. Victor said about love and will or Berkeley about relativity. In
over a hundred years (and those the years of more free scientific enquiry than in all previous history), nobody had
found an exception to that great equation. *Force* was equal
to *mass* times *acceleration,* everywhere, every time: Newton had seen through appearance to a coherent order that
was real and eternal. Like the compass and the square used
in the Craft, this equation was a demonstration that behind
every tragedy and beyond every possible doubt, there was
some core of rationality at the heart of existence. The human mind did not wander forever among vain imaginings:
it could find truth sometimes.

His new rope was growing very slowly; they would not
give him extra blankets again. The bars installed on the
window could be dented and scratched with metal from the
bedsprings, but it might take years to cut through even one
of them.

Sigismundo began writing his autobiography—in the third
person, to get outside and look at himself with detachment:

Being both a fool and a bastard, our melancholy subject
was always somewhat alienated from normal social standards. Since he knew the world was mad, he could laugh at
it; but since he suspected that he was a bit mad himself, the
laughter had a morbid edge.

His first soul, the vegetative part of him, had been formed
by a loving mother, so he had learned a capacity for tender-
ness. This, however, was balanced by an equal capacity for
anxiety, also learned from his mother; for she knew who and
what his real father was, and she worried that the devil's taint
would show in the blood eventually. So it came to be that our
quixotic hero was inclined to love, to almost feminine pity

and sympathy for others, and to fear and mistrust himself. In short, we find in this case a fine candidate for martyrdom, or for messianic delusions.

The second soul, the emotional, animal part of a man that seeks to capture space, had been undernourished by a weak and timid ostensible father. Perhaps this was overcome, somewhat, by expert fencing technique learned from Giancarlo Tennone, a great master of the sword. He could be brave, then, this fellow, but he could never fully believe in his own bravery. He suspected always that he would turn coward at some crucial test. This may explain the extraordinary idiocy with which he involved himself in pointless escapades calculated only to risk his neck again and again.

The third soul, the human reason, was formed by a most cynical uncle who subtly undermined his faith in the Church and led him step by step to the precincts of Freemasonry and natural philosophy. Thus, he analyzes everything—busy, busy, busy—and even analyzes himself to the point where he has quite split in two, the one who would act and create, and the one who questions each action and creation as an Inquisitor would question a suspected heretic.

The fourth soul, the true Self, which is asleep in most men, was violently awakened by his real father, who filled him with Satanic drugs and cast him into the abyss—so that out there alone, beyond the first three souls, he would find in himself the power that creates and destroys whole universes. An old mystic named Orfali tried to teach him how to use this knowledge to become a Saint instead of a Satanist, but the issue is still in doubt.

He does not know, of course, which soul is writing this. After studying at the University of Paris, among the atheists, he is not even sure the souls really should be called *souls*. Perhaps they are just different physical parts of the brain.

The next morning Sigismundo awoke on the ceiling of his cell.

He also noticed that he was no longer cold, even though he had no blankets on him.

Sigismundo looked down at the floor. His bed was there, the writing table and chair, even the chamber pot.

He did not panic. His first thought that was that he had somehow triggered an explosion of *baraka,* and had levitated himself in his sleep.

He secured a grip on the nearest wall and tried to climb down to the floor.

He immediately lost his grip and slid back up to the ceiling.

By then he was fully awake and beginning to try to reason about this. He tried another experimental descent, clutching the wall desperately and trying to ease himself down toward the floor. He slid slowly and inexorably back to the ceiling.

Then the terror began to grip him.

Thirteen

I must reason about this, Sigismundo thought. *Up* and *down* are relative, as Berkeley says: what is up to a European is down to the colonists in Australia. On a spherical planet there is no absolute up and down.

But the sense of up-and-down was created by gravity, which was not relative.

And yet the floor was far below and he could not get back there from the ceiling.

Sigismundo reminded himself of the Real and Eternal:

$$F = m\,a$$

That was the great equation, the foundation stone on which the Great Architect built. Applied to planetary systems, it yielded the formula for gravity:

$$F = \frac{M_1 M_2}{d^2}$$

Sigismundo began to notice other details. He could not see the city gate through the window. The window had been boarded up.

Gravity had not been abolished. They had moved him, during the night, to a specially prepared room, just like his room in the Tower of Liberty, but upside down.

They?

The international conspiracy, of course.

But believing in *them* was almost as bad as not believing in gravity. He had been trying to convince himself that thinking about *them* was a symptom of madness, which he should resist.

Nonetheless, either gravity had been abolished and he was really stuck to the ceiling; or *they* did exist, in some form, and *they* were able to bribe the governor of the Bastille, move Sigismundo out in the night, just as easily as they acquired the *lettre de cachet* that placed him in the Bastille in the first place. As easily as they stopped Sartines's investigation.

The Duc de Chartres, the cousin of the king; the "friend of the people," as he was called. He was part of the conspiracy. He had to be. That was the only way to make sense of this.

That is the way all madmen think, Sigismundo told himself.

But suppose *they* put you in a situation where sanity did not apply, where only the madman's logic could account for what you experienced? Then you must either give up entirely on trying to understand, or admit that *only* the madman could understand what was happening.

To be sane was to be mad, at a time like that.

Sigismundo sat on the ceiling, looking down at the floor—which was really *up*, of course—and tried to reason logically.

The *Rossi* had given him the devil-drug, belladonna, once. That had been cruel but not pointless. They wanted him out in the abyss, beyond the constructs of space and time, so that he could discover his True Self, the fourth soul. What the atheists would call the latent part of his brain, if they admitted it existed at all.

The *Rossi*, of course, were not still working on him. They had been destroyed by the Neapolitan police.

But somebody *was* working on him, finishing up the *Rossi*'s job of tearing him loose from all socially conditioned constructs of "space" and "time" and "objects."

Therefore, there really was an international conspiracy, and the *Rossi* were only one branch of it.

That was perfectly logical, given what Sigismundo had perceived and experienced.

Of course, the delusions of all madmen seemed perfectly logical to them, given what they had perceived and experienced.

I am *not* mad, Sigismundo told himself. I am in an upside

down room that somebody has constructed to make me think I am mad. And it is not necessarily mad to think of international secret societies; the Knights of Malta are international, and every Freemason is sworn on oath to combat their intrigues. For that matter, Freemasonry itself is international and probably looks like a conspiracy from the outside, to those who do not understand its true and noble mission.

Sigismundo suddenly felt total vertigo.

Suppose Freemasonry itself were the conspiracy? He had only reached the fourth degree, after all. Suppose those at the very top—above the Rose Cross degree, say, or above the Royal Arch—had purposes and plans that were not noble at all? Suppose they managed Masonry with one hand and groups like the *Rossi* with another, and had puppet strings on which danced dozens of other secret societies of which he knew nothing? Suppose Uncle Pietro and old Abraham Orfali, for all their shrewdness, were not aware of the true manipulators behind the scenes?*

And suppose I am still in the Tower of Liberty and they really can abolish gravity?

Sigismundo went and deliberately stood "under" the chamber pot. Nothing foul leaked "down" on him and, straining, he could ascertain that the pot was in fact empty. It had not been empty when he went to sleep.

It is easy to nail an empty chamber pot to the ceiling, he thought, if you want to make the ceiling look like a floor. You can't do that with a full chamber pot without giving the

---

*Cf. *Jack the Ripper: The Final Solution*, by Stephen Knight, Grenada, London, 1977. Knight argues that Jack-the-Ripper murders were actually part of a Freemasonic plot to cover up the existence of an Irish Catholic heir to the British Throne (by way of the Duke of Clarence, Victoria's grandson). According to this thesis, the Freemasonic killers (three of them, Knight claims) were protected by their Freemasonic collegues in Scotland Yard; in a later book, *The Brotherhood*, op. cit. (see footnote p. 104). Knight claims the Freemasons in Scotland Yard are still up to the same skullduggery, covering up the facts about the murder of Roberto Calvi, the Freemasonic banker whose Banco Ambrosiano embroiled the Vatican Bank in various high crimes including stock and currency fraud and drug running. But of course the founder of the Freemasonic group to which Calvi was pledged, P-2, was Liccio Gelli, who was a CIA operative according to Penny Leroux (see footnote pages 290–291), and the CIA seems to be largely a fishing expedition by the Knights of Malta (see footnote page 100). It fairly makes one's head whirl, it does.

show away. So: they were human—tricky, yes, but human—and they could not abolish gravity.

Sigismundo stood "under" the writing table. With some uncomfortable stretching and squinting, he was able to assure himself that there were very small, very thin nails, but nails nonetheless, holding the paper and quill to the desk.

So the paper and quill would not fall "up" to the ceiling.

It was all trickery, then.

Of course, people who could smuggle you out of the Bastille could also build an upside-down room and have it waiting. They were rich, very rich—the king's cousin was part of it—which meant that the next shock would be even more incredible—

It is that damned fool astrological prophecy, Sigismundo thought. They are very rich and very clever and very bloody superstitious. They really think they need to move me to a certain square on their chessboard before their vast scheme, whatever the devil it is, can be completed. And every "coincidence" in my life may have been part of this manipulation.*

---

*Cf. again the strange death of Roberto Calvi, former President of Banco Ambrosiano and key figure in the Freemasonic P-2 conspiracy. If, as many have claimed, this death was not suicide but murder, the murderers—whether they were Freemasons or, as La Tournier says, "ardently wished" us to think they were Freemasons—had to lure Calvi to a bridge, in the hours between midnight and 2 A.M., in order that his hanging body be submerged in the rising tide before being found at dawn, in keeping with the first degree Masonic initiation, which calls for that form of death for anyone who betrays his fellow Freemasons. (See *Unsolved*, by Foot and della Torre, op. cit., pp. 93–95.) Calvi had been a go-between in the transactions by which Leopold Ledl secured one billion dollars in counterfeit stock for the Vatican Bank. According to Yallop's *In God's Name*, op. cit., Calvi was also part of the group, including Archbishop Marcinkus (director of the Vatican Bank), that poisoned Pope John Paul I. See also Father Malachi Martin's *The Decline and Fall of the Roman Church* (Bantam, New York, 1983), which supports Yallop's thesis and argues further that the Freemasonic infiltration of the Vatican began under Pope John XXIII, whom Father Martin believes was himself a Freemason. Baigent, Leigh, and Lincoln, op. cit., pp. 132–136, suggest peculiar links between Pope John XXIII (whom they also suspect of Freemasonry) and another "John the 23rd"—Jean Cocteau, whom they name as the twenty-third Grand Master of the Priory of Sion. The fact that literally billions of dollars in illicit money were gained by Calvi, P-2, and the Vatican Bank in these clandestine activities does not rationalize the ritual manner of Calvi's death, which seemingly demonstrates mys-

They did not send the *Rossi* to kill Uncle Leonardo for any of the reasons I thought. They killed Uncle Leonardo to start me moving in a certain direction, the direction that led to Freemasonry eventually. They did not kill Uncle Pietro, for instance, because he was to be my guide into Freemasonry.

And did they send the Englishman, Babcock, to marry Maria, just to get me drunk and involve me in a duel?

That is a little bit too extravagant, Sigismundo reflected. I am thinking like a real madman when I let my fancy carry me that far.

He remembered how, eight years ago, at the start of all this, he had theorized that behind everything was a Jacobite plot to restore the Stuarts to the throne of England. It was more reasonable now to assume a multiplicity of conspiracies. Every history of every royal family was a story of treachery: a wise prince kept a food taster. Many plotters, then, and nobody at the "top" controlling it all? Perhaps he was looking at chaos and trying to impose a form upon it.

He wondered again what the next shock would be.

Once the King of France got lost while hunting and found himself in Scotland . . .

That was the legend of the origin of the *Carbonari*, who were the first Masons, some said. Sigismundo had always believed the legend was a code, but now he realized it was very similar to his Masonic initiations and to what was happening to him right now. The king had been moved in space, without understanding how he had been moved—without passing the English Channel, for instance. He had been riding on dry land and suddenly the space between France and Scotland did not exist for him.

"And Enoch was, and he was not." That was what the Bible said. Enoch was there, and then he was not there.

Space was relative to the human mind. Plato and Berkeley and Hume had all proven that in different ways.

I am an ideal victim for this kind of game, Sigismundo

tical obsessions on the part of *some* of the conspirators. (Full details on the counterfeit stock swindle managed by the Vatican Bank, with P-2 and the Mafia, are given in Hammer's *The Vatican Connection,* op. cit., but that book does not cover the other crimes of the Vatican/P-2 cabal, which are still coming to light as investigations in Italy continue.) See also footnote page 151.

thought. My head is full of philosophy and I am not at all sure what is real and what is human imagination.

Then he began to wonder more practically: Of course, they will have to feed me. They do not intend to let me starve, after setting up a mind-trap like this for my special benefit.

Whoever brought the food could not really walk around the "floor," since the "floor" was in fact the ceiling. That would give away the whole masquerade, would it not?

Sigismundo imagined the jailer sliding upward to the "ceiling" to join him there, while the food flew in a mess "up" to the same destination.

The King of France suddenly found himself in Scotland . . .

Sigismundo remembered the peasant in Napoli, back in '65, who claimed a hot rock had fallen out of the sky. That was at the time when Sigismundo, beginning to doubt the miracles of the Church, was not sure what he believed; he remembered thinking, *Well, at least I know rocks do not fall out of the sky.* But suppose he had been that peasant. Would he have believed his own eyes, or would he have believed the opinion of the experts?

I thought I was on the ceiling of my cell—but then I deduced an explanation. That explanation involves an incredible, almost unbelievable conspiracy. Would it not be more *economical*, as the natural philosophers say, to seek a simpler explanation, and just accept that I have gone mad?

All coincidences have meaning: Abraham Orfali had insisted on that, over and over, when instructing Sigismundo in Speculative Masonry. So the rock fell, or the peasant hallucinated it, *just when* I was asking what was "real," because—because God wanted to cause me even more puzzlement? It was rather conceited to assume God put on such spectacles just for the benefit of one young, confused, fifteen-year-old musician.

But it was equally conceited, was it not, to assume that some vast international conspiracy had built an upside-down room just to further vex, or instruct, the same musician at the age of twenty-two?

Sigismundo remembered another of the things that seemed certain when he was fifteen: *I am Sigismundo Celine, not the man in the moon.*

A few months later he had learned that he was Sigismundo Balsamo, the son not just of a peasant, but of a

Sicilian peasant, and not just a Sicilian peasant but a murderer and Satanist.

If I ever get out of here with my mind still functioning, he thought, I will change my name to Sigismundo Malatesta—just like my famous ancestor who built the Tempio in Rimini. It was another incredibility, as bad as the upside-down room, to be "Celine" in public and *Balsamo* in the privacy of his own mind: Sigismundo Balsamo, son of the Satanist, Peppino Balsamo . . .

And Malatesta was indeed a noble name. They had not only ruled Rimini but had governed the whole Western Holy Roman Empire in the ninth century. They were descended from the Merovingians, the priest-kings of ancient Gaul.

And the Merovingians came out of the sea, originally, like the mermaid that washed ashore in Napoli that time and was seen (THEY say) by sober and scholarly men; but you know the sort of things THEY say . . .

Or the character in Babylonian mythology—what was his name? Oh, yes: Oannes—who also came out of the sea and taught the Babylonians agriculture and astronomy and other sciences . . .*

The whole world is as incredible as this room, Sigismundo thought. Merovée** and Oannes were just myths, of course, of course, but why was it that no matter where you looked, history and oral tradition always trailed off into absurdities and allegories and impossibilities—one king was half fish, and another was in France and then he was in Scotland—I was in the Bastille and now I am—where?

And Enoch was: and he was not.

*The King of France got lost while hunting and found himself in Scotland . . .****

*Robert K. G. Temple argues in *The Sirius Mystery* (St. Martin's Press, New York, 1976) that Oannes was actually an extraterrestrial from a planet in the system of the double star Sirius; see footnote, page 27, for the Argentum Astrum/Sirius theme in Freemasonry. Hanfkopf has written almost as many diatribes against Temple as against de Selby; see *Werke*, IV, 36 ff., and V, 3–107.

**The alleged ancestor of the Merovingians, half man and half sea-creature.

***Dagobert II, the last Merovingian king, spent his youth in Ireland, then called *Scotia*. When he returned to France and resumed the kingship, he was murdered, apparently by agents of the Vatican, for unknown reasons. See de Sède, *La Race fabuleuse*, op. cit.

Anyway, it will be interesting when they finally feed me, he thought. Will they actually *walk on the floor?*

That question was not to be answered. In a short while, Sigismundo began to feel drowsy. At first he wondered why he should be sleepy again, so soon after waking, but then he realized the answer.

They had drugged him, of course, when they moved him here. The shock would not work if he were not totally oblivious, if he had any memory of being moved.

Abraham Orfali, back in Napoli, had explained to him once that there was a way of mixing drugs—discovered by the Sufis in Cairo, Orfali said—so that they acted in different time-delayed stages. It was drugs of that sort, Orfali said, which had been used by Hassan i Sabbah, "the old man of the mountains," to convince his duped disciples that they had traveled to heaven when actually they had just been under the influence of various drugs in a garden in his palace.*

Oh, Lord, Sigismundo thought. Maybe it is the Assassins, the secret order founded by Sabbah seven hundred years ago. An incredible life demands an incredible explanation; maybe I have been a pawn all along in a secret Moslem plot.

"As for the 'foul Mohammedans,' you have joined them already." Peppino had said that, long ago, but almost all Peppino said was a lie—

Maybe they will put me in the Garden of Delights now, Sigismundo thought as he lost consciousness. That was Hassan i Sabbah's private brothel, where the Assassins were deluded into thinking they had had sexual intercourse with angels.

That would not be bad, he thought, half-asleep and visualizing an angel who looked like Maria Babcock. If they must mess around with my mind, some of it should be seductive instead of terrifying. I could use some seduction now.

Maria, the angel, was dancing for him. Then he saw her webbed feet and knew she was from the sea and would drag him down, down into watery death, as he had always feared. And then a blue lion walked past and not just his body was

---

*See Akron Daraul, *History of Secret Societies*, Citadel Press, New York, 220 ff.

blue, but all about him was a blue, luminescent aura; and he said slowly, distinctly: "Mark my words, you will come to know God." And a bell bullowed, "Look, look, look: Too leaf is to sea." And a seagull sang, "John peeked with his goat so grey and a hney nonny nonny hney!" And the angel mermaid said: "Matter of space, matter of time, matter of mind. You will come to new good."

And Sigismundo was marked, and crossed the lion, and was unmarked: and Sigismundo was: and he was not.

Fourteen

Sigismundo woke with a hellish, headsplitting hangover.

He did not know where he was, but the place, alas, was not the Garden of Delights in any respect. At least he was on the floor, instead of the ceiling.

"Damn, damn, damn," he said sincerely. It was the only adequate comment. Abraham Orfali had taught him how to cure headaches by visualizing white light, but he was too drugged and tired to make the effort. Go on and ache, for all I care, he told his head.

He was in a cell of some sort, and in every feature it was worse than the Tower of Liberty. It stank; it was dark and filthy and probably underground; he heard rats scuttling in the corners.

From the Tower to the Abyss. It was like some hellish caricature of a Masonic initiation.

There were footsteps in the hall—a bit too loud. An act for his benefit. They had been waiting for him to wake, to drag him out of here for the next masquerade when he was half-asleep. They probably even knew that the drug, whatever it was, would leave him with a hangover.

Lovely people.

The door was unlocked and two Neapolitans in Italian jailers' costumes stood there.

"The Holy Office will examine you now," one said, with a gaze of unmitigated hatred.

That was acting, of course. They had been hired to give a good performance. They had no reason to hate him, actually. And he was not in Napoli, of course, but somewhere in France, probably not too far from Paris.

The King of France finding himself suddenly in Napoli . . .

Sigismundo, head throbbing in pain, was led down a hall, around a corner to another hall, and into a room set up for a trial by the Holy Office of the Inquisition. Monks with typical Neapolitan faces sat at a long table, in Dominican garb, the black that always reminded Sigismundo of the Satanic *Rossi*.

Sigismundo was dumped rudely into a chair facing the Inquisitors.

Maybe I *am* in Napoli, he thought. God knows how long the drugs have been working on my head.

"Read the charges," said the monk at the center of the table. The Grand Inquisitor himself.

Except that this was all a masque, of course.

"Item," another monk began reading from a long scroll, "That the accused, Sigismundo Celine, has consorted with Jewish sorcerers and with the forbidden heretics of the Free-masonic and Rosicrucian orders; that he has abjured Christ and joined his fellow heretics in worship of the demon Baphomet.

"Item: That the accused, Sigismundo Celine, did, in his initiation to Satanism, spit upon the crucifix and call upon the devil as his Lord and Savior.

"Item: That the accused, Sigismundo Celine, has written alleged music which is so hideous that Doctors of the Church, having examined it, pronounce it the result of diabolical possession.

"Item: That the accused, Sigismundo Celine, has often and repeatedly and habitually indulged in the sin of Onan; and has, in contravention of divine commandment, coveted another man's wife; and has consorted with whores; and has looked at certain alleged works of art, depicting the female nude, with lust in his heart, and has indulged that lust by further excesses of Onanism.

"Item: That the accused, Sigismundo Celine, is now obsessed and possessed by so many devils that he does not know where he is, in Europe or Asia or on the moon, and does not know what year it is, or how old he is, and will claim, as the devils prompt him, that this is France in 1772 and not Napoli in 1765.

"Item: That the accused, Sigismundo Celine, allowed the devils to enter him by drinking a potion of diabolical drugs prepared by his father the *Rossi* Satanist Peppino Balsamo, and has been obsessed and possessed since that day, and cannot stand trial in the normal manner until the devils are driven from him by the use of whips.''

There was a pause.

"Item," Sigismundo said calmly. "That you are jointly and severally the greatest collection of touring mountebanks and players I have ever seen; and I applaud your art, but do not take you seriously for a moment.''

"That is the devil prompting him," one monk said quickly. "It should not be regarded as a sin of insolence. We must drive the devils out before we judge the boy at all.''

"Allow me to examine the boy a moment or two," the Grand Inquisitor said kindly. "Tell me, lad, do you know who I am?''

"A remarkable player," Sigismundo said sincerely.

"That is not intended as deliberate insult?''

"Not at all. I admire your skill. You do not overplay the role at all.''

"Do you know where you are?''

Oh, well. Let me try *my* game on them. "Space is a creation of the human mind, some philosophers think. I have often puzzled over the question and have come to no definite conclusion yet.''

"They often talk that way," one monk muttered.

"On the other hand," Sigismundo said, "the first time I was *given* a drug *against my will* was indeed in Napoli in 1764. I will entertain the hypothesis that I am still in Napoli in 1764 and that all that has transpired since then has been the hallucinations of the drug.''

"The human soul survives in him," a monk said quietly. "He can reason, despite the demons that inhabit his body.''

"But the people who give you this kind of work," Sigismundo said more cheerfully. "I wonder about *them.* I wonder if *they* play games with you, too. I wonder if any of you are totally free of their drugs and deceptions. Have you considered that you might be fellow victims along with me?''

I'm not doing too badly, he thought, for a man with the grandfather of all murderous hangovers, who doesn't know where he is, and is almost starting to doubt that he knows *when* it is.

"My child," the Grand Inquisitor said gently. "You recognize that you have been possessed by devils—"

"I rather suspect I have been tricked with drugs."

"You know that evil men gave you evil drugs, in any case," the Inquisitor said softly. "Do you not realize that we represent your Church, your hope of salvation, and that it is these evil invaders of your body that seduce you to distrust us?"

"I have no church," Sigismundo said angrily. "To put a church between a man and his God is the laziest form of atheism. To obey a church is to stop listening to the voice of God entirely."

"That is the Protestant heresy," the Inquisitor said sadly. "Do you not realize that it is devils that make you speak thusly?"

Most marvelous, Sigismundo thought. Now we can have a nice theological debate. "It is possible that you are right," he said blandly. "It is also possible that there are devils in you that have made you think you are a Dominican monk and not a strolling player hired for some dirty tricks. Do you have any memory left of being a player hired for this role?"

Hume had said somewhere that "reality" is our word for those inferences that have become so habitual that we forget they *are* inferences. Maybe, Sigismundo thought, it is he, David Hume, who is "the Secret Chief in Scotland" from whom all Masonry springs. Maybe he invented these shocks and rites of transition to make clear to all that there is absolutely nothing that can be taken for granted in this world.

Maybe after the fourth degree initiation you don't have to go to a lodge for further advancement in the secrets. Maybe *they* come and get you, just to demonstrate that you never know what is real and what is a game somebody's playing with you.

The monks whispered among themselves briefly.

"The accused, Sigismundo Celine, is not able to present a defense or plead for mitigation of punishment," the Grand Inquisitor pronounced finally. "The devils must be driven out of his body first. Take him to the exorcist."

Sigismundo knew that whips were the first device used to try to drive demons out.

This is not really another Masonic initiation, he told himself. These bastards actually are out to drive me off my skull.

"Wait," he said. "Your Reverence, I wish to recant and repent. The devils have left me."

"They often play tricks like this," one monk muttered.

"These were cowardly devils," Sigismundo said urgently. "The mere mention of the whip frightened them away."

There was a pause. Sigismundo wondered if this would be considered tragedy or farce by an unprejudiced observer.

"Are you ready to give us the names of your cohorts in heresy—all of them in Napoli?"

They know all about me already, Sigismundo thought. And they are not real Inquisitors, only players. It is not a real betrayal.

"You have nothing to gain by protecting those wicked men who led you into sorcery and evil," the Inquisitor said solemnly. "They are your true enemies, not we."

"You cannot deceive us," another monk said. *"We know more than you think."*

"We are holding your uncle, Pietro Malatesta, and Giancarlo Tennone, and many others," a third monk said. *"Nobody will ever know who confessed first."*

"Tell us the names," the Grand Inquisitor prompted.

Tell us the word, the three ruffians had said to Hiram, the widow's son. It was the same story, over and over, in every land, in every age. They are not tormenting me, Sigismundo thought wildly: they are merely teaching me what history is all about.

Many years ago, another Dominican—a *real* Dominican, not a player—had almost terrified Sigismundo into betraying the men of the Craft in Napoli. That had been done with threats of an imaginary Hell, that time: now it was threats of real whips.

"The names?" the Grand Inquisitor repeated, impatiently.

First an imaginary Hell, then real whips, Sigismundo thought. Maybe you have go through the ritual over and over, until you discover it is not a ritual but the essence of real life.

This is *not* Napoli in 1765, Sigismundo reminded himself. It is (I think) somewhere in France in 1772.

But the Inquisition does exist, both in Napoli and here

and in other places. Maybe the names will find their way back to the Dominicans in Napoli.

"I cannot betray those who have trusted me," he said uncertainly. It seemed ridiculous to act heroic in what was, after all, only a staged imitation of an Inquisitorial trial, not the real thing. Except that they might be going to use real whips—

"The men who seduced you from the True Faith are not your friends but your enemies," the Inquisitor said gently. "They have placed your immortal soul in jeopardy. We are your true friends, trying to save your soul. You must not try to evade the choice. Eternal salvation or eternal damnation depends on what you say now."

"But you are threatening me with whips," Sigismundo said. "That is not very friendly, reverend sir. I grow confused and am not sure who is my real enemy in this situation."

"You see?" the suspicious monk cried. "The devils never left him. He was only playacting."

"I imagine that it is you up there who are playactors," Sigismundo said. "Can you not remember when you were hired for this job?"

"The devils have destroyed much of his mind," another monk said sadly. "He can no longer tell what is real and what is fantasy."

"Whips are absolutely necessary in such cases," the suspicious monk said. "It is stated clearly in the *Malleus Maleficarum*. Kramer and Sprenger say that only the whip brings such persons back to their senses."

The Grand Inquisitor motioned for silence. "The names," he repeated firmly.

Am I making a real moral decision, Sigismundo wondered, or just making the next move in an insane farce they are staging to terrorize me?

Sigismundo forced himself to relax, and spoke without a tremor:

"The Lord is my shepherd; I shall not want. He maketh me to lie down in green pastures; he leadeth me beside the still waters. He restoreth my soul; he leadeth me in the paths of righteousness for his name's sake."

The Grand Inquisitor's mouth set in a tight, grim line. "Take him to the whipping post," he said.

The jailers dragged Sigismundo from the room. A few of

the men at the table looked uncomfortable as his voice came back from the hallway:

"Yea, though I walk through the valley of the shadow of death, I will fear no evil: for thou art with me—"*

---

*Cf. de Selby, *Golden Hours*, II, 33: "Naive realism, such as is found among savages and some Germanic scholars, accepts the data of perception without question. Philosophy began with the distinction between the 'apparent universe'—the universe made up of the data of perception—and the 'real universe'—which allegedly underlies the universe of perception and 'explains' it. The 'real universe,' then, is assumed to be by definition more 'real' than the 'apparent universe.' But philosophy turns on itself and the mind whirls when we remember suddenly that this so-called real universe is made up entirely of our theories, our guesses, and, as I have explained previously, the *instinct to gossip*. It then appears that the 'real universe' like the 'apparent universe' is the creation of our brains. We then have to assume a triple, or three-headed, cosmology, made up of the 'apparent universe,' created by our senses, and the alleged 'real universe,' created by our guesses and gossip, and the *real* 'real universe' which our 'real universe' may or may not resemble greatly. But if the 'real universe' is made up of theories, this *'real* real universe' can only be a *theory about theories*, namely a theory that some thing may correspond to some theories. Thus we go from inference to inference, and find certainty nowhere." Hanfkopf comments, as usual, "What can you expect of a dope addict who has conversations with goats?" (*Werke*, IV, 37). La Puta (*Estupidad*, op. cit. 44) adds the helpful comment: "De Selby is perhaps trying to say that 'reality' is an assumption and never becomes totally factual."

Fifteen

After several months of insistent correspondence, Sir John Babcock was finally allowed to show his "thunder-stone" to the Royal Scientific Society at Somerset House.

The rock was of irregular shape but vaguely spherical and about five feet across at the broadest point. There was nothing very special about the Damned Thing at all, except that Sir John insisted that he had seen it fall out of the sky. It is not square, he thought ironically, but it has a singular beauty.

James Moon had been brought along for the occasion, to corroborate Sir John's paranormal story, and to wheel the rock, in a cart, into the enquiry room.

Moon, Sir John could see, was visibly nervous. The lad was no doubt aware that most Englishmen regarded the Irish as incurable liars and swindlers and also as superstitious Papists. In truth, Sir John thought anxiously, Moon did look much like the stereotyped Irish criminal or rebel: the eye and hand that had been ruined by violence, the typical red-headed Irish features. It would be difficult to get ordinary Englishmen to believe anything Moon said.

But they were not facing ordinary men, of course. They were before the Royal Scientific Society, where each man selflessly obeyed the harsh dictates of logic and reason. In these men, Sir John knew, all prejudice was ruthlessly suppressed in the disinterested search for pure objective truth.

The questioning was begun by Sir Charles Nagas, who was widely known as a great astronomer, although actually nobody knew of any great discoveries he had made. Nagas wrote a great deal for the papers and magazines and, hence, he was the one astronomer that most people knew. He was a handsome man, with an expensive wig, dressed in the latest fashion, and he spoke kindly and gently, with a wry smile. "You actually claim that you saw this rock *fall*, with your own eyes, Sir John?"

"Yes. And I have brought my coachman with me, as a supporting witness."

Nagas nodded. His smile was more wry, slightly pitying. "Have you ever studied astronomy, Sir John?"

"Not *per se*. I did have courses, at Oxford, on general physics and mechanics, and how the Newtonian laws apply to planetary systems." Sir John took a breath. "I do not claim to be an expert. I claim that I am telling you honestly what I saw."

Nagas sighed. "You saw a light, as I understand it. Then you found the rock. You deduced a connection between the light and the rock. Do you not think it possible that you deduced incorrectly?"

Sir John smiled. "You are implying that the light was only *coincidentally* connected with the rock? Gentlemen, in the abstract, far from the scene, that may seem possible. It does not correspond with all I saw and all I heard. There was a distinct sound as the rock fell and a crash when it hit the earth."

Herbert Sharper spoke up. He was a young, pock-marked dandy with a great deal of impatience in his voice. "How do you expect to use this incident to advance Whig politics, Mr. Babcock?"

The "Mr." was no accident, Sir John realized. Sharper was being deliberately insulting, stripping away the knighthood of a man who dared to challenge his prejudices.

Sir John spoke carefully. I'll be damned if I'll remind him of the "Sir," he thought; that would just make me appear pompous. "I had hoped," he said, "that this phenomenon could be examined impartially, in the spirit of science, with no politics entering the matter at all."

"There are no rocks in the sky," Sharper said angrily. "Why should we not treat you as any other fraud who comes here to impose a hoax upon us?"

Before Sir John could reply Nagas interrupted. "Without casting any aspersions on your honor, Sir John, I must admit that my learned colleague has a legitimate doubt. It would be easy for us, and possibly lazy, to dismiss this whole matter by accusing you of such deception. I assure you, I do not want to take the easy and lazy way, not do I wish to insult you gratuitously. I prefer to think you did see something that night, but I suggest that all you saw was lightning striking this rock.''

Sir John realized that he was nervously adjusting his weskit. I must not become rattled, he told himself. It is natural that an event of this nature should arouse some initial skepticism. ''The noise I heard was not at all like the noise of thunder which normally follows lightning. It was the noise I have heard when a projectile falls, such as a cannonball, for instance.''

''Do you think an angel in heaven was shooting cannons at you, Mr. Babcock?'' Sharper asked angrily. He is quite perturbed, Sir John thought; it is as if he were a Catholic and I were questioning the Virgin Birth.

''I do not suspect that this singular object was literally fired from a cannon,'' Sir John replied. ''I merely observe that the noise was like that of a projectile, not like that of thunder. And the rock was not on the ground before the light fell, I am sure. My man and I both heard the impact as it hit.''

A third member spoke up—a mathematician named Gardner Marvins. He seemed amused, like Nagas, rather than actively furious like Sharper. ''That is how you recollect your impressions, sir,'' he said simply. ''Is it not more prudent to assume that your impressions might be slightly awry, rather than to rush in unseemly haste to the conclusion that, um, all the known laws of celestial mechanics are false?''

Sir John remembered not to straighten his weskit again. ''I do not have adequate knowledge of theory to comment at length upon that,'' he said evenly. ''But I thought it possible, in ruminating about this singular object, that perhaps there are more masses circling the sun than our present instruments reveal. Perhaps the gravitational law and other laws can accommodate this object if, for instance, there are many unknown masses in the solar family, of various sizes, and if the smaller one may be attracted to our earth by the gravitational law itself.''

''You are offering us a whole new astronomy,'' Nagas said, struggling not to sound too patronizing. ''That is most ingenious and heroic of you, especially since you do not possess the requisite mathematics and other knowledge to create such a system. However, before we eagerly accept such a large and, um, ill-defined gift, we must still ask if your *impressions* about this rock are correct. We have heard that Lady Babcock presented you with a fine healthy daughter that night, whom you have named Ursula. I congratulate you, sir; but you must forgive me if I wonder whether such an emotional occasion may not have confused your faculties a bit?''*

"There are two of us here who saw the Damned Thing fall," Sir John said, keeping his voice level and remembering not to shout. "There have been hundreds, maybe thousands, of such reports throughout history, as you know, and I know, and anybody who has ever read Pliny or Aristotle knows. Is it not time to consider that such reports might be veridical instead of blithely attributing them all to disordered perception?"

"*Mr.* Babcock," Sharper said in a voice of venom, "I am not as charitable as some on this panel. I know there

*Hanfkopf makes much the same point in his discussion of the Betty and Barney Hill UFO case in his *Werke*, VII, 64-137, arguing that since Barney was black and Betty white and they lived in a racist country, both were perhaps unreliable under emotional stress and therefore unreliable. La Puta commented (*La Estupidad*, 78), "What can you expect of a man who lives in a city from which have emanated so many slanderous anonymous letters?" (There are reasons to believe this sentence was somewhat stronger, before La Puta's publisher showed the text to his attorneys.) It was shortly after this that La Puta become the target of another poison-pen campaign, in which the University of Madrid received many allegations (in envelopes postmarked Frankfurt Airport—a twenty-minute drive from Heidelberg) about Professor La Puta and certain female students. It is sad to note that La Puta did not handle his temper at all well when University officials questioned him about these charges, and his subsequent behavior (including the absurd and unmotivated duel with Flahive, over the trivial question of the dating of the *Quadruped Quatrains*) was not always that of a perfectly rational man. However, his mysterious flight to Heidelberg, under the assumed name of Kowalski, has never been proven to be connected with the unfortunate poisoning of Hanfkopf's dogs. La Puta drank heavily thereafter until the night of his unfortunate accident, mentioned earlier. The man from Langley, Virginia, at the scene of the accident has never been positively identified and Ferguson's attempts to prove the same men was one of the "three tramps" on the Grassy Knoll, November 22, 1963, are certainly not conclusive. Anyway, nobody yet has explained why La Tournier's *De Selby: Homme ou Dieu?* was published ten years before the generally accepted date of de Selby's birth.

are liars and frauds in this world and I am determined to expose them. I have been investigating you, *Mr.* Babcock. Would you care to tell my learned colleagues what your nickname was, when you were at Eton?''

Sir John flushed. "Better Logic Babcock," he said stiffly.

"And how did you earn that euphonious sobriquet?"

"I said once, in geometry class, that perhaps, just as Copernican astronomy replaced Ptolemaic, someday another logic might replace that of Aristotle."

There was a long pause.

"You *are* an original and daring thinker," Nagas said finally, his smile more wry and pitying than ever. "Would you enlighten us, pray, as to what term such an improved logic might place between *true* and *false?*"

"I merely meant that all old systems are eventually found somewhat defective and replaced by improved systems."

"And is your wife not a Papist?" Sharper asked, flushing with anger.

"That is not a crime, although it may be a disadvantage," Sir John said. "Are you implying that my lack of religious bigotry and the normal sectarian hatreds makes me an unsavory character?"

"You marry a Papist," Sharper went on, louder. "You come here with another Papist, as a witness to a story that is palpably fraudulent on the face of it. You speculate wildly about astronomical subjects you admit you do not comprehend fully. You claim you are not bound by ordinary logic. Did you not second the Jacobite conspirator, Burke, in his recent efforts to arm the Irish Papists against us?"

"What?" Sir John asked. "To arm the Irish . . . Are you referring, sir, to the bill that would permit Irish Catholics to *buy property?*"

"To buy *guns*. That is the secret purpose of the bill, as well you know."

"Burke is not a Jacobite," Sir John exclaimed, trying to keep track of all the accusations. "He is a good Church of England communicant. He has nothing to do with this damned rock, anyway. You are dragging red herrings all over the trail, and I begin to resent you."

"There is no need for acrimony," Gardner Marvins said, frowning. "I had thought you wished a rational discussion, Sir John."

"I did. But he—"

"Have you not visited extensively in Papist nations?" Sharper demanded.

"And in Moslem nations, you idiot. What has that do with this *solid, tangible, physical* rock that is right before your nose?"

"Please calm yourself, Sir John," Nagas said. "I understand that you have passionate beliefs and find normal scientific skepticism somewhat offensive. You must understand that we receive many strange communications, from people who claim for instance to have evidence that England was once under water and therefore Noah's flood really happened." He smiled sadly again, at the idiocy of unscientific people. "We have done you a singular courtesy in enquiring at all into your extremely strange assertions."

"I do not resent normal scientific skepticism," Sir John said, measuring his words carefully. "I resent this Sharper creature muddying the waters with irrelevant and untrue political innuendoes. Surely you all remember that this society was founded by a Papist, or at least a man suspected of Papist sympathies? If Mr. Sharper's bigotry is to replace evidence here, then are not all of you under the same suspicion as myself? Is that not the sort of sectarian folly that science wishes to replace with detached and impartial reason?"

"I knew he would start attacking *me*," Sharper said. "They are all like that when their frauds are exposed. What have Charles II's religious convictions to do with this matter?"

"No more than Burke's politics," Sir John exclaimed. "You are the one who keeps raising political and religious bogeys."

"Pray," Nagas said, still smiling, "why do you believe the late Charles II was a Papist?"

"I do not say he was. It was a common rumor, and still is. My argument was merely that if my testimony is to be impugned because my wife is Papist, then the same transferred guilt can apply to this Society. It is well known that Charles II despised the anti-Papist fanatics and his own brother, James II, *was* a Papist. I deplore the absurdities of all sectarianism, when the rock is before us and exists independently of sects and politics."

"Have you ever visited with the Pretender, Charles Edward Stuart, in Rome?" Sharper demanded.

"My God," Sir John said to Nagas, "how much time will you allow him to waste on these irrelevancies?"

"You refuse to answer," Sharper said. "Have you donated money to Charles Edward Stuart or other Jacobite traitors in Rome or in France?"

We know more than you think, Sir John thought wildly. *Give us the names.* It is the same in every time and place.

"I have never visited the Stuart Pretender," he said steadily, "and I have never contributed to Jacobite causes. This is idiocy. An examination of the rock might show something of objective validity."*

"I think politics might better be left out of this matter,"

---

*Ferguson's attempts to link Hanfkopf to the CIA via the Gehlen *apparat* (a team of ex-Nazis, under General Reinhard Gehlen, who served as a CIA conduit to right-wing Russian exiles while keeping them at a distance from the agency itself) has been as exhaustive and controversial as Hanfkopf's charges concerning de Selby's role in the *Propaganda Due* bank frauds, the alleged poisoning of Pope John Paul I, and the attempted assassinations of Pope John Paul II. All that is clear at this point is that either the Italian Secret Police had infiltrated *Propaganda Due*, or P-2 had infiltrated them, or each had infiltrated the other, but in any case, the current Italian government now charges that the secret police, or SISMI, were involved for twenty years in aiding the terrorist bombers they were supposed to be trying to suppress. See *Irish Times*, 23 October 1984, concerning the charges against General Musumeci, head of SISMI, now known to be also a member of P-2 along with Roberto Calvi, Michele Sindona (sentenced for 65 counts of stock and currency fraud in the U.S. and convicted of murder in Italy) and Licio Gelli, the Grand Master of P-2, who recently escaped from a maximum security prison in Switzerland. Archbishop Marcinkus, who has been repeatedly named as co-conspirator in these frauds and who refuses to come out of the Vatican to answer questions for the Italian magistrates, is named by Yallop, *In God's Name*, op. cit., as one of the murderers of Pope John Paul I, but the exact connection or connections are still unclear between Archbishop Marcinkus's "Vatican Bank" (or Institute of Religious Works), Calvi's Banco Ambrosiano, and the Gray Wolves, the right-wing Moslem group named in Banco Ambrosiano—Mafia heroin-dealing exposés. Mehmet Ali Agca, who attempted to assassinate Pope John Paul II in 1981, was a member of the Gray Wolves, according to recent charges by the Italian government (and Thomas and Morgan-Witts in *Pontiff*, op. cit.) Father Juan Fernandez Krohn, who attempted to assassinate Pope John Paul II at Fatima in 1982, was a disciple of Archbishop Lefèbvre, who has been linked with the Priory of Sion and the Merovingians by Baigent, Leigh, Lincoln, *Holy Blood, Holy Grail*, op. cit., pp. 184-187. It is all most mysterious.

Gardner Marvins said with a smile. "Let us all try to proceed with more dispatch and less passion. May we question
your man, Sir John?"

"Certainly."

Moon had an angry look on his face. Of course, Sir John
thought, a Jew who had been listening to wild talk about
Jewish conspiracies might have the same look. But it was
not a good omen.

"Your name is James Moon?" Marvins asked.

"Yes, Your Honor."

"And you are a coachman for Sir John Babcock?"

"That I am."

"He pays your wages."

"He does that, Your Honor."

"Do you like him?"

"Well, Your Honor, he seems to have less prejudice than
many I've met, including some in this room. He deals honestly with me."

"Is it your impression," Marvins asked softly, "that you
saw this rock, ah, literally *fall,* ah, out of the sky?"

"Aye, as sure it is my impression that I am talking to a
man who has made up his mind in advance not to believe
me. Your Honor."

Moon is making the same mistake as I did, Sir John
thought. He is allowing them to provoke him.

"Would you tell us, James, what unfortunate accident
happened to your right hand?" Marvins asked.

There was a pause.

"A cart fell on it," Moon said.

"Did a cart fall on your eye also?"

"That was a disagreement with a fellow named Murphy."

"Have you ever been charged with seditious activities?"

"No, Your Honor."

Every man in the room, including Sir John, felt intuitively
that Moon had been lying. His voice lacked something; he
was afraid of this line of questioning.

"Have you been involved with White Boys or groups of
that sort?"

"No, Your Honor. Never."

There was another pause. "You think we in England are
unfair to Ireland," Marvins summarized. "You feel Sir John

has more sympathy with Papist nations. You feel he treats you well and honestly. Would you lie for him?''

"My da told me the only excuses for lying are to please a homely woman and to save a life. I have told the truth about the rock.''

"Where do you think it fell from, James?''

"I was hoping learned men like yourselves could answer that question.''

"Do you think it perhaps fell from the city of heaven?''

"I doubt that they are so careless up there.''

"You do believe in heaven?''

"I have hope, as all religions teach us to hope; I doubt that heaven is in the sky.''

"You are not an orthodox Papist, then—''

"Aquinas said that heaven was a state of being, not a place.''

There was another pause. Sir John knew what the committee members were thinking. Sharper said it for them:

"You sound like a learned man, for a servant. Where did you acquire this education in Papist theology?''

"I made my living as a sailor for a few years,'' Moon improvised. "Many nations do not have laws against an Irish lad reading a book.''

"And did you visit Rome in your travels?'' Sharper pursued.

"No. And I never met Bonnie Prince Charlie either, if that's what you're thinking.''

"Have you conversed with Jesuits?''

"No, Your Honor. Never.''

"An Irish lad who reads theology but has never spoken to a Jesuit,'' Sharper said. "The dimensions of the swindle here grow larger as we look into it.'' He addressed the committee. "I have no further doubts, gentlemen. What we have here is a man with a Papist wife and a Papist servant, who is probably a secret Papist himself. This is some Jesuit or Jacobite plot to deceive us into endorsing the idea of a heavenly city in the clouds, to encourage superstition and advance the frauds of the Church of Rome.''

"Gentlemen,'' Sir John said quietly. "I belong to the Church of England, and to its liberal faction. I have no ties with Rome or with Jacobite plots. As a statesman, I have made enemies, and they would have exposed me, and driven me out of the House of Commons long ago, if such foreign conspiracies could in fact be connected to me. I do not for a moment believe, or urge you to believe, that this object descended from the heavenly city or was cast down to earth by an angel or anything of that sort. On the contrary, I have a firm persuasion that it is a natural product of natural causes and can be explained scientifically. I entreat you to cast aside prejudice, consider the possibility that my man here and myself are honest observers, and exercise your knowledge—which is far greater than mine—to find the scientific explanation for such objects as this, which, I remind you one more time, have been recorded in all known ages and lands.

"If I may add one more word," he went on smoothly, having decided that he was not dealing with detached and impartial rationalists but with a group much like the opposition party in the House, "I would beg your attention to turn itself upon the following observations. My man and I both agree that the rock *glowed* when it was falling, although it became cool very rapidly after landing. We agree that the noise was like that made by other heavy objects when falling. We agree that it buried itself partly in the ground when landing. These observations agree with those made by countless men and women in many other places. It is possible that all these witnesses were confused and misperceived what they saw, as I may have been confused and misperceived; but it is also possible that there are more planets than the seven we know, and that there are other, miscellaneous masses in the sun's family, and that some of the lighter ones might be pulled to earth by our gravitational field. I can only repeat that an impartial investigation would consider both possibilities, and not quickly dismiss all inconvenient testimony as hallucination or fraud. I thank you, gentlemen, for your patience."

"You speak well, as befits a member of Parliament," Nagas said with equal smoothness, still smiling sadly and condescendingly. "The man who claimed England had been covered with water during Noah's flood, alas, used many of the same arguments; but all the evidence he had were some *seashells* found atop Beachy Head. It is more economical to assume some boy carried the shells there and lost them than it is to assume Bible miracles are literal facts. It is more economical to assume that when lightning strikes rocks some people will misperceive what they saw, than it is to assume that rocks can *glow* and that the solar system is full of these shining strangers and that they occasionally fall out of their proper orbits into ours. As a layman, Sir John, you cannot imagine the technical mathematical problems the existence of such objects would cause in the theory of gravity. However, I think the spirit of free inquiry is our most precious national heritage and I am sorry that some here have perhaps treated you roughly. I propose to this committee that we appoint a subcommittee to examine this rock chemically and otherwise. If it came from elsewhere it should show signs of a non-earthly origin and we will have to revise our thinking. If, as I suspect, it is just an orginary rock, I hope you will understand, Sir John, that we can waste no more time on it after that is established.''

There was a short, whispered conversation among the committee. Sir John distinctly heard Sharper mutter ''Papist plot'' one more time. Gardner Marvins said something which caused a few muffled laughs. Then Nagas addressed Sir John again.

''The investigation will be made,'' he said. ''We will notify you of the results.''

Sir John was elated. He was sure that, since the rock had fallen from elsewhere, it would show chemical irregularities that would confirm his assertions. He did not know that the whole universe was composed of the same ninety-two chemical elements and that no scientist of his time was aware of more than seventeen of them.

Sixteen

Sigismundo Celine knew that he had dreamed of upside-down rooms and talking lions and Inquisitors.

He knew that there were drugs in his food. Nevertheless, he ate, since the only other choice was to starve, and he intended to live long enough to find out who was moving him around in space and time and distorting his memories and playing all these games with him.

Sigismundo had not been whipped, although he vaguely remembered that it had been threatened many times. He *thought* he had actually been strapped to the whipping block once, but then that might have been another dream.

He also *thought* they had given him an injection of some sort when he was strapped to the post and waiting for the whip to fall, but he also *thought* he had been back in Napoli and aboard a marvelous boat that sailed under the water.

He had been given drugs so often—and, he suspected, he had been given so many different drugs—that he was no longer sure what was memory and what was dream or hallucination.

Right now, he *thought* he was back in the dungeon. That was where he usually found himself when his mind cleared for a while.

The last dream—if it had been a dream—involved a group of Doctors of Medicine. They were part of the conspiracy, of course. Everybody he met these days were part of the conspiracy; he was shrewd enough to remember that. The doctors, or conspirators—or dream-figures—seemed to be treating him for some illness, and they were most sympathetic. It was not clear what his disease was, but it had something to do with his frequent suspicion that they were all part of the conspiracy.

They told him he was in St. John of God's Hospital for the Insane, in London.

Sigismundo sometimes thought that that might be true. The doctors might be real doctors and not conspirators at all. If he had been brought here by the real conspirators while totally deranged by drugs, the doctors might sincerely think he was mad.

If he told them any of his recent adventures, they would be even more convinced that he was mad.

On the other hand, deep down, Sigismundo really didn't believe any of that.

I don't think this is really a hospital, he told himself stubbornly. I don't think they are real doctors. I don't think this is the year 1814, as they keep insisting; I think it is 1764 or 1771 or something like that. Or 1772 or 1773. Somewhere around there.*

*Prof. Dhuigneain argues (De Selby and the Celtic Imagination, op. cit., 42-3) that de Selby, Erigena, and Berkeley were "merely being consistently Irish" in their rejection of ordinary time as objective; he instances the notorious fact that no two clocks in Dublin ever agree, and the more notorious case of the four clocks atop the Cork City Hall which always give four different times (and are locally called "the four liars"). Prof. Vinkenoog's de Selby: De Onbekende Filosoof, op. cit., pp. 109-113, indicates that just as it is only the twentieth century to Christians (being the fifty-ninth century to Jews, the thirteenth century to Moslems, the first century to Crowleyans, etc.), and just as two events on Earth and Sirius cannot happen "at the same time' in Special Relativity—there being a nine-year difference between them, if they are perceived as "simultaneous"—the "eternal now" of the mystics and the "plenumary time" of de Selby are both "closer to existential reality than the conceptual time of calendars and positivist science." Vinkenoog is especially clear on the obscure subject of de Selby's backward/sideways "vortices" and explains concisely (pp. 115-16) how the teratological molecules, moving backward from the Big Bang at the end to the chaos at the beginning, produce more and more "monsters" (dragons, cyclopeans, dinosaurs, etc.) as one follows them in their headlong flight into remoter and remoter antiquity. The serious enquirer should also see Prof. Vinkenoog's amusing "Personalized Synchronicity," in Jungian Journal, IV, 3, in which he recounts the mysterious sequence of taxi accidents that occurred to him on a recent visit to Heidelberg; Ferguson is probably extravagant and subjective in insisting that these accidents are somehow connected with Vinkenoog's letter to him, expressing interest in his unpublished notes on the Knights of Malta and the Gehlen apparat. However, to be fair, the objective student should consult also Oglesby's

He heard footsteps. *They* were coming again.

He wondered what it would be this time.

It was two men in white.

Oh, yes, he remembered, I am supposed to be in a hospital.

The two men in white dragged him from his cell and marched him quickly down a dimly-lit hall. It was not the "same" hall that had been outside his dungeon before, he thought. Not quite.

But he wasn't really sure, of course.

They came to a door marked "Dr. Sanson." Sigismundo remembered that door, or thought he did. Dr. Sanson was a jovial, red-bearded man who seemed sincerely concerned with curing Sigismundo's delusion that he was being held prisoner by conspirators.

But this time Dr. Sanson was not in the office. In his place was a shorter, darker man, a Southerner, without a beard.

"Who are you?" Sigismundo asked.

"Dr. Sanson. I spoke with you just yesterday, Joseph."

"You've lost some weight since then."

"Have a seat and tell me why my weight is important to you."

Sigismundo sat down. "It is a matter of gravity," he said. "Without gravity we might all float up to the ceiling."

"I see," the doctor said thoughtfully. "Do you often worry that you might, ah, float up to the ceiling?"

"Why, no," Sigismundo said innocently. "Do you?"

"But gravity is important to you?"

"Not as important as levity."

"You wish to levitate, to go to the ceiling? To, ah, be above other men, as it were?"

"Pardon me," Sigismundo said, "but why are you so

discussion of the Gehlen *apparat* in *Yankee and Cowboy War*, op. cit., pp. 38–43, and Oglesby's further discussion of Mafia/CIA links (pp. 28–37, passim) should be compared to the Mafia/Vatican links in Nino Bello's *Vatican Papers* and Hammer's *Vatican Connection*, both op. cit. The links between the Mafia, the Vatican Bank, and the Gray Wolves, as asserted by Thomas and Morgan-Witts in *Pontiff*, op. cit., do not perfectly explain why an agent of the Gray Wolves, Mehmet Ali Agca, tried to assassinate Pope John Paul II, but they give one much to ponder. Leaving politics out of it, the Vinkenoog thesis certainly helps one to understand how La Fournier could be writing about de Selby before de Selby was born, if de Selby was not the Prince of Wales after all.

concerned with the ceiling? Is there something up there that bothers you?''

"What does Newton mean to you, Joseph?''

"He reminds me of you.''

The doctor made a note. "Why is that?''

"He asked a lot of questions, too.''

"What does the ceiling mean to you?''

"Ceiling wax,'' Sigismundo said at once. "It contains secrets.''

"I see. What does Charles Radclyffe mean to you?''

"That you are about to ask me about the widow's son.''

"And who was the widow's son?''

Sigismundo shook his head. "Not until you give me the sign of the third degree,'' he said furtively.

The doctor made the square gesture correctly. "Now,'' he repeated, "who *was* the widow's son?''

"Hiram, the builder of Solomon's temple.''

"Was it a physical temple, or symbolic?''

"Symbolic.''

"What does it symbolize?''

"The Father lives in the Son.''

"That is orthodox enough. Does it have a secret meaning also?''

"Yes. The reproductive act is itself literal immortality. The Church has forgotten this and lost the *gnosis.''*

"That is most heretical, Joseph.''

"That is why it is only passed on in symbols and allegories and codes. The *gnosis* has been underground for centuries.''

"In what sense does the Father live in the Son?''

"Literally and concretely. The seed is alive and intelligent.''

"Yes?'' the doctor prompted. "Go on.''

"Our intelligence is small, comparatively. The intelligence of the seed is vast, because it is old, very old. Each of us is a temporary mansion in which the seed lives for a while, in its journey across the aeons. 'In my Father's house are many mansions.' ''

"You refer to the human seed only?''

"No. The apple seed knows how to become an apple tree. It is intelligent and alive too. There are many orders of intelligence in addition to those we normally recognize.''

"This was explained to you by an initiate of the Rose Cross?"

"No. I deduced it gradually by meditating on the symbols of the Craft."

"The Rose Cross image, for instance?"

"Yes. That is rather obvious, when you think of it. Especially when you remember the alchemical formula, 'It is only on the Cross that the Rose will bloom.' The rose is the womb, and the cross is the male organ. I first began to perceive this dimly in that seemingly silly joke in *The Key of Solomon*—the formula for making a homunculus, an imitation man, out of your own seed. Like most of the jokes in hermetic literature, that is really a concealed clue, to make you think about what the seed contains."

"Very good, Joseph. What other clues have you found?"

Sigismundo plunged straight ahead. "The genealogy of Jesus beginning at Luke 3:23. That makes Jesus the son of God not directly but through Joseph and Joseph's father, Heli, and so on, back through the generations to the beginning of mankind. That is to teach us that the seed lives in many bodies in its journey to eternity."

"What else?"

"*The Alchemical Marriage of Christian Rosycross*. The clue is right there in the title, and the text makes perfectly clear that both a man and a woman, together, are necessary to produce the First Matter. The eye in the triangle, of course. The writings of Nicholas Flamel, that old joker. He states very explicitly that his wife, Perenella, was assisting in the laboratory each time he produced the elixir of immortality. The symbolism of the stone that is rejected becoming the cornerstone: the stone that is rejected in Christianity is the female."

"I congratulate you; you have done well. What is the Grail, then?"

"It can only be the womb of the beloved."

"And Parcifal, the pure fool?"

"He is pure because he has never learned the guilt and shame that the false *gnosis* of the churches has imposed on the rest of us. The symbolism of his lance redeeming the wasteland is rather overt."

"What is your conclusion, then?"

"The *baraka* is hidden, forbidden, sealed with seven seals, because power is wielded by those who do not want us to know these things. There *is* an international conspiracy to blind and deceive us, and it is thousands of years old. It is the 'tyranny and superstition' that we swear to combat in the first degree oath. It is made up of all those men who have learned to raise the *baraka* and have become drunk and maddened by it, because they are only men. The true *gnosis* requires the union of male and female in the working. That is the alchemical marriage of Christian Rosycross.''

''You have almost all of it. Who was the wife of Osiris?''

''Isis.''

''In India, the wife of Shiva?''

''Kali.''

''The wife of Zeus?''

''Hera.''

''Who was the wife of Jupiter?''

''Juno.''

''And what do all these symbolize, Joseph?''

''The alchemical marriage, as I said. The fusion, when a man and a woman use the *baraka* together.''

''Is it the seed only that is intelligent, Joseph?''

''No. I see now. The egg is intelligent, too.''

''And what did the Knights Templar find in Solomon's temple?''

Sigismundo sighed. ''That is the part I haven't figured out yet.''

''I see. I'm sorry, Joseph. You were close but . . . I'm afraid your case is hopeless.''

The doctor rapped on his desk three times, Masonically.

''Who is it? Who is it? Who is it?'' chanted a voice in the hall.

''The son of a poor widow lady,'' the doctor responded, ''who has become lost and seeks the Light.''

Three ruffians, dressed like Jubela, Jubelo, and Jubelum in the third degree initiation, rushed into the room, seized Sigismundo and dragged him out into the hall.

Now they throw me in the well again, he thought.

But they merely threw him back in his cell.

Seventeen

From AN HONEST DEFENSE OF FREEMASONRY, by Henri Benoit:

Aristotle, then, only knew of three souls (the vegetative, the animal, and the human; *viz.*, the survival-and-nourishment faculty, the emotion-and-aggression faculty, and the pure reason), but the function of the Craft is to form a fourth "soul" or higher mental center. This, I do verily believe, was the purpose also of the Mysteries, the secret rituals practiced at Eleusis in which Plato and many another ancient philosopher were initiated; it was the original purpose of the sacraments of the Church; it was, and is, the purpose of the ordeals of the Red Indians and the *derwishes* of Africa and the Near East. I suspect also that many of the strange practices of the alchemists had similar intent.*

*The basic alchemical process was to separate the "soul" (or "First Matter") from the body and then return it in "sublimated" form back into the body, producing what is nowadays called an OOBE, or out-of-body experience, and to accomplish this during prolonged (Tantric) sexual dalliance. See *Works of Thomas Vaughn*, op cit., and the footnote on page 60. It is doubtful that de Selby ever accomplished this, given his dismal record with women, but Le Tournier's insistence on an "alchemical code" in *Golden Hours* seems to have some sort of validity. One recalls Hanfkopf's claim that the Royal Sir Myles na gCopaleen Institute, whose branches published de Selby's works and many of the first commentaries thereon, was nothing more than a postal "drop" in Dalkey; and Ferguson has sound evidence (*Armageddon*, 14–56) that "Sir Myles na gCopaleen" was O'Brien himself, author of the questionable *Dalkey Archive*. The only mention of the Sir Myles na gCopaleen in all the Irish newspapers consulted by Hamburger (op. cit.) deals with "the Royal Sir Myles na gCopaleen Archeological Institute" and their astounding discovery of "Corkadorky Man," a prehistoric denizen of County Kerry

The need for this fourth "soul" or higher faculty is that mankind today is not a *finished* creature but a being in the process of transcending its own past. ("For the earnest expectation of the creature awaiteth the manifestation of the sons of God," Romans 8:19.) We are still, as the mystics say, asleep: we do not know who we are or what it is possible for us to do. . . .

From THE SPAWN OF THE SERPENT, by *John J. A. MacKenzie*:

. . . And the light of which they speak is not the light of reason nor yet the holy light of faith, which the Craft is intended to unite in alchemical marriage as we become increasingly aware of the *design* of the Great Architect; no, with these *Illuminati* such as Weishaupt and Cagliostro and the vile liar, Robison, who alleges that he is *exposing* these fiends while in fact he is recruiting for them (and that right under our noses), and others whose names we know not (the hidden chiefs of this infamous brigade), no, I say, with these

who allegedly constructed all the megaliths of Ireland and the British Isles, just to puzzle future archeologists. This definitely has all the earmarks of a Hibernian hoax or "sendup"; and if both na gCopaleen and O'Brien are creatures of de Selby's own humor, then the Prince of Wales theory is untenable, unless the Prince of Wales himself can be shown to be a member of the Knights of Malta, or if the multiple de Selbys of Swenson were, in fact, the same person but not at the same time. Still, the theory of plenumary time stands on its own two or three feet as the one mathematically sophisticated and consistently existential explanation of such puzzles as how meteorites (only accepted by nineteenth-century science) found their way back to the eighteenth century (when they were officially nonexistent), how La Fournier could write a book about de Selby before de Selby was born, why the most ancient epochs contain the greatest number of paranormal and "miraculous" happenings together with the largest stretches of time when apparently nothing was happening; or the fact that, e.g., John Adams was born on both 19 October 1735 and 30 October 1735, and indeed that everybody born before 1750 had two birthdays; or the inconsistencies and improbabilities of all history (as contrasted to the orderly universe of novels and Romances), etc. Cf. also Gribbin's *In Search of Schrödinger's Cat*, op cit., pp. 184–94, where it is shown that the Feynman diagrams of quantum mechanics make as much sense mathematically if one assumes the particles are moving backward in time as they do if one assumes they are moving in the conventional direction. The serious student should consult also "Turning Einstein Upside Down" by John Gliedman *(Science Digest*, October 1984), in which is given Professor John Archibald Wheeler's demonstration of how events in the future can, by Bell's nonlocality theorem, influence the events of the remote past.

it is the light of Lucifer, son of the morning, fallen angel, King of Hell. For just as the impertinent Danton and the mad Marat and the abominable Robespierre were but tools, so, too, were the villains who began this conspiracy against God; they served powers they knew not. It is an easy thing, once the techniques of shock and mystery are understood, to alter the consciousness for good *or for ill*, and those methods that can raise the mind to glory and redemption can also be deliberately perverted to incite it to madness, violence, and revolution.

Sir John Babcock was in Camden Town, outside London—a long walk from Parliament, but he did not want to meet anybody he knew.

He was in a tavern habituated by the Irish, run by a loud, foul-mouthed old Irishwoman whom her clients addressed familiarly as "Mother Damnable." Sir John gathered that Mother Damnable had other commerce besides the running of a public house; some of the customers brought her not cash but commodities, of a sort they did not seem prosperous enough to have acquired honestly.

The old lady was a "fence," and the pub a den of thieves. It did not matter. Sir John was in a snug—a closed room, off from the main room—and he was sincerely devoting himself to the occupation of becoming blind drunk.

"Why, damn my eyes, if it ain't Doll Cutpurse," Mother Damnable howled. "Whatcher been up to, dearie?" Everybody in the place seems to have been inspired by *The Beggar's Opera*, Sir John thought—or had this crew inspired Gay when he wrote that satire?*

Sir John banged the wall with his walking stick, signalling that he wanted another pint of Guinness's. *Wine of the country,* they called that in Ireland; or sometimes just *the customary*.

—*What'll your pleasure be, Pat?*

—*I think my physician would recommend the customary.*

How many times had he heard that in his youth?

I am not only a "leading figure" according to the Press but a husband and a father, he told himself. Father of the most adorable little girl in the British Islands.

A flunky brought in the pint. Sir John rolled a penny across the table at him.

*Yes.

Alone again, Sir John looked at the wall and mentally addressed it.

Adultery, he said in his best Parliamentary style, while admittedly not as common here as it is in France, is certainly not unknown; some have even observed that the strangest thing about our strange German king is that he actually appears to be faithful to his wife.

Furthermore and in addition to that, I call your attention to the scandals connected with Wilkes and Dashwood and the Hell Fire Club, which are well known to the general, and included the distinguished Earl of Sandwich as an eager participant, at least until the orangutan bit him.

I add significantly that the Bible Itself says all men are sinners.

"Why, damn my eternal soul, it's Dick Stickpigs," Mother Damnable howled in the main room. Sir John took another strong swig and addressed the wall again:

The greatest folly of all, I submit, is to continue to torment oneself about something already done, which cannot be changed, nor blotted out, nor erased from the Eternal Ledger of Time Past and Time To Come. Whatever that means.

I always knew this was part of my nature and only sentimentalism ever deceived me into thinking it could be changed permanently.

And finally, in summary, let me say, gentlemen of the jury, that he was absolutely irresistible (and he knew it, the bitch!) and I do truly love my wife and, furthermore, I will never, never do it again.

"God blin' me," Mother Damnable howled, "if it ain't Flossie Burner,* big as life and twice as dirty."

I think I must be quite drunk by now, Sir John reflected. My father, after all, was a judge, and I know that no sober jury would accept such a defense. The simple fact of the matter is that one of the bravest proponents of progressive politics in England is a hypocrite and a scoundrel, and he is hiding out and drinking himself senseless in a low Irish tavern because he is afraid to go home and look his adoring young bride in the eyes; and, worse yet, he is now about to

*Current slang for a lady who distributed syphilis along with her favors.

get even more drunk because he loathes the thought of remaining conscious, knowing what he knows about himself.

Ladies and gentlemen of the World's Greatest Christian Empire, I give you Sir John Babcock, defender of the oppressed, champion of liberty, husband of the beautiful Contessa Maldonado, father of the angelic Ursula, owner of God knows how much land here and in Ireland, and clandestine devotee of boy's bottoms. I give you the man with two faces, two souls, two natures fighting in one heart. I give you the Compleat Machiavellian, the practitioner of that Vice which is so terrible and unspeakable that God destroyed two whole cities for it if we are to believe the inspired authors of Holy Writ.

I give you the man who will someday blow his brains out with a pistol and leave everybody standing around saying, "Why would he do that, a man with so much to live for?"

I give you the bifurcated man.

"By the sacred chamber pot of Our Lady," Mother Damnable howled, "if me poor old eyes ain't gone entirely on me, it's Captain Comegrass."* There was an instantaneous silence.

Sir John felt his spine prickle, wondering what was happening. Then he heard a thunderous crash, and Mother Damnable shouted again:

"Good man yourself, Mike!"

Conversations began again, and there was a sound of a body being removed. *I deduce that the colorful names around here are functional rather than ornamental*, Sir John thought, *and that an informer has just been dispatched by someone named Mike.*

He banged for another pint.

I am overly histrionic, he told himself calmly. *I have good reason to know that there are not a few but in fact many men who share my tastes. I have met them in Paris and Rome and Cairo and Athens and Baghdad (especially in Baghdad), and even here in Honest Protestant England. The truth is (and there is truth in alcohol, as the proverb says) that I do not really hate myself quite as much as I make out.*

His pint arrived.

The truth is . . . ? Oh, yes: the truth is that I do not hate

*Because *to come grass* meant to be an informer.

myself, really. I only think I *should* hate myself, and that is the benefit of a Good Christian Education. I have been castigating myself so that I might feel remorse, and that is necessary so that I may next proceed happily to forgive myself.

"The Necessary?" the flunky said.

Sir John came out of his trance and rolled another penny on the table. A dirty hand pounced and snatched it; he was alone again.

Looking with the undeceived eyes of drunken self-knowledge: I know that I am what I am.

Yes: I am what I am. As a roach is a roach: and a whale is a whale: and a tree is never a tiger: and a fish is a fish and not a rosebush. Every part of nature must be necessary or it would not exist, could not exist. Is the House of Commons less *natural* than an ant-hill? *Au contraire, Rousseau:* I very much doubt it. "God is no respecter of persons"; the mind behind the cosmos does not share in conventional morality, or it would not make so many bizarre variations and permutations. Wisdom is to know what you are and accept it. And I do not tailor my politics or my philosophy to the constraints of the mediocre average: why should I try to trim and clip the most vital function of my living flesh to such standards?

I wonder if I really believe all that?

Anyway, he was an attractive lad, and good sport.

No: more than sport. Love. A kind of love. Or if not love, need, but do not degrade it by calling it mere play.

Gentlemen of the jury, call it what you will: I throw myself on your mercy. Or my mercy, since I am in fact the only jury here.

Oh, stop this, he told himself tiredly. Just drink and don't think: the best plan in times of stress. You are as trapped by your desire to be "good" as you are by this drive which tells you it cannot be satisfied by the female only but needs the male as well. You don't understand, and you didn't create, either your conscience or your drives: you are merely owned by them. You will, of course, try to be faithful to Maria in the future, of course. Being the person you are, you will *try.*

And God only knows if you will succeed.

Eighteen

I certainly congratulate you on enduring that torment so nobly," Uncle Pietro said.

"It is just a matter of the will," Sigismundo said grandly. "The general of an army can be kidnapped, but no amount of coercion can kidnap the will of a true man of the Craft."

" 'Learn to Know, Learn to Dare, Learn to Will, Learn to Keep Silence,' " Uncle Pietro quoted. "You have mastered the whole arcanum. You deserve the Rose Cross degree immediately."

"Oh," Sigismundo said modestly, "I already understand that. Maria has the rose and I have the cross. When they are united the alchemical marriage is complete and the drama ends. Then we wake from history and enter eternity."

"You have indeed penetrated to the secrets of secrets," Uncle Pietro said softly. "Horus, the crowned and conquering child, springs from the union of Father Osiris and Mother Isis. The sun and moon together."

"The union of priest and priestess, that means," Sigismundo said. "I've figured it all out. Well, almost all."

"What do you still lack?"

"I haven't guessed the identity of the real widow's son from whom all this derives."

"Just trace the genealogies back," Uncle Pietro said, eyes like diamonds. "The house of Stuart, the house of Lorraine, the Bourbons . . . the Malatestas . . . *Et in Arcadia Ego* . . . no wife, no horse, no moustache . . ."

"What?"

Uncle Pietro's voice seemed to come from further away:

"They came from the stars and they brought their images with them."

"Wait, don't go yet . . ."

"Dinner, Joseph." The guard was outside, inserting the metal plate through the judas window. Uncle Pietro was gone.

Sigismundo glared, growling back in his throat, lupine.

"Take your plate, Joseph."

Sigismundo took the plate. He was a bit dazed and somewhat frightened. Vaguely, he remembered that he had begun an imaginary conversation with Uncle Pietro, in his head, just to pass the time. But he had no idea how long ago that was. It was unnerving to realize that Uncle Pietro had become so solid and tangible, there in the cell with him, that he had forgotten the conversation was imaginary.

It is easy to hallucinate when they leave you alone in a small room for many days, he had learned. It was rather difficult, in fact, to avoid slipping off into the hallucinations as one empty hour followed another.

They were not playing games with his head lately—except that business about calling him "Joseph" when food was served.

They had simply locked him up to let him see what kinds of games his head played by itself when in isolation from humanity.

Well, he still knew he was "Sigismundo," not "Joseph," although, of course, it was clear that he wasn't really "Sigismundo," since that was only a convention. The True Self was invisible, unspeakable, so it didn't matter whether you were called Ivan or Henri or Therese or Fionula or whatever.

Still it was important to cling to the convention of "Sigismundo," because if you let that go, all sorts of other things might go with it.

Uncle Pietro had encouraged "Sigismundo"—that is, the invisible being manifesting on this plane under the name "Sigismundo"—to read Vico, when he was only fourteen, before he did any traveling. That was wise. Vico made clear that every group of men and women is a separate reality-neighborhood: the Neapolitans create one reality-city by talking in Neapolitan words and concepts, the Spanish create another by talking in Spanish words and concepts, the English have a third reality-tunnel, and so on. All reality-grids were created by people talking to each other. They make their history out of forgotten poems, Vico said.

So Sigismundo—or the formless, infinite consciousness temporarily manifest as "Sigismundo"—was not too surprised that all reality-tunnels start to collapse and fall apart when there is nobody to talk to. The third soul, the reason, was the joint product of people talking. When the talk stops, the fourth soul, the silent self, begins to manifest. And the fourth soul knows nothing of "time" or "space" or "matter," which are all words by which the third soul creates a reality-mesh by talking to other third souls.

Sigismundo noticed that he had finished eating. That was odd; he had hardly tasted the food.

But that was because food was the concern of the first soul. Sigismundo, the entity calling itself "Sigismundo," had lost interest in the first soul a long, long time ago. Not that he had any idea how much "time" had actually passed since the change in him had begun. But the first soul is concerned with food because it is the body-soul and wishes the body to survive. Survival was no longer important. What was important was *understanding*.

They are either torturing me or educating me. They are tormentors or teachers.

And the paradox was that not even they could say which was true.

He was certainly being educated, whether that was their intent or not.

The judas window in the door opened again.

"I'll take your plate now, Joseph."

The creature in the cell passed the plate through the window.

He tried to remember what it was that he was trying to remember.

Oh, yes, I am Sigismundo Celine, not the man in the moon.

But then he *was* the man in the moon. Earth was a distant light in the sky far, far away. Various famous Lunatics were gathered around explaining moon-logic to him. "You never get 'outside.' What you call 'outside' is another part of 'inside.' See?"

"Yes," he said. "I have never experienced another human being. I have experienced my impressions of them. Even in sexual intercourse with Fatima, the black goddess at the Maison Rouge, I did not, strictly speaking, experience Fatima: I experienced my experience of her."

THE WIDOW'S SON 289

"Then the whole universe is inside my head?"

"But your head is inside the universe. How do you explain that?"

"Well, then, I must have two heads, so to speak. The universe is inside my actually *experienced* head, but that head and the universe itself must be both inside my logically necessary *conceptual* head. Is that it?"

"Yes. My conceptual head contains the universe, or a model of the universe to be strictly precise, and inside that model is the *model of my conceptual head*, which is of course also my *experienced* head."

"Careful now. You're building up to an infinite regress."

"I can see that, but it must be because consciousness itself is an infinite regress. I think that explains coincidences."

"Are you quite sure you know what you're saying?"

"Yes. A coincidence is an isomorphism between the contents of my conceptual head, outside the universe, and my experienced head, inside the universe."

"And why should there be such an isomorphism?"

"Because, damn it, my two heads are really only one head. I've just separated them for logical analysis."

"But how can your conceptual head, outside the universe, be your experienced head, inside the universe?"

"Because, because . . ."

"Yes?"

"Because concepts are experiences, too. My conceptual head is experienced, and becomes my experienced head, whenever I think about mathematics or pure logic. Yes, by God. When I see a spotted dog, that is inside my experienced head, as Hume demonstrated. But when I think about the actual dog that creates that image in my experienced head, I must be expanding my conceptual head to include the actual dog, not the image of the dog. So the dog, and the rest of the universe, are actually in my conceptual head, not in my experienced head, which only has their images."

"But then my experienced head is both inside and outside my conceptual head—which means it is both inside and outside the universe."

"You're still in the infinite regress."

"I can appreciate that. By the way, am I talking to you or talking to myself?"

"Is there a difference?"*

"Yes," Sigismundo said, feeling certain. "When you talk to others, an average group reality is maintained, as Vico says. When you talk to yourself, there are as many realities as you want."

"Then anybody who makes an impression on you, enslaves you. Total freedom is only to be found by keeping silent, sitting alone in a dark room, and making up your reality as you go along."

"That sounds plausible," Sigismundo said "But somehow I think it would get lonely after a while."**

Another Lunatic spoke up, "Reality," he said precisely,

*O'Broichain (not to be confused with the devious O'Brien, although their names sound alike) points out (*A Chara*, op cit., p. 93) that de Selby's system is entirely *phenomenological*, as distinguished from *theoretical*. That is, teratological molecules are banished by electric light, in de Selby's patapsychology, because one is apt to see strange and sometimes monstrous shapes in a darkened room (especially if one is as nervous as de Selby) and these *phenomena* (sense experiences) are removed when the light is turned on. Patapsychology also argues (see *Golden Hours*, III, 23 ff.) that objects shrink as they move away from us, railroad tracks converge as they approach the horizon, all literary and artistic judgments, however contradictory (e.g., "Beethoven is greater than Mozart" *vs.* "Mozart is greater than Beethoven"), are strictly accurate *scientific* observations (about the nervous systems of those who write them), and everybody who interferes with what one wants when one wants it is "unfair" and "unreasonable." It is because of this unflinching acceptance of what is actually experienced, rather than on theory, that La Tournier regards de Selby as "a brutal empiricist" and Conneghen defends him as "the one totally consistent Irishman." Indeed, de Selby named this aspect of his cosmology "patapsychology" in tribute to Alfred Jarry's "pataphysics"—the science of unique (nonrepeating) events. Patapsychology begins from the detached, objective, and passionless contemplation of unique neurological events that can neither be forecast nor precisely remembered if one is asked about them later—e.g., what one was thinking when one took the first bite of dinner last Thursday, or what impressions one had while paying a bus fare on this day last year, etc. De Selby defines "existence" (he did not believe in "the universe" as an object) as "the sum total of such states as encountered and endured, before magnification or exaggeration by the instinct to gossip."

**In this connection, and as a homely American contrast to the Banco Ambrosiano scandals with their Mafia drug running, terrorism, murders, etc., one should contemplate the case of the Penn Square Bank of Oklahoma City, which failed in 1982, as revealed by Penny Lernoux in *In Banks We Trust*, Anchor Press/ Doubleday, New York, 1984. The vice president in charge of loans at Penn Square was William G. Patterson, who was in the habit of wearing Mickey Mouse ears to the office (Lernoux, p. 12), and once startled executives of Seattle First Na-

"is the name we give to those inferences that have become so habitual that we have forgotten they are only inferences. Hume proved that."

"Yes," Sigismundo agreed, tentatively.

"You once believed in the Thomist universe, with God at the top and Thrones and Dominions and all sorts of angelic choirs in between and man at the bottom, looking up. But that was only a set of inferences."

"Yes."*

"More recently you believed in the Newtonian universe with forces and masses and accelerations and all sorts of abstractions like that governing the assumed movements of alleged objects in hypothetical space and conjectural time. But that was only another set of inferences."

"Yes."**

---

tional Bank by arriving for a conference dressed as an Arab shiek (p. 12 also). As Lernoux explains at length (pp. 100–142), the drug industry is now the third largest moneymaker in the U.S., and many American banks have found, like Banco Ambrosiano and the Vatican Bank, that "laundering" drug money can be profitable. The World Finance Corporation of Florida, for instance, went bankrupt after investigators traced the drugs, as well as the drug money, back to its offices. Lernoux summarizes (p. xix), "The drug trail led all over the world, from the Caribbean to Miami, Australia, and eventually the Vatican . . . mobsters, right-wing terrorists and CIA agents, all . . . used the same banks and bankers." When Penn Square went belly-up, the catastrophe cost the tough, shrewd old Chase Manhattan a pretty penny, because the boys at Chase had covered most of the unsecured loans which led Penn Square to being forty-six million in hock when the bubble burst. It was revealed later (see Lernoux, p. 19) that Chase had agreed not to investigate the soundness of Penn Square's loans in order to reap the hoped-for later interest on them. *The Wall Street Journal* for 27 July 1982 quotes one borrower from Penn Square as saying Patterson kept tugging the strings that made his Mickey Mouse ears wiggle while they discussed an unsecured loan for seven million. The loan was granted.

---

*As Prof. Han says *(De Selby Te Ching,* p. 31), "Tao fa t'ien; t'ien fa ti; ti fa jen; po de Selby fatzu-jan." (Roughly, "Universal process produced the stars; the stars produced the earth; the earth produced human consciousness; de Selby is his own creation.")

**Which reminds me of a funny coincidence. Over in Italy, Michele Sindona started his career as a conduit of CIA funds to right-wing political groups (see Penny Lernoux, *In Banks We Trust,* op. cit., p. 170, 188, passim). Down in Florida, the World Finance Corporation was founded by Guillermo Cataya, who served the CIA in the Bay of Pigs invasion; its lawyer, also a director, was Walter Surrey, a former employee of the OSS (the CIA's parent organization). According to both Lernoux, pp. 143–169, and Jonathan Kwitney *(Endless Enemies,* Congdon and Weed, New York, 1984, p. 26), when the World Finance Corporation collapsed during investigations of its role in international

"The night before the duel with Carlo Maldonado, your mind went into a state you had never experienced before, and you thought that was the fourth soul and you were perceiving True Reality at last, in capital letters. But that was just another state of mind. All states of mind are equal."

"Yes."

"No wife, no horse, no moustache."

"What?"*

"Then what did the Knights Templar find in the Temple of Solomon?"

"The birth certificate."**

drug smuggling, eight members of its executive staff were protected from prosecution by CIA intervention on their behalf. Although the World Finance Corporation was involved principally in laundering money from the drug business, serving as a conduit for CIA funds to terrorists, and (oddly) certain mysterious transactions with the KGB, the Banco Ambrosiano/Vatican Bank crowd, under Sindona's management, seems to have gone into such sidelines as gun running, terrorism, and murder, as well as infiltrating over nine hundred of its agents into the Italian government. (Sindona was recently in prison in the U.S. for 65 counts of stock and currency fraud and for faking his own kidnapping while under investigation; the Italian government then convicted him of murder.)In both cases, the same link between banking, drugs, and the CIA appears, and in both cases links appear with "Odessa," the underground Nazi group of former SS officers, and with Klaus Barbie, the Nazi war criminal who was mysteriously protected by the CIA for over thirty years. (See Lernoux, pp. 150 ff.) But don't forget good old Bill Patterson back at Penn Square Bank (see footnote, p. 290) wiggling his Mickey Mouse ears as he doles out millions of dollars in unsecured loans. "Reality," as de Selby says, "is what you can get away with."

*Nothing is more controversial in patapsychology and theo-chemistry than de Selby's insistence that King Kong, the Holy Ghost, the photons of quantum theory, and Kant's Categorical Imperative are all equally real because human minds have "encountered and endured" them *(Golden Hours,* CXII, 333–36). This is entirely consistent with his advocacy of a flat earth, on the grounds that nobody has "encountered and endured" a spherical earth (which is a theory generated by "the instinct to gossip"). As Flahive points out, de Selby would change that latter opinion today, while remaining true to his Phenomenological Principle of Variable Constants, because various astronauts and cosmonauts have now "encountered and endured" sphericity. Hanfkopf's comment that "such an ontology is only the result of encountering and enduring too much Irish whiskey" *(Werke,* I, 3) is merely snide and sarcastic; I cannot imagine why Prof. La Puta spent so many years investigating de Selby's bar bills to refute it, especially since La Puta did not explore the bar bills of O'Brien and La Fournier, who may also have been de Selby. And if de Selby was the Prince of Wales, that's a whole new ballgame.

**The reader should recall the remarkable pamphlet called *Le Serpent rouge,* privately printed in Paris in 1967 and deposited in the Bibliothéque

"No wife, no horse, no moustache."

"I heard you the first time."

"Then what did the Knights Templar find in the Temple of Solomon?"

"The birth certificate."*

"Whose birth certificate?"

"The widow's son's."**

"And who was the widow's son?"

"I don't know," Sigismundo screamed. "I don't know. I don't know."***

"I'm sorry," the Lunatic said. "You're not ready to be one of us yet."

Nationale. The authors of this egregious work were Louis Saint-Maxent, Gaston de Koker, and Pierre Feugère, and all three were found hanged within two days after the pamphlet appeared in the Bibliothéque. (They were not submerged in water with their pockets full of bricks like the unfortunate Roberto Calvi of P-2, however.) Baigent, Leigh, and Lincoln in *Holy Blood, Holy Grail*, op. cit., pp. 74–76 examine this peculiar matter inconclusively. (*Le Serpent rouge* deals with astrology, the Merovingians, and Mary Magdalene.)

*The population of India (1985) is estimated at 700,000,000.

**Contrary to popular belief, the leaning tower of Pisa does not lean; the tourists are all staggering when they photograph it.

***Georg Cantor demonstrated mathematically that if an infinite set is removed from an infinite set, an infinite set still remains. The American mathematician Eric Temple Bell pointed out that, by the same reasoning, if a lecturer lectures every night for an infinite number of years, he will not only come to a night when every person in the audience is named Murphy, but he will by sheer chance come to a second such night eventually, and a third . . . and so on, for an infinite number of Murphy-nights, which is still a subset of the infinite number of both non-Murphy-nights *and* Murphy-nights. More radically, the German philosopher F. W. Nietzsche (1844–1900) argued that, in a mathematical infinity of time, every possible event must recur, not once or many times, but an infinite number of times, including the moment when, gazing at "this very spider in this very moonlight," that thought first came to him; e.g., in an infinite number of years, a second Nietzsche would be born, live without that notion for many years, then come again to the spider and the moonlight and the thought that it would all recur; and a third Nietzsche, and a fourth, and so on, to an infinity of Nietzsches contemplating an infinity of Nietzches (Richard Wagner, however, offered the cogent rebuttal: "Nietzsche masturbates too much.")

Nineteen

*From a letter by Sir John Babcock to Charles Nagas, Ph.D.,
F.R.S.:*

. . . and I assure you, sir, that I do understand Occam's Razor
and do appreciate the centuries of experience which justify & en-
dorse the scientific principle that the least complicated explanation
is the preferable explanation. I must point out, however, that by
this principle the lack of extraordinary chemicals in my thunderstone means nothing, or even supports my case, since it is less
complicated to assume that all bodies in the universe are made of
the same elements than to assume that the objects of daily experience on this planet are made of special elements not to be found
elsewhere.

That is not the issue between us, however. The issue is that
people in all lands continue to see things that do not fit into the
Newtonian system as currently understood; and among the things
they commonly see are these controversial thunderstones. I consider that by Occam's Razor, it is less complicated to accept that
Newton's system, for all its excellence, is only a temporary way
of organizing our knowledge, than it is to hypothesize (with great
extravagance) that people of all ages and races, in many lands, are
strangely prone to having this one special hallucination. I beseech
you to remember that reports of these thunderstones do come from
all classic authors and today continue to pour forth in abundance
from France, from Ireland, from the German states, from Italy,
from Greece, and in short from every land from which we receive
news regularly. I beseech you also to recollect your history, sir,
and to remember that, just as the Newtonian system seems complete today, so did the Keplerian system a century ago, and the
Copernican system earlier, and the Ptolemaic system before that.
The question is, I dare to think, and I implore you to ask your-

self also: Do we worship a system, any system, or do we "sit down before Nature, like a little child" (as Newton himself recommended in his *Principia*, which I have been studying lately) and think it possible that we still have things to learn? Do we recognize that Newton's system must eventually be superseded, as it superseded earlier systems? Or do we close our eyes to new data and offer them as sacrifices (as it were) at the altar of Saint Newton? Are we thinking freely, or are we creating a new cult?

I assure you warmly, sir, that since this experience with the thunderstone, and with your Society, I have really come to know what philosophical doubt means, and you have nothing to teach me on that subject. I realize that I had once believed in Newton as naively as a prattling child believes in those parts of the Bible that the educated now know to be but fable and allegory; and it is my suspicion (and my growing conviction) that any system believed in with that innocence, or that fervor, becomes a blindfold, a hoodwink, yea, a mental prison. Do you appreciate that danger, sir? Do you conceive that if a thousand thunderstones can be dismissed as lies or hallucinations today, then ten thousand greater wonders can be dismissed with those disparagements tomorrow, until all informations not compatible with the system are rejected and (God save the mark) worship of Newton perhaps might stop thought in its tracks, as worship of Aristotle did in earlier centuries?

We have lost a great deal, I fear, when we are no longer capable of being shock'd by the universe; when we *clip* and *trim* all our perceptions to fit some abstract system pre-existing those perceptions; when we disregard and defame all reports that do not suit our system; when we no longer believe that the universe contains mysteries and is capable, in the next half-hour, of such prodigies that we must reverse all that we hitherto have taken for granted.

In this connection, I call your attention, sir, to the criticism of Newton by the ingenious Bishop of Boyne, Dr. Berkeley, who has noted the salient points that A, the whole mechanics of Newton depends on the differential calculus; B, the differential calculus depends on the notion of the infinitesimal; and C, the notion of the infinitesimal, as given by Newton, contains a clear fallacy. That is, the infinitesimal, defined as a thing infinitely small, is, so defined, something we have never encountered and never can encounter, *viz.*: experimenting upon this both mentally & practically, I find that if, *exempli gratia*, I take a piece of wood and cut the smallest possible section from it, and then repeat this operation continually, at any point I always have a *very small* piece left, but a piece of definite dimension, not an *infinitely small* piece. And if I cut and hack further and ferociously, I still have a piece that is *very* small but not *infinitely* small: I never reach a world of *no dimension* such as is posited in the definition of the infinitesimal. (The piece may be so small that it requires magnification to be seen, but it is still of definite dimension; it has not become infinitesimal.) All in candor, sir, have you ever yourself seen an infinitesimally small section of anything? Then must we not admit that in this particular, Bishop Berkeley has been more perspicacious than Sir Isaac Newton? And if this flaw has been found by one clever Irishman, what other flaws in Newtonian mechanics might not the future discern?

Twenty

One day they came and took the creature, Sigismundo or Joseph or whoever he was, out of his cell and led him to a room where there were two beautiful women, naked. The guards tied the creature to a chair. The women did not speak to him, or look at him; they pretended he was not there.

The shorter, blonde woman began, slowly and languidly, to masturbate. The other, darker woman watched with growing excitement; so did the male creature tied to the chair. After what seemed a very long time, in a room totally silent except for occasional moans of pleasure, the blonde woman achieved her first delightment. Immediately, the second woman, dark as a Sicilian witch, began to masturbate. The male creature watched, unable to move, fascinated.

Vaguely, he had heard of such exhibitions; some "houses" provided them for men who liked to watch. He had wondered about the quirk that inclined such men that way; now he saw the quirk in himself. Unfortunately, he had only a minor trace of it—watching became increasingly uncomfortable: he wanted to participate. He wished that at least his hands had been untied, so he could relieve his own mounting need. But, of course, that was the whole point of this performance: he had to endure and discover what happened when the passions rose higher and higher and he could neither relieve nor contain them.

The dark woman reached her delightment, panting a bit, flushed. The blonde woman immediately began to caress her own thighs and belly again, moving her fingers gradually inward. He watched.

This is most educational, he told himself, and I do not have to pay for it.

But he still wished his hands were untied.

Time passed—a long, very long time, he thought—and all he saw was naked female flesh, all he heard was soft female sounds of self-delightment, all his mind was a panorama of the rise and fall and rise again of female sexual excitement.

All through this, the women watched each other but never spoke, never touched; and they never looked in his direction.

The male creature, Sigismundo or Joseph, whoever he was, began to notice that he was beginning almost to enjoy his state of passive excitement, which was different from active excitement, but had its own unique pleasure. It was as if he were floating, not in the ocean but in the air, gliding, soaring, every part of him a-tingle, as if his whole body were experiencing what only his penis experienced in active excitement. And time was moving as slowly as the growth of crystals.

Then there was a chime—a single note that hung in the air for six thousand years while civilization rose and fell, it seemed—and the women moved closer to each other, masturbating simultaneously now, and still they did not touch, yet, until each had enjoyed one more separate delightment. Then they were upon each other—as the gong chimed again— and the dark witch-woman knelt and spread the blonde's thighs, her head between them, and the creature saw that a woman can do for a woman part of what a man does (and understood at last those rumors about certain noble ladies who, it was said, had female lovers instead of male lovers), and this also went on for a long, long time, while the creature tied in the chair watched passively but alertly, very alertly.

When the guards came and took him back to his cell, he did not tear open his fly at once (as he might have if the performance had been a few hours shorter) but lay back on his cot, soaring, still gliding through the air, tingling and happy and quite incapable of wishing to focus all this delightful energy into the mere genital explosion.

He trembled occasionally. Once or twice he moaned—as the women had moaned: in pleasure—but mostly he just floated.

It must have been about four hours before he slept, still without ejaculating.

As usual, he did not know how long he slept. Suddenly, the guards were in the room, shaking him awake, and then there was the usual quick trot down the corridor; he noted that the walls had been painted a new color (blue this time) or else that they had moved him in his sleep again and he was really in a different corridor.

They arrived in a courtyard. From the direction of the sun, he knew it was little after dawn—his first clue, in what seemed aeons, as to the "objective" time in the "real" world.

There was a scaffold in the courtyard.

He realized that he was still somewhat in the passive-excited state, floating, noticing every detail.

Another prisoner was brought into the yard, struggling, desperate, almost weeping. They trotted him quickly up the steps. A "priest"—or somebody dressed as a priest—gave the last rites. The noose was fixed, in place. The trap was sprung. The man hanged.

Sigismundo giggled. He was trying to convince himself it was all an elaborate fake—like a mountebank making a horse disappear at a fair—but he also giggled because he noticed that he had just experienced, finally, a small, slight dribble of ejaculation.

They marched him down the hall again, to the "doctor's" office.

The original Dr. Sanson was there, red beard and all, jovial and fatherly as ever.

"Well, Joseph," he said kindly, "how are we today?"

Sigismundo giggled again. "Not very steady on the feet," he said, taking his usual chair. "A bit wobbly, in fact."

"What has disturbed you, Joseph?"

"The fellow being hanged in the courtyard."

"You imagined a hanging . . . ?"

"Yes. And before that I imagined other things. There was another Dr. Sanson in this room, asking me questions about the Craft."

"The craft? What craft?"

"Forget it. How long does this go on?"

"Until you are cured, of course."

"How will you know when I am cured?"

"Oh, there are many different signs. For instance, do you still think we are trying to harm you in some way?"

"Not in the least. I am sure this is all for my own good."

The doctor frowned. "I seem to detect irony in your voice. Surely you realize that you need help. You are quite confused, are you not?"

"What makes you think I am confused?"

"But," the doctor said, "just a moment ago, you were claiming you saw a man hanging in the courtyard. Hangings do not happen in hospitals, but in prisons."

Sigismundo gave a Neapolitan shrug. "Only a fool argues with his own doctor," he said.

"Good; on that basis we can make progress. Now I will admit that I am no ordinary doctor, just as this is no ordinary hospital. We deal here not with those who are *known* to be mad, but with those who wander the world passing themselves off as perfectly sane."

"I am honored to participate in such a worthy endeavor."

"You were selected because you are a very special person."

"I know. My horoscope is extraordinary."

"Indeed. But for those of extraordinary destiny, extraordinary trials must be passed. Hercules had his twelve labors, Moses had his forty years in the wilderness, Jesus had his trial and crucifixion—"

"And I have this special 'hospital.' "

"Exactly."

"All because of my horoscope. Isn't life mysterious?"

The doctor leaned forward. "It is not just the horoscope," he said intently. "It is the special ancestry. 'The Father lives in the Son.' "

"I understand that."

"The Mother lives in the Son also."

"The alchemical marriage. Yes."

"Imagine a poor widow lady. She does not tell her son who his father was. But there are those who are pledged to help her. The son grows to manhood, not knowing who he is. There is a time when he must be told. But he must be prepared first."

"I know who my father was."

The doctor raised an eyebrow. "But I was only talking about Parcifal and the Grail."

"No you weren't. You were giving me another hint."

"Perhaps." The doctor caressed his crimson beard. "What do the three knocks represent, in the third degree initiation?"

"The Holy Trinity."

"Which symbolizes . . . ?"

"The union of male and female and the new soul that is created."

"Is a new soul created in each sexual union?"

Sigismundo laughed weirdly. "This almost makes sense," he said, becoming a bit shrill, to his own surprise. He had thought his voice was still even and under control. They're getting to me, he reflected uneasily.

"What happens to the souls that are not born as bodies?"

"Why is a duck? You must be toying with me."

"No. Think, Joseph. All the symbols have meaning. You know that. Think."

"It still sounds like 'why is a duck?' 'Because one of its legs is both the same.' Is that the answer?"

The doctor rapped three times. The medical attendants, not the three jailers dressed as Jubela, Jubelo and Julelum, entered this time.

"They will return you to your room, for meditation," the doctor said somberly. "You should ponder this: What is the literal meaning of the stone that was rejected becoming the center of the arch?"

Sigismundo was taken back to his cell.

It gets more subtle as it goes along, he told himself, but I still know that they are my enemies. They do not mean well by me.*

---

*Cf. de Selby (*Golden Hours*, IV, 57): "Mr. A. is very good at quaternions, Mr. B. can read Homeric Greek, and Mr. C. has never shown any talent except for falling off bar-stools. (These are not hypothetical, but real people I have met in Dalkey.) From the point of view of patapsychology, each of them has encountered a different type of existence, the first made up largely of mathematical symbols, the second of barbaric-heroic poetry, and the third of pints of Guinness stout; and that is all. To go further and say that one type of existence is more 'real' or 'meaningful' than another is to enter into metaphysics and depart from the empirical status to which patapsychology, as the science of encountered states, aspires." According to Ferguson (*Armageddon*, 17), Hanfkopf, whose English was never perfect anyway, owned only the first edition of *Golden Hours*, in which the word "patapsychology" is consistently misprinted as *"parapsychology,"* and this (Ferguson claims) is the entire foundation of Hanfkopf's unending assaults on de Selby and on anyone who ever said or wrote anything favorable about de Selby. O'Broichain cites O'Brien (who either knew de Selby or *was* de Selby), who in turn cites de Selby as saying the study of parapsychology "is a waste of time entirely, because this part of Ireland has enough spooks and the problem is to get rid of them, not to invoke more of them," and that "the power of electrical lights to banish teratological molecules is all the light I care to cast on that subject." Hanfkopf was also deceived, it appears, about the "spirit rapping" often heard in de Selby's Dalkey house, which appears to have been normal *hammering*, connected with the time-machine on which de Selby worked so long and fruitlessly, although (as O'Brien notes) the hammering went on for so many years that many fanciful theories about it were once current throughout County Dublin.

Twenty-One

Seamus Muadhen awoke in terror, his heart pounding wildly.

Time and space were still twisted, as in the dream; he was neither quite "in" the coachman's cottage of Babcock Manor nor "out" among the stars. He was still lost *between* space and time with the voice chanting in singsong—"Who are you?" "We are one" "When does this end?"—and Corporal Murphy was banging his rifle-butt on the bucket in the interrogation room.

Seamus sat up and concentrated on lighting a candle without dropping a match, although his hand shook.

I am James Moon, he told himself as the light came up and the room appeared solidly in ordinary space again. I am James Moon, and that poor booger Seamus Muadhen died of excessive interrogation in Dun Laoghaire over a year ago. They had done that trick with the bucket that drives the mind a-kilter and Seamus Muadhen never came back.

I am James Moon, and I am in bloody England.

But he remembered the six tarry corpses swinging in the Dublin Bay wind that whipped across Dun Laoghaire that day. He remembered himself saying, "The truth is that I just this moment joined the White Boys, Your Honor." He remembered that he had come here to murder Sir John Babcock and to do it so cleverly that he would escape and never be suspected.

Lord, he thought, we are such great fools and idiots, every man jack of us.

It was easy to hate "Sir John Babcock" when he was just a name on a deed, the owner of some properties south of

Dublin that the White Boys were fighting over. It was harder
to hate the man himself with his soft and lazy voice, his
endless curiosity about everything under the sun, and that
imbecile smile on his face (the smile of all new fathers)
when he rocked little Ursula in his arms; aye, and he was
not even aware of the contested properties in Ireland, being
so involved in politics that he left business affairs in the
hands of his solicitor. It was even hard to hate the solicitor,
Seamus had found, because that person had never been in
Ireland in his whole blessed life and had left those properties in the care of a manager—who was himself an Irishman,
even if a black Protestant Irishman.

The only thing left was to hate the bloody sheep that had
been moved onto the lands when the farmers were driven
off. That made as much sense as hating the manager, Al-
exander McLaglen, who was just trying to show a profit so
the solicitor would not replace him with a more able manager.

And it wasn't even Seamus Muadhen's fight, as he had
told the sergeant in the interrogation room. It was a farmer's
fight.

And Seamus Muadhen, the fisherboy, was dead anyway.
He was James Moon, coachman, who had been saved from
committing murder by learning so many facts that his mind
was confused and he no longer knew who or what to hate.

All that was left of Seamus Muadhen was these nightmares of the interrogation room and the crazy space between ordinary spaces.

James Moon got up from the bed and started putting his
breeches on. When the nightmares were this bad, the only
thing to do was to walk them off. Even now, with the candle
blazing and the room quite solid around him, he could feel
part of himself being pulled back toward that interrogation
room and the hallucinations of the abyss.

In a few moments he was dressed and outside the cottage, and he could see the pink pre-dawn flush in the east.
The summer solstice was near, and the nights were getting
short again. It could not be later than three. He wondered
what it would be like to live in a southern country where
the nights lasted until five or six even in the summer.
Sure, they miss half the beauty of nature and they don't
even know it.

He walked toward the stables. The smell of horses was

always refreshing; it brought you firmly back to this earth and out of the witch-world of pandemonium the bucket had imprinted on his ears and brain.

It was strange that noise alone could do such things to a man's mind. But then, music—the opposite of noise—could send you into ecstasy sometimes. And it was not just the noise, probably. It was the vibrations of his skull when the bucket was hit. The bastard who first thought of that trick must have been fathered by the devil himself.

One of the horses whinnied enquiringly.

That was Candy, the old mare. She never missed a thing.

"Quiet, girl," James called softly.

Candy whinnied again, but briefly. That was her way of saying she recognized his voice.

James wondered if O'Lachlann the shanachie could really talk to animals, or was that one of his tricks? Shanachies would teach you a great deal, if they liked you, but they always kept some mysteries. James had asked once if O'Lachlann really believed in the Gentry, or wee folk, the creatures of light who lived under the hills. "That I do not," O'Lachlann had said, "and they do not much believe in me either." What could you make of an answer like that? It was like the answer the hedge-priests gave if arrested by the English—the famous Jesuit equivocation, "I am not a priest and *if I were* I would lie to you about it." That was not, strictly interpreted, a lie, and O'Lachlann's answer, strictly interpreted, was not saying what it seemed to say either.

James smiled suddenly. Sir John was writing letters lately, to the Swedish Scientific Society and the Academy in France and other places; the Royal Scientific Society had found his rock normal and refused to discuss the matter further. Be damned, but if he took the rock to Ireland he would find a score of shanachies to believe his story, and each would have a different explanation of where it fell from.

James knew a great deal of classic literature, thanks to the shanachies, but he was aware that his ignorance of science was vast. He had no idea, himself, where the damned stone came from, but he was sure that in addition to its "natural" cause it also had a "supernatural" or spiritual cause. He had been alone with Sir John, far from witnesses, and he had realized then that he could not kill this man.

The trouble with the English, James thought, was that

they believed finding *one* cause explained something. They
did not realize there were always many causes. They had
never learned to pay attention to *coincidences,* as every
shanachie taught you to. They saw only the surface of things.
They could not imagine that the rock had fallen partly to
make James Moon face the fact that he had no real appetite
for murder. Nor could they imagine it had also fallen because the girl, Ursula Babcock, had an important destiny.
One cause explained everything, to them. They looked at
one side of the rug and did not realize the intricate design
on the other side.

James decided to turn back toward his cottage. He could
sleep now, without the nightmares coming back.

He would save his money and eventually have that shop
in Liverpool he had planned. Ireland's problems would
probably last another century or more, before any mortal
man could make a difference. If you could not save a whole
nation, at least you could make the best life possible for
yourself under the circumstances. Just last week he had read
of more White Boys being hanged, this time in the far west,
in Donegal. It would go on like that, on and on, for a long,
long time before there would be any true chance for successful rebellion in that country. Seamus Muadhen had
sworn to fight seventy years, like Brian Boru, if that were
necessary; but James Moon knew better. The average rebellion lasted six months before the English hanged all the
leaders.

And the song they sang was of Ireland free

The tune came back to him with shocking pain, like the
face of a woman who has been loved and lost. *Shan Bhan
Bhocht,** some of the shanachies called Her in their songs,
so the English would think they were mourning a dead
woman and not their own half-dead nation. "Cathleeen ni
Houlihan," "the woman shapely as a swan," sometimes
even "the fair colleen"—any code would do, to deceive the
galls; Irish listeners would know at once what the song was
really about.

The galls? James Moon had stopped thinking of them that
way, since he lived among them. It was strange to be think-

*"Poor Old Woman."

ing in Gaelic again, and to be carried away by a sentimental tune. The makers of such songs were dangerous men. Every city and town and hamlet in Ireland had had brave lads hanging from the trees, because they had been maddened by songs like that. The songs could tear the heart out of you, they were that seductive. And with those songs in your ears, Ireland was a woman to you, a woman who had been cruelly raped and beaten, and you had to rush to her defense or you could never again think yourself a man; and that was the way you ended on a rope, covered in tar, swinging in the breeze.

And the dead men knew it, Seamus Muadhen thought, forgetting all about being James Moon: the men who were hanged were not all fools. They knew it would end that way—"You will surely piss when you can not whistle, my lad," they told each other; it was a favorite joke—aye, they knew what they were doing, and what would happen, but when the music drives you mad and Ireland is a woman to you, mother and wife and daughter and all in one, you can look right at the corpses of the last rebels and know you will hang beside them, and still you will rush to your execution, knowing all along how it will end. Not because the gall landlords have made us poor; and not because they have persecuted our religion; and not because they are after driving out whole families to make grazing land for their sheep and cattle; but because She possessed you with Her beauty and Her need, because She was wise beyond mortal women and you could not let Her die, for She is more than a nation, more than an island bounded by waters: She is all that Europe no longer understands, all that the world is perishing for the lack of, all that the myths of the shanachies and the music of the harpers and the great paintings in the cathedrals are longing for and hinting of and trying to bring back into the minds of men numbed by calculations and ledgers. She was all the wild and fugitive and beautiful things that could not be put into calculations and ledgers. To love Her was madness, when the whole world could no more see Her than those fargo-bawlers of the Royal Scientific Society could measure mercy on their scales; but not to love Her was to be blind and deaf and dumb and not even know it. She was Eire, now, but She had not been born Irish. It was Ireland's misery and affliction and burden to be the last place in the world where She could be seen and heard and felt in the blood, ineluctable as thunder's hammer and lightning's shock.

Aye, they are dangerous and deadly fellows, the makers of songs. Not two minutes ago Seamus was ready to settle for a shop in Liverpool and now he was again thinking of throwing his life away for Her, for "Dark Rosaline," for a myth, a metaphor, a *figure of speech,* as the calculators and ledgerkeepers would say. Gone, gone and by the wind mourned . . .

But She was not a myth or a metaphor. She was the dark river Anna Liffey dancing and prancing through the green Wicklow hills and rushing through Dublin like a new song each morning; She was the Shannon glittering more turquoise than green, and the giant waves like sea-hags leaping in Dingle Bay; She was the land, not as calculators measured it on their maps but the living mother who teaches shanachies to sing and incites the beasts and birds, and men and women, to mate and recreate life out of life. And the men who rose with Silken Thomas FitzGerald two hundred years ago had known their cause was hopeless, doomed in advance, as Seamus knew that the White Boys and Heart of Oak Boys and all the others fighting today were doomed and hopeless. But you could not remember death and defeat waiting for you down the road, when Her songs called to you: you followed the songs, because you were mad with the love of Her.

The Poor Old Woman. A figure of speech. An idea no more substantial than swamp gas. It was thinking like that, as if a poem were more real than a high gallows and thick hemp rope, that made all Europe say the Irish were mad entirely.

Venerandum, Seamus thought. That fellow knew how to swing the bloody Latin, he did; no Gaelic bard could teach him anything. *Venerandum:* the strongest declension of the adjective: in English you would have to say it in many words. She-who-must-be-venerated. No: more like She Who Must Be Adored. Dark Rosaline, Isis, Venus: She had a thousand names once, but now She was the exclusive possession of the Irish because all the world else had forgotten her. Even the simplest country folk in Ireland said on meeting, "God and Mary and Patrick and Brigit be with you," not knowing they were using two of Her names in that greeting. She was in every mouth that spoke Irish whether they knew they were calling on Her or not.

And now more verse ran through his head: *I am Ireland and great is my pride* . . . . In poverty, in filth, in ignorance, as a conquered province of a great and foreign Empire, half-dead and dying more every day, we can still say it and mean it. Great is my pride. They have stolen our wealth and taken our lands and beaten us in every battle, but they have only the surface of things and we have the living soul.*

"And would you die for me?"

The voice was so startling that James Moon jumped, thinking he was hallucinating again. But it was not Dark Rosaline; it was a human woman and he recognized the voice as soon as his hair stopped standing on end. It was Lady Babcock.

"Procure me a pistol from the stable," said Sir John's voice, "and I will prove it at once."

James hardly dared to move for a moment. It was unethical to eavesdrop, of course, but it was embarrassing to stumble upon one's employers as if one *had* been eavesdropping. He tried to place their voices exactly, before moving quietly away from them.

"I was only teasing," Lady Babcock said. "But I am not perfectly convinced, sir, that you are not mad enough to do it."**

---

*Nothing could be more typically American than Hamburger's claim that de Selby *must* be O'Brien because "De Selby is not an Irish name." Actually, in addition to two de Selbys the Dublin phone book lists several de Barras, de Burghs (from whom Edmund Burke was sprung), de Brits, de Bruins, de Courcys, de Lacys, de Lasas, de Loughrys, de Paors, de Veres, etc., all the spawn of the Norman invasion of August 23, 1170, which also brought in the FitzGeralds, FitzMaurices, and dozens of other Fitzes all over Ireland. But don't forget Bill Patterson at Penn Square Bank with his Mickey Mouse ears: banks can legally loan eight times more than they have on deposit, thereby creating money out of nothing, but many of them loan much more than that when they think the controllers aren't looking.

**The hammering that went on so persistently during the seventeen years that de Selby worked on his time machine has baffled commentators. Ferguson claims that "although gifted mathematically, the sage of Dalkey was too clumsy to be a talented experimentalist" and that de Selby had trouble driving the nails in the wooden box that held the "teratological neuro-galvanizer"; but La Puta claims that the hammering was a blind to deceive curious neighbors about the actual workings of the

They were walking in the labyrinth—the hedges designed
as an amusing puzzle—and hence they could not see James.
He started backing away slowly.

"God, is not the dawn a lovely sight," Sir John said.
"The rosy-fingered dawn. *Rhododaktylos eos,* as Homer
said."

"I am glad we took this stroll," Lady Babcock said. "But
it is probably time for sleep now. Unless . . ."

"It is quite impossible," Sir John said.

My mother, sainted though she be, brought forth one
scoundrel son, James Moon thought. He stopped backing
away. The temptation was irresistible.

"But, my love," Lady Babcock said, "when you have
given me such pleasure, I wish I could . . ."

"Men are capable of fewer enjoyments than women.
Nature ordained it," Sir John said, sounding vaguely
guilty.

They had been making love all night, Seamus Muadhen
thought, and the lady was well-pleased but the gentleman
could not please himself.

"I would be happy to . . ." Lady Babcock evidently con-
veyed the rest of her meaning with a glance.

Shame came over James Moon again. He could listen to
no more of these intimacies without feeling himself a total
swine.

He backed away more rapidly, being as silent as possible.

Ah, well, he thought, all of us have that problem once in
a while. But it was, in the name of God, a terrible embarrassment to know it about another man, when he is your
employer.

I will forget this, he told himself. I will banish it from
my mind entirely. Every servant learns such things occa-

device. De Selby's own remark (to O'Brien) that "hammering is anything
but what it appears to be" has not been helpful and grows (in fact) more
inscrutable the longer one contemplates it. The alleged appearances of
de Selby at the storming of the Bastille, in ancient Rome, etc., adduced
by the credulous O'Broichain, are inconclusive and implausible. Hanfkopf of course remains convinced that what was involved was "spirit
rapping," and adduces this as proof of the "mental collapse of the mystic"; but he never found out that de Selby was a patapsychologist, not a
parapsychologist.

sionally. One can keep the knowledge out of one's eyes and voice.

And one could forget all about the Poor Old Woman and all those lovely, autochthonous songs that send lads out to get themselves hanged.

Twenty-Two

Sigismundo or Joseph—the creature who was buried alive—was wakened by a blue light.

He hadn't heard the cell door open but there was a man in the corner, with a hammer in his hand and a strange machine before him. And a strange-looking man he was: he wore neither the bright-colored silks of the nobility nor the dark rags of the poor. He was wearing midnight blue, and his jacket was almost as short as his shirt (which was light blue); his breeches did not stop at the knees but fell all the way to the floor. And he was wearing neither boots nor sabots but bizarre things that seemed to be of leather, like boots, but were ridiculously short and reached from the floor only to his ankles. When he spoke it was in English and with a peculiar intonation Sigismundo had heard only once before, when he met Edmund Burke in London: a brogue, that was called.

"Quick, man, what year is it?"

Not that again, Sigismundo thought.

"I am still convinced," he said firmly, "that this is 1772, or 1773 at the most. It is not 1814."

The man looked at him oddly. "Be damned," he said, "are you a *traveler*, too?"

"Not lately," Sigismundo said. "Your friends won't let me go."

"My friends?" The man seemed puzzled.

"What sort of game is it this time?"

"Faith," the stranger exclaimed, "you know my friends but you don't know what year it is, and you claim you are not a *traveler?*"

"When do you get around to the widow's son?"

The man hesitated. Then he pulled himself together and announced in a stentorian voice. "I am an Angel of the Lord."

"Of course."

"I am an Angel of the Lord," the man repeated sternly, "and you will tell nobody of this encounter, not even your confessor."

"At least this is a new routine."

"Silence, blasphemer! I come in the name of God and you must answer my questions, and devil a joke or sarcasm I will be taking from the likes of you!"

"You do that awfully well. It might work at a fair in Rouen."

"First question," the man said, ignoring this. "Have you ever seen a dragon?"

"No."

"A unicorn?"

"No."

"People with goat hooves or goat horns?"

"Of course not."

"Have you ever seen anything strange in a darkened room?"

"Once I thought I saw crocodiles. I was young then."

"Crocodiles? In Paris? Just as I suspected . . ."

"Not in Paris. In Napoli."

"You are Italian, *Signor?"*

"You know who I am."

"Be damned to that. All I know is you're the strangest coot I've ever interviewed."*

"When do they bring in the naked women again? Or will it be another hanging?"

The man was now doing a good imitation of confusion and anxiety. "Ah, sure, now," he said vaguely, "this would not be a . . . hospital . . . of some sort, would it?"

"That's what they keep telling me."

"Bejáysus, I set the controls wrong again!"

"I thought angels didn't make any mistakes."

"Ah, faith, you don't want to believe everything I say when I have a few jars on me, do you know that way of

---

*Contrary to the general impression, the whale is not a fish; it is a symbol of divine inscrutability.

it?'' The man pondered and then said, "It would not be the
wisest thing to be after telling the doctors all about this.
They might think you had taken a turn for the worse, if you
get my drift. I don't want to be causing any trouble on my
travels. Ah, *orra*, it might be the best thing to just forget
all about this. Do you know that way? I mean, just *forget*
about it entirely.''

"I'll file it under It Never Happened."

"Good man yourself! Well, I must be off now . . . check
the neuro-interossiters, don't you know . . .'' The man
made some adjustments on his machine.

Nothing happened.

He made some more adjustments.

Still, nothing happened.

The man waved his hammer wildly and began pounding
on the side of the machine. "Be damned to you, sir. I designed you, sir. You bloody well will work, sir.''

Amid loud hammering the machine and the man slowly
rose from the floor and ascended to the ceiling.

Sigismundo watched, entranced, as the range duo ascended right through the ceiling and disappeared. The sound
of hammering continued from above and then shifted quickly
to the east and faded away.

I'll never figure out how they managed that one, Sigismundo thought, but it is certainly a lot classier than the
upside down room.

It must be the drugs they are always putting in my food.

Next it will be little green men with egg in their beards.

The same night, James Moon had an equally astounding
experience.

Sir John had been at the House of Commons until quite
late; he announced that he would be staying at his club in
London. James was given the night off and would pick Sir
John up in the coach at seven in the morning.

James tried a few pubs first and then went down to the
East End and found Madame Rosa's. There was a new girl
there, with a Liverpool Irish accent, and she as young and
sweet as a fresh rose with the dew still on it, and it was so
grand and wonderful entirely that he wrote her a short poem
in Gaelic and left it with the two shillings, and staggered
out into the night feeling for all the world like the Sultan of
Turkey himself.

And then he sat down in the doorway and lowered his head, pretending to be blind, falling-down, stinking drunk.

Yes: the man who walked past, all in fine green velvet and with a blue cape, like Boswell himself was Sir John Babcock.

Bejesus.

James did not raise his head even an inch until Sir John's footsteps died away in the distance.

It could not be true. You could recognize that type: they all had high, effeminate voices and moved their hands in exquisite, artificial gestures.

James went back inside Madame Rosa's.

"God's nightshirt," Madame Rosa said. "It *is* true what they say about you Irish! Twice in one night?"

James grinned. "Faith, it is the same night, woman?"

"You jest with me. You are not drunk, fellow."

"Tell me," he said. "The house next door—is it what the sailors say?"

Madame Rosa sized him up again. "It is not the place for a lad such as I thought you were," she said bluntly.

"It is for sodomists then? It has boys for men who like boys that way?"

"Twice in one night," she said, rolling her eyes heavenward. "And a change of flavor in the middle of it."

"I am not that sort," James said, flushing. "I just wondered about the gent I saw coming out of there."

"You would be wise not to wonder about what *gents* do, a fellow of your class," Madame Rosa said. "You might end up floating in the Thames."

Seamus, back on the street, looked at the house next door. I thought you could recognize *them*, he told himself. I didn't know they married and had families and sat with their daughters in their laps, chortling over them just like normal men. I didn't think they made noble speeches in Commons about the rights of the Irish and the American colonists.

The shop in Liverpool suddenly seemed very close. Sir John was the sort who would pay; he would not arrange for Seamus to be clubbed and dumped in the Thames.

My God, Seamus thought, am I really that sort of blackguard?

You don't know who or what you are until you are tested, he remembered. He had learned that in the interrogation room and alone with Sir John in the dark on the night the thunderstone fell.

But, he thought, can I be the brave fellow who kept his mouth shut through the torture and the poet who hears the Lady's voice in every brook and birdsong and also the villain who gets rich by blackmail? Can I?

Ah, Dark Rosaline, the woman shapely as a swan, you will turn your back on me entirely and I will hear no more tunes of glory.

But I will have money. I will be master of my fate.

Twenty-Three

Before Abraham was, I am."

Yes, Joseph thought, *of course.*

"I am yesterday, today, and the brother of tomorrow."

Yes.

"I am you. We are one. The Living One."

You are talking to yourself again, you fool.

"No, I am talking to my other self. My real self."

He heard footsteps. They were coming for him again. I wonder what it will be this time, he thought wearily.

It was two Neapolitans: he could recognize them from their complexions, their style of clothing, everything about them.

"Are you Sigismundo Celine?" the taller one asked him at once, looking concerned.

Joseph had to think about it. "In a manner of speaking," he said carefully, "according to certain conventions, yes, I think I am. But I am also Joseph. There are two of us, you know."

"Thank God," the tall Neapolitan said. "We have been searching for months."

They lifted Joseph from the bunk, gently. "Can you walk?" the tall Neapolitan asked sympathetically, or with a good pretense of sympathy.

"Yes," Joseph said impatiently. "What is the game this time?"

"We have come to rescue you. Your Uncle Pietro sent us," the shorter, sandy-haired one said.

Uncle Pietro! At the name, Joseph felt a wave of helpless longing—he saw Uncle Pietro's face, and Mama's face, and

Papa Guido's face, and the house in which he had grown up, and the bay at the bottom of the hill, and the apple trees in bloom, and twenty years of Napoli and music and being the star pupil at Sacred Heart College—and then a sudden panic, because that was not his life, it was Sigismundo's life, and being Sigismundo again was a dangerous business. It was safer to be Joseph. People were always trying to kill Sigismundo, or drive him mad, or generally vex him.

"When we get outside," he asked craftily, "do I find another man hanging from the gallows? Or do you just hit me with a bladder while the whole crowd laughs? I mean, is it a gothic novel or a circus or what, this time?"

The two men exchanged uncertain glances, or glances that skillfully aped uncertainty.

"They must have given you a hellish time," the tall one said after a moment. He had a moustache and laugh-wrinkles around his eyes and was older than the other one: noting these details Sigismundo realized that he hadn't looked at anyone closely for a long time. He had been shutting himself off in his own head, closing out the insane world around him. "I can understand your doubts and confusions at this time," the tall man went on. "Let me reassure you." He pressed Sigismundo's hand and made the grip of the fourth degree.

Sigismundo knew that at each initiation, from the first degree onward, a Freemason swore most solemnly never to betray or harm a Brother in the Craft. He knew also that he had considerable doubts lately about French Masons and their Grand Master, the Duc de Chartres. But he reminded himself that the state of mind in which you see betrayal everywhere was an illness, and that it had killed his cousin Antonio.

"I thank you," he said. "I am sure that my uncle will see that you are well rewarded."

"Come," the sandy one said. "Let us get you out in the fresh air. It will revive you."

Sigismundo accompanied them down the hall to a room he hardly recognized: probably, he thought, it was the room of the Inquisitors with a few changes in furniture. They stepped out into a courtyard.

The sky was a brilliant blue, painful to his dungeoned eyes, and in a green tree a little, red-chested, brown bird sang merrily, as if he had never been told there were hawks in the world. There was an oaken table built around the tree and on it was a yellow clay pitcher decorated with a rose imprint. The cobbles looked half as old as Rome; and from far off there came the angry liquid sound of a rooster's braggadocio.

I am drinking impressions as a parched man drinks water, Sigismundo thought: it was as if each object had been illuminated from within, and he remembered his wild, irrational, but ineluctable sense of invulnerable immortality on the morning of the duel with Carlo Maldonado.

"Where are *they*—my captors?" he asked warily.

"Some are being held by our friends, downstairs. Others were killed in the fight," said the tall Neapolitan.

"How did you find me?"

"We were searching the countryside north of the Bastille. This villa was supposed to be deserted, but we saw lights and got curious."

The sandy blondish man fetched water from the well. "Here," he said, offering the bucket in gnarled ex-peasant's fingers. "You probably need this."

Sigismundo drank a pure deliciousness, sweet as a fresh apple, and reminded himself to be sly. This was probably just another masque, but they had grown accustomed to his skepticism. It would be interesting to see what they would do if he pretended, this time, that he was capable of believing that a human being was what he seemed to be, or that those who acted like friends really were friends.

A door to the opposite wing of the villa, across the courtyard, opened. A man crossed the garden rapidly and trod on the cobbles, beginning to smile in welcome. He was extremely well dressed in the cornflower-blue silk that was fashionable, with gold brocade, and had all the jewels and accessories of a noble. He was tall, hawk-nosed, and very dark. The last time Sigismundo had seen him he was dressed as a carnival mountebank.

Dippel von Frankenstein.

Or, rather, the man who in Napoli in 1764 had pretended to be Frankenstein. The real Frankenstein had died thirty years earlier in 1734.

Unless, of course, he had only pretended to die then and was still walking around, like the legendary creature the Bavarians claimed he had made by means of Black Magic.

Here we go again, Sigismundo thought.

Frankenstein, smiling inscrutably—but then all mountebanks smiled inscrutably—extended his hand. Sigismundo took it and was not surprised when the grip of the fourth degree was formed.

"I am glad we were able to save you from these *cowans*," Frankenstein said. "Greetings on all three points of the triangle."

"Thank you," Sigismundo said politely. "I am supposed to believe you and your friends are my protectors, and you are not another part of the gang that has been holding me captive all along, is that it?"

Frankenstein gave him a shrewd glance from dark, sympathetic eyes, or from dark eyes that imitated sympathy. "You have been ill," he said. "Perhaps you will need to recuperate."

"It is true," Sigismundo said. "I have been in a room where gravity is reversed. I traveled across space and time and returned to Napoli six years ago. I have been in a hospital in London forty years in the future. I talked to a man in strange clothes who flew away through a solid ceiling. I need somebody older and less nervous, such as yourself, to tell me what is real and not real."

"They were heartless villains who did this to you," Frankenstein said, putting sadness in his voice. "Men without mercy or the love of God in their souls."

Sigismundo looked him straight in the eye. "You describe them accurately," he said mildly. "But tell me, when do we leave these walls and return to the normal world?"

"In a few moments," Frankenstein said quickly. "There is much that I must explain to you. I fear that you still do not trust me."

"I will listen to what you have to say. It does not appear that I have much choice."

"Sit down," Frankenstein said, motioning toward the table. He turned to the tall Neapolitan: "Get him some cheese and wine from my traveling bag."

Sigismundo sat, looking at this man who would be ninety-nine if he were the real Frankenstein. He did not appear any different than in Napoli eight years ago: he might be two or three years on either side of thirty. But his face had the same attentive serenity as old Abraham Orfali: as if he had forgotten how to desire or fear or prefer one thing to another. Uncle Pietro increasingly had that look in recent years, and

Sigismundo thought of it as the result of many decades of working with the mind-sciences of the higher degrees of the Craft.

"You might start," he said carefully, "by telling me who you really are."

Frankenstein gestured impatiently. "You would not believe me, and I have more important news. It is time for you to learn who *you* really are."

"The man who will shake the earth? The one foretold in the stars? Is it that again?"

The tall Neapolitan brought the cheese and wine. He put it on the table with a look of what seemed genuine concern as he registered the suspicion in Sigismundo's tone.

Sigismundo took a swig from the winesack, ignoring the cheese. The wine was dry and almost sour to his Neapolitan palate, which meant it was probably the sort of thing the French nobles liked.

"It is more than a matter of the stars," Frankenstein said softly, perching on a corner of the table and hacking at the cheese with a *banditto*-style dagger. "Do you know who the Malatesta really are?"

"We came out of nowhere in the ninth century," Sigismundo said, drinking again. "No historian ever heard of us before that. For some reason, Charlemagne made us rulers of what are now the northern Italian states."

"Charlemagne had a reason. You have heard the legend."

Joseph answered him; it was becoming uncomfortable being Sigismundo again. "We are allegedly descended from the French royal family. The old one. The Merovingians. The ones who came out of the ocean." Joseph smiled cynically, and took another drink. Being drunk might not be the best defense, but it was *a* defense. Maybe I have discovered a Great Principle, he thought: Stay Drunk All The Time. How to deal with a barbaric, Machiavellian planet. He quickly drank again, applying the idea.

"Charlemagne had a reason," Frankenstein repeated. "There is another version of the legend. You have heard it."

"The Merovingians came from the stars. Is that what you mean?" Joseph drank again. Might as well relax and enjoy the sun and the sky, before they put me back in the dungeon again.

"Yes," Frankenstein said simply. "From another planet, far away."

There was a silence. He knows how to milk a moment for the drama, Joseph thought.

"I was terribly shocked when I found out I was part Sicilian," he said finally. "Now are you telling me I am part *something else?*"

"What does Genesis say about the sons of God and the daughters of men?" Frankenstein munched some cheese, as if they were talking about the price of cows in the market of Rouen.

Sigismundo drank again; he wasn't sure Joseph could handle this. "I believe there was a certain amount of carnal knowledge involved," he said. "Most people are just people, you are saying, but some of us are, ah, more than that? This gets better and better."

"What do you feel when you look at the stars at night?" Frankenstein asked.

"The same as anybody else. Feelings that I cannot put into words."

"Not the same as anybody else. Try putting it into words."

"I feel," Sigismundo said, "something powerful and urgent, and a sense of absurd desire. I have tried putting it into my music, but I know I have failed."

"What is the desire that seems absurd?"

Sigismundo drank again, deeply. He looked at the little brown bird, so fragile, but not more fragile than himself. "I feel invulnerable and detached. I want to feel that way all the time. I don't want to come back to my messy little life and the petty little problems of this stupid, violent little world."

"You think all people feel that?"

"All with enough education to understand what the stars are, and how *contingent* this little planet is."

Frankenstein laughed. "Few feel that as you do; few even have the concept of contingency. Those who feel that special cosmic yearning are those whose ancestors came from the stars originally."

"I see," Sigismundo said, finishing the bottle and realizing that he did not need to hide behind "Joseph" anymore. "Naturally, that is why we have been kings and princes in so many lands, right? We have the right to treat the rest of humanity as dirt beneath our feet. I know this scene. You take me to a mountaintop soon and show me all the kingdoms of the Earth waiting to be ruled by me.''

Frankenstein waved that aside tiredly. ''They have to be ruled by *someone,*'' he said simply. ''There must be an Emperor of the World, eventually. One who can say to each and every local prince, 'Thou shalt not arm, thou shalt not make war on thy neighbor, thou shalt not disturb the peace,' and make it stick. Do you see any other end to the international anarchy of our feuding nation-states?''

''I am not interested in power. I am interested in art. And science.'' Sigismundo remembered his *autokinoton*—his carriage-without-horses—for the first time in over a year; someday he would make that damned contraption work.

''That is another sign that you are the elected one. Anybody who *is* interested in power is not to be trusted.''

''That is quick and apt and almost convincing. You must have been rehearsing this scene for years.''

''You had the *baraka* all your life,'' Frankenstein said. ''That is the first sign of the star-seed. Even when it appears in those whose genealogy is unknown, it always means relation to the Tree, as we call it: the royal blood. Do you really think all men are as brave as you, as intelligent as you? Have you been completely seduced by democratic sentimentality, just because you liked the Whigs you met in England?''

Sigismundo shook the empty winecask, hoping somebody would take the hint. ''I am not very brave: I cry easily. I am just good at killing men who are trying to kill me, but that is because I was well trained by my fencing teacher. As for intelligence, my Uncle Pietro is wise: I am only clever.''

''Everything you say proves our intuition has been right all along. Few men know themselves as you do; most live in a myth and grow violently angry if anyone dares to tell them the truth about themselves. You have the humility to see yourself objectively.''

''And when I use the pissing conduit it smells of roses for three hours after. Don't lay it on too thick.''

''Stop shaking that winesack and trying to convince me

you are a drunkard. You are not the first to be abashed when your destiny beckons.''

"My destiny is music, and some mechanical devices maybe. I know nothing about politics and care less. It seems to me the art of herding people like cattle.''

"Do you want to see this planet governed by fools and knaves forever?''

"Who else would want to govern it? I just want to escape it and do my own work. Once or twice a week I will promise you to sit quietly and wonder why every hermeticist and alchemist and mountebank in Europe wants to recruit me for his own favorite conspiracy.''

Frankenstein waited a moment, saying nothing. That always gets the attention of the victim, Sigismundo thought.

"Some do not want to recruit you,'' Frankenstein said finally, "and you have reason to know that well. Some want you off the board entirely. To them, you are a pawn that does not fit their strategy.''

"I know. Some want me dead, and some are satisfied if I am just buried alive, and you represent the nice, friendly crowd that merely wants to overthrow every government on the planet and make me the Universal Emperor. Why won't any of you just agree to leave me alone if I agree to pay you the same courtesy?''

"Because of all those with the blood, you are the one marked by the stars in this generation. And because we have watched you, and seen that your behavior confirms the stars.''

"You would make a better Emperor than me. You have the outstanding quality a politician needs: absolute inability to hear anybody saying 'No' to you.''

"I am merely a friend of the widow's son, a guardian of the blood. I do not have the blood myself.''

"Very bluntly and simply, may I ask if I am still a prisoner?''

"You may leave at any time you wish.''

Sigismundo arose and walked toward the gate, knowing what to expect.

"Wait,'' Frankenstein said, only raising his voice slightly.

I knew it, Sigismundo thought. Back to the dungeon.

"I will show you all the evidence after a short trip,''

Frankenstein said earnestly. "The treasure that the Knights Templar found in the Temple of Solomon the King—all the books and documents that were hidden when the Black Sorcerers took control of Rome and the Gnostics had to go underground. But if I judge you correctly, you have guessed the secret for yourself by now. Am I right?"

"Perhaps." Sigismundo stood by the gate, not moving back toward the tree-table.

"Who is the bridegroom in the Alchemical Marriage of Christian Rosycross?"

"It can only be Christ himself. Of course. The best place to hide something is right out in the open, because nobody looks there."

"And the bride? The widow, after the crucifixion?"

"It can only be Mary Magdalene."

"And the widow's son—the one who survived the crucifixion and brought the *gnosis* to Europe?"

"Their son. Merovée. The first Merovingian. My ancestor. No wonder historians are confused and say he was more priest than king."

"The legend that he was half-fish means . . . ?"

"It is a code. The fish is a symbol of Christ."

Frankenstein smiled. "I congratulate you. You have broken through seventeen hundred years of lies and false teaching."

"It was right out in the open all the time, as I said." Sigismundo stayed by the gate. "Even in the forged gospels the Roman conspirators dumped on us, he is called *rabbi* many times. No man could be a rabbi in Orthodox Judaism who wasn't married. The Church forgot to cut out that word 'rabbi' because they didn't know enough about Jewish law to realize it was a giveaway."*

"We have the real gospels," Frankenstein said. "By James, the brother of Jesus, and Jude, his other brother, and the one by Magdalene, his wife. And the other documents the Templars found. They have been hidden in the vicinity of Montségur since the Templars were smashed."

"You will let me see them?"

*See W. E. Phipps, *Was Jesus Married?*, New York, 1970; and *Holy Blood, Holy Grail*, op cit., pp. 301, passim.

"Whatever your ultimate decision, no man living has more right to see them."

Sigismundo took a step back into the yard.

"Well . . . ," he said.

Twenty-Four

From THE GOSPEL ACCORDING TO MARY MAGDA-LENE:

These are the words which the Living Jesus spoke and I, Mary, his spouse, wrote down.

And whosoever finds the meaning of these words shall find the Living One.

He said: When you remember well, you will know that you are children of one father and one mother. But if you do not remember, you are in poverty; yea, you are poverty.

The first shall become last, and the last shall become first; they shall be a single one. When you see the first and the last, you will have no doubt: it is like seeing your own face in a glass.

He said: The seed was scattered on many worlds. Some seeds were on rocky worlds and did not sprout. Some seeds were on sandy worlds and did not bear fruit. Some seeds were consumed by the flame. Some seeds became the Living One. Who has ears, they shall hear. Smash the old laws and wake from the Lie that all men believe.

And he said: These words are simple, but they shall set the world on fire. I have started the fire, but the woman, my spouse, shall bring forth the bread.

He said: That which is in the sky is that which is in the earth. That which is in the sun is that which is in the moon. When face beholds face reflected, it is in balance, and the Living One comes forth.

He said: The heavens that men see shall pass away, and the heavens that they do not see shall pass away, but the Living One is life and does not become death. There is that which does not die, but you cannot hold it in a tight fist.

He said: You were in the light, you were the light, you were one. Now you have become two, and can reflect the light unendingly, but you think you are in darkness.

And he said: Tell me what I am like.
And Peter said: You are like a flaming angel. And Matthew said: You are like a mother who loves her children. And his twin brother Jude said: I dare not speak the words to say what you are like, Master.
Jesus said: I am not your Master. You have drunk too much. You are drunk and talk like a fool.
And he took Jude aside and spoke to him in secret.
And the others asked what Jesus had said; but Jude answered: If I repeated it, you would take up stones and kill me.

Jesus said: If you fast, you will create great evils. If you pray, you will be cursed. If you obey the law, you will lose your souls.
But act from the light within and you will do well. Heal the sick, console the dying, make jokes in the face of the wise, and teach only one thing: the Kingdom of Heaven is here and now. Smash, smash the old laws and wake from the Lie that all men believe.

He said: I will give you what eye has never seen and it will consume you. You will burn in it.

Peter asked: What shall be the end?
Jesus answered: Have you discovered the beginning, that you may comprehend the ending? Where the beginning was, there the end shall be.

I said to Jesus: What are the disciples like?
He said: They are like children who play at war. They fall down and play dead; they rise up and play life again. But they have not died nor lived. But you, beloved, have died in making life out of life, so you are truly alive.
He said: It is right in front of their noses, but they do not see it. Their mothers gave it to them at birth, but they have misplaced it. It is louder than thunder, but they do not hear it. They are all drunk in this world; even the ones who do not drink, they are drunk still.
And he said: Life is real only to the man or woman who is real. The rest is dreams and drunken ravings.

The way out is by means of the door. But they dig tunnels and burrow deeper into darkness.

Jesus said: My soul is full of pity because they are too drunk to see the beginning and the end.

He said: If the spirit gave birth to the flesh, that surely was a miracle, was it not? Or if the flesh gave birth to the spirit, that was a miracle of miracles, was it not? Can an apple become a plum, or life become death?

I am astounded that such great wealth has come here to live in poverty. The Kingdom of Heaven is before you: wake, wake from the Lie that all men believe.

He said: What you thought yesterday is what you are today. A drunken man lay in straw and dreamed he was in an emperor's bed: was his error unusual? I say it was most usual in this world. Who has ears, they shall hear.

He said: The criminals who are not caught cast stones at the criminals who are caught. The ordinary mind breeds nothing but criminals: it is like a dream: yea, it is dreaming.

And he said: When the two become one, they shall say to the mountain: ''Be moved,'' and it will move.

Matthew asked: When will the new world come?

He said: It has already happened but you were looking the other way. Your cellar is full of gold but you are seeking among the cobwebs in the attic.

And he said: A certain landlord took his money and bought many new fields and bought seed also and sent his workers to plant the seed. And he planned to have abundant harvests and become rich. That night he died. Who has ears, let them hear.

Salome asked: How shall I know the Living One?

He answered her, saying: The Living One is full of light. Those who are divided, they are full of darkness.

I tell the mysteries to those who are ready. Let not your left hand know what your right hand is doing.

And he said: Two will lie down in one bed. One will become a corpse, the other will live.

He said: It is easy to be a criminal. In this world, it is very hard work to be human.

They are drunk, and they do no work, and they are all criminals.

If you try to wake them or sober them, they will be terrified, and they will try to kill you. Be as gentle as doves and as subtle as serpents.

Peter asked: Who sent thee?

Jesus answered him and said: The cornerstone that the builders rejected is the place from which I came. The gate that is not a gate is the source of the Living One.

A man said to him: Tell my brothers to divide my father's possessions with me.

Jesus said: I am not a divider.

And he said to the disciples: Do you think I came here to make divisions? I came here to sober the drunks, and wake the sleepwalkers, and rehabilitate the criminals.

He said: There is more violence in the ordinary mind than in a twenty-year civil war. They are all drunks fighting in a tavern. They all cry "Fool, fool!" and plan murderous revenges in private.

Many stand at the door but only the bridegroom enters the bridal chamber.

I tell you that he who says, "Fool, fool!" is already a murderer.

And he said: They do not see the Living One because they are in a fever. They do not hear because they are asleep.

Jesus said: I have come to put an end to revenge. They who see the next thing, and the thing after that, their quarrels cease at once.

He said: Be silent, and listen to the inner voice. Then silence even the inner voice. The Living One will come forth, and the bride will join the bridegroom.

Great wealth and the Living One are here now, amid the wars and poverty. The Garden of Eden is not around the next corner, and Heaven is not the day after tomorrow. Who has ears, let them hear.

Jesus said: A man thought, "My neighbor has wronged me," so he killed him. Another thought, "My neighbor has wronged me," so he slandered him. A third thought, "My neighbor has wronged me," so he robbed him. Are these unusual or remarkable thoughts? They are not unusual or remarkable.

The ordinary mind, drunk with passion, creates all the violence in the world. Judge not and there will be an end to violence.

He said: If you can see heaven in a mustard seed, then you can be said to know heaven. If you can see what is going on around you for an hour, then you can be said to have entered eternity.

It is so vast that you cannot climb over it. It is so deep that you cannot crawl under it. It is closer to you than your pulse; it is more intimate than your blood.

And He said: I see infinite knots, yes, but I see also that there is only one string.

There is one flesh and one mind; one light, and many reflections.

A city that is on a mountain, is that hidden? Does any man light a lamp and conceal it under a bushel?

He said: If you ask your mother for bread, will she give you a stone? If you ask her for light, will it be denied?

The desires of the human heart were not put there without reason.

Peter asked: When shall you reveal to us the mysteries you have only told to Mary, your spouse, and Jude, your brother?

Jesus said: When you take off your clothes without being ashamed, you will know the Living One; you will see the unborn and the undying. You will not need me to tell you.

Smash, smash, smash all the old laws and wake from the Lie that all men believe.

He said: Beware of false prophets. They are wolves disguised as sheep. They have made themselves eunuchs for the Kingdom's sake, but they do not know the Kingdom, nor does the Kingdom know them.

He said: Take in the bitch that moans at your door and care for her puppies. Then the Kingdom is within your house.

Pass by praise and blame as a horseman passes a village at night. Then the Kingdom will never leave you.

He said: Who rejects me shall be forgiven. Who rejects prophets and sages shall be forgiven. Who rejects *Sophia*, the Mother, shall not be forgiven in all the eternities.

Peter asked: Are you the Living One?

He said: I am the One. I am the All. Before Abraham was, I am. Cleave a piece of wood and I am in the middle of it. Lift up a stone, and I am there. Empty a bucket and you pour me on the ground.

He or she who understands these words will repeat them and not lie in so speaking.

He said: There is long memory and short memory. I have come to teach long memory.

When you find the world, you will find the body; and when you find the body, the world will hate you.

Jesus said: Who can say No to others is strong. Who can say No to himself is wise.

And he said: The foxes have their holes and the birds have their nests, but the Living One does not stop and rest.

He said: The Kingdom is like a woman who has taken a seed and made a loaf of bread.

He said: You have become what you thought. All good and evil in the world began as thoughts.

There is no angry thought that does not bring forth violence sooner or later.

The disciples said: Come, it is time to pray and fast.

He said: What sin have I committed, that I should pray and fast? When the groom comes out of the bridal chamber, the guests celebrate; they do not pray and fast.

And he said: If you know your true mother, the world will call you the son of a whore.

Our Kingdom is not of this world. We are in the world, but our home is in the stars.

Jesus said: These words shall not be understood until the male becomes female and the female becomes male.

He said: The angry man lives in an angry world. The sad man lives in a sad world. The Living One lives in eternity.

He said: The Kingdom is in the sky but is also in the earth. If it were in the sky only, the birds would get there before you. If it were in the earth only, the worms would get there before you. The Kingdom is within you.

Jesus said: The drunken man looks everywhere for the key that is in his pocket. The dreamer sees dragons and monsters but does not see the room in which he dreams. The ordinary mind is so impoverished that it is no mind at all.

They all hate one another, because they have not known themselves. They hate one another, because they all believe the same Lie that all men believe.

Peter said: Let Mary go out from among us, for women are not worthy to sit here.

He said: I have taught you the mysteries and you heard them not. I have put the food in your mouth and you will not chew.

Jesus said: You cannot drink the ocean up in one gulp. You cannot walk to Egypt in one day. Do you think you will understand the Living One without effort?

He said to his disciples: They are planning to kill me. Are you afraid?

Peter said: I am sore afraid. Matthew said: What will become of us? And all muttered and were downcast.

Jesus said: What is of the world, the world can kill. What is not of the world, the world cannot kill. I am not of this world.

After the crucifixion, Peter went to Jude, the twin brother of Jesus, and asked: What shall we do?

And Jude said: It has been done. Lazarus has done it. He has protected the widow and the widow's son. They are gone where Caesar and his great armies shall not find them.

They are in the world, but the world does not know them.

Many shall have the Cross, and bow down and worship it, but only the wise shall find the Living One.

PART FOUR

The Thing with Feathers

△

Emily Dickinson was wrong: hope is not the thing with feathers. The thing with feathers is my cousin. We're sending him to a specialist in Vienna.

—Woody Allen, *Getting Even*

Harry: I've had a team working on this over and over the past few weeks, and what we've come up with can be reduced to two fundamental concepts . . . One . . . people are not wearing enough hats. Two . . . matter is energy; in the Universe there are many energy fields which we cannot normally perceive. Some energies have a spiritual source which act upon a person's soul. However, this soul does not exist *ab initio,* as orthodox Christianity teaches; it has to be brought into existence by a process of guided self-observation. However, this is rarely achieved owing to man's unique ability to be distracted from spiritual matters by everyday trivia.
Max: What was that about hats again?

—Monty Python, *The Meaning of Life*

△

One

Luigi Duccio said yes, he would very much enjoy a bottle of wine. He took a seat.

"The thing is," Honoré said, still speaking to François, "you got to give her credit. She was the only one would go near him, at the end."

"She's a whore," François said.

"Yeah, but still," Honoré said. "It took guts, to do what she did. The stink would knock you on your ass. You ever been there when somebody died of smallpox? It would knock you on your ass. The others wouldn't go near him. Hell, even the dauphin stayed way the hell the other end of the palace, what I hear."

"You are talking about Madame Du Barry," Duccio said, pouring from the bottle.

"Yeah," François said, turning back to Honoré at once. "It took guts, I admit that. But she's still a whore. Best thing the dauphin did was throw her the hell out of the palace as soon as the king was dead."

"I know more about it than you do," Honoré said. "It wasn't the dauphin did that, it was the dauphine. The Austrian bitch. She's the one wears the pants in that family, you know what I mean." He lowered his voice. "Louis XVI is going to be one hell of a weak-livered king, my friend. That Austrian, she treats him like dirt."

"What do you think, Luigi?" François asked.

"Well, I'll tell you, guys, I never take much interest in politics."

"What you're saying," François said to Honoré, "is that a whore like that Du Barry is great in your book. I don't see that, not at all. A whore is a whore. She was a national disgrace."

"You telling me you never been to one of them houses?" Honoré demanded. "Pardon me while I laugh. What it is, is you're some kind of hypocrite. Of course, she was a whore. Kings have whores just like you and me have whores, but the kings get the really high-class ones. So what's the difference, is what I mean. I known a lot of whores I like better than some shopkeepers."

"You been reading this Spartacus," François said. "Or Voltaire. Or somebody. Ideas like that, they're going to make a lot of trouble for guys like you and me. You're a shopkeeper yourself, remember."

"That's what I say," Honoré said. "I'm a shopkeeper and I know lots of whores I like better than some shopkeepers. This Du Barry, she had what it takes, going in there, the bedroom, and staying with him until he croaked."

"The family got to him, I heard," François said. "They made him take the sacrament, you know, and the priest was all primed by them. Wouldn't give the absolution until the king renounced his sins. And then, you know, he had to renounce, what do they call it, sinful companions. That was the beginning of it, how they got Du Barry out of the palace. What it is, Honoré, is you got to keep up appearances. A new king, he's got to look good at first, and having his grandfather's whore hanging around the palace, that does not look good. That looks like hell, is what it looks like."

"It was the dauphine," Honoré said. "Because she's Maria Theresa's daughter, thinks she should be Empress. Queen isn't good enough for her. What do you think, Luigi?"

"Well," Luigi said, "I'll tell you, the dauphine is going to make one hell of a good-looking queen. I will say that. She's a beauty."

"From the lips up," Honoré said, lowering his voice. "She's got that Hapsburg jaw like the rest of them. Too much inbreeding, is what that is. Her brother, the Emperor Joseph, he'd be a good-looking guy, too, if it wasn't for that jaw."

"They're all over Europe now," François said. "Them Hapsburgs. Joseph, he's got Austria. His sister, what's her name, Maria Amelia, she's queen of Parma. The other sister, Maria Carolina, she married Ferdinand of Naples, so now they got Naples too. And now with Marie Antoinette as dauphine, they got France. Them Hapsburgs."

"Every royal family in Europe going to have them jaws in a few generations more," François said.

Honoré lowered his voice still further. "You heard the rumor about the dauphin, guy that's going to be our king soon as they get around to crowning him?"

"Don't say it," François said. "I heard it. I don't want to hear it again. Jesus, the walls have ears."

"Well, Jesus, you think it's true?"

François looked over his shoulder. "Just watch that dauphine, that Marie Antoinette. She starts swelling up, then it ain't true."

"Or else," Duccio said softly, "she will have found somebody to do for the king what the king can't do for himself."

"They say it's because of his grandfather," Honoré whispered. "Old Louis. He had the, you know, the other pox. When that's in the blood, hell, two generations and everything happens. You got an idiot, you got a blind one, you got a cripple, you got the works."

"That's why I don't like whores," François said bitterly. "They're spreading it all over the country. That's why I never go to them houses, even if you think everybody does. Some of us have more sense."

"Oh, shit," Honoré said. "Here comes Pierre."

"Pretend you don't see him. Maybe he's looking for somebody else."

"He's got a shop of his own now," Honoré said. "He's respectable. Oh, shit. Here he comes . . . Hello, there, Pierre. Good to see you."

"Evening, Pierre," François said.

"Health," Duccio said.

"You guys, mind if I sit down? Let me order another bottle. Hey, innkeeper. Some good red here. Goddam dogs. You know what I just stepped in?"

"No," Duccio said innocently. "What did you just step in?"

"What I heard," François told Honoré, "the dauphin, and I heard this from Chartres's coachman, who ought to know, the dauphin when they told him old Louis was dead, he said, first thing, 'But I don't know anything about being

king.' That's what he said. Chartres's coachman heard it
from a guy works at the palace.''

''. . . dirty, filthy animals,'' Pierre said.

''Well, old Louis,'' Honoré said, ''he never had much
use for the dauphin. Thought he was feebleminded, what I
hear. And also he's, you know, too fat. Nobody takes a fat
boy seriously.''

''We're all going to have take him seriously now,''
François said. ''Soon as the coronation.''

''Here, try some of the red,'' Pierre said. ''This is good
stuff. Eh, Luigi? Isn't the diego red the best stuff?''

''If it is your ambition to be taken home in a wheelbar-
row,'' Duccio said, ''then yes, it is the merchandise you
want.''

''Want to see the paper, Pierre?'' Honoré asked.

''Hell, can't read in this light.''

The other three looked at each other uncomfortably. It
was not dark yet, not really.

''Well,'' François said heartily. ''How's tricks, Pierre?''

''That Sardines,'' Pierre said. ''I hear they're moving him
up. Right into the palace. Minister of something-or-other.
They're putting the other guy, Lenoir, in charge of the whole
police setup.''

''Well, things change,'' Honoré said. ''Sartines is a very
able man.''

''That's one way of putting it,'' Pierre said.

''You don't like Sartines?'' Honoré said. ''Best man in
the government, you were to ask me. Kept the prices stable
all the time he was in charge of the markets. God knows
what'll happen now.''

''What it is,'' François said, ''is Sartines was breathing
down Pierre's neck for a few years there. Isn't that it, Pierre?''

''Well, every businessman has to cut corners now and
then,'' Duccio said smoothly. ''People have bought merchandise from Pierre that didn't come through customs first,
maybe. But you have to cut corners now and then. It's a
jungle out there.''

Honoré lowered his voice again. ''You think the fat boy
will do any better than his grandfather?''

''God only knows,'' François said.

''It remains to be seen,'' Duccio said.

''That Sardines,'' Pierre said. ''With him in the palace,

whole country will end up with spies under every bed. You wait and see.''

"Well, say what you want," Honoré said. "There was no inflation while he was in charge of the markets.''

Two

Gabriel de Sartines was indeed a minister of something-or-other. Nobody ever remembered what he was supposed to be a minister of, because his real job was taking the lunatic system of interlocking and competing spy services of old Louis and rationalizing them into one efficient, modern intelligence network.

One of his more colorful employees was P.A.C. de Beaumarchais, who, since we last saw him, has been going up in the world, and going down, and going up-and-down. First, just when his *The Barber of Seville* was about to open in Paris, the *affaire Goezman* exploded in his face. It started as a simple lawsuit: some people were claiming Beaumarchais had defrauded them, all slander (he always insisted), but annoying. Beaumarchais did what any sensible man would do—he bribed the judge, Goezman. To his horror and outrage, the verdict went against him. It seems that the other side had given the judge, that damned Goezman, a bigger bribe. An ordinary man would have accepted that he was outclassed at that point, paid over the disputed money, and chalked it up to experience. But Beaumarchais is not an ordinary man, of course, and he commands a mean, sarcastic pen. He writes pamphlets about the case; he asks all France to be the judges of his judge, this damned thrice-cursed Goezman who is bought and will not stay bought. He documents similar corruption throughout the judiciary; he is carried away by his own eloquence—he calls fire and brimstone from the heavens. When Voltaire praises his courage and his wit, he even thinks he is making an impact on the world.

What could you expect? De Beaumarchais's title was bought; he is a commoner, in fact; he does not know the rules. When the case got to the Court of Appeals, the whole judiciary hated him for what he had been writing about them. They rub his nose in it. First, he loses the case, and must pay his opponents in full. Second, he must pay additional fines to the royal treasury, for writing lies about French judges. Third, he must kneel all day on the steps of the Palace of Justice while the public executioner burns all copies of his pamphlets. Fourth, he is enjoined forever against writing further pamphlets about this case or any case before the courts. Fifth, and gratuitously, he is not allowed to produce *The Barber of Seville* in Paris or anywhere else in France.

That was in February 1774; by May, Beaumarchais has embarked on a new career, as special agent for Minister Sartines. He is sent on a secret mission to London, and performs well; another secret mission to Holland, and he performs better. By 1776, money was being secretly funneled out of the royal treasury into the bank account of P.A.C. de Beaumarchais, whence it moved into a fictitious bank account of a minor character in *The Barber of Seville* (he has a sense of humor, this Beaumarchais; nobody ever doubted that), and from there—it becomes guns and munitions, bound for America. Louis XVI has decided to support the American Revolution surreptitiously, so as not to openly offend the English. It was many, many decades before historians determined that not all the money got turned into guns for America; some of it, a large part it appears, went into the founding of a bank of which P.A.C. de Beaumarchais was sole owner and proprietor.

They even allowed him to produce the *Barber* in Paris after all.

And none of them, not even the icy and illusionless Sartines, seems to have ever guessed that all this time Beaumarchais was a high degree initiate of the Grand Orient lodge of Egyptian Freemasonry and serving it more faithfully than he ever served the government.

King Louis XVI—the fat boy, as everybody called him behind his ovoidal back—was finally crowned in June 1775, nearly a year after he had become king *de facto* due to his grandfather's death. Although his brother-in-law, the shrewd and debonair Emperor Joseph of Austria,* once claimed that Louis was "not actually feebleminded, but hesitant," most of the palace staff and soon all of France took the surface for the reality: everybody accepted that there was a dunce on the throne. It is hard to get people to take you seriously when you are only twenty, grossly overweight, and terribly shy.

That the fat boy was, in fact, "not actually feeble-minded" is indicated by his appointment of Sartines to make something rational out of the chaos of Louis XV's espionage system. Indeed, one of Beaumarchais's early assignments, it appears, was to negotiate the respectable retirement of that embarrassment in London, the "lady knight," the Chevalier d'Éon. Both Beaumarchais and d'Éon bargained well; the contract they drew up between them was fifteen pages long, in the best Gallic legalese. The king undertook to pay d'Éon, for the rest of his or her life, a sum equivalent to £1000 sterling per month (1991: corrected for inflation), and d'Éon agreed to remain a woman once and for all, stop confusing people by switching back and forth between male and female, and keep his or her mouth shut in general. (One section specified that he or she would never write his or her memoirs.) D'Éon, ever quixotic, insisted on, and got, the right to wear over his or her female gowns the medal he or she had won for bravery when he or she was an ordinary soldier and (apparently) an ordinary male; Beaumarchais

---

*Joseph was everybody's model of "the enlightened despot." Beethoven hymns him as the foe of superstition in the *Emperor Joseph* Cantata (commissioned by the Illuminati, as mentioned in the footnote on page 154). Although possibly a descendant of the widow's son (if one believes the genealogies in *Holy Blood, Holy Grail*, op. cit., and *La Race fabuleuse*, op. cit.), Joseph spent so much time in oedipal feuding with his mother, Maria Theresa, that between them they wrecked the government and economy of Austria; when asked his opinion of the American Revolution, he said dryly, "I am a monarchist by profession"; drove the Catholic Church out of the education business and replaced them with secular scientific schools; also legalized Freemasonry; was a Freemason himself, according to many authorities; decided in cold-blooded rationality (he thought) that wives and mistresses were more trouble than they were worth and confined himself to whores for life; and one of his current descendants seems to be a member of the Priory of Sion, according to *Holy Blood, Holy Grail*, again op. cit.

agreed to that placidly, to end the whole scandalous business.

The Chevalier d'Éon later wept on the shoulder of the Comte de Broglie, "In fact, I have always been a woman, and would have functioned as one all of my life, if politics had not forced me into a most wretched career of duplicity."

De Broglie believed it. So much feminine charm, and so many feminine tears, he felt, could not be a deception.*

From THE REVOLUTION AS I SAW IT, *by Luigi Duccio:*

. . . And when the fat boy (as everybody called him) was returning from the coronation ceremony, there occurred one of those remarkable coincidences that linger in the memory precisely because reason can never decide whether they are significant or not. The school of the rue St. Jacques, run by pious Benedictine monks, had held a contest to select one student to deliver a patriotic address to the king as he passed. The boy who won was chosen both for his high marks in all his studies and also for his exemplary character and good habits; everybody believed that he was also elected because the monks pitied him: he was an orphan.

Alas, when the king passed that way, it had already begun to rain. Protocol insisted that the boy should nonetheless kneel, and so he did, ruining his only good breeches in the process. There was a mistake somewhere; nobody had told the king that there would be a schoolboy presenting an address on that street. The royal carriage rolled by; the boy knelt in the mud—and, I might add for vividness and total accuracy, in the excreta of horses, dogs, and cattle, for there was no part of a Paris street in which these could be avoided; the cold rain poured down on the boy, kneeling there in the filth, dutifully reciting his stentorian oration. Neither the king nor Marie Antoinette ever gazed even for a second in his direction.

The boy never spoke of that incident; as I say, we can never know if it was important or not, or what it meant to him. But we all knew him in later years, that serious, pedantic, ascetic boy; he was my friend, the great hero of

*When d'Éon finally died in 1810 twelve doctors officiated at the autopsy, to settle all the wagers about the lady knight's real gender. They found normal male organs and no signs of physical hermaphroditism.

1791, the great villain of 1793, Maximilien Robespierre, who tried so passionately to inflict enough Terror and Virtue upon our nation to save us from the whirlpools of coincidence and conspiracy that make up the muddle of actual history.

Three

The Marquis de Sade had been living quietly in his estates in Provence, while all the police of France were seeking him. The local inspector had called on the marquise once, asking if she knew where her infamous spouse was; she had claimed she had no idea—he might be on the moon for all she knew, she said. It was unthinkable for a mere inspector to doubt the word of a lady of her rank, especially one so closely related to the royal family. After a year, however, rumors began to leak out; the police could not ignore them, even if this meant calling a marquise a liar to her face. They resolved to search the villa and root out "the modern Bluebeard," as de Sade is now called.

Alas, rumors run in *all* directions; de Sade was tipped off that they were coming, and fled to Italy. The inspector and his men had to apologize to the marquise after searching the place and finding no de Sade.

De Sade was in Rome, it appears, for the death of Pope Clement XIV.

In 1773, His Holiness had made a terrible mistake—he issued a bull, *Dominus ac Redemptor,* officially dissolving and extinguishing forever (he *hoped* forever) the Society of Jesus.

The Catholic princes of Europe had all insisted on it—Don Carlos of Spain, who had thrown the Jesuits out of his own kingdom in '68, Ferdinand IV of Naples who had followed suit a few years later, the dukes of Parma and Genoa, the lot of them. The Jesuits were secretive; they had separate loyalties, it was believed. Every Jesuit, of course, took an oath of absolute obedience to God, the Holy Virgin, the

Pope, and the General of the Jesuits, allegedly in that order. Of course, THEY said (but you know the sort of things THEY say) that actually the General came first, with God and the Pope and even the Virgin in distinctly inferior positions. Besides, there were too many rumors, *altogether,* about linkages between the Jesuits and the Freemasons, or Jesuits even teaching Galileo's heretical astronomy in their schools. The Society of Jesus might be the most intelligent and erudite men in the Church, as all agreed; they might actually obey their vows of poverty and chastity, as other orders only pretended to do; they might have served the Vatican well in the past; but now their day was done.

And yet Pope Clement XIV was said to look wan, *ghastly,* when he pronounced his ban. Old Ganganelli—everybody called him that; he was the first pope in centuries not of noble birth, a barber-surgeon's son, a liberal—knew the legends about the Society of Jesus as well as any northern anti-Papist did. Their reputation was sinister; good lord, no prince could die anywhere, of any cause, without people whispering that probably the Jesuits had poisoned him. Some even claimed that Ganganelli's voice actually *trembled* when he read the bull. THEY said (but you know the sort of things THEY say) that he even muttered afterward in a hoarse voice, "This will be the death of me"—a legend, almost certainly, like Galileo's putative "But still it moves"; but like the Galileo yarn, this invention will live longer than the facts.

In Ferney, among the foothills of the Alps, Voltaire rejoices. "In twenty years," he writes in an ecstatic letter, "the Catholic Church will have ceased to exist."

Within a week the infamous graffiti begins to appear all over Rome, all over Italy next: de Sade sees it as soon as he arrives—

I S S S V

Nobody will admit they know who is doing it, but somehow everybody knows what it means, even poor old Ganganelli himself: *In Settembre Sara Sede Vacante:* in September the throne will be vacant. His Holiness cannot stick his pontifical nose out of the Vatican without seeing it: I S S S V. All up and down Italy: I S S S V. Everywhere, everywhere: I S S S V. A smallpox of walls with initials as the scabs. In September the throne will be vacant. In September the throne will be vacant. In September . . .

Repetition. Repetition. Repetition.

In September the throne will be vacant.

I S S S V.

Ganganelli gets a minor cold—a few sneezes, hoarseness, nothing more, for God's sake—and everybody immediately has a knowing expression. He sees sly eyes, quickly turning bland, everywhere he looks. *They are clever fellows, the Jesuits,* they are all thinking: why, any damned fool can commit a murder, but it takes an artist to arrange a convincing natural death. Ganganelli sees that everywhere; they are waiting for him to fall.

The pope decides to go horseback riding, to demonstrate his vigor publicly. He deliberately gallops ahead of the party, leaving younger men behind, to show them all: *I am still a tough old bird.* But everybody looked concerned because he was out of breath afterward: that could be another symptom. And it was still there, wherever he looked: I S S S V. In September the throne will be vacant. And he could see the pity and the malice, the genuine concern and the theatrical excitement, the delicious *suspense,* in every face: When will the old man drop in his tracks?

Long before September, Ganganelli—liberal, skeptical, tough—was in an altered state of consciousness and seeing as many conspirators as old Louis XV in his poxy last years. He suspects *everybody* in the Vatican. His closest confidants, his oldest friends. The servants. The Swiss Guard. Every visiting priest. I S S S V. He cannot eat a morsel without wondering. I S S S V. His digestion suffers as his inner organs try to *taste* for possible poison in time to vomit it. He has hiccups, belching, heartburn, insomnia. I S S S V. He staggers about exuding dyspepsia, and all eyes are full of sympathy and the theatrical suspense. Some try to reassure him, but he wonders: Were they lying about his good health to cheer him up, or because they were in on the plot? Every time his gut aches—and it aches increasingly—he wonders, and wonders, and wonders.* I S S S V: In September the throne will be vacant.

---

*Cf. the more recent death of Pope John Paul I. According to Yallop's *In God's Name,* cited in previous footnotes, John Paul I was considering the removal of Archbishop Marcinkus from the Vatican Bank when he

But he was a tough one, this barber's son. He would not let them worry him to death; he vowed it.

It surprised everybody when he survived September 30.

In the Massachusetts Bay Colony, in Boston Town, a group of men dressed as Indians invades the docks and pours several tons of tea into the harbor. Nobody believes they really were Indians; everybody knows it is a protest against the new tea tax. In London, Lord North has no doubt about that at all. And THEY say (but you know the sort of things THEY say) that the alleged Indians were seen coming out of Freemason's Hall . . .

In Russia, strange rumors have circulated throughout the army for several months. It is said that the late Czar, Peter III, did not die of natural causes, as the government stolidly claims—nor was he murdered by his wife, that German whore who now rules under the name Catherine II, as the aristocrats whisper in Moscow. No, no. The Czar, the Little Father, is *alive* and among us. He is clever: he went into hiding when Catherine plotted his death. Many have seen him with their own eyes.

Soon the rumors grow more specific. The Little Father is living under the alias Yemelyan Ivanovich Pugachev, pretending to be—of all things—a Cossack. The German usurper will get her comeuppance; you can bet on it. How can he be defeated, the Little Father who has returned from the dead?

In Salzburg, Mozart produced his 23rd symphony and then rushed merrily along to write his 24th, 25th, 26th, 27th, 28th, and 29th. He celebrated his eighteenth birthday in the midst of this creative frenzy and acquired a minor distemper at a brothel, which he believed was promptly cured by the quack he consulted.

was poisoned by Marcinkus and his confederates in P-2 *(Propaganda Due)*—the notorious Calvi, Sindona, and Gelli—and with the connivance of Cardinal Villot. Father Malachi Martin in his *The Decline and Fall of the Roman Church*, also op. cit., adds that John Paul I had received, and was studying, documents about the Freemasonic/P-2 associations of several top cardinals, these documents having been submitted by Archbishop Lefèbvre of France; the same Archbishop Lefèbvre who is considered a possible member of the Priory of Sion in *Holy Blood, Holy Grail*. Father Martin also says Lefèbvre had previously submitted to the Pope such choice items as "photos of cardinals with their boyfriends, cardinals with their girlfriends," and such *hot stuff*. Cardinal Villot arranged for the pope to be embalmed before an autopsy could be performed.

Ever since joining the Ancient and Accepted Order of Freemasons, Mozart has had a higher ambition for his music, a mission to bring to all people some prismatic reflection of the light he has experienced. The Bishop of Munster, another Freemason and a Hapsburg,* has been encouraging this ever-accelerating crescendo of light, love, liberty, and laughter that Mozart pours forth.

Quietly, without attracting the attention of the world, a marriage was celebrated in Bavaria: Adam Weishaupt, Professor of Canon Law at the University of Ingolstadt, wed Eve Barth, the daughter of a local judge.

Everybody said they were a beautiful couple.

And now the "Pugachev uprising," as it is called, has swept across half or more than half of Russia. Of course, nobody but the rebels themselves believes that Pugachev really is the late Czar Peter III, but—the rebels are led by Cossacks, who know strategy. They keep on winning. Everybody says they will be beaten soon, but they still keep winning—and winning—

In Rome the graffiti still appear on new walls every day:

I S S S V

*It was another Hapsburg, distantly related to this Bishop and to the Emperor Joseph, who visited the controversial priest, Father Saunière, in Rennes-le-Château in the 1890s and thereafter paid into Saunière's bank account enough money to make the priest rich. This matter is discussed in *Holy Blood, Holy Grail*, op. cit., and the authors examine the possibilities that Saunière was either blackmailing the Hapsburgs or being paid by them for his part in an anti-Vatican conspiracy. De Sède in *L'Or de Rennes-le-Château* relates the whole Saunière mystery to various Freemasonic and Rosicrucian activities, and hints at the "Ancient Astronaut" theory expressed in his later *La Race fabuleuse*. Father Saunière, curiously, used some of the Hapsburg money to build a church dedicated to Mary Magdalene, and over the door inscribed on it the words *THIS PLACE IS TERRIBLE.*

Four

Sir John Babcock poured himself another glass of brandy, not noticing that his hands shook slightly, and then slowly, viciously, tore the letter from the Royal Scientific Society of Sweden into small bits, and then into smaller and smaller bits; then he allowed himself to drink the brandy in a gulp. He quickly poured another without noticing what he was doing.

The same blind prejudice exists everywhere, he thought angrily. Nobody was willing to believe the damned rock had actually fallen out of the sky. Nobody, nobody, nobody!

Well, that was not completely true, he reminded himself ironically. He had found a few believers in the course of extended correspondence with twenty nations; and a choice lot they were. Some were British Israelites, who held that the English, not the Jews, were descended from the Old Testament Hebrews; some had found the formula for the Philosopher's Stone coded into Shakespeare's plays, along with such sentences (in acrostic) as "I, Francis Bacon, from the planet Mars, wrote this"; some assured him that they communicated daily with angels. There was small comfort in having such intellectual associates.

"I do not fully accept that we are living in an Age of Reason," Dr. Ben Franklin, the American, had said at a recent conference with Whig leaders about the worsening political hostilities between England and the colonies. Sir John remembered, with a smile, the rest of Dr. Franklin's animadversions on that subject. A purely rational being is a contradiction in terms, the doctor had said. Imagine such a being: he is in his laboratory conducting experiments, of course The servant knocks. "Sir, dinner is ready." "Dinner, dinner—what dinner?" mutters the rational man, not wishing to break off his thoughts. "Ham and chicken, sir." What, Franklin said, does the purely rational being reply to this? "To hell with your ham! I will not disturb my reflections to gnaw on a damned hog's arse!" Thus, the American went on, without at least one appetite to constrain him, this rational being would not eat to survive, and without another appetite, he would not reproduce his kind. "And so we see that the exalted dignity of human nature is dependent upon our being driven by the same instincts as horses and dogs . . ."

Sir John looked around his study, not realizing the cunning expression that had come over his features. Safe. Maria had not entered quietly while he was lost in thought. He poured another brandy and drank swiftly.

Silly damned thing, that; but women were temperamental creatures. Maria lately had this notion that he was drinking too much. Perhaps that was because she was pregnant again; that did provoke strange emotional shifts in the female at times. Lately, he could hardly pour a glass in her company without her saying, "Do you really need another?" Or, even worse, that sad, worried look in her eyes. The one thing more unbearable than a wife who scolds, he thought, is a wife who just looks at you that way and does not say a word.

Well, he thought, I must be charitable. She's six months gone now and it's only natural to be jumpy then. Everything will be normal again after the child is born.

He rammed the cork back into the decanter. There, he thought, I am finished for the night. Not another drop. I can stop any time I *decide* to stop. Women and their fantasies!

He carried the brandy back to the liquor cabinet, not noticing that he was staggering. See? I can stop just like *that*, the minute I make up my mind.

Meanwhile, he decided there was no real harm in one more short drink before going to bed.

After all, he told himself, I have amended my life. No more boys—not for nearly a year now. He drank happily.

He almost slipped once, going up the stairs. He clutched the banister firmly the rest of the way. Perhaps I did have one or two glasses too many, he thought; well, it will be a lesson to me. I will be more moderate tomorrow night.

When he passed Maria's door, her voice called, "John?"

Oh, lord. It was suddenly like being at Eton, waiting for his interview with Father Fenwick, during the investigation of sodomy among the students. He remembered his fear that the guilt would show on his face; but then he remembered how cool he had been, and how he had escaped unscathed. He pulled himself together with an effort, and entered the bedroom without wobbling in the slightest.

Maria, bloated but beautiful, was sitting up in bed; he noticed that the book in her hand was something called *Not The Almighty*. "Pray," she said, "were you still in correspondence about your singular rock, my lord?"

Sir John eased himself into a chair—not too close, so she could not smell the brandy. "I was reading correspondence," he said carefully, "but not answering it. I fear, my lady, your husband has become a cynic. I no longer care to correct the follies of the world; they seem incurable to me."

For barely an instant the sad reproach came back into Maria's eyes; then she briskly banished it. "A person without some cynicism in this world must be a dunce," she said, "but a person governed entirely by cynicism is in danger of becoming a poltroon. I know you too well to think that is your ultimate destiny."

"We are all poltroons. None of us ever dares to utter half of what he knows and thinks." Sir John heard the shrillness in his voice as he said it, and knew that despite his efforts he had sounded exactly like a surly drunk.

"Nonsense," Maria said. "On our wedding night—do you remember, my lord?—you made a similar speech, although less melancholy in tone, and we pledged never to hide our thoughts from each other. I have hoped that we have been true to that oath."

"Madam, I was as moonstruck as Quixote on that occasion."

"You wish me to despise you, because you despise yourself this evening. But I am no child any longer. I know that playing that game will solve nothing. You will feel better if we have a grand opera scene of howling and shrieking, but in the morning the problems will still be there and will have to be confronted."

"Forgiveness can be the cruelest of all punishments."

"Only to the weak. And you are not truly weak, John. It

merely suits your present mood to think of yourself as such.''

"Madam, do you have any concept of what it is that torments me?''

"I think I do.''

"If you did you would loathe me.''

Maria closed her book and set it on the bed table. "It was two or three months ago,'' she said directly. "We were at a ball at the Greystokes'. The Earl of Pembroke was there, and he mentioned the Irishman, Moon, who once worked for us. He said he had been in Liverpool and saw Moon there, running a shop of his own, a victualler's and greengrocer's. He thought Moon was extremely frugal and clever to save enough on his salary to buy a shop. But I saw the look on your face, John. And the word *blackmail* came to me as clearly as if it had been spoken, or as if somebody had written it in paint on the ballroom wall.''

Sir John closed his eyes, wishing he had not drunk so much brandy, wishing his throat were not suddenly cramped with anxiety.

"Who was she, John?''

He opened his eyes and was not surprised at the slight wetness in them. *Living with a half-truth is better than living with a total lie,* he thought; *it gives one more room to maneuver.* "It is better not to name her,'' he said in a hoarse voice, real emotion making the lie sound true. "Her husband is one of the most powerful men in the kingdom.''

"It started when I was pregnant the first time, and inaccessible?''

"You guessed even then?''

"No, but that is when it usually starts. You would be astounded at the confidences women exchange with each other. Do you know that there is not one lady of our acquaintance who believes her husband has been consistently faithful?''

Bleeding Christ, Sir John thought. He was relieved that the whole truth was not coming out; he was guilty; he was drunk; he was irrationally afraid that the truth would slip out accidentally. He gave up all control and let his tears flow for a moment. "I am a swine,'' he said, realizing that he was still lying, still hiding.

"The affair began when I was carrying Ursula,'' Maria said flatly. "When did it terminate?''

354   *Robert Anton Wilson*

"A long time ago. Over a year."

"And do you go on drinking because you wish you had not terminated it?"

"I do not drink as much as most of the men of my class in this nation."

"Most of the men of our class are drunkards and you know it. John, John, darling, you are not a drunkard yet, but you are tormenting yourself and tormenting me by teetering on the edge of becoming a drunkard."

Sir John abruptly perceived truth amid his many masks. "I was teetering on the edge, as you so accurately phrase it, because I needed help and did not know how to ask for it. Do you understand? It was like walking with a limp, waiting for somebody to say, 'Sir, you need a crutch, or you should see a surgeon.' "

Maria smiled for the first time that evening. "You would rather I despised you as a drunkard than hated you as an adulterer."

"Yes. Something like that."

Maria rearranged the pillow, to sit more erect. "I think I have been talking like some heroine of a novel I once read. Perhaps I rehearsed this scene too often in my mind before I decided to speak out. John, John, it is not in my nature to withhold forgiveness. You know that."

"Yes. But—"

"But forgiveness can be the worst punishment, as you said?" Maria smiled again. "Do you want me to beat your buttocks with a birch rod first, as in those strange erotic novels only men read, since no woman in her right mind can take them seriously for a moment?"

Sir John almost laughed, almost sobbed, and then stared into Maria's exasperated but still loving eyes. "I am not that sort of idiot," he said finally, "but I suddenly believe I understand the men who are. I think I did want something of the sort, on a more subtle level—perhaps the grand opera screaming that you mentioned."

"Very well," Maria said. "I am not inclined to that unbridled childishness. Since coming to England, I have learned to recognize what is puerile in both this nation and back in Italy, and I know that the way people express emotion or hide emotion is usually the way they have been trained and is therefore always a trifle dishonest. I will not offer you Neapolitan opera but I will not hide in ambush

and seek revenge later in cold little nastinesses as so many
of you English do. I have been angry and hurt, John. The
infidelity itself only hurt a little, I think, and I am persuaded
that it hurt only because of false ideas that I never examined
critically before this incident. What hurts more is that you
have been dishonest in a low and sneaking way. No: stop
looking so absurdly repentant and don't interrupt. I am not
finished. A man my father knew back in Napoli once found
his wife had been unfaithful and he stabbed her to death.
Of course, he was hanged for it. Do you know what is truly
tragic in that story? Its total *stupidity*. That man did not
think for one second of any reality but his own emotions.
He did not think, for instance, of his children, and what
would happen to them when both parents were dead by violence and subjects of scandal. Your playing around the
edges of becoming a drunkard is the same variety of emotional blindness, John. You think you are punishing yourself, and you are waiting for pity and forgiveness, but you
do not reflect at all that you are punishing me also and will
soon become a liability to your political party, at a time
when they need your talents and the unselfish dedication you
once exemplified. God only knows what the distress you
have caused me has done also to the child in my womb.
Your child.''

Sir John was sober and dry-eyed. ''I am not going to take
another drink, I am not going to blow my brains out, and I
am not going to commit any further imbecilities. I merely
have an urgent need to visit the water closet.'' His face was
white but he walked steadily now.

When he returned he sat and said, ''Truth is not as unbearable as the pessimists say. It is only painfully shocking
at first. In the long range, it is easier to live with, I think,
than lies. There was not one affair of the heart, as I just
allowed you to think. There were several brief and sordid
encounters. This began, not during your first pregnancy, but
shortly after the birth, when I was most deeply and passionately in love with you, and with our new daughter. I do
not understand why I behaved so. The last encounter of this
sort was approximately eight months ago. I resolved then
that it would never happen again. It has not happened again.
I told you long ago that my father was a drunkard. I do not
understand why or how I decided to substitute his weakness
for mine, but it is obvious in retrospect that that is what I

have been doing. I will do it no more. I will never touch another drop of liquor."

Now Maria's eyes were wet for a moment. "I think our vices and our virtues are both derivative," she said carefully. "Under stress, you imitate your father, the man who impressed you most as a child. Under my own stress, I imitate Mother Ursula, who was always rational and forgiving; she was the woman who influenced me most after my mother's early death."

"Yes," John said. "Even my politics, my highest ideals, are imitations of my father at his best."

"I do not know why so many husbands are unfaithful, but I know it is the fact. Few of them punish themselves as you have done."

"That is because their wives punish them. They are always found out sooner or later There are no real secrets in society, these days."

"I suspect, sir, that guilt is a counterfeit of responsibility, just as punishment is a sham of correction."

"I do believe I understand what you mean, madame."

"Come closer."

"Yes." He sat on the edge of the bed.

"Hold me a moment."

"Cara mia."

"Caro mio."

After a while, Maria said, "I think you became wild and wicked for a time because you were too happy. The world was too comfortable for you, and you had to make a problem for yourself."

"No," he said. "Those French atheists who say we are machines have half the truth, as your dear, quaint, old-fashioned religion has half the truth when it says we are free. We are free only through terrible struggle, and when we are emotional or lazy, we forget to struggle and become machines again without even noticing it. I became lazy and reverted to the type of machine I had been before I met you."

"Mother Ursula says we are asleep most of the time. I think she means what you mean when you say we easily become machines."

"I cannot believe this," John said. "You were always a remarkable girl, but you have become a more remarkable woman."

"Plato says the wicked do what the wise only imagine. I can be asleep or a machine, too. I imagined some terrible revenges, at first. Then I woke and remembered that I still love you."

"Yes. I woke up, in that sense, when you were telling me what my drinking had been hiding from me."

After a while they slept. But John woke toward dawn with a brandy hangover; and he thought: seven days to a week, fifty-two weeks to a year. God knows how many years left to my life. And I will have to struggle against relapse every day of every week of every year.

Five

His Holiness Clement XIV will not survive a second September. He is ill all winter and spring, and becomes worse in the summer. Everybody in Rome is saying the Jesuits had got him. Nobody doubts it; and he believes it himself. I S S S V: it haunts him the way *Pepsi-Cola hits the spot* will haunt later victims of Signal Saturation. He is a wreck, a caricature. Was it only a year ago that he rode out ahead of younger horsemen to show his continued vigor? He is almost a skeleton now, and his eyes look rattish, furtive.

He has even become religious.

A religious pope! Nobody in this day and age can believe it;* It is like a vegetarian tiger or a square circle. It is true nonetheless; he prays incessantly. He has nightmares about hell and wakes up screaming.

The old joke has returned to haunt him, the story of how representatives of all the different orders of the Church—Franciscans, Dominicans, Capuchins, the lot of them—once prayed together to God, asking which order He loved best. In the morning they found a note saying, "I love you all equally," signed "God, S.J." It is not funny to old Ganganelli, the dying pope. He has always tended to believe in

---

*As Colin Wilson notes *(Criminal History of Mankind,* Putnam, New York, 1984, p. 340), murder in the Vatican has been "commonplace." Wilson goes on: "The pope was, in effect, the Roman emperor, the Caesar. With enormous revenues flowing in from all over the civilized world, he built palaces, employed great artists, hired armies, poisoned rivals, fathered bastards, and gave away important Church appointments to members of his family."

some form of Higher Intelligence, on philosophical grounds, even if it is absurd (and profitable) that ignorant people believe that Intelligence can be influenced by dressing up in costumes and chanting and singing at it. Now he has begun to wonder, anxiously, if that Intelligence might take an interest in human affairs *occasionally*, and might even be in cahoots with the Jesuits. Why not? If there is one thing certain about a Higher Intelligence, it is that its workings will be inscrutable to us. Who knows what tricks it might be up to? He fears that he has offended it by pretending to speak on its behalf. It doesn't matter by autumn whether the Jesuits poisoned him or God make him sick to punish him for impiety: he accepts that he is doomed. He prays, and prays, and prays, but without hope.

He died on September 22, 1774. The graffiti had become true: I S S S V.*

De Sade observed the whole psychological drama; it was his main study during his first months in Rome, and it would play a large role in his later philosophizing about power and the men who wield it.

The little blond experimentalist also attended the coronation of the new pope, Pius IV, at Saint Peter's. Everybody who met him at the time commented later that he had exquisite manners, even for a Frenchman; they also took his minute curiosity about every detail of the ritual as a sign of piety.

Back in his hotel, de Sade wrote into his journal, where it may be seen today, a poetic, if overly flowery, description

---

*Cf. de Selby, *Golden Hours*, XVI, 1904: "Witchcraft has certainly increased, rather than decreased, since the medieval age. A doctor says a man must die, and the man obediently takes to his bed, wastes away, and is soon dead. The same doctor pronounces that another man shall recover, and that man is soon back at his job and stopping off at the pub for a drink on the way home. An economist announces depression, and factories close; another economist later announces recovery, and the factories reopen. It only takes an 'expert' to claim a city has a crime problem, or air pollution, for crime and respiratory diseases to increase at once. We have only recently discovered iatrogenic distempers; we need to ask whether consciousness is not *per se* iatrogenic." It was in his diatribe against this paragraph *(Werke*, VI, 47–334) that Hanfkopf first suggested that De Selby's enigmatic "hammering" or "spirit rapping" might be "the sound of a victim of Korsakoff's psychosis banging his own head against a wall in frenzy."

of the Pope's throne, which he considered gorgeous. "What a divan to be buggered on," he added raptly.*

The same month Clement XIV died in Rome the Pugachev rebellion was finally defeated in Russia. Pugachev was hanged; his followers were pursued and methodically exterminated; and yet fear remained. THEY said in Moscow (but you know the sort of things THEY say) that an ignorant soldier like Pugachev could never have raised such an insurrection without powerful and unrecognized supporters *somewhere* . . .

The following spring, in England, the Whigs made their final effort to stave off the oncoming war with the American colonists.

John Wilkes, back in Parliament at last (he said in his first speech that the Constitution had suffered worse wounds than he had by his removal and imprisonment), led the onslaught against Tory prejudice with his usual fiery eloquence. He was voted down. The only immediate results of his speeches were that Wilkes-Barre, Pennsylvania, and Wilkesboro, North Carolina, were named after him; and in France, Diderot praised his oratory and his devotion to libertarian principles. A more ironic result, later, was that the actor Julius Booth named his son John Wilkes Booth.

Pitt, Sheridan, Babcock, all the Whig leaders made their attempts to persuade the House to negotiate, to conciliate, to stop the plunge toward war; all failed.

In march, Edmund Burke made his last, and greatest, speech on the subject. Sir John Babcock thought it was the most eloquent and resonant argument ever heard on the floor of the House.

"The proposition is peace," Burke said in his heavy Dublin accent. "Not peace through the medium of war; not peace to be hunted through the labyrinth of intricate and

---

*The current Pope, John Paul II, has finally commented on the scandals that have recently rocked the Vatican. Now that the managing director (Mennini) and the chief accountant (de Stroebel) of the Vatican Bank are under indictment for fraud, while Archbishop Marcinkus and Monsignor de Bonis are still under investigation for fraud and possible murderconspiracy-drug offenses, and Cardinal Poletti is accused of tax fraud, His Holiness has explained to the faithful, "Many incredible things can be read in the newspapers, things that have no basis in truth. Your faith must never be questioned because of what you read in the newspapers."(*Irish Press*, 23 June 1983).

endless negotiations; not peace to arise out of universal discord, fomented from principle in all parts of the empire; not peace to depend on the juridical determination of perplexing questions, or the precise marking of the shadowy boundaries of a complex government. It is simple peace, sought in its natural course and its ordinary haunts. It is peace sought in the spirit of peace and laid on principles purely pacific.''

It is marvelous, Sir John thought, that a man can speak like that without notes. It would take me hours to write a paragraph so lucidly yet limpidly elegant.

But a voice from the Tory bench cried, ''Go back to Dublin, Paddy!''

Burke, as usual, ignored that kind of heckling. He went on with simple dignity, arguing against the Tory position that the colonists had violated the letter of the law and must be punished. Such metaphysical doctrines, he said with Swiftian scorn, are ''the great Serbonian bog where armies whole have sunk.'' He insisted on the realities of the situation:

''When driven to desperation, the boar turns on the hunter. If your sovereignty and their liberty cannot be reconciled, which will they choose? They will fling your sovereignty in your face. No man will be *argued* into slavery,'' he said emphatically.

There was a steady rise of hissing. Lord North, Prime Minister and known to be the king's illegitimate brother, remained poker-faced, but Babcock knew the order to hiss had come from him.

Burke insisted that reconciliation meant concession on both sides. There was louder hissing and a shout of ''Bograt! Traitor!''

''Go back to Dublin,'' came the first heckler again.

''The proposal ought to originate from us,'' Burke said, raising his voice now. ''Great and acknowledged force is not impaired, either in effect or in opinion, by an unwillingness to exert itself. The superior power may offer peace with honor and with safety. In large bodies, the circulation of power must be less vigorous at the extremities. Nature herself has said it. The Turk cannot govern Egypt and Arabia and Kurdistan as he governs Thrace. The Sultan gets *such obedience as he can*,'' he thundered. ''This is the *im-*

mutable condition, the eternal law of extensive and detached empire.''

A mocking voice sang out:

> Paddy was a Dublin man
> Paddy was a thief

Burke went on to discuss the principles of bargaining and negotiation known to all businessmen. He demonstrated, as if to children, that all society and all peaceful relations are based on compromise and pragmatic give-and-take. He said the world would be at war forever if men did not choose rather to be happy than to pursue every quarrel to the death.

"In all fair dealings," he said, "the thing bought must bear some proportion to the purchase paid.

"None will barter away the immediate jewel of his soul.

"Man acts from adequate motives relative to his interest, and not on metaphysical speculations. None of us would not risk his life rather than fall under a government *purely arbitrary.*"

He went on, and on, with eloquence that centuries were to admire, arguing that no policy totally obnoxious to the colonists could be enforced. The hissing grew louder as he spoke.

When the vote was taken, forty-nine members accepted Burke's peace plan; 572 voted to send troops across the Atlantic to put down the insubordination of the colonists. It was March 22, 1775.

Sir John Babcock wrote in his daybook, "Newton explained politics as well as mechanics. *The universal law is inertia.* A parliamentary body in motion continues in the same straight line until deflected by a countervailing force. God help us, the only such force now is the armed resistance of the colonists."

He was sure that the colonists would be defeated, but he saw the victory of England as a black tragedy, since it would be the triumph of might over right. The other Whigs saw it that way also.

Beaumarchais, alone in Europe, was sending reports back to Minister Sartines in Paris, that the Americans would defeat the English troops. He said that if France played her cards shrewdly, this could be the beginning of the end of the English Empire.

In April, Benjamin Franklin was declared *persona non grata* and expelled from England like a common criminal.

There would be no further negotiations.

Franklin, finding no maids to fondle, spent the long month of the stormy North Atlantic crossing playing checkers with his grandson in their cabin and chatting with the sailors, learning all he could about the technical side of ships and navigation. He was sixty-nine, but still avid for knowledge about all things he hadn't had time to study yet.

Every day Franklin took temperature readings of the water, using a thermometer on a long stick he had devised. He had no theory to guide him; he simply thought such precise knowledge might be valuable for its own sake. As he jotted the temperatures down each day, a pattern emerged. By the time the ship *Pennsylvania Packet* docked in Baltimore, he had deduced the existence of the Gulf Stream.

There was a huge crowd to greet him: Old Ben was the colonists' pride, the man whom David Hume had called the greatest scientist since Newton: he who had tamed the lightning and explained electricity, who gave Philadelphia its library, its hospital, its paved streets. He is more of a hero than ever, now that perfidious London has cast him out like a dog.

And the crowd has news for him, after he has been feasted on Maryland lobsters and spicy clam chowder. While he was on the seas, on April 19, English troops were sent from Boston to Lexington to arrest Sam Adams, of the Sons of Liberty. When they entered Lexington, hidden farmers in the woods opened fire. The redcoats lost 247 men out of 2,500, could see nobody to shoot back at, and retreated: the first time since the religious wars of the early 1600s that a civilian insurrection has defeated an organized professional army.

Now the colonists want him, Dr. Franklin, to go to Philadelphia at once. Approaching seventy, he had planned to retire and philosophize; but, no, he must attend a Continental Congress.

An organized anarchy, it sounds like to Ben. He sees that the hotheads are rushing madly into dangers they do not comprehend; some demagogue named John Adams, who must be wilder than his cousin Sam, is trying to stampede the Congress into declaring independence from England.

Somebody with common sense and moderation has to go to Philadelphia and head off the catastrophe. Dr. Franklin resignedly agrees to accept the responsibility.

Already in Philadelphia, John Adams, who regards himself as a conservative and is always astonished that others think him a radical, has bluntly told the Congress, "We are in the state of nature." The words created exactly the terror that he intended. At the age of forty, Adams, an attorney and a admirer of Lord Coke's theory of rational justice, has no patience with euphemism and wishful thinking. This is what he sees: the dam has burst, the flood waters are rising, the earth is shaking beneath our feet. The *state of nature*— a term from Hobbes—means the state of anarchy.

Right now, in summer 1775, Congress does not see any of that. They are convinced that Mr. Adams is merely an extremist, an alarmist, and an obnoxiously pugnacious debater, overly given to sarcasm and invective.

When the urbane Dr. Franklin arrives, all are convinced that now, at last, some sort of reasonable compromise with London can be achieved.

In France, bread had remained at four to six sous a loaf throughout Sartines's paternalistic administration of the markets, but now things are changing. Turgot, who controls the markets now, is a radical, a *philosophe*, a believer in the utopian new theory of *laissez-faire*. He knows that the average worker earns fifteen to twenty sous a day, but he believes that with benign neglect the market will self-regulate itself. The fact that some parts of the economy are not *laissez-faire*, but monopolized, does not enter into his calculations.

The price of a loaf reached twelve sous by March 1775, and continued to rise. By April it was fifteen sous.

By mid-April it was twenty sous.

The first riot occurred April 18 in Dijon, the capital of Burgundy. The workers wrecked a mill, then attacked the miller's house, wrecked that also, and tossed the furniture out into the street. Two days later the army arrived and order was restored.

In Beaumont on April 27, another mob breaks into a bakery and seizes the bread they need. They are not exactly stealing it, by their understanding; they scrupulously left behind what they considered a fair price—six sous a loaf, the maximum allowed under Sartines's rules.

By the time the army arrived in Beaumont, the story was all over France. Between April 29 and May 6, the pattern had been repeated in dozens of towns. The mobs attacked the bakeries, broke the windows, took the bread, and left behind the old pre-inflationary price—six sous a loaf.

In Paris, Jean Jacques Jeder took part in the attack on the Gilbert bakery. He was earning eighteen sous a day; there was no way he could buy a daily loaf at twenty sous.

It was the first time Jeder had broken the law since his career of grab-and-run during his unemployment in 1771. He did not feel guilty; the whole mob had an exhilaration and sense of righteousness about it. Those rich bastard bakers could not expect people to *starve,* could they?

But by then, May 6, the mobs were not leaving money behind anymore. They were grabbing all they could carry and running—partly because they had to move fast to get the bread before the army and police arrived; partly because they had entered the state of nature.

It was also on May 6 that other mobs rampaged in Versailles, where they did not attack bakers but government buildings. Some said later that these rebels were led by known Freemasons; but you know the sort of things THEY say . . .

In Paris alone thirteen hundred bakeries were looted.

Government officials gradually stopped speaking of "riots" and began speaking of "rebellion," then of "civil war." Eventually, in retrospect, the whole three weeks of mob action was to be called simply "the grain war."

The price of bread came down to its old level for a while.*

Meanwhile, the grain war of 1775 gave birth to a legend. In 1761, Rousseau had written, to illustrate his thesis of the ignorance of the rich, that "a certain noble lady, in the last century," told that the poor had no bread, remarked innocently, "Well, let them eat cake." Somehow, after May 1775, this story got attached to the new queen, Marie Antoinette. Those who remembered the original, in Rousseau,

*Then it started to climb again, slowly at first, and continued to climb until August 14, 1789, when it reached twenty-one sous again and Paris exploded irrevocably.

were a minority. The majority believed the pretty, extravagant, willful daughter of Maria Theresa had actually said it when the mobs were rioting in Paris.

After the riots were suppressed there were ritual hangings in various cities, to remind the populace that the government would not tolerate such lawless behavior. In Paris, it appears, only two were hanged: Jean Denis Desportes, twenty-eight, and Jean Claude Lesguiller, sixteen.

They were hanged on May 11 at the Place du Greve. An unusually high scaffold was built for the occasion, to make the greatest possible impression on the citizenry.

The executioner, Charles Henri Sanson, wore his usual well-cut suit of green. Two lines of soldiers surrounded the gibbet, with rifles, since there was still fear of further mob unrest.

Both the man, Desportes, and the boy, Lesguiller, indeed shouted to the crowd for help. Why not? Most of the crowd had also participated in the looting and were as guilty as these two symbolic sacrifices. But the soldiers had rifles. Nobody tried to rush them.

Desportes shouted again. They say he was claiming he was innocent. Whether he meant that he hadn't done any looting or that he felt blameless about seizing bread to feed his family—who knows? Nobody cared what he meant.

Lesguiller, the boy, sixteen, was sobbing like a child as they dragged him up the steps. They say he was telling the hangman's assistants that he had always been hard-working and honest and that he was sorry he went with the mob that day. He said he would never do it again.

A priest prayed for their souls. At that point, nobody could hear him, because the boy was weeping hysterically now, almost screaming in terror.

Jean Jacques Jeder, in the crowd, was wet with perspiration. He kept thinking: It could be me up there.

"O clemens, O pia, O dulcis virgo Maria," the priest intoned, finishing his prayer.

Everybody close enough to the scaffold smelled the stink and knew that the boy, Lesguiller, had shit himself. The hangmen yank the *jets* and the two bodies dangle, strangling slowly. Sanson, in his splendid green, gives the signal for mercy, since he has not been ordered otherwise. The hangmen grab the knees of the culprits and pull down hard, ending the agony.

The "grain war" is over. The lessons remain. That night, Jean Jacques Jeder re-read the pamphlet by Spartacus that Luigi Duccio had given him long ago. The mob had controlled Paris for three days, he knows. If there were more of them, if the soldiers had come over to their side, if they had been better organized . . . Jeder is thinking of America, and of the struggle there, which is growing day by day.

Is it possible, he thinks, that this Spartacus is right, and the people can seize power themselves if they are determined enough?

From THE REVOLUTION AS I SAW IT, by Luigi Duccio:

Thus, the revolution did not begin on August 14, 1789, as conventional wisdom says, but in the weeks between April 18 and May 11, 1775, when the so-called "grain war" was fought in every major city of France. The *index of desperation,* the ratio of population to prices, had reached the explosive point. All the rest was just a matter of organization and the deployment of forces; and here the dread "secret societies" of Freemasons, &c. play their role; but only after the social conditions were such that out of the usual maelstrom of coincidence and conspiracy one new dominant tendency could come to the fore.

At the Kytler Inn in Kilkenny, Ireland, Sean O'Lachlann, the greatest shanachie in Meath, had presided over a clandestine meeting of White Boys, Jacobites, and rebels from all four provinces. There had been a great deal of drinking, of course, but there had also been a great deal of very serious discussion and planning.

"We will die of old age, if the galls do not hang us first," said O'Lachlann, "before Ireland is free. If any man jack among you doubts that, let him leave now for Christ's sake and not turn the colors of his coat later. What we are doing is for our children, and I even misbelieve that at times. Before God, it may be only for our grandchildren. It is a long and desperate struggle ahead and it is not to be won by bravery or high hopes. It is planning and perseverance we need."

"You need not tell us that, Sean O'Lachlann," said the giant O'Flaherty of Connacht. "We have seen enough high hopes smashed and enough brave lads hanged. We do not expect freedom to drop into our laps as a faery's gift, by God. Not any more. We know what is ahead.''

Nobody disagreed.

Toward the end, the third day of the confabulation, O'Lachlann became the traditional shanachie again and told them the fable of the widow's son. "Some say he was Hiram in the Old Testament, some say he was Parcifal, the Grail Knight, and others there be who say he was someone even more glorious whose name dare not be mentioned. But all the wise men and wise women of the Craft say his descendants survive. 'They are in the world, but the world does not know them,' it is promised to us. They always come forth to give help, one way or another, visibly or invisibly, when men fight for justice and for freedom.''

Men need realism in a desperate struggle, O'Lachlann told himself while raising another pint later: but they also need a hope and a dream and a myth set above them in the stars.*

---

*As we go to press, the terrible news of the death of Prof. Hanfkopf has just come from Heidelberg. Apparently, the Herr Doktor was accidentally killed while trying to assemble some sort of explosive device or "infernal machine." He lived long enough to dictate a statement to the police, which has been translated by an officer whose knowledge of English is not, perhaps, perfect: "All that I have struggled for truth and logic has been . . . reason, pure reason . . . *(unintelligible words)* . . . The conspiracy worldwide is and the evidence faked has been for telepathy and spoonbending and all nonsense . . . History before about 1920 they have faked and myths they have made . . . Gurdjieff the leader I think was . . . *(unintelligible)* on the Masonic buildings the G in the compass . . . Mr. G. it means . . . From Tibet it unfolds the conspiracy world-wide and in my food lately poisons I know. Today is the leader of the conspiracy named—arrrgggggggh!'' Prof. Hanfkopf has been cremated in accord with his will, but the executors and court have agreed to set aside the codicil requesting that his ashes be thrown in the face of Dr. Hans Eysenk, the English psychologist who recently published statistical studies allegedly validating some basic claims of astrology. It is a sad case.

Six

Dear Uncle Pietro,

I am leaving tomorrow for what is called the Northwest Territory, where it is my plan to seek friendship with the Red Indians and live among them for a time.

(Isn't it strange, by the way, that this should be mailed from Philadelphia City? Do you remember, ten years ago, when poor Antonio first went mad, he predicted I would go some day to Philadelphia—and I did not even know where that was at the time. Well, it proves again that, just as most of what the world calls sanity is really a hypnosis or dream, much of what is called lunacy is a terrible perceptiveness.)

I spent over a year, or seventeen months to be precise, with your friend "Frankenstein" and his associates in the Priory, and I must admit that the Egyptian climate agreed with me, and that their teaching techniques are indeed formidable. As you have no doubt learned from them, I left without saying farewell—rather hurriedly, in fact—and I have changed my appearance in a number of ways, as well as obtaining all the *documentia* to establish a new identity for myself. In a word, I am tired of secret societies and occult mysteries and all varieties of *magical politics*. I do acknowledge and accept that the men and women of the Priory are in the position of the invisible keepers of the armed madhouse that is our planet, and that their techniques are necessary and inescapable for those taking on such a dreadful responsibility. I wish them well, and am grateful for such light as they passed on to me, but their Way is not my Way. In fact, I can summarize my thoughts now by simply saying each must find his or her own Way *because "the Way" does not exist.*

I will not be too astonished if I eventually learn that such words do not come as a shock to you; I will not even be truly amazed if I someday discover that the function of the Priory is to provoke students to escape from it and seek their own paths. Meanwhile, however, I suspect, and am almost persuaded, that the Priory, like every similar order throughout history, has lost its original light and *seeks* so passionately for the King of the World only because its members no longer know how to *find* themselves.

I will tell you more of my heresies, not at all certain of whether they will shock you or just cause you to nod and grin and say, "The boy is finally coming to his senses."

There are gods, but there is no God; and all gods become devils eventually.

One of the first gods—perhaps the very first, and certainly the greatest—was she who *created* beauty in the world. It is her image that is still worshipped as the Great Mother in the eastern lands, and among the underground witch cults in rural parts of Europe. I rather imagine she was suckling her newborn at the time she became a god and a creator; this is how the Egyptians showed Isis, their image of her, and it is the favorite Christian icon of Mary, the same archetype of the same long memory. She was, of course, one of the cave people Dr. Vico has told us pre-existed civilization. As she suckled, she went deep, deep into that voluptuous revery which even we men may know when we make love to women, and then she *saw* for the first time. A single rose, a gorgeous sunset, the intricate design of what had previously been an "ugly" insect—I cannot guess what she saw, but she *saw*. And in excitement and rapture, she cried out to her mate (whatever form of "marriage" they had in those days) "Oh look at this, look!" and he looked and he *saw*. And beauty was created in a world that had been flat and dead and meaningless until that moment.

(Incidentally, we can all go backward in history, and uncreate her creation. We can do this by getting very drunk and waking in the morning with a vile hangover; or by worrying continually, until all things become tinged with our own gloom; or by numerous methods well known to the devotees of self-pity everywhere.)

And why do I say that all such creatures become devils eventually? Any musician knows the answer to that; and so does any other artist. *"Smash, smash the old laws":* habitual beauty becomes narcotic eventually; it can be rediscovered, but only dialectically, by contrast, by the creation of new, brutally shocking beauty, beauty that seems barbarism at first. And the creation of such new beauty is the first step for anyone who would *be* a god, and not a slave of dead gods. It is in the war between great seeking and great boredom that new beauty is born.

Another god, who has become the worst of all devils, is he—I am rather sure this god was male—who first put truth and law into the world. It is this genius, this demonic visionary, whose worshippers have killed or tried to kill every "blasphemer" against *his* truth and *his* law who tried to invent new truths and new laws. And another god put love into the world, and the deviltry of this can be seen in the police records: it is astounding how many murders are committed "for love." Another god put justice into the world; and we have been at war ever since; another created mercy, and every coward has flocked to that banner.

And even in the corrupt gospels of the Church, from which the true *gnosis* has been largely expurgated, the text still stands: "I said: ye are gods" (John 10:34) and a million fools gape at the page and have not the wit or courage to understand. For the most diabolical of all gods, the creator who towers above all creators, the tyrant who enslaves the world, is *he who invented guilt.* I am rather sure that this Moloch, this creator-monster, was the first priest, or the first swindler (in those days the concepts may not yet have been distinguished). Human beings then *learned to judge and despise themselves;* an uncomfortable state, from which they chronically sought escape by judging and despising one another. And of all creations, this is the hardest to *uncreate,* because it left the deepest wound; it left, in fact, that festering suppuration that is normal consciousness in our species today. It is this creator of evil in the world, I think, who is remembered allegorically as he who said, "Thou shalt have no gods but me," and who thereby reduced the other gods to devils and worms crawling in the dust: to humanity as we know it.

For, once evil and bad conscience were invented, "the one became two"—the mind was split against itself, the cosmos was split into fictitious and antagonistic oppositions; everything was turned upside-down and backward and the world became populated with the hallucinations of mania. This raving lunacy, this hatred of self and others, is the "sleep" and "dream" and "illusion" against which the sages warn us; it is the "drunkenness" against which Jesus rails in the gnostic gospels; it is coded into the parable of the fall in Genesis. And all this suited the first priest-swindler very well, as it has suited all other priest-swindlers ever since; it made them rich; it gave them that which, for small souls, is sweeter than wealth—*the power to control others;* and they have been most industrious, ever since, in inventing new "sins" so that more gloom and horror and despair will be spread over life, so that the number of human sacrifices on their altars will never cease.

(How am I doing, dear uncle, first and best of my teachers? Have I seen through the illusions of the millennia, or am I just inventing my own grand opera like all the other gods and devils before me?)

Now, I have asked myself: What is the "fourth soul," if there are no gods but men and women who are able to create, out of meaninglessness, *meanings?* The fourth soul, like the first three, can only be part of our brains. The proof is that every known method of activating it acts upon our bodies first, which in turn acts upon our brains. All these techniques are methods of stress and exhaustion. The fakir and yogi in the east drives his organism to such a pitch that a spasm of involuntary relaxation ends the stress. The repetition of chants, whether *Ave Maria* or *Om,* exhausts the candidate into this relaxation. Terror, as in many initiations, leads to the same stress-and-relaxation. I encountered the fourth "soul" first while waiting to fight a duel, and history is full of cases of those who found it when they thought they were about to die. Almost all have fleeting glimpses of it in the glow after orgasm.

And now I utter my worst heresy. This higher "soul," or higher faculty as I would prefer to say, *has absolutely no value in itself.* Many who have attained it have remained imbeciles or worse; some have "graduated" to higher imbecility, or fanaticism. (That is the reason for grades and ranks and teachers in the Craft, is it not? To guard against unleashing more lunatics upon an already deranged world.) The "vegetative soul," or oldest part of the brain, merely perceives simple sensations: hot or cold, damp or dry, seemingly safe or seemingly noxious. The "animal" soul, or middle brain, perceives the body language of similar organisms and can, somewhat, predict their behavior from this. The "human" soul, or later brain, perceives structures of a simple, mechanical kind. The "fourth soul," or emerging brain, perceives the invisible web of connections between all things; *but it is no more infallible than the rest of the brain, or the gut, or the liver, or the gonads.* It merely works without effort, unlike the more primitive parts of the brain, which is why *meanings seem to flow into us,* when this is activated, and we forget that we are still creating the meanings. We imagine we are "receiving revelations," and hence we do not *take responsibility* or exercise any prudence or common sense. This is why there are so many "holy fools" and so few holy wise men.

Perhaps this is like explaining cow dung to a farmer, but for the sake of clarity let me stress again that the creative faculty, the god-power, is not used here with anything less than *total literalness.* When beauty was created by a godly mind, beauty existed, as surely as the paintings of Botticelli or the concerti of Vivaldi exist. When mercy was created, mercy existed. When guilt was created, guilt existed. Out of a meaningless and pointless existence, we have made meaning and purpose; but since this creative act happens only when we relax after great strain, we feel it as "pouring into us" from elsewhere. Thus, we do not know our own godhood and we are perpetually swindled by those who assure us that it is indeed elsewhere, but *they* can give us access to it, for a reasonable fee. And when we as a species were ignorant enough to be duped in that way, the swindlers went one step further, invented original sin and other horrors of that sort, and made us even more "dependent" upon them.

I have described the result as an armed madhouse; I might go further and call it an abattoir in which the cattle have been persuaded to slaughter one another. "I have

come to put an end to revenge,'' said Jesus, but revenge
is the obsession, the compulsion, of all those who, having
been *told* they are guilty, have *become* guilty. The criminal is not an exceptional type, but the normal type in a
world in which evil has been invented; as cynics like
Shakespeare and Swift and Cervantes have all remarked,
the criminals on the bench sentence the criminals who
come before the bench. The criminal mind is precisely
the average mind in this world, after the priests invented
sin. ''He who cries, 'Fool, fool!' is already a murderer.''
''Judge not.'' The illusion of Sin and Guilt, the madness
of our species, is the act of *cursing the world under the
misapprehension that one is cursing only one part of it.*
To curse the fig tree, as in the funniest and most misunderstood parable of Jesus, is to curse the soil in which it
grew, the seed, the rains, the sun; the whole world, eventually—because no part is truly separate from the whole.
The fallacy that one can judge the part in isolation from
the whole is ''the Lie that all men believe.''

As I have said, of all lies this is the hardest to undo: of
all creations, the hardest to uncreate. Yet I have done it.
Whether the Priory intended this result or not, I have
found, in their meditation practices, that I can not only
go back to the void mind before beauty and then recreate
beauty, and back before ''space'' and ''time'' and ''order'' and recreate them, etc.—all normal phenomena of
those who have any activity of the fourth faculty at all—
but I actually went back before good and evil, before
priestcraft. I saw the world in all innocence again: you
can imagine my tears of joy, my ''holy idiocy,'' my in-
coherent enthusiasm. When I came to my right mind
again, I realized what the *ev-angel*, the ''good news''
of Jesus, had been; and why the priests of his time crucified him and why the priests ever since have exercised
such ingenuity in obscuring and concealing the *good
news.*

I saw, in short, that he who created good and evil was
indeed a god and the greatest of geniuses, even if it is
necessary now to denounce him as a devil; I saw that,
because we are all gods, we can all create our own good
and evil and our own beauty and meaning, &c. All may
say, ''This is *my* way, this is *my* good and *my* evil''; none
may say, ''This is *the* way, this is *the* good and *the* evil.''

The judge speaks the truth without knowing it, and acknowledges his own divinity without realizing it, when he says, "I *find* you guilty"; he lies the oldest and most terrible of all lies when he says, "You *are* guilty." The god creates meaning and value; the devil is a god asleep who imagines meaning and value *exist in themselves elsewhere*.

And I understood, of course, the darkest of all Jesus's dark sayings, "Who is near me is near the fire." To know that men and women are the gods they imagine *elsewhere*, the creators of meaning and value, is dangerous in itself; to act, or even to speak, of such knowledge is almost certain to be fatal in the present state of sleep, dream, illusion, and madness of humanity. I understood why Jesus ran away when the disciples wanted to make him king; and I ran away from those who want to make me emperor.

As for the enemy (the Black Sorcerers, or the Knights of Malta, or whoever they are): their attempts to kidnap my mind seem to me, now, no "worse" than the Priory's desire to educate and liberate my mind. Let each of them pursue their own notion of illumination, and promote their own candidates for the Illuminated Monarch. I go to live with the Red Indians only because I do not know enough to socialize with the wolves and bears. I must escape to the clean air for a long, long time, for I am *sick with pity*. I cannot read a printed article without wanting to vomit; I cannot look at theology or politics or art criticism without wanting to shake the fools who write such sentences as "This is sin," "This is injustice," "This is beauty," and scream in their ears, "You fools, you have just created sin and virtue, and justice and injustice, and beauty and ugliness, when you spoke." But they would not understand. In their dreams, they would dream I said something else, something they could hear and make sense of. In the dream the old gods have created, we all see our creations as outside ourselves; it will take a struggle to awake, and a longer struggle, before we can see the glory and the stupidity of the universe we have created and then learn to make one more glorious and less stupid.

I say again that he was the greatest of gods who created good and evil, and the greatest god is the greatest devil, because gods enslave those who come after them.

I go now to seek my own good and my own evil in my own way.

If I return to Europe, ever, it will be to serve my own goals and not those of any order of illuminated beings who know what is best for me and for the world.

Seven

I am a wife deserter," said Tom Paine. "That is the sort of scoundrel I am."

"Have some more rum," James Moon said. "We all become scoundrels in this world, sooner or later. Events it is that conspire against us. Sure the holy man of Nazareth would be a bit of a rogue if he had lived long enough."

Paine drank some more of the sweet, dizzying rum. "My wife had no children," he added. "I would not have been that much of a blackguard. I would not desert helpless infants like Monsieur Rousseau did."

"You would if you were tempted *enough*," Moon said. He drank some more of the rum, too. The ship heaved again, and he told himself he had better make this his last drink before he became ill.

"Strange, is it not, how being together on a journey like this makes for sudden confidences?" Paine mused.

"Jesus, man, we will probably never meet again. America is a big continent from what I've heard." Moon hesitated. "I'm a blackmailer, myself."

"Because you were tempted *enough*," Paine said thoughtfully. "I see where your tolerance of wife desertion comes from."

"It was years ago," Moon said. "My conscience did not die. I eventually sent the money back and told the man he would never hear from me again and I would keep my mouth shut forever." We confess, he thought, and then we add the extenuating circumstances. "I wanted the money to become a shopkeeper. I was in service before."

"And you gave up your shop to return the money?"

"Sure, there's no joy in life with a conscience chewing you every day like a dog worrying a bone." Moon took another drink after all. "So I tried to undo what I had done. But, don't you know, man, the way of it? I know now that I can be a scoundrel. I can never forget that."

"So," Paine said. "We are two scoundrels who wish we could be more than scoundrels. Well, sir, that is what the New World is for. To give men a new chance."

He had spoken very somberly and slowly. Jesus, Moon thought, he's drunker than me by a long league.

"I have failed at everything," Paine went on, somber still, not indulging in self-pity; with the clarity of alcoholic self-examination. "I have been a shopkeeper too. And a customs agent—which means, as you no doubt know, a bribe-taker. A teacher, for a while. A sailor once. Many things. I was always discharged for insubordination or incompetence or laziness or one damned thing or another. Or I simply got bored and wandered off to seek something else. The truth is that I would rather think than work. That is a dangerous vice for a poor man; only the rich can afford that taste." He drank again. "God knows what I will do in America. Try other jobs and fail at them, I suppose."

"Ah, Jesus, man, don't be a pessimist. Have some more rum."

"To tell you the truth, sir, I was just being morbid for a moment. I still have the wonderful illusion that someday I will discover my true destiny. Perhaps in America."

"If I believed in destiny," James Moon said, "I would look forward to hanging. A wise woman saw that in my cards once."

"I do not believe in fortune telling by cards," Paine pronounced. "Or in the stars, or any such devices. Tomorrow morning we dock in Baltimore. I do not believe that any human device can predict the *first five minutes* of what will happen to us upon shore, much less the whole rest of our lives. The universe may be preparing an enormous surprise for both of us."

"Drink up," Seamus Muadhen said. "To two scoundrels in an unpredictable universe."

"Two scoundrels," Paine said cheerfully, "in an unpredictable universe."

NATURE'S GOD

VOLUME 3 OF
The Historical Illuminatus Chronicles

Clontarf 1014

A Danish Norseman or Norwegian Dane named Brodar, who wasn't particularly brilliant or scintillating and never did anything else that got into the history books, killed an old man around the hour of sunset on April 23, 1014 in a bull-grazing field called Clontarf, on the north coast of Dublin Bay. Brodar, whatever elements of Danish and Norse were mixed in him, was a Viking and he killed the old man with an axe through the head. Vikings seem to have liked to kill people with axes. Historians agree that, when not combing the lice out of his beard or getting drunk, your average Viking preferred to spend his time cracking skulls with axes.

Incidentally, we know the Vikings spent a lot of time combing lice out of their beards because archaeologists have made careful scientific catalogs of the Danish and Norse artifacts found around Dublin Bay, and lice combs outnumber swords and all other implements of war about a hundred to one. As Sherlock Holmes would tell you, "Observing thousands of lice combs, one deduces the existence of many, many lice." When the Irish said, "Here come those lousy Vikings again," they were probably being literal.

I know the movie people left the lice out of that epic adventure, *The Vikings*, starring Kirk Douglas and Tony Curtis, but Hollywood has a tendency to glamorize things.

Although the historian Snorri Sturlusen has the kind of name you would expect to belong to a troll in a Norse myth, he appears to have been a real person, and he left us our best records of the Viking invasions or incursions in Ireland. All that the euphoniously titled Snorri chronicled about Brodar, besides his deed of valor in the Clontarf field that memorable April day in 1014—it was Good Friday, curiously—is that Brodar was dark haired. The Irish tradition agrees, and calls Brodar a *dhuv-gall*, which in Irish means "dark stranger." The Irish never knew whether the invaders were Norse or Danes, they just called them *dhuv-galls* or *finn-galls* (dark strangers or blonde strangers) and generally ran like hell when they saw them coming.

The old man who got Brodar's battle-axe through his brain—he was sixty-four actually, but still blonde and bursting with vinegar and venom, due to unusual genes—was named Brian Caeneddi of Borumu, but is usually remembered under the English version of his name, which is Brian Boru. He was not the sort who ran like hell when he saw the Vikings coming. In fact, Brodar killed him in revenge, because Brian (Caeneddi) Boru had just defeated the Vikings again, which was a nasty habit he had developed over the decades. Brian Caeneddi (Boru), in fact, had been killing and vanquishing Danes and Norsemen, all over Ireland, for forty-six years, starting in 968 when, at the precocious age of eighteen, he had led a small band of guerrillas to the Viking stronghold at Limerick, killed every Dane and Norwegian in sight, and then burned the whole town down afterwards, leaving nothing behind but cinders.

That was just for starters.

During the next forty-six years, Brian marched around Ireland constructing simulated lunar craters—large smoking holes in the earth, full of charred bones and ashes—wherever the Vikings had previously had towns and strongholds. If Brodar hadn't axed him at sixty-four, Brian (Boru) Caeneddi might have gone on killing Danes and Norsemen for another ten or twenty years probably. Although much about that period of Irish history is clouded with legend and mystery, it is quite clear that Brian Boru had a distinct ethnic prejudice against Danes and Norsemen, or anybody with a Viking helmet on his head.

Some say one of these Scandinavian invaders had raped Brian's mother, others, that he was simply an early Sinn Feiner and believed in Ireland for the Irish.

Brian of Borumu was also politically ambitious, and, starting out as a local "king" or chieftain in the Shannon River valley, had made himself High King of Ireland by bribing all the other local "kings" who could be bribed (of which Ireland had God's plenty) and burying the ones who could not be bribed, and then persuading the previous High King, Malachi Uj Naill or O'Neill, to abdicate.

There are many different stories about how Brian Caeneddi persuaded Malachi O'Neill to give up the throne, and they are all incredible. The safest verdict is that Brian was a very persuasive talker, who could put even a radical idea like abdication across with enough unction and lubricating oil to make it go down smoothly, and besides, after Limerick, he never went anywhere without an army of about 500,000 loyal supporters.

After becoming High King, Brian Caeneddi of Borumu consolidated his genetic potential by marrying his sons and daughters into royal or noble families all over the British Isles and even in France. You've encountered his granddaughter in English Lit class; she was Lady Macbeth. The Caeneddi genes were actually carried by the later O'Neill kings, the royal Stuarts of Scotland and England, the Hapsburgs, the Lorraines, and, eventually, by the Hanovers, the Mountbattens and the Minority Whip of the U.S. House of Representatives, Tip O'Neill.

The name Caeneddi was by then spelled, English-fashion, Kennedy, and Brian Boru's pugnacious and charismatic seed had found its way to the presidency of the United States.

An axe in the skull can stop even a man like Brian Boru, but it does not stop the genetic vector in time of which he is an expression.

To be Continued...

About the Author

Robert Anton Wilson is the co-author, with Robert Shea, of the *Illuminatus!* Trilogy, recognized as a New Age classic. In addition, he is the author of more than fifteen other books, including *Sex and Drugs*, *The Schroödinger's Cat Trilogy*, and *Cosmic Trigger: The Final Secret of the Illuminati*. He is a former *Playboy* editor, a philosopher, a poet, a playwright and a well-known lecturer.

WORLDS AT WAR

☐ **THE LOST REGIMENT #1: RALLY CRY by William Forstchen.** Storm-swept through a space-time warp, they were catapulted through Civil War America into a future world of horrifying conflict, where no human was free. (450078—$4.95)

☐ **THE LOST REGIMENT #2: THE UNION FOREVER by William R. Forstchen.** In this powerful military adventure, soldiers from the past are time-space-warped to a warring world of aliens. "Some of the best adventure writing in years!"—*Science Fiction Chronicle* (450604—$4.95)

☐ **DAWN'S UNCERTAIN LIGHT by Neal Barrett Jr.** In a devestated, post-holocaust future filled with Wild West savagery, civil war, and irradiated mutant humans, orphan Howie Ryder grows up fast while searching to rescue his sister from an inhuman doom inflicted by a government gone awry. (160746—$3.95)

☐ **JADE DARCY AND THE AFFAIR OF HONOR by Stephen Goldin and Mary Mason.** Book one in *The Rehumanization of Jade Darcy*. Darcy was rough, tough, computer-enhanced—and the only human mercenary among myriad alien races on the brink of battle. She sought to escape from her human past on a suicide assignment against the most violent alien conquerors space had ever known. (156137—$3.50)

☐ **STARCRUISER SHENANDOAH: SQUADRON ALERT by Roland J. Green.** The United Federation of Starworlds and its most powerful enemy, the Freeworld States Alliance, must prepare for a war they hoped would never start. (161564—$3.95)

Prices slightly higher in Canada.

Buy them at your local bookstore or use this convenient coupon for ordering.

NEW AMERICAN LIBRARY
P.O. Box 999, Bergenfield, New Jersey 07621

Please send me the books I have checked above. I am enclosing $_____
(please add $1.00 to this order to cover postage and handling). Send check or money order—no cash or C.O.D.'s. Prices and numbers are subject to change without notice.

Name_____

Address_____

City _____ State _____ Zip Code _____
Allow 4-6 weeks for delivery.
This offer, prices and numbers are subject to change without notice.